Surendra Mohanty's
Neeladri Vijaya
The Glorious Homecoming

Surendra Mohanty's
Neeladri Vijaya
The Glorious Homecoming

Translated by
Gurudev Meher

BLACK EAGLE BOOKS
Dublin, USA | Bhubaneswar, India

 Black Eagle Books
USA address:
7464 Wisdom Lane
Dublin, OH 43016

India address:
E/312, Trident Galaxy, Kalinga Nagar,
Bhubaneswar-751003, Odisha, India

E-mail: info@blackeaglebooks.org
Website: www.blackeaglebooks.org

First International Edition Published by
Black Eagle Books, 2025

NEELADRI VIJAYA:
The Glorious Homecoming
by **Surendra Mohanty's**

Translated by **Gurudev Meher**

Translation copyright © Gurudev Meher

Cover & Interior Design: Ezy's Publication

ISBN- 978-1-64560-797-7 (Paperback)

Printed in the United States of America

CONTENTS

Preface

Although *Neeladri Vijaya* is the latter half of the novel *Neelashaila*, apart from the sequence of events and the continuity of characters, it has no other connection with *Neelashaila*. It can be read as an independent novel.

I had never imagined writing the latter half of *Neelashaila*. After the death of 'Saradei' in *Neelashaila*, I had no desire to write further on this subject. Saradei was my daughter of the mind; in her creation and embodiment, all my emotional wealth was exhausted.

But about ten years ago, I happened to meet the historian and distinguished littérateur Parmananda Acharya suddenly on the road. He called me, seated me in the verandah of an iron warehouse at Chauliaganj, and without any preamble said: 'Shri Jagannath has been cast into the midst of Chilika. He returns thereafter to the Shrimandir. That portion you must write.' How could I explain to him that after Saradei's death, I was utterly empty, my creative power silent? Before his death, the late Acharya wrote an article on *Neelashaila* for the journal *Jhankar*, in which he also gave me this directive.

After his death, his affectionate request became for

me an unbreachable command. Many readers, too, met me personally and requested that I record the account of Shri Jagannath's return. *Neeladri Vijaya* was written against this background. To gather the broken threads of *Neelashaila,* I had to spend many nights halfawake. By the boundless compassion of Lord Jagannath, this work could be completed amid my busy, turbulent life; for me, it is a matter of supreme inner satisfaction.

The background of *Neelashaila* is vast—hence its epic expanse. The background of *Neeladri Vijaya* is not very broad; it is limited. Therefore, in terms of structure, it is more tightly woven. While *Neelashaila* is based on the *Madala Panji* and historical facts, *Neeladri Vijaya* also relies on the details from the *Madala Panji.*

When I wrote *Neelashaila,* I was not well acquainted with the Puri dialect. The speech used by the temple priests and servitors has a native vitality of its own. In truth, the Puri dialect as used in *Neelashaila* contains some imperfections. Learned readers from Puri had drawn my attention to this. In the fourth edition, I attempted to address these matters. But I did not have the time required to conduct the kind of research into the servitors' spoken language that was necessary. In this regard, I encouraged the writers of the Puripublished group, *Anam,* to take up the study. As a result, in some issues of *Anam*, Shri Siddheshwar Mahapatra wrote essays on the Puri dialect. The use of the servitors' living Puri speech in *Neeladri Vijaya* proved helpful to me. On this occasion, it would be a lapse of duty not to express my gratitude to him.

Apart from the servitors' language, the temple's ritual practice contains many words whose origins and meanings would be a challenge for any linguist to determine. Some of the temple servitors assisted me in this work; I am grateful to them as well. Yet more research is needed on the language used in the Shrimandir. The universities of Odisha should take an earnest interest in this, so that the historical and traditional aspects of the Jagannath element can be illuminated anew.

Publication of *Neeladri Vijaya* was not possible for me; Lakshmi, Saraswati, and Vishnu may dwell together in a household, but not in the world of a writer like me. Yet my family insisted that they would publish *Neeladri Vijaya* as an offering of their devotion. Through their collective effort, it has been published by Shivani Prakashan. The artist Shri Bibhuti Kanungo executed the book cover in the Odissi style. He deserves thanks. Like *Neelashaila*, may *Neeladri Vijaya* receive the esteem of Odisha's readers, and may my labour be vindicated.

Shivani   **Surendra Mohanty**
Cuttack-8
11.5.1980
Jalakrida Ekadashi

Preface to the
Third Edition

In the meantime, the second edition of *Neeladri Vijaya* had long since become scarce, yet for various reasons its subsequent edition could not be brought out until now. Since Cuttack Students' Store, the publisher of almost all my books, has taken responsibility for the prompt publication of this edition, I extend my heartfelt thanks to its authorities.

It has come to my notice that many critics compare *Neeladri Vijaya* with *Neelashaila*. Anticipating such comparisons, I had already indicated in the preface to the first edition the fundamental differences between the two novels. In truth, *Neelashaila* is a pure outpouring of emotion. It contains the loose expansiveness of a horizonspanning epic. But in *Neeladri Vijaya*, such intensity of emotion is absent, nor is there scope for it. Moreover, in *Neeladri Vijaya*, the unity of time, event, and character has been preserved in a way that *Neelashaila* could not achieve. The two novels are independent of each other in style, presentation, and temperament. Because of its compactness and unity, some readers even assign *Neeladri Vijaya* a higher place than

Neelashaila; yet even with them, I do not agree. These two novels must be recognized as distinct from one another.

Since Saptarshi Printers has taken special care to ensure error-free printing, I express my gratitude to its proprietor, the distinguished litterateur Shri Baikunthanath Acharya.

Shivani   **Surendra Mohanty**
Cuttack-8
14 January 1988
Makar Sankranti

Prelude

Neelashaila closes amid the waters of Chilika Lake, upon Gurubai Island, in the forest of hental palms. To shield Odisha's presiding deity, Shri Jagannath, from the fanatical assault of Taqi Khan, Ramachandra Dev carried Him into the heart of Chilika.

Yet Ramachandra Dev's path remains undefined—where shall it lead? Where? Before him lies brimless Chilika—ashen in hue—beneath the cloudless firmament, a boundless blue desert!

Within only a few days, Chilika's island ceases to be secure for Mahabahu. In conspiracy with Lalita Devi, Taqi Khan plots to complete the Navakalevara and enthrone the new wooden images upon the Ratna Simhasana in the Shrimandir.

At that very time, Bhagirathi Kumar will be consecrated upon the throne of Khurda.

But shall the images, infused with the *brahmashila*, lie abandoned in the wilderness, forgotten? Ramachandra Dev has sworn: in Utkal's struggle for liberation, Lord Jagannath Himself shall be the charioteer!

The Lord shall be enthroned upon the Ratna Simhasana—even if he must remain outcast.

This solitary struggle is the story of ***Neeladri Vijaya***.

Chapter I

The sun sank below the horizon, a fiery orb vanishing into the landscape's embrace.

Across the vast expanse of Chilika, the sky stooped with an oppressive weight, its golden farewell fiercely etched upon the ragged wings of departing birds—flocks of garganeys, swans, and countless others, carrying the desperate whispers of day's demise. In that tense embrace between sky and lagoon, the sunset gasped as one—a tortured exhalation steeped in hues of crimson despair.

The waters lay unnervingly still, as though paralyzed, holding their breath. Even in the biting winter of Pausha, the air—drenched in an icy grip—hangs frozen, refusing to stir. No sharp bite of frost dared to venture in the northern winds. A canvas of gentle serenity stretched around. Yet within Ramachandra Dev, a storm brewed—a deep, restless sigh. An ache. Ah, Shri Jagannath—an untamed flame, an unfathomable, formless void! That abyss was terrifying, boundless in its depth, sending violent tremors through the soul. A solitude so vast, so unrelenting that even the body quaked before it.

Ramachandra Dev wiped away the feverish beads of

sweat at his brow, abandoning the oar momentarily. Rising from the boat, his gaze raked the sky. The heavens pulsed with the unbroken garland of birds—some soaring, some plunging, weaving a frantic rhythm through the sky. Their ivory trails carved fierce strokes upon shadowed islands—Gurubai, Varunakuda, Mausa Brahmapur—a sanctuary even for them. Yet, unlike the birds, he had no refuge. And disconcertingly, their voices, once brimming with the warmth of homeward flight, were eerily absent today. As if devoured by an unseen disquiet. All around, silence, solitude, and emptiness stood vigilant.

Mist clutched the dusky veil of evening, smothering Chilika's sun-scorched isles, commanding them into slumber. Yet against the twilight's oppressive backdrop, mountains surged—Soleri and Ghantasila, their peaks awakening in silent defiance.

Inside Ramachandra Dev raged a merciless storm of hope and despair, anxiety and defiance, twisting his heart in relentless turmoil. Clad in a once-stately ochre dhoti, its folds stained and frayed, and a scarf cinched tight around his waist beneath tattered, soiled rags, he carried an air of tragic dignity. Yet his noble features—etched now with lines of fear and resolve—shone through the grime, for since the day he had plunged into Chilika's labyrinth with Lord Jagannath, exile and flight had stolen every trace of softness from his face. At a glance, he might have passed for one of the ragged oarsmen drifting among the brackish marshes.

His broad forehead, rendered a yellowish hue by dust and sweat, and his once-resplendent countenance—where a nose, once as keen as a sword's edge, had lost its subtle gleam—spoke of a fading glory. Even his once-glittering moustache now lay dry and in disarray, while the tufts of hair rising on either side like proud horns had succumbed to chaotic disorder.

Each dawn found him returning from the Maluda Ghats, eyes straining towards the horizon for Lakshmi Paramaguru and Vishnu Paschim Kabat Mahapatra. He had sent Vairiganjan of Gangapada in search of them, but he was also lost somewhere. He went to Maluda yesterday, hoping to collect some news about their whereabouts, but his allies had vanished as though swallowed by the lake itself. Jaguni, whose own wanderings seemed as lost as his prayers, warned that the deities were no longer secure in Chilika's hallowed crest.

Generations ago, at the height of Mughal wrath, the idols had been repeatedly secreted deep within Chilika's hidden coves. For this reason, now every island and crag lay under the watchful glare of Maluda's faujdar. Patrols carved pincer-strikes around Gurubai Island. But the waterways held no charted passage, the lagoons lay sealed, and the primaeval forest formed an iron ring. A cape-like ridge jutted into the lake, its stony spine half-swallowed by reeds. Under the ancient banyans' tangled canopy, no glint of Lord Jagannath betrayed a hiding place.

The god's safety trembled on a knife's edge. Where, then, could true refuge be found?

Many times, in moments of helplessness and distress, keeping himself as far as possible from the plot where the idol of Lord Jagannath had been installed, and gazing into his large, rounded eyes, Ramachandra Dev had asked that same piercing question—Where? In which direction?

Across his mind flashed the image of Lord

Jagannath's face—serene, impervious, curved in that silent, inscrutable smile. As if hoisting his hand in the gesture of fearlessness, he was saying, 'Fear had no foothold here; this dark night would soon break into a new dawn.'

He drew a ragged breath and plunged anew into Chilika's chaos, each step an act of defiance.

All since the month of Margashira, Lakshmi Paramaguru had journeyed to Murshidabad, leaving no whisper of his fate. Had Shuja Khan seized him? The thought turned Ramachandra's blood to ice—yet Jagat Seth Fatehchand still wielded power in Murshidabad, and as long as he was there, Ramachandra Dev had no fear that Shuja Khan would imprison Lakshmi Paramaguru. Jagat Seth, a Jain whose faith bowed only to the one true god, had declared Shri Jagannath the living Rishabadeva. At every summit, Lakshmi Paramaguru, honoured as Rajaguru, stood at the epicentre of worship. In Purushottam's sacred precincts, Jagat Seth knelt before him, offering him gold coins and gifts. His influence over Nawab Shuja-ud-Din Muhammad Khan ran deep; as once he had helped him procure a Shahi firman from Delhi by paying a handsome *nazrana* to the imperial throne, and nothing, it seemed, could undo it.

A few days after the deities were lodged in Gurubai Island, Lakshmi Paramaguru, in an abrupt revelation, announced his decision—'I am leaving for Murshidabad!'

'You walk into the tiger's jaws!' Ramachandra had seized his arm. 'Your journey there at this moment is nothing short of perilous. Having thwarted all of Taqi Khan's schemes, outwitted the Mughal faujdar and deceived the watchful eyes of the imperial army to ensure Lord Jagannath's safe disappearance, if you now fall into Shuja

Khan's grasp, rest assured—he will not let you go so easily!'

Paramaguru's eyes burned with calm fire. 'Shujauddin Khan is a despot—though he may be lacking in character, he is not, like Taqi Khan, bound by religious scruples. I am convinced that through Jagat Seth, we can sway Shuja Khan regarding the safeguarding of Shri Jagannath.' With this conviction, on the auspicious sixth day of Margashira Shukla, Lakshmi Paramaguru embarked on his journey to Murshidabad, faith as his only shield.

Yet, it was Shuja Khan, far more than Paramaguru, who anguished over Lord Jagannath's return to Shrikshetra. Ever since Shri Jagannath had departed from his sacred abode, the flow of revenue in Odisha had dwindled to a mere trickle. The once-prosperous coffers, where a sum of ten lakh rupees was customarily amassed from Jaziya and offerings, now lay barren—for how could tribute be gathered when Lord Jagannath no longer resided in Shrikshetra?

Shrikshetra, once pulsating with divine grandeur, now stood bereft of its soul, hollow in its sanctity. Without his presence, the land had lost its sacred allure. Pilgrims, who once journeyed with fervent devotion, now hesitated— what remained in a realm where the very essence of its holiness had been stripped away?

On the Murshidabad Nawabi *masnad*, Shuja Khan's investiture was by no means free. Following the death of his father-in-law, Murshid Quli Khan, he was forced to incur vast debts—drawing upon his in-laws' fortune—to pay a staggering sixty-one lakh rupees as a bribe to Bahadur Shah Farukh Siyar at the imperial court in Delhi. It was then that he received the imperial mandate, which conferred upon him the governorship over Bengal, Bihar, and Odisha. Thus, adorned with the title Nawab Shuja-ud-Din Motamman-ul-Mulk Shuja-ud-Daula Asad-Jung Bahadur, he ascended as the Nawab of the Murshidabad *masnad*. Yet, all these acquisitions added a heavy burden, for he still maintained a plush woodland estate and palace in Fararabagh, not to mention the expense of another splendid garden in Roshni Bag.

Ceaseless demands were made, moment after moment, for the collection of peshkash and the jizya tax from Odisha. 'Yet until Shri Jagannath, returns to Purushottam Kshetra, not even a single cowri shall be extracted from Odisha,' was the recurrent warning issued by Jagat Seth Fatehchand.

There was no doubt in the minds of either Shuja Khan or Taqi Khan. Even before Shri Jagannath abandoned Shrikshetra, Ramachandra Dev had already halted the peshkash; and now, all the more, Shri Jagannath has sunk into the nether realms. Consequently, spies and lashkars were dispatched far and wide to trace his elusive trail. Moreover, numerous unscrupulous miscreants—driven by the slightest measure of selfinterest—would not hesitate to capture him once more, binding him with leather cords and dragging him ingloriously as they pleased.

A trembling, deep sigh escaped from Ramachandra Dev's breast as the azure veil of dusk descended slowly upon the rosy-hued waters of Chilika. From Gurubai Island, two boats were setting forth—one bound for Maluda and the other for Parikuda—while, from the opposite direction, Ramachandra Dev's own vessel drifted across the deserted Chilika like an emblem of solitary desolation.

At Murshidabad, the power of the Nawab now

waned and lay on the brink of decay; Shuja Khan had grown old, and an unspoken struggle for the throne raged between him and his son, Sharfaraj Khan. The influential elite—Diwan Haji Muhammad, Rai Rayyan Alamchand, Jagat Seth Fatehchand, and others—were embroiled in this covert contest against Sharfaraj. The moment Shuja Khan's flame flickered and was snuffed out, preparations were already underway to seat Bihar's Naib Nazim, Aliwardi Khan, in Murshidabad. Fortune's capricious wager was in full swing here, and if destiny tilts its scales towards Taqi Khan, who could fathom its mysterious designs? Accordingly, he too had accelerated his frantic dash towards Murshidabad.

Rowing steadily, Ramachandra Dev mused: What if, in these dire circumstances, unity were to coalesce in Odisha against Mughal might? 'Rebellion… Rebellion…' echoed in his agitated mind, as though a torrent of fervour and blood had been unleashed. Countless sleepless nights had been spent envisioning this unity, dreaming of an uprising. He had long engaged in clandestine consultations with Vishnu Paschim Kabat Mahapatra; yet, while the spark of revolt might seem natural, its consummation appeared profoundly intricate and daring.

Independence is an unyielding, arduous toil—its history inscribed by countless tears. No eminent fort lord had ever been truly prepared for its demands. In hushed conclaves, regional chieftains of forts such as Gangapada, Banousagarh, Kamaguru, Bangaroba, Rathipur, Ghatikia, Gadmanitri, and others had already deliberated with Vishnu Paschim Kabat Mahapatra over the prospect of rebellion. Yet the majority of these potentates, for now, remain preoccupied with preserving their own security and petty interests rather than embracing a genuine quest for freedom.

Harihar Uttar Kabat of Bangaroba even remarked, 'Have you forgotten, Mr. Mahapatra, the uprising against the Mughal Subedar Khan-e-Duran in the days of Mukundadev? The fort keepers of Ranapur, Saranga Garh, Dampada, Khalikot, Banki, and others joined that revolt. But many other fort keepers, abandoning the struggle against Khan-e-Duran, instead fell into disputes over their boundaries. In the end, KonkalaBharat Patnaik exploited their divisions, handing them over to the enemy, and Mukundadev was captured. Has it slipped your mind? Lord Jagannath never ordained unity as our destiny. Trivial betrayals and internecine skirmishes have repeatedly led us to selfdestruction. Otherwise, why should the oncemighty Utkal empire—from the Ganga to the Godavari—now languish in such lamentable condition?'

Uttar Kabat's apprehensions were not unfounded; for many a chieftain, whose words promised one thing while whose actions suggested another, left the common folk indifferent and resigned. Year after year, tormented by famine and the relentless onslaught of Mughal forces—as if struck by a swarm of locusts—they struggled solely for survival, with little time to ponder the causes of nationhood, social order, or true freedom. Without igniting in the hearts of the people that fierce thirst for liberation, a revolution on a national scale remains impossible.

Yet, the spark of rebellion had not completely left Ramachandra Dev's heart. With that in mind, he dispatched Vishnu Paschim Kabat Mahapatra to reconvene, in secret, with all the chief custodians and fort lords to prepare for an uprising. But ever since Kabat departed, not a word has been heard about his return—who knows when he might reappear? And until Lord Jagannath could provide some semblance of order, how might Ramachandra Dev dare to plunge into the conflagration of revolt? For at the very core of all things lay Shri Jagannath, and until he was secured from Taqi Khan's iron grip, Odisha's hunger for freedom would continue to burn.

Yet Lord Jagannath's sanctuary amid the heart of Chilika cannot endure much longer.

Ramachandra Dev had sent Upendra Bahubalendra of Siko Garh to Tikali Raghunathpur. He believed that if Govind Jagadev could provide the deities with even a few days' repose in Tikali, Taqi Khan would find it exceedingly difficult to track them down. The northern frontier, slothfully guarded by the Kutub-sahi Nizam, lay so lax that no matter how far Taqi Khan's arms reached, those regions remained beyond his grasp—a counsel echoed by Mahuri Narendra. Ramachandra Dev, having weighed all considerations, found this reasoning sound. Yet, where had Bahubalendra vanished? Had disillusionment with Tikali driven him towards Jarada Khemandi? Every day, as Ramachandra Dev journeyed to Malakuda only to return in despair, there was still no sign of Bahubalendra.

Then, as the full moon of Purnima ascended from the deep blue waters of Chilika, Ramachandra Dev was suddenly startled. It dawned upon him—today was Pausha Purnima! In the saffron hues of dusk upon those waters, the silver festival of the full moon unfolded in all its resplendent glory. Today, in Shrikshetra, the Pushyabhishek of Lord Jagannath would be celebrated in magnificent pomp—the deity's worship graced by elaborate vestments and ceremonial attire:

the finery of Kanakalagi, the sacred abhishek raiment, and garlands interwoven with flowers and the delicate fragrance of camphor, so lavishly arrayed that even the wooden structures would seem to stir with the pressing throng of pilgrims. In the inner chamber, the venerable Bhitarachha Mahapatra, rising upon the bejewelled throne, would bear the ceremonial umbrella staff like Lakshman, while Palia Mekap, in a manner reminiscent of Hanuman, would kneel with bowed knees to hold the umbrella's lower section.

As the divine sovereign of a nation where Dharma pulses at its very heart, Shri Jagannath now stood as the living embodiment of Raghunath Ram, the ultimate symbol of supreme kingship. His ceremonial coronation would unfold with grandeur, an unyielding affirmation of his role as the Rajadhiraj. In a fervent display of devotion to the nation's deity, ministers and officials would engage in the sacred ritual of 'Shadhi Bandhan,' a powerful testament to their unwavering allegiance to Dharma and divine governance.

Yet in the Hental wood, Shri Jagannath now remained as a solitary recluse, exiled from the grandeur of his former abode. Where from could one bring him the sumptuous vestments or the celebratory feasts befitting the Pushyabhishek? Beneath the ancient banyan adorned with a tangled mesh of aerial roots on Gurubai Island, Shri Jagannath would have endured in a state of complete fasting. It seemed as though the rising Pausha Purnima moon itself cast a bitter, ironic mockery upon his modest living.

Gurubai Island, fringed with wild date palms, Jevla shrubs, and nala grass, lay beneath the morning sun like heavy eyelids furrowed with lashes.

Ramachandra Dev surveyed the barren desolation stretching endlessly around him, then, with silent urgency, set off towards the ridge.

He recalled that when Lord Jagannath first came to Gurubai Island, a veritable retinue of servitor communities—Sagnik, Brahmin priests well-versed in the Vedas, Udgatas, Purana Pandas, water-bearing servitors, Pushpalak Singhari, attendants of Shriang, Garabadu, and others—had been in attendance. Now, none of these faithful retainers remained. Once, if even a mere fistful of coarse rice or a single day's ration—drawn cautiously from that aged, briny well—had been their only sustenance, how long could they have endured in such unrelenting barrenness? Not even a solitary pilgrim would venture here. And how then could provisions be gathered? The days of bhang, revelry, music, and sumptuous feasting had long receded into the mists of memory. The meagre amount of bhang leaves they brought with them had already dwindled into nothingness. Jaguni, infamous for his stinginess, scurried about all day, yet despite repeated entreaties to procure some bhang, he turned a deaf ear to all appeals.

Their resolution to uphold the honour of Mahaprabhu was never in doubt; yet, they found themselves grievously bereft of the indispensable means. What, indeed, is the value of a resolve that is starved of resources?

The Puja Panda remarked one day: 'Lord Jagannath now dwells deep in the impenetrable forest, as though veiled by the curtains of misfortune. Vedic rites are no longer properly performed here—the sacred flames of the Yajna refuse to kindle, not ever achieving that pure, transformative conflagration of the Divine. Instead, we are left with merely the feeble blaze of burning wood. In such circumstances, what profit can there be for us to remain?'

Purana Panda, Pushpalak Singhari, and Garabadu all concurred. They voiced but one singular question, reaching a resolute decision: For how long shall we tarry in this bleak solitude?

Pushpalak Singhari and Harihar Patjoshi, sensing the urgency of the moment, put forth a solution: 'Ever since the fall of Telenga Mukunda, through the storm of Mughal onslaught, devoted servitors have kept vigil over the empty temple of the Unsullied Purushottam in that forsaken sanctuary. But now, with the deity exiled to the wilderness, let us return to that sacred ground. How many more days can we allow this state to persist? Moreover, there are children to consider.'

The arguments of the Brahmin servitors were irrefutable. What purpose would it serve to remain here, amid the relentless torment of mosquitoes, doing nothing? Especially when Lord Jagannath's service and rituals had lost all connection to the Vedic tradition, and even the sacred *Panchopachara* rites lay abandoned. The truth is evident—in the void of the forsaken temple, at least there was the duty of guarding the holy seat, a distant hope of earning even the smallest coin. But here? There is nothing. At least within the temple grounds, whether the deity be present or not, there remains the possibility of livelihood—of some meagre sustenance, a humble offering to keep them from utter destitution.

Hearing the decision of the Panda servitors, Ramachandra Dev, overcome with helplessness, turned his gaze towards Junior Parichha Vishnu Paschim Kabat—as though in him lay the answer to this vexing problem. Yet Vishnu Paschim Kabat, having long discerned that detaining the Panda servitors here was a futile endeavour, knew they wished to depart. Who could possibly bar their way? In truth, leaving in itself was a kind of benediction. From the standpoint of the deities' security, a large crowd clinging to this barren island was far from desirable—the more people who remained, the more they would draw prying eyes. Naturally, where there was a scarcity of provisions for Shri Jagannath, the problem of securing sustenance for the servants would become even more intractable.

'The Panda servitors may depart if they so desire,' Vishnu Paschim Kabat declared, 'and as for the Daita servitors—there are two—they, too, may leave.'

Turning his gaze towards Jaguni, his eyes alight with a wry smile, he continued, 'While Jaguni stands firm, what reason have you to fret? He is here—a steadfast Parichha, a devoted sevak of Shrianga, a diligent Suara, and a sincere priest! Even the service dictated by '*Vastrabhave Sutram Dadyat*' (in the absence of cloth, one should offer a thread) falls woefully short of true worship without him. Tell me, what profit is there in lingering amid this barren expanse, entangled in the ceaseless dance of mosquitoes? Let the deities carve out a permanent sanctuary; then you will all reconvene here with due earnest.'

Whatever might be the intended meaning, Junior Parichha Paschim Kabat's words sent a thrill through Jaguni's very being—a vivid pulse of significance, as he recognized that in this desolation he remained, once again, the solitary servant of the Great Mahaprabhu—a servant whose essence bore the fruits of penance from a previous lifetime. In the very next moment, the memory of Saradei surged forth unbidden, filling his heart with melancholy. How earnestly had she longed, in days past, to catch a glimpse of Shri Jagannath with eyes brimming with wonder! Yet amidst this raging storm, she vanished without a trace. After all, if she were here, she would be weaving garlands of wild blossoms for Shri Jagannath.

Saradei's insatiable soul seemed then to awaken in every whisper of the forest breeze, in the plaintive lament of a solitary dove. Yes—like the tearful call of a mourning dove, her sorrow dripped in tender compassion.

Jaguni exhaled a deep, lingering sigh, wondering where in the vast expanse of Chilika Saradei had vanished— as if swallowed whole by the mysterious currents of space and time.

Noticing Jaguni's sudden silence, Ramachandra Dev asked, 'Arey, Jaguni, why have you fallen mute? Are you afraid?'

He did not dismiss Junior Parichha's words with a laugh; rather, they resonated deep within him—a blend of deep loyalty, inner conviction, and heartfelt trust. Tossing back his receding hair from his brow, he declared, 'What is there to fear? Whom should we fear? Lord Jagannath encompasses all directions.' Whether in jest or in solemn earnestness, Junior Parichha's proclamation was made before all the servitors—his heart swelling with quiet pride and profound purpose. Jaguni then added, 'Let those who wish to leave depart; I alone shall assume the full responsibility of Lord Jagannath's governance and the sacred ritual proceedings.'

'Will you then assume the mantle of overseeing

the sacred ritual proceedings? Tell us, how?' Jaguni's confidence struck at the very core of their pride. With casual nonchalance, he replied, 'What more is required for Shri Jagannath's holy rites? Simply douse him with a few brisk splashes—a couple of quick spritzes, adorn him with a garland of forest flowers, and present him with a handful of coarse rice on a leaf platter—and that is sufficient. What more can the Puja Pandas offer?'

'Oh, you fool!' Patjoshi Mahapatra interjected sharply. 'Is this all that the service of the Mahaprabhu entails? Do you even know the Lord's true mantras? Can you recite '*Gopijana Vallabhaya Bhagavate Vasudevaya...*'

'Mantras? What of it?' Jaguni countered. 'Must we really utter 'Om Swaha' to beckon the Lord?—Can we not, instead, invoke him by purifying our mind and expecting him to heed? Yet I have learned a few stotras along the way. Should I recite the very stotra that I intone each day—will it be hearkened?' With a sudden burst to dispel all apprehension and agitation, he began to recite—his voice raw and unsteady:

> *Mahambhodhestire kanaka ruchire neelashikhare*
> *Vasanaprasadante sahajabalabhadrena balina*
> *Subhadramadhyastha sakala surasevavasarado*
> *Jagannatha swami nayanapathagami bhavatu me.*

In Shrikshetra, every morning at the time of Sarvasadharan Darshan, or mass viewing, an elderly devotee—whose age might well be measured in decades, his face deeply etched with wrinkles—stood by the Garuda pillar with hands folded in supplication and eyes closed, intoning this very hymn. What of it would bring tears? Jaguni himself could not rightly fathom; yet, as the aged man's eyes suddenly burst forth like waterfalls, the repeated cadence of the verse moved Jaguni profoundly.

Hearing the resonant repetition of Jaguni's recitation, all fell silent. That day, for the first time, Ramachandra Dev perceived in the impassive eyes of the deities a spark of lively effulgence—the tender glimmer of a smile tugging upon their lips. An ineffable sensation enveloped him! The gods, it seemed, were very much alive; their invocation is born of the union of heart and soul, revealed through the tears of that venerable devotee standing at the Garuda pillar— not in the mere recitation of stotras, nor in rote ceremonial formulas, nor through the customary *Panchopachara* or *Shodashopachara* pujas.

Jaguni then said, 'And I know even more…!'

Patjoshi Mahapatra's spirit could not be so easily uplifted. 'Oh, foolish one!' he chided. 'This is but a verse—a mere recitation, not the true mantra. Without knowing the mantra, the simple utterance of verses does not consummate the act of worship.'

Ramachandra Dev interposed and said to Jaguni, 'Enough, enough—speak no more. Each day, let us offer a modest serving of coarse rice in a leaf platter, sprinkle a few droplets of water—this will suffice! Just as in the days of Vishwavasu, when worship of Neelashaila, the Sapphire Deity, was conducted beneath the Agaru tree, in like manner.'

One by one, the Brahmin servitors took their leave. Yet two among them lingered on Gurubai Island—they were not like the Brahmin servitors bound by the lineage of Vidyapati, those who, seizing each historical opportunity, had hoarded all rights, privileges, and even the spoils of serving and worshipping Shri Jagannath. Their bond with

Shri Jagannath was as if forged over countless lifetimes—a connection unalloyed by selfish desire.

Since time immemorial—since some unrecorded, primordial age—was it not the case that Shabara Vishwavasu, the forest dweller, used to worship the supreme form of Shri Jagannath, in a similar fashion? Beneath the Aguru tree, in a practice devoid of the *Pancharatra* element, without the esoteric mystery of tantra, lacking the chanting of mantras and the lavish embellishments of ritual verses, there were no prescribed rites of *Panch* or *Shodashopachar*. Jaguni himself had, at best, memorised a few couplets from elsewhere—a recitation imbued not with contrived fervour but with genuine, unadorned devotion, tenderness, and heartfelt love. Such worship was not a mere formality but a profoundly personal expression.

Over the course of time, through evolving expressions of dharma and devotion within the Utkal realm, Shri Jagannath of the forest-dwelling Shabaras gradually emerged as Maha Buddha, then as Maha Rudra, and ultimately as Maha Vishnu. He came to be recognized as the national deity—a unifying symbol of all faiths. With this, evolved a whole servitor community comprising Acharya, Mahanta, Panda, Padhiari etc. to perform the elaborate rituals of worship. The Shabaras found themselves deprived of their erstwhile, intimate service; apart from the most meagre Anasara ritual, the unqualified right to perform his worship remained reserved solely for the Brahmins. Shabara Vishwavasu would simply juggle a pot of water and arrange a modest repast upon a leaf platter, and thus the ritual of Shri Jagannath's worship would be fulfilled. There, the Sagnik and learned Brahmins ignited the eternal flame of the Yajna.

Where formerly the worship simply sufficed with a few succinct words in the form of affectionate address to the deities as 'O Kalia, O Balia,' was replaced with an entanglement of machinery-like mantras, verses, and contrived procedures—from invocations rooted in the Shat Chakra to recitations such as '*Gopijana Vallabhaya Namah*'—a veritable medley of ritualistic worship, accompanied by the elaborate prescriptions of *Panchopachar* and *Shodashopachar* rites.

Yet, in all that elaborate ceremony of worship and adoration, the Hental forest offered no proper setting. The Brahmin servitors had departed one by one, but how could the Daita attendants leave? Their connection with Shri Jagannath was so profound, as if bound by the umbilical cord, together with whom they share space inside the Anasara quarantine, dining side by side and offering even meagre leftover fruits in a ritual act of surrender. How could they abandon him and seek shelter elsewhere? For these Daitas, the Hental forest, which in their eyes now transformed into the Anasara bamboo matting, was their only refuge—the sole place where they may feel the intimate presence of Shri Jagannath. In their delight at this possibility, a Daita burst forth, exclaiming, 'What a divine play this is, O Jagannath!'

The two Daitas' faces shone wild and fierce, almost monstrous in countenance. During Rath Yatra—at the moment of the *dhadi pahandi*—the mere pair of them sufficed for carrying Shri Jagannath's wooden idol to the altar on the chariot along the temporary stairway; no further attendants were needed. With a simple scarf wrapped around their waists, these two mighty figures could hoist Shri Jagannath upon their broad shoulders as though he were a mere doll, crying out, 'Come now, arise, O Kalia—why do you resist so?' Then, like an obedient child, Lord Jagannath would effortlessly ascend the grand chariot.

And yet here, with only scant sustenance—half meals or even occasional fasting—their muscles remained robust, their bodies unyielding; it is nothing short of a marvel. These devoted servitors of Shri Jagannath were clad in nothing more than threadbare, soiled dhotis, a sweat-dampened gamchha secured around their waists, and a towel tied upon their heads in the manner of a humble turban.

There was no elaborate extravagance of the Shrivatsa Khandashala temple ritual with its full *Shodashopachar* pomp; instead, a simple rite was observed. They would merely pour water over the altar, sprinkle it on Lord Jagannath, perform a brief dental cleansing and a modest ablution—without the trappings of ornate garments, costly adornments, or sandalwood smearing. Such ornaments would serve no real purpose here. Every day, as Jaguni roamed aboard the boat from Manikpatna, he would collect plump rice and fresh greens, boil them in the kudua (earthen pot), and thereby prepare a humble repast for the Daita attendants. Occasionally, even Jaguni would partake in their modest fare. And yet, one would marvel that the pot never ran dry—the store never depleted. There were days, too, when Jaguni would return from Manikpatna bearing milk and cheese to create a special *chakta* so that the occasion resembled a festival of the revered Lord. When dishes like a simple yoghurt pudding, rice pudding, and cheese *chakta* were provided, one Daita would remark, 'Arey! With so many ingredients at hand, couldn't you manage to fetch some hemp leaves with black pepper and spices?' To which Jaguni would reassure, 'I shall bring them next time.'

Today was the day of Pushyabhishek. If the deities were in the temple, their divine forms would have been adorned with the markings of the ritual—*tadapa*, *khandua*, *pheta*, and *chemedi*—in accordance with the *Panchopachar* rite. How many times would the Ashthan Paḍhiari, accompanied by the Mekap, have ventured forth to the victual room for the bhog offering? But today, a complete fast was observed. Since yesterday evening, Jaguni had been absent. Early this morning, the Daita servitors stripped the weary, worn-out adornments from the deities' form, dressing them instead in tattered cloths; wild oleander flowers were plucked and fashioned into garlands, yet—where was the offering? Not even a single handful of coarse rice appeared in the prasad, nor were the customary dayana garlands to grace the deities, or the essential camphor available to conduct the arati. Still, as evening fell, casting the full moon's silver glow like crushed camphor strewn across the earth, Jaguni remained nowhere to be seen.

'Fie!' cried one voice. 'A ship without a rudder, drifting aimlessly.'

'What a divine play this is, O Mahaprabhu!' exclaimed another.

Between Gurubai and Barunakuda, along the banks of the stream, Ramachandra Dev secured his boat to a Hental tree and leapt onto the sandy shore. Dense, youthful mists descended upon the bosom of Chilika. What a day had passed—it felt as though an entire epoch had been spent. A long, soulful sigh escaped Ramachandra Dev's chest— was it one of relief or of despondency? It carried with it the simple consolation that yet another day was done.

Winding his way along a labyrinthine forest path,

Ramachandra Dev recalled that it was Pushyabhishek day. The grand temple lay barren—the seat of Ratna Simhasana was empty—while Shri Jagannath dwelt, lost somewhere in the unfathomable vastness of Chilika, in that great immensity. A sudden realization struck him: he must bear responsibility for this bitter irony. It was, after all, his own pride and inflated ego that had left the mighty Mahabahu wandering in the vast expanse.

Ramachandra Dev reclined against a tree, seeking a brief respite from his profound weariness. He could not summon the courage to approach the image of Shri Jagannath beneath the ancient banyan, for guilt and uncertainty had almost paralyzed him. His inner soul rose in stern indictment: 'O greedy king, you have cast Lord Jagannath, the tutelary deity of Odisha, into this immensity! It is your own petty selfishness, your trivial pride, your desperate craving to gratify your limited ambitions! Aminchand might have seized Shrikshetra, the sacred seat, or even become the royal servitor of Shri Jagannath—but on a day such as Pushyabhishek, they would not have been present in this vast darkness!' In that silent moment of anguished introspection, Ramachandra Dev deemed himself culpable.

Deep in the forest, a flock of birds cried out in unison and then fell silent. In their restless cries, it was as if the answer to Ramachandra Dev's inner dilemma was whispered—was his act justified? For Shri Jagannath is the unmistakable symbol of Utkal's invincibility, Odisha's cherished object of liberation! How, during his lifetime, could he allow Shri Jagannath to fall into Taqi Khan's clutches? Yes, by consigning Shri Jagannath to this vast exile, perhaps he had indeed committed a grave sin. For that, if he must endure hellfire, so be it—but not sorrow. Had he abandoned Shri Jagannath, the emblem of the humanitarian spirit, to the merciless hands of the oppressive Taqi Khan, he would not only be branded a traitor to Shri Jagannath, but his name would be forever etched among those who betray humanity itself.

Ramachandra Dev pressed onward, moving beneath the sprawling banyan towards the vicinity of the shrine. In the full-moon's gentle light, the sand's glimmer took on the hue of camphor. As his footsteps rustled the fallen leaves along the forest path, the two Daita servitors instinctively tightened their grip on their makeshift maces, ears sharpened in alertness—was it a spy from the enemy's ranks? They also observed that the lashkars of the Maluda army had begun to encircle Gurubai Island with evil intent. Yet fate had preserved a secret: concealed beneath the verdant canopy of Hental and Sundari trees, a slender stream charted a hidden course—a clandestine water route destined to lead the servitors to Shri Jagannath's sacred shrine. Remarkably, the enemy had yet to discern this covert passage, leaving the divine sanctuary unscathed by their intrusion.

One Daita suddenly screamed out, 'Beware—I shall sweep you away in a single stroke!'

In response, Ramachandra Dev bellowed, 'Hail, Shri Jagannath!'

The Daita servitors knew that Ramachandra Dev was returning from somewhere. Today, on the sacred day of Pushyabhishek, the deities embraced a complete fast! But alas, what use was it to disclose this fact to him? Perhaps he, too, had spent the entire day wandering like restless whirlwinds, consumed by the hunger of abstinence.

Beneath the ancient banyan, the wooden images of the deities loomed on the lofty shrine. From a branch, a torch swayed like an *akhanda* lamp; in its soft, wan light, the deities' pallid, almost besmirched form was discernible—his vestments tattered and his robes sullied. The once-proud attire of the Boirani, the worn *khandua* cloth, had all been reduced to shreds. No *tadapa* or *uttariya* was adorning his hallowed form, no string of dayana leaves, malati or nageshwar, which were so endeared to him; even the garland of forest flowers around his neck had withered.

With a deep, sorrowful sigh, Ramachandra Dev lamented the sight before him. Was this truly the regal semblance of Shri Jagannath—the cherished deity of the Utkal empire—on such a sacred day as Pushyabhishek? A wave of grief washed over him as he mourned the diminished splendour of the divine forms.

And yet, in his pair of big, rounded eyes was etched the gesture of *abhayamudra*, which conveyed that same gentle assurance in a soft murmur: 'There is no fear! Absolutely none! Every suffocating night is conquered by the blazing light of dawn!' With these stirring thoughts, Ramachandra Dev advanced towards the shrine.

In the flickering glow of the torchlight, the Daita servitors cast their gaze on him and voiced their accusation. 'Where has that wretch vanished? Not a single trace! He is utterly oblivious—completely ignorant—that today is the sacred Pushyabhishek of Lord Jagannath. The Lord himself is in rigorous fasting! Not even the humble offering of coarse rice could be presented. Had he been in the temple, by now he would have undergone his vital ceremonial purification, and the Gopalaballabh bhog would have been reverently placed before him.'

It was as if this lament laid the blame squarely at Ramachandra Dev's feet; after all, he was the root of the matter.

Speechless and at a loss, what answer could he give? Today, in every corner of Utkal, famine and drought reigned supreme. When a hearth might burn once and then never again, how could we silence the cry for nourishment? Like lashes raining down upon those bound, the Mughal army's demands for tribute had laid waste to villages with plunder and cruelty. When even the very lives of people hang precariously, how could our beloved Shri Jagannath—enshrined on the throne of Ratna Simhasana and celebrated with thrice-incensed offerings—fulfil his role? Alas, like the ill-starred denizens of Utkal, he too remained today as hungry, gaunt ascetics. And what words could he offer to console the Daita attendants, who looked upon Lord Jagannath with a bewildered sense of duty? His heart falters; he knew not how to ease their despair.

'Let the tired soul move forward and behold the visage of Shri Jagannath!'

From deep within the Hental forest, the rapt strains of Jaguni floated on the breeze, carrying with it the weight of longing and devotion.

In that mist-drenched evening, as if the very dusk had been steeped in rain, the Daita attendants and Ramachandra Dev, their hearts united in silent accord upon that desolate patch of forest land beneath Lord Jagannath's shrine, seemed to pour forth a floral tribute befitting the Pushyabhishek. In a single, fleeting moment, that numb, sorrowful stillness was swept away.

The eyes of the Daita servitors lit up as they exchanged long-awaited signals: 'Jaguni has arrived! Look—the hymns he intones resound like the plaintive call of a koel! O deity, you who have fasted this entire day!'

Jaguni hefted an oar over his shoulder like a makeshift staff, balancing two small baskets on either side, and searched for a proper place to set them aside.

One Daita, his temper rising, demanded, 'Scoundrel, where have you been since yesterday evening?'

Finding a suitable spot at last, Jaguni lowered the oar from his shoulder and replied in a matter-of-fact tone, 'I went to see the fair—where else could I have gone? It has become exceedingly difficult to gather even a fistful of rice from one village to the next; yet here you sit idly beneath the banyan's shade, issuing commands with ease, while I toil from dawn till dusk to procure the sacred offerings for the deities.'

Indeed, his words were no falsehood. Some semblance of Lord Jagannath's ritual practice was being upheld—whether promptly or belatedly, his bhog had arrived, all thanks to Jaguni, who roamed from village to village collecting a few handfuls of rice. The Daita servants understood this, and Ramachandra Dev himself recognized it.

Steadying himself amid these unfolding circum-stances, Ramachandra Dev declared, 'Here, Jaguni is our trusted aide; Lod Jagannath's worship—the entirety of his ritual upkeep—rests upon him. It is solely by his roaming about and gathering rice that we manage to subsist. To cast blame upon him would be an injustice.' And yet, Jaguni remained wholly detached from any desire for personal praise.

Then Jaguni spoke with a tone of mirth and earnestness: 'I have brought an offering of milk, cheese, and bananas from Manikpatna today, carried in that vessel. On this sacred Pushyabhishek day, should the Lord be served merely with coarse rice? No—mix the cheese into the milk to prepare a *chakta* offering; kheer, indeed, would be a marvel if only it could be made!'

'Let me prepare a banana *chakta* with these.'

Yet there was no means here to prepare kheer—for where among the devoted Daita servitors was any expertise in the delicate art of preparing kheer?

'Let me prepare a banana *chakta* with these.'

The two Daitas tied a gamchha around their waists and began preparing banana *chakta*. After all, presenting the deities' bhog was the realm of the Suara, and what the humble Daitas knew? During Anasara rituals, the Daitas would only serve fruits to the deities. Now, however, preparing even a mere banana *chakta* proved a monumental task for them.

As the Daita mashed the banana in a manner that resembled doing push-ups, he recalled how, in the temple, before the evening dhup, there was always the camphor arati—followed by the ceremony with twenty-one lamps—and then the Mangala Arati, culminating later in the evening with the kahali arati, after which Lord Jagannath's golden attire was revealed in the majestic Suna Vesha! During Lord Jagannath's golden ceremony, the offerings were truly bountiful. In the glow of the evening dhup, the deities were presented with *dahi-pakhala, shakar, parijatak, mandua, mathapuli*, *chadheinada*, *bada-pitha*, and *sana-peeta* in abundance.

'Ah, Jaguni,' a Daita exclaimed with a mix of amusement and urgency, 'couldn't you procure some black pepper—or perhaps some camphor—for the banana *chakta*?'

Yet, Shri Jagannath today had assumed the guise of the nude Mahabhairava. With this drastic change, how should one ever behold his resplendent Suna Vesha?

Then, with a playful glint in his eye, the Daita fixed his gaze on the dark visage of Lord Jagannath and continued, 'And what are you watching, O Kalia, Balia! This very banana *chakta* shall serve as your evening dhup, and with it, the grand Badasinghar dhup will be accomplished! What wondrous *leela* is unfolding here—only you can truly fathom it!'

But for the arati, camphor had long run out. From a torch, one Daita lit a brass lamp.

'Hold on,' Jaguni shouted. 'I've brought a little camphor for the arati. Today, the deities shall have a proper camphor arati!' Unfastening a corner of his dhoti, he produced a few diminutive bundles of camphor, murmuring to himself, 'Tonight, at the time of the dhup, a modest camphor arati will finally be held.'

The Daita preparing the banana *chakta* remarked, 'Do you see, Mani! Had the deities been in the sacred precincts of Shrivatsa Khandashala temple, there would be a lavish cascade of offerings—*kanika*, *arisa*, *pana*, *pitha*, and kheer flowing in abundance. Lord Jagannath's Pushyabhishek would have been celebrated with 108 copper vessels brimming with the purest cow's ghee. And here, a little camphor is all that we have, and that is sufficient.'

The Daita knew no sacred stotra or mantra. Standing humbly beneath the shrine, with clumsy, unpractised hands, he began to perform the camphor arati, swaying it in an erratic up-and-down motion before the deities. His gestures followed no set cadence and possessed none of the elegance one might expect. In the background, not a single instrument—the resonant conch, the solemn *bheri*, the hallowed *mahuri*, nor the veena, *rava*, *singha*, gong, and *pakhawaj*—joined in harmonious unison. Instead, in the depths of the Hental forest, the voices of countless cicadas swelled into an impromptu medley, as if nature itself were offering a Mangala Arati with its own enchanted refrain.

Suddenly, as if overtaken by wild fervour, Jaguni seized a gong and began striking it. Ever since the day Shri Jagannath went into hiding, not even the gong had tolled at the time of the arati—let alone the sound of a conch. In the desolation of Chilika, enemy spies might well seize upon even the faintest sound and track the deities. Yet today, Jaguni had become utterly resolute, his doubts completely dispelled. In the silken glow of the arati, the mighty arms of Mahabahu appeared to rise in the Varabhaya gesture—no fear... no fear!

The Daita placed the arati lamp beneath the shrine. Now, prasad will be presented to the deities. How could Ramachandra Dev—once cast out from Hinduism for embracing Islam—remain present during the sacred offering of dhup?

'Your Majesty!' the Daita implored to Ramachandra Dev. 'Dhup will be offered!'

Ramachandra Dev grasped the silent signal ingrained

in his words. Letting out a weary sigh, he descended from the shrine and stepped towards the sandy expanse.

In the dappled darkness and crystalline silver moonlight of the Hental forest, a spectral figure advanced steadily towards the sandy expanse. Was it an enemy, drawn by the echoing resonance of the tolling gong, stealthily advancing upon them? Oh, Jaguni—his untamed spirit and fevered frenzy had yet to abate.

Ramachandra Dev, his instincts sharpened, reached for the curved dagger at his waist, gripping it tightly in his fist.

The shadowed figure called out, 'Jai Shri Jagannath!'—a cry, a signal laden with meaning.

Bahubalendra ascended the sandy expanse. 'Let me return after darshan. There are many urgent matters to attend to.'

He soon returned, his expression marked by quiet resolve. Ramachandra Dev regarded him keenly and spoke, 'Where have you too disappeared into secrecy all this time? Each day, I wait and return empty-handed from Maluda Ghat. Even today, I arrived mere moments ago. What arrangements have you made? The deities will not remain safe here for long!'

After Taqi Khan's assault on Khurda, even when only a handful of regional chieftains remained loyal to Ramachandra Dev amid countless calamities, none had been as steadfast as Bahubalendra. Through every crisis, he had stood by Ramachandra Dev like an inseparable shadow. Now, standing at the very twilight of his maturity, Bahubalendra's muscles remained firm and his resolve unbroken. Though his broad head showed the marks of time, his eyebrows still gleamed with youthful lustre, and the saffron line of vermilion on his face shone on. His rugged visage was complemented by thick moustaches and a tangled beard on either side.

With deliberate grace, Bahubalendra stroked his moustache and said, 'I have come after meeting with the chieftains from Mahuri, Khemndi, and Jarada. That is why I have been delayed for so long. They are all deeply concerned for Shri Jagannath's sake, yet none of them is willing to take on the responsibility of sheltering him within their own domains.'

Ramachandra Dev frowned and retorted, 'Then venturing there was nothing but a waste of time! Do you not remember the days of the Tikali war? When the Faujdar of Chikakol, Zulfiqar Khan Nasrat Jung, hot on our trail, pursued us relentlessly? Had those allied forces been with us when I organized our defences and advanced towards the Chhatradwar Valley, the course of Utkal's history might have been changed. How could you so easily forget such a simple fact, Bahubalendra?'

Bahubalendra replied gravely, 'For this, their conscience gnaws at them. But, Maharaj, when fate turns against us, even our dearest friend may become our foe.'

In a troubled tone, Ramachandra Dev asked, 'And what of Tikali? I have longed to ask this for some time now, but have been unable to speak.'

Narayan Jagadev of Tikali stands ready,' Bahubalendra explained, 'his resolve unwavering, untouched by hesitation. The Nizam, troubled by the relentless Maratha onslaught, finds himself ensnared in the throes of conflict. The faujdar of Chikakol, too, is preoccupied, leading his forces against the advancing Marathas. Thus, in consideration of Shri Jagannath's safety, the northern frontier under the governance of Chikakol stands as a more secure refuge. If the deities were to remain concealed in Tikali, neither Taqi Khan nor Chikakol's Faujdar would readily discern their whereabouts. Until the Mughal assault upon Odisha abates, Jagadev is prepared to assume the responsibility of safeguarding Shri Jagannath within the sanctuary of Tikali.

A visible weight seemed to lift from Ramachandra Dev's brow. He breathed a sigh of relief and said, 'Bahubalendra, you have freed me from my deepest worries! Yet I still wonder—how will the deities ever reach Tikali? A snake in the grass is more perilous than a lion in the open. The traitors within our own ranks—the spies of Mansingh who sit by the gates in Ganjagarh—stand ready. Should they find even a moment's chance, they will not hesitate to have Shri Jagannath dragged away on leather ropes!'

'I have already made the necessary arrangements,' Bahubalendra reassured. 'The chieftains of Muhari, Chikiti, and Mahendragiri have pledged to escort the deities with their soldiers to ensure their safe passage. Their promise is more than sufficient. The route to Karandimala is treacherous enough, and once the deities are conveyed through the dense jungle and placed upon a chariot for the journey to Tikali, no further inconvenience will be encountered.'

'Then let us move with all haste!' Ramachandra Dev declared, with determined urgency. 'It's unwise to keep the deities here even for a single day. Once his sanctuary is arranged, we must prepare for the final battle for our independence against the Mughals—there is no time to waste.'

With his hands clasped behind his back, Ramachandra Dev paced restlessly along the moist, camphor-sprinkled sands of Chilika. In the desolate cries of the coastal gulls and the languishing wails of home-bound swans rising from the empty shores, his inner urgency and longing reverberated as if echoing the very heartbeat of destiny.

Abruptly, he turned to Bahubalendra and queried, 'Tell me, can we escort the deities from the Malakuda Ghats along the road to Ganja and then to the Karandimala Valley? Have you devised a plan for that, Bahubalendra?'

With serene resolve, Bahubalendra replied, 'The Lord shall arrange it as his will decrees—for we are but instruments in this grand design.'

*****

Chapter II

In the relentless whirl of history, the village of Malakuda on Chilika's shore had been scattered to the winds—as if it were nothing more than a handful of withered, dry leaves.

To the south, in times when the deities' temporary dwelling was sought, a modest temple had been raised here. Its upkeep was entrusted to a chowpadhi, and the village of paikas came into being at Malakuda. But amid recurring calamities—persistent drought, aridity, fierce tempests—and the repeated plunder by the raiding armies of the Maluda's faujdar, the village had largely been emptied of life. Only four or five paikas' dwellings and the stone-stepped chowpadhi of the village accountant, Arjun Jenamani, remained, while all the other houses lay abandoned. The mounds were now overrun by wild growth—dense brush, thorny scrubs, rank vegetation—and bore the scars of countless brutal assaults by both man and nature. From one crumbling house drifted a lone, sorrowful cadence—the plaintive voice of a woman, like the mournful coo of a dove:

> My husband rides to war—receive my prayer,
> Let valour rest upon his shoulder wide.
> Let vermilion grace his brow so fair,
> And guard his soul through battle's raging tide.

Hearing this sorrowful lament on repeated occasions, Ramachandra Dev inquired, 'Jenamani, who is weeping thus?'

Jenamani answered, 'She has lost all sense. Her husband had gone to battle in the Chhatradwar Valley, alongside the intrepid general. In that fight, he was slain. The villagers urged her, "Snap the bangles, and wipe away the sindoor from your brow!" But she believes with all her heart that her husband is not dead—that he will return!'

Ramachandra Dev shuddered and observed, 'Never, in all the forsaken abodes of Utkal, have I heard such lamentation!'

'My husband rides to war!' she wailed again…

Beyond that ceaseless lament, all that remained was a silence so absolute, a stillness so profound, that no other sign of life endured. The nurturing love of the village's earth had long since withered away—even though a few houses still stood, sustained by the sparse pursuits of salt cultivation and modest trade. To the east of the village lay a few habitations, the settlements of the Noliyas and the Kandaras.

As the chill winds of Pausha whipped along the road through Malakuda, they sent a whirlwind of desiccated leaves skittering before them.

Further east, where the temple once proudly stood, the Maluda's faujdar—driven by impotent rage—had reduced it to a mere pile of stones. And yet, the ruined vedika remained unscarred. In the relics of the temple's threshold, the gnarled, Champak tree—its contorted form mirroring the twisted limbs of Sage Astavakra—stood unyielding. It remained a silent witness to every cruelty meted out by man and by nature—a detached spectator on the stage of a thespian tragedy, reminiscent of a jester. In its strange, distorted posture, every moment of sorrowful parting seemed to emerge with a secret, imperturbable resignation.

Ramachandra Dev wandered in a fruitless, restless agitation along the lonely road from Malakuda Ghat to Jenamani's chowpadhi in that forsaken hamlet. On the day following Pausha Purnima, the Daitas and Jaguni had set the deities adrift from the shrine beneath the ancient banyan in three boats, their destination being Malakuda. From there, by overland route, the deities were to be clandestinely transferred to Tikali; yet, an easy passage from Gurubai to Malakuda was nowhere to be found.

The deities had now been absent from Gurubai for two days. On the first day, they would linger at the uninhabited Nalavan Island; on the following night, they would be conveyed in the boat to Chadheihaga Island. Had they departed from there yesterday evening—taking refuge for a while near Barakuda Island—they would have managed to reach Malakuda Ghat by nightfall after what felt like three long *pahers*.

Above, the heavens were awash with a scattering of clouds, as if formed from shattered fish scales, while the mist over Chilika slowly parted, revealing in its midst the emerging crescent of the waning moon. Its pale, silvery radiance cast a lonely, sorrowful pall over the desolate landscape.

With troubled, unsteady steps, Ramachandra Dev retraced his path along the ghats towards Jenamani's chowpadhi. His feet halted before the ruins of a weathered house. In the fractured moonlight, the abandoned home to the west appeared like the hump of a camel—its walls, once washed by rain, now long swept away by capricious winds, leaving behind only a skeletal remnant. The courtyard was choked with accumulated earth, creepers and tangled scrub, while on the outer wall, two lotus motifs, half-hidden by slanting moonbeams, still barely glimmered. The ravages of countless past assaults had been unable to erase these vestiges completely.

Deep within Ramachandra Dev's consciousness lay the indelible scar of life's suffering—a wound long dried yet still bearing its mark. This crumbling wall stood as a silent witness, a mute testimony to the shattered fragments of his own existence.

Memories drifted back of that searing noon in the month of Jeshtha—of the scorching gusts of heat that once lanced over his face, leaving behind an echo of thirst and weariness. For on that day, he had set out from this very path, seeking a boat along the route to Malakuda Ghat. How he had yearned for a boat to appear, to carry him across the lake.

Amid the silence of that ruined house, a trembling, ragged cry erupted—a harsh utterance filled with curses and screams. "Oh, you wretched, doomed soul! Die… die! Again and again, you are warned not to join the battle—is this a war fought for the nation? Here, it is the common man who slays the king, and the king, in turn, who dispatches the common man. Brothers even tear each other's throats apart! Everyone is turning over to the Mughals."

"Clear the way…" came a voice, laced with suspicion and quivering apprehension.

Startled, Ramachandra Dev stopped in his tracks.

In the fog-laden moonlight of that cold Pausha night, beneath a silver curtain of mist, the loose pallu of a graceful woman fluttered.

With a tremulous murmur, she inquired, "Clear the way—who are you? A paika? Or a bandit?"

Deep in the recesses of Ramachandra Dev's memory emerged a forlorn, haunting image of that bride of the household—unadorned, eyes betraying a deep, wistful helplessness.

"O evil Sara, the damned one."

How utterly she had been swept away by the relentless cycles of history! Yet on that very day, that pitiable figure had been his life□giver, his refuge! In his pride, Ramachandra Dev's heart turned bitter and venomous—for not even for a single day had he inquired after her welfare, consumed as he was by matters of greater urgency, his days swallowed by duty and pressing affairs.

'Your Majesty, why do you stand here in the open in this bitter cold?' echoed a startled cry.

'Oh, Jenamani! How long must we wait for them to arrive?'

In an indifferent tone, Jenamani replied, 'Between Malakuda Ghat and the waterway of Barakuda, there are four kos—about ten kilometres. If the boat was set afloat at dusk, and with the westerly winds battering like errant gusts, they should reach Malakuda Ghat within five or six hours tonight, Maharaj. Until then, waiting here serves no purpose.'

'High atop the Ghantshila hills, the Maluda faujdar, Fateh Muhammad, has now established a fortified outpost. From this stronghold, his forces unleash sudden raids upon merchant boats bound for Ganja Port, plundering without warning. I fear for the deities' boat if they attack…' Ramachandra Dev's tone quivered with both apprehension and agitation.

'If it is indeed the immutable wish of the Lord,' Jenamani responded curtly, 'for him to be bound with leather ropes—what can be done, Maharaj? What can you and I possibly do?'

There was a slight lessening in Ramachandra Dev's agitation upon hearing Jenamani's detached reply. A battle must be fought, of course, yet its outcome is intricately woven into the will of fate itself, with its threads held in the hands of the divine. So why should he be agitated?

Yet, had he not already surrendered himself before the Almighty? Had he not raised his hands in earnest supplication? 'Look—I have raised both hands… may your wish be fulfilled!' And yet, even as terror and anxiety burned like tiny flickering embers within him, every moment of the future was filled with a rising dread.

Oh, this restless soul! This feeble, aimless heart!

Ramachandra Dev came to feel that it was not Taqi Khan himself who was his enemy, but rather Taqi Khan's terror and anxiety that had become his foe. With that thought, Ramachandra Dev silently set off towards Jenamani's chowpadhi.

Outside Jenamani's house along the roadside—even before dusk—a line of some twenty to twenty-five bullock carts, each draped in cloaks from top to bottom, stood haphazardly in a blockade. The road lay impassable. In Jenamani's fields of salt that stretch into Huma and Ganja, salt merchants would stream in from all around to purchase their wares. Observing the long queue of carts at Jenamani's gate, one might surmise that eminent traders from distant lands had arranged these vehicles to collect salt. The oxen, once unbound, now grazed a short distance away; in the pallid moonlight, the mass of oxen appeared as if a heap of salt itself.

Yet, when one gazed closely at the well-appointed merchants sitting at Jenamani's door on the chowpadhi, wrapped entirely in double-layered blankets from head to toe, their figures bathed in the flickering glow of lanterns suspended from the posts, one might harbour suspicions—they seemed almost like impostors. Beneath some of these double-layered shawls, the bound tiger skin would occasionally catch the eye. The sheen of oil and turmeric on their foreheads shone like vermilion. Arrayed haphazardly at the corners of the chowpadhi were piles of weaponry: blades with their reversed edges, daggers, long swords, leather shields, iron bucklers affixed with bolts, bows, additional daggers, iron spikes, double-barreled guns, and a collection of sixteen different arms and weapons. All these, assembled from various quarters by Upendra Bahubalendra, were intended to ensure that the deities' passage to Tikali was secured.

'Where is Bahubalendra?' questioned Ramachandra Dev.

In a low, enigmatic tone, Arjun Jenamani replied, 'Two detachments armed with paikas will be waiting for you just outside Ganjagarh—in a screwpine forest.'

Ramachandra Dev's thoughts turned to the perilous valley of Ganjagarh. Mansingh stood firmly with Taqi Khan, his predatory gaze ever fixed on Chilika, while their spies and clandestine agents scour every corner for any sign of Shri Jagannath.

With a note of anxious inquiry, Ramachandra Dev asked, 'But what if Mansingh of Ganjagarh catches even a faint clue?"

'Then war will be upon us,' Arjun Jenamani responded evenly. 'We are ready.' Observing Jenamani's unruffled confidence, Ramachandra Dev found a modicum of relief.

'Our soldiers are positioned at every key stronghold along the valley, stretching all the way to Karandimala,' Jenamani continued. 'And once we cross Mahuri, there will be no further cause for worry—we are secure here!'

Leaving the chowpadhi behind, Ramachandra Dev advanced towards the Ghat, his mind heavy with concern. In the interplay of fog and moonlight, Chilika appeared adrift—directionless, devoid of life, sprawled across an endless, murky expanse. Jenamani followed closely at his heels, as Ramachandra Dev intermittently lifted his eyes to the fog-laden heavens where the evening star flickered faintly in the Nairata—southwest quadrant—out of clear view. 'It is now five hours into the night,' he murmured, just as Jenamani's resounding voice boomed from behind, 'Look—they are coming!'

Ramachandra Dev cast his gaze towards the shrouded form of Chilika. From Malakuda Ghat, a burst of flame had momentarily leapt from a rugged outcrop before extinguishing—a prearranged signal that, upon drawing near, they would leave such a blaze behind. As though a weight had been lifted from his heart, Ramachandra Dev raised his voice in fervour, 'Jai Shri Jagannath!' Meanwhile, three bullock carts rolled in and took their positions along the water's margin, and after a long, tense wait, three boats finally reached Malakuda Ghat. No sooner had they docked than both Daitas and Jaguni sprang onto the earthen bank.

Gasping slightly, Jaguni announced, 'By the time the evening star had risen, we had already reached Barakuda. Then, after navigating through the shadowed expanse of Ghantashila, we ferried the boat in such a manner that—thanks to the oppressive fog—we mistakenly headed for Kadakani Ghat rather than our intended destination, Malakuda. Only after leaving Kadakani did we promptly kindle a trail of fire, a beacon that unerringly guided us to Malakuda. Without that signal, discerning our path in that mist-shrouded, moonlit night would have been exceedingly difficult!'

In that charged moment, neither Ramachandra Dev nor Jenamani entertained any further appeals; their sole preoccupation now was the swift transfer of the deities from boat to bullock cart. For they knew that by securing the Mahuri frontier this very night, all peril beyond would vanish.

The paikas, assembled on the chowpadhi, had reached the bank, and amid their heightened clamour, the silent night resounded like a waking nightmare.

Amid the tumult, Jenamani bellowed, 'Quickly, secure the contrivance—lay the bamboos across the channel and add the side-railing! We have no time to waste!'

'Do you think we've been dawdling on purpose?' Jaguni retorted sharply. 'We've all been rowing together from Barakuda, yet your men are sluggish in setting up the structure!'

Despite their clashing words and disputes, they hastily arranged the bamboos and constructed the side-railing—securing the contrivances that artfully spanned the gap from the three boats to the Ghat. Meanwhile, three bullock carts stood ready in quiet reverence at a distance.

Yet a new challenge emerged: disembarking the deities from the boats and conveying them along the bamboo pathway into the awaiting bullock carts proved a formidable and laborious undertaking.

'*Apasara! Apasara!*' Jaguni shouted, his mind was swept away by a vivid recollection of the sumptuous cushioned pillows employed in the *pahandi* that gently ushered the deities into the chariot during the grand Rath Yatra.

One of the Daitas snapped, 'Where in this very place do you expect to find *apasara*, you scoundrel?'

At the outset of the journey from Gurubai Island—reminiscent of that moment on the sandy slope when the Daitas gracefully hoisted the deity aloft in his *pahandi*—they now faced an altogether different ordeal. They were confronted with the vexing task of safely conveying the deity—waist-deep in water and mire—across the contrivance and into the shelter of the bullock cart's cover.

A Daita, cradling Sudarshan firmly against his chest, carefully eased it into the shelter of the covered cart. Retrieving the idol of Subhadra and ushering it into the cart was also not a troublesome endeavour. As for the venerable Lord—Balabhadra—the two Daitas, together with Jaguni, toiled in concert, heaving and dragging him onto the supports fashioned for the purpose until, with unyielding resolve, they finally nestled him safely within the protective shroud of another bullock cart's cover.

But Shri Jagannath remained immovable! It was utterly impossible to hoist him even upon the contraption designed for dragging. In that cool, shivering night, one Daita, dabbing sweat from his brow in exasperation, grumbled, 'O Kalia, you revel as if this were the carefree splendour of Chandan Yatra, while we toil under its crushing weight.'

Another Daita, his tone soft with supplication, urged, 'Oh Kalia, lift yourself! Why are you dawdling so heedlessly?' Even the paikas, stalwart in their duty, were drenched in perspiration.

By the riverside steps of the Ghat, Ramachandra Dev beheld the Daitas' harrowing struggle—a soul burdened by duty, torn between devotion and peril. Tightening a scarf around his waist, he strode forward, resolved to lend his strength in lifting Shri Jagannath. But as he approached the scene of the arduous dragging, a voice rang out from the turmoil—a Daita's urgent cry:

'Maharaj! Hold—fall back!'

Like the searing sting of a scorpion's tail, that sharp command reminded Ramachandra Dev all too painfully that he was denied even the slightest privilege of touching Shri Jagannath. Dispirited yet resolute, he returned to the Ghat, inwardly lamenting, 'Why, time and again, this obstinacy, O Jagannath! How deep into the unfathomable abyss of misfortune must one be plunged to have your will done?'

'Necessity knows no law!' another Daita called out. 'Lend your hand, Maharaj, will you not?' And with that, Ramachandra Dev clambered once more to the contraption.

The solemn night trembled beneath the unified chant of Haribol. In the shadows, none could discern how the Daitas and paikas, moving as one, lifted him aloft—securing him within the enclosure of the bullock cart's cover with an almost imperceptible grace.

In a jubilant chorus, the paikas raised their voices in unison: 'Jai Jagannath!'

Once the deities were firmly nestled within the cart, the combined might of the paikas and Daitas pulled all three carts through the mist-veiled, moonlit expanse towards Arjun Jenamani's chowpadhi. The moment they arrived at his threshold, yet another band of paikas sprang down from the chowpadhi, encircling the carts with swift precision.

Inside the cart coverings, the deities were packed with straw before layers upon layers of coarse salt were generously sprinkled over them. Numerous carts, burdened with salt, stood ready. Soon after, the oxen were yoked to the bullock carts, and they set forth along the Malakuda road towards Ganja. In disciplined formation, paikas from forts such as Mahuri and Jarada, weapons concealed, advanced ahead, behind, and flanking the carts—disguised as salt merchants and drivers. Amid the hush of night, the clamour and scraping of the carts rose—a mournful lament echoing the tragic strains of Utkal's fate.

From the very edge of Malakuda village to Ganja, the route was marked solely by salt carts strung along a path intermittently bordered by screwpine hedges. The bullock carts, sometimes winding through the salt flats, sometimes navigating the narrow passages between the hedges, trudged onward towards Ganja. By the time they arrived at

Ganjagarh, the eastern sky was ablaze—the morning star flared like a fiery ember, pulsating in the dawn.

As the hour of daybreak arrived, Ganjagarh lay silent, eerily deserted. The rhythmic creaks of the bullock carts pierced the stillness. In the watchtower, the sentries, half-asleep, glimpsed the approaching caravan of salt traders. Recognizing them at a glance, they stirred momentarily, only to shut their eyes once more, indifferent to the quiet procession.

After passing through Ganja, they crossed Mahuri. Beyond lay the expanse of Karandimala—a forest of jujube, screwpine, cashew, and tamarind—where manoeuvring the bullock carts over whispering, shifting sands proved increasingly arduous. Gazing upward at the vast heavens, Ramachandra Dev silently vowed that by morning, they would indeed reach Karandimala.

As the party neared Mahuri, emerging from the dense clusters of screwpine, a detachment of paikas led by Upendra Bahubalendra materialized. Their collective cry rang out in harmony—'Jai Jagannath! Jai Jagannath!'—and the moustachioed wilderness itself seemed to resound with that victorious intonation. In that resonant sound, as if summoned from the very womb of the dark night, a new, vigorous dawn was being born. Even amid potential storms of a hundred assaults, this invincible cry emboldened the paikas, who had laboured to convey the deities through the black, impenetrable night—moving like a band of dacoits. At the close of every night, as the nascent light of dawn broke in resplendent hues, their voices once again heralded its arrival with the fervent refrain, 'Jai Shri Jagannath!'

Suddenly, a Daita was struck by a realization—'The hour of the morning repose has arrived!'

Ramachandra Dev, progressing slowly on horseback behind the grand procession, was similarly reminded. In the temple, it was indeed time for the *Prabhati Mailam*—a sacred moment of vestment transformation at the Shri Mandir. Yet, in this barren wilderness, where were the blooming flowers, the sacred tulsi, the cooling sandalwood, or the tangy amla? Where were the customary servitors—the Suarabadus, the Khattuli attendants, the Amla carriers, the Ghatuari custodians, and the Pushpalak—each entrusted with the sacred duties of tending to Lord Jagannath's hallowed presence?

In the salt-laden shelter today, the deities were granted their morning reprieve!

Had Shri Jagannath acquiesced to Mughal subjugation and remained within the temple's sanctum, his dawn hours would have been graced with the ceremonial camphor arati and the prescribed sixteen rites. Yet, through the ages, the price for the struggle for liberation has been marked by such a bitter, salt-washed reproach—a price the Odia people themselves are paying. How, then, could the cherished deity of the Odia, the exalted bulwark of this fierce campaign, ever find solace amid the majestic security of the temple's Meghnad ramparts and the resplendence of the sacred rites?

The eastern sky blossoms with vermilion hues. On the horizon of Mahuri, the Karandimala mountains shimmered like undulating waves of blue stone—a silent herald to the coming day.

Ramachandra Dev spoke with resolute calm, 'I now

take my leave from here, Bahubalendra! Jaguni and the Daitas shall escort the deities to Tikali; the responsibility now rests with you.' He added confidently, 'There is no hint of disaster here. Once we have traversed Karandimala, we shall remove the deities from the bullock cart and carry them to the palanquin. For, immediately after crossing Chikiti and Mahendragiri, Tikali awaits—truly, the path through the forest beckons!'

One by one, the bullock carts melted away into the forests of cashew and screwpine, swallowed by verdant mystery.

Ramachandra Dev slackened his reins and lifted both hands skyward in solemn surrender, his voice ringing out in fervent devotion—'Now, with both hands raised, I offer myself in reverence to Shri Jagannath!'

*****

Chapter III

In Tikali, Shri Jagannath was secure—there was nothing to fear. Jagadev had sent word, and neither Taqi Khan nor the faujdar of Chikakol—or even the Nizam-ul-Mulk—could glean a hint of that hidden sanctuary. Shri Jagannath, having emerged from Chilika and enshrouded himself in Tikali, had veiled his presence so entirely that it defied the imagination—not just of his pursuers, but of anyone. Taqi Khan's secret agents prowled in every direction, yet from Banapur to Junagadh, Bolgarh to Mantiri, not a single trace of him could be unearthed.

On every tongue rose the same mournful lament: 'Ah, hapless Jagannath—now hidden from all eyes!'

Rautapada stood as a revered stronghold of paika heritage, its soil steeped in the legacy of valour and tradition.

Ramachandra Dev had spent the previous night on his journey towards Puri, taking refuge at Fakira Mangaraj's Bhagavata house. Now his state of being was aptly encapsulated by the venerable verse: *Ahara yatra tatrascha, shayanam hattamandiram*— Where sustenance is found, so too is shelter. Drifting in disguise from one village to the next, from chowpadhi to chowpadhi, and from fort to fort like an unsettled storm, he assumed the guise of a wandering dervish or the austere renunciate at will. Changing his appearance posed little challenge: his wild, unkempt hair, his beard, and his moustache had grown on their own; whether he donned a sombre black garment with a glimmering glass bead necklace around his neck or transformed into a saffron-clad exile adorned with rudraksha beads and smeared with vermilion on his ample brow—the metamorphosis was as effortless as it was enigmatic.

Utkal stood in turmoil. Chaos gripped Khurda, Barunei, and Cuttack, where Taqi Khan's faujdar, Hashim Khan, lurked in ambush. The revered deity of the Odia people remained in exile, severed from his sacred abode.

The paikas—once freeholders by right—were now stripped of their lands and livelihoods, while Mughal forces, under the guise of tax collection, unleashed cruelty, plunder, and fire upon them. They burned slowly—inch by inch—yet their voices, robbed of language, failed to rise against the oppressor. Their limbs, paralyzed in anguish, were rendered powerless in defiance.

Odisha had become a mute, silent convulsion—a wounded beast bearing an unutterable pain. In a desperate bid to dull their anguish, the villages hummed the lax, intoxicated strains of kirtan, following the tradition of Nadiya: 'Brother, when does the golden bird grace the sky?'

Under the once-dynamic leadership of Shri Chaitanya, Nagar-kirtan had erupted as a battle-cry against the sanctimonious nawab Husain Shah of Gauda; yet in the span of two centuries, that fervour had withered into the anguished final cry of a people robbed of virility. But Shri

Chaitanya was never to be blamed—it was the absence of steadfast, fearless leadership that had doomed them.

In Rautapada too, Ramachandra Dev beheld the same spectacle unfolding once more—a haunting echo of the past. Yet, no circumstance arose to introduce himself. Where had the thunderous roar of the Paika Akharas vanished? O brave paikas…!

In the subdued glow of the Bhagavata house, Fakir Mangaraj yawned deeply, cracking his knuckles with deliberate ease as he murmured 'Ram, Ram,' and then observed sorrowfully, the deities have forsaken the sacred shrine of Shrivatsa Khandashala, abandoned the regal seat of Ratna Simhasana, vanishing into some unknown realm. The king went into exile. Would Utkal not be left orphaned, bereft of its guardian?'

Voices of resolute support joined in.

'Beware of the thirteen! Now, wait and see what unfolds.'

'Hari Bol!'

A forlorn procession of the disheartened—a caravan lacking in self-assurance—carrying the echoes of despair!

That night was spent beneath the verandah of the Bhagavata house. At dawn, Ramachandra Dev set off towards Puri. Fakir Mangaraj spared no effort in his eloquence and hospitality, warmly attending to Ramachandra Dev, who had assumed the garb of a sadhu from the western lands. Ramachandra Dev expected that perhaps in Puri, he might at last receive an audience with the elusive Vishnu Paschim Kabat Mahapatra—a meeting of destinies long deferred.

As long as Lord Jagannath remained secure, Utkal would continue to survive by some grim miracle. But until the Supreme Lord once more graced the Ratna Simhasana with his sacred presence, the soul of Utkal would remain ever aggrieved—the bitter scorn and smouldering flame of exile would persist unabated. Until the Mughal oppressors were driven from the land and true independence was restored, this acrid reminder would burn on, relentless and unyielding.

'But how…? By what twist of fate?'

Ramachandra Dev, his eyes void, beheld before him a barren, ashen path—a stretch of obscurity that stole the very breath from his lungs.

Lakshmi Paramaguru had yet to return from Murshidabad. It was not beyond the realm of possibility that he had been taken captive. Even Vishnu Paschim Kabat Mahapatra remained unreachable. Ramachandra Dev drifted alone, as solitary as an errant comet—a lone, withering leaf caught in a relentless gale—venturing from village to village in a desperate attempt to rekindle the very spark of life in a people marching steadily towards demise. Must our beloved deity, Shri Jagannath, remain exiled for all eternity? Would Odisha never break free from the yoke of the Mughals? Would the lands stretching from the Ganga to the Godavari, in forsaking their ancestral legacy, meekly accept Mughal servitude—as if it were some indelible inscriptions upon the forehead? And what could you do, Ramachandra Dev? In the very fabric of Odia society, you were an outcaste, unwanted. Who today should answer your earnest call?

Last night in Rautapada, the echo of Fakira Mangaraj's observation still resounded: "The king has lost his caste and gone into exile." Caste! Caste! How had it come to be that upon this sacred soil where Shri Jagannath abides, adherence to caste had become so narrow-minded? Today, Hindus themselves had become the most formidable adversaries of Hinduism, even as they continued to celebrate their revered identity. What a bitter irony of history! Is caste defined by faith or by deed?

There was no need to spur the horse; Ramachandra Dev pressed on steadily, though his brow was creased with worry.

At Atharnala Ghat in Shrikshetra, the acting administrator Naib Aminchand had levied the jizya and appointed an ijaredar for its collection. The ijaredar's collectors—those who had fastened a strip of red cloth around their heads—perched like vultures in the makeshift shelter at the ghat, waiting hungrily for travellers. But where were the travellers?

Since the deities were sequestered from the temple, all festivals and sacred celebrations had fallen silent. Not even the pilgrims, hailing from within a radius of ten miles from Puri, now visited Shrikshetra. On the rare occasion when a pilgrim from the western lands dared to arrive, the collectors would swarm about him as vultures encircled a fallen corpse.

Yet these tax collectors, mistaking Ramachandra Dev for a mere dervish, did not bar his passage—instead, they saluted him. Could they have failed to recognize him? Ramachandra Dev exhaled a quiet sigh of relief— for recognition itself carried danger. Had Aminchand imprisoned him in that hour of helplessness, not even a crow would have let out a cry of protest in his defence.

Two halves of the day slipped away. The sky was heavy with clouds, shrouded in unyielding fog, and there was no means to divine the time. On both sides of Grand Road, houses stood mute—no trace of life, no murmur of daily bustle. In that frozen hush, uncertainty, apprehension, and terror reigned, as silent as the depths of a cavern. Not a single child wept, and even the crows remained unusually quiet.

An unrelenting desolation held dominion, vast and absolute.

Some western pilgrims, unaware of the enforced seclusion, would make their way to the temple, only to circumambulate its empty courtyard in despair.

'Did you see the twelve-armed deity housed within a temple barely a hand's breadth wide?'

'And what of the Kaliyugi sheep?'

'Here stands the primordial Narasimha!'

'Chaitanya Mahaprabhu! Will you not behold the eight-armed Gauranga?'

'Bow your head at the edge of the Ratna Simhasana! The primordial void has Himself unravelled into infinite nothingness. Cannot you visualize the deities in the *senapata*?

The pandas and temple servitors left no stone unturned in urging the pilgrims, coaxing them with the promise of divine revelations—always with an eye towards offerings. Some reached into the folds of their garments, producing a few copper coins. Occasionally, from others, a Jahangiri rupee surfaced. They were lavish in their promises of a worthy darshan. And yet, after traversing such barren, inaccessible mountains and fording rivers on a long and arduous journey, they received no vision—only a burning disappointment that lingered unspoken amid the bickering of the pandas and servitors.

Within the modest confines of the *gumat*, a glimpse of the Patitapabana—Saviour of the sinful—temporarily quenched the pilgrims' thirst for the divine vision of Jagannath, though the rapture remained unassuaged. For it is only once, upon the hallowed Ratna Simhasana, that the eternal thirst of countless lifetimes may be momentarily still. Yet in the oppressive, musty atmosphere of that humble shrine, even the very breath seemed to choke them further.

Meanwhile, Ramachandra Dev, having once more altered his guise, now appeared as an ascetic from the western lands—a hardened, Aghori renunciant. Outside the *gumat*, facing the sacred Patitapabana, he cast a yearning gaze towards the hallowed Baisi Pahacha—the flight of twenty-two steps leading into the temple complex—a sacred destination he was forbidden to cross. Though branded as one estranged from his dharma, still counted among the traitors to Shri Jagannath, he could not—nor did he wish—to entirely repel the magnetic pull that emanated from within.

In the Mukti Mandap, many dignified Mahajana Brahmins, with sacred *upavita* draped across their shoulders, sat, carefully tallying tithis, nakshatras, and astrological positions, expounding their penance with solemn elegance, and accepting offerings of *pavalas* and *dhelis* as payment for their decrees. For one exiled from the Shri Jagannath Temple—where even the Lord had been banished and calamity prevailed in every corner of Odisha— the custodians showed no parsimony in prescribing penance, for no misfortune could render their meticulous rites futile. Clad in coarse tusser robes, they bore the old monastic marks upon their foreheads—a sandalwood tilak signifying an ancient legacy. When pilgrims rested their heads upon the edge of the Mukti Mandap, an elderly Mahajana, his voice thick with a drawling nasal lament, exclaimed:

'This is Mukti Mandap! Why do you offer mere *pavalas* and *dhelis*? Cast a charani instead! Sola Shashan Brahmins that we are! Salvation shall be yours. For the king has lost his caste, and the deity has gone clandestine—our very earnings have dissolved!'

The pilgrim agent, guiding a few weary western pilgrims through their circumambulation, suddenly bared his teeth in a strained grin, sensing the dwindling weight of his earnings. With a half-mocking tone, he grumbled, 'We, too, are not sailing in the abundance of kheer and khichdi? Mahajana Gosain! Let us be content with whatever grace Kalia has bestowed upon us.'

Ramachandra Dev entered the sanctum through the South Gate, his steps laden with a deep, heart-rending longing. Although there was no obstacle preventing him from proceeding as far as the Ratnavedi, something seemed to check his progress towards the empty jewelled throne—as if invisible hands barred his path. The throne lay desolate! And yet, the Akhanda lamp beneath it still burned, its unwavering flame lit in steadfast vigil for the Lord's reappearance. That flame, unsullied by suspicion or defilement and brimming with inexhaustible confidence, remained immovable. There was no doubt that the empty throne would one day be filled; until that auspicious arrival, the Akhanda lamp would burn on in endless expectancy.

Nearby, a learned panda, offering drops of Tulsi water to a western pilgrim, explained in hushed tones, 'The formless Lord, silent and void, has dissolved into emptiness.

He cannot be seen with mortal eyes. And yet, it is on the Ratna Simhasana that he still resplendently abides. Offer your tribute—one Jahangiri rupee, at least!'

It appeared as though touching his forehead against the edge of the Ratna Simhasana would bestow Ramachandra Dev's burning existence with a tranquil release. But he found himself bereft of the courage to attempt such a blessing. His inner voice rose in protest, lamenting, 'Now you are forsaken by dharma! Branded an outcaste! Your name is inscribed among the *yavanas*! What right do you have to lay hands upon the Ratna Simhasana of Shri Jagannath—the very chosen deity of the Hindu world?'

Yet, is Shri Jagannath solely the beloved of those who bear the Hindu standard? He is, in truth, Jagannath—the deified soul of all humanity. He is revered by every seeker, from the uncompromising ascetics who dwell in untamed groves to the erudite Smarta Brahmins. And yet, within the Mukti Mandap, the ruling sovereigns who rendered verdicts on purity and impurity sat like solemn sacred crows, their presence testament to a corrupted order. Would they allow him passage to that hallowed Simhasana?

Ramachandra Dev made his way back to the Garuda pillar, where, from that solemn height, he beheld the Simhasana—silent and unclaimed. The Garuda pillar was deserted—bereft of any seekers. From Vasant Panchami to the Dola festival in Phalguna, the temple teemed with pilgrims; now, however, it lay abandoned. Who would gather by the Garuda pillar? And yet—who had lit these lamps that flickered around it?

At the very sight of the vacant Ratna Vedi, his eyes involuntarily closed. Upon the throne of his heart, the mighty

Lord was enthroned, consecrated in eternal presence. He beheld him upon the empty seat—gazed upon him to his heart's content. Yet the thirst for divine vision remained unquenched.

'This is no enigma,' he mused bitterly. 'Who claims that the Simhasana is empty? There, resplendent plenitude abounds—indeed, it is not merely the throne that preserves such majesty, for not even a single corner of the temple is left devoid of divine grace.'

Ramachandra Dev's heart was not stirred merely by devotional fervour. For Shri Jagannath was not only the cherished deity of Odisha—he was the very soul of the land, the spark of liberation itself. In his eyes, the long-dried barrenness of his absence finally gave way to a miraculous descent onto a life-scorched wilderness—a deluge of compassion. In that moment, his weary body and tempestuous spirit were animated with a thrilling exhilaration, as if the dormant sinews of his being were newly awakened by the blessed touch of new life.

For several moments, he stood transfixed, lost in rapture, until his emotions broke forth.

'Maharaj!' A temple servitor spoke in a quivering, indistinct tone near his ear, the voice laden with terror and apprehension.

Startled, Ramachandra Dev could not at once recognize the man—it was Bentabindha Raut. There were a few other servitors like him, serving in the temple, who, during Vijayadashami and the Chaitra Yatra of Shri Jagannath, would march in the procession, armed with heavy weaponry. A murky memory surfaced: that dreadful night when the deities were conveyed from the temple to

Chilika, and Bentabindha Raut had accompanied them. The haunting image of that fateful journey swept over him.

'Y–you?' Ramachandra Dev's question faltered in alarm.

'I am Neela Dalabehera—the Bentabindha Rauta of the revered Lord!'

Yet the Dalabehera's face was not marked by the robustness of earlier days. Ever since the deities had departed from the temple, the stoves in the servitors' homes struggled to keep even a meagre flame alive, and the temple no longer partook in the lavish feasts of old; every household was gripped by scarcity. The Dalabehera himself now wore the weariness of disillusionment: his veins stood out on his emaciated frame, his eyes sunken, his once vigorous face now gaunt and skeletal.

In a hushed whisper, the Dalabehera confided in Ramachandra Dev, 'There is no deity in the divine abode; in the void, Raja Aminchand rules in proxy. In the Garad house, his court limps along with only a few trailing servitors.'

'But, what manner of oversight does the Naib claim to exercise when the temple itself stands desolate?' Ramachandra Dev's tone dripped with sarcasm.

The Dalabehera cast a furtive glance around and replied, 'Many matters are at hand. Maharaj, let us proceed to the Pataleshwar temple—I will lead the way, and there, in seclusion, we may speak freely.'

At that moment, Madan Mahapatra, the Parichha overseeing the Eastern Gate, strode in through the Southern Gate, his voice ringing with authority as he sought to assert his command over the gathering.

Upon seeing Madan Mahapatra there, it was as if a

fiery sting had been smeared across Patjoshi's body at the edge of the vacant Ratna Vedi. He erupted, his voice sharp and unyielding, 'Why have you come striding in like a raging bull, Mahapatra? Aminchand has devoured the Lord, and now he feasts upon his throne. What remains to be taken?'

Madan Mahapatra responded, 'This morning, some western pilgrims offered Jahangiri rupees and gold mohurs—where is the tribute? The Naib Aminchand is furious with me.'

It was his duty to ensure that all offerings were deposited with Aminchand.

'Not a single pilgrim hailing from within a radius of ten miles from Puri has come for darshan since morning,' Patjoshi observed, his tone edged with irony. 'Yet the western pilgrims have arrived, piling up silver and gold. And now you come running to collect the tribute!'

'Tell me, Mahapatra, even if the pilgrims offer gifts, what right does Naib Aminchand have over them?' he added.

Mahapatra stiffened. 'As the Parichha of the Eastern Gate, I am responsible for the tribute.'

'Spare me your morning quarrels, Mahapatra!' Patjoshi scoffed. 'The temple is shrouded in emptiness— you see it yourself. Until Dola Purnima, the Purushottam Kshetra would have been teeming with pilgrims, the fairgrounds bustling. But now, silence reigns.' He had no desire to engage in a war of words with Mahapatra.

But Madan Mahapatra was not one to yield. With a cutting remark directed at Patjoshi, he declared, 'Then let us proceed to Garad—to the court of Naib Aminchand. Let you and him settle matters there. The Naib has stationed sentinels at all four gates, keeping close account of every moment. Even a fly cannot escape unnoticed. Do you think you can deceive them?'

In a defiant glare, within a room upon the Ratna Vedi, Patjoshi tightened a red gamchha around his waist and proclaimed, 'You have sold yourself to Naib Aminchand, Mahapatra! But I serve the mighty Lord. Beneath the Ratna Vedi, men like Aminchand have grovelled before. Who here acknowledges that wretched scavenger, licking the scraps of the Mughals?'

Such defiance was intolerable to Mahapatra. Two sturdy Lenkas stood beside him, ready to enforce orders. If a servitor refused to obey, if he did not come when summoned, it was their duty to seize him. The Parichha of the Eastern Gate turned to them and commanded, 'Has ghee ever been extracted with a straight finger? Bind Patjoshi and take him to the Garad, Lenka! Let him flaunt his wrath there.'

Then, as if summoned by chaos itself, Shendha Suara appeared out of nowhere, swooping in like a hawk. With a gamchha wrapped around his head, slapping his thigh with his palm and puffing out his throat, he roared, 'Gone mad, have you, vulture? Since when did you grow so arrogant, Mahapatra? Call your master Aminchand here! If I don't twist his neck, I am no son of a priest!'

'Go if you must—but if you linger, blood will spill in the temple. There will be carnage!' he added.

With a face carved from solid, hardened black stone—its rugged strength unmatched—a broad, formidable chest, arms as mighty as an elephant's, and two thick, blazing red eyes smouldering under the haze of bhang, Shendha Suara stood there like an immovable force. His sheer presence alone was enough to freeze any challenge before it could arise. Madan Mahapatra scarcely mustered the nerve to utter further words. Fuming in silent frustration, he felt as though the sheer audacity had left him battered—black and blue without a single blow. With indignation simmering beneath his breath, he stormed off towards Aminchand—to plead, to protest, to reclaim whatever authority remained to him.

Muttering, he grumbled, 'It is because of the defiance of men like this that the servitors have grown disobedient!'

Meanwhile, standing beneath the shadow of the Garuda pillar, Ramachandra Dev beheld this disheartening spectacle. The bare, almost brutal derision of the Parichha towards the priests and servitors of Lord Baliara Bhuja stirred in him deep disquiet. Exhaling slowly, he murmured inwardly, 'It seems that most of the Parichhas and servitors have now aligned themselves with Aminchand.'

'There are many matters afoot; let us head over there,' the Dalabehera interjected. 'Remember—as the walls have ears.'

Within the temple courtyard lay the Pataleshwar Temple—a dark, fathomless abyss where the descent through numerous flights of stone steps led to the sanctum. The lamp burning beside the Linga only deepened the mystery of the sanctum's darkness. It was within these ancient walls, on the fateful night of the deities' deposition, that Ramachandra Dev, Vishnu Paschim Kabat Mahapatra, and a handful of servitors and paikas had sought refuge, their presence concealed in the temple's depths. Outside, the storm had raged—a howling tempest, sweeping through the night in furious silence, leaving no herald of its coming. And, with each flurrying blast of wind, the flame of the solitary lamp trembled, quivering as though seized by an unseen terror.

In his inexperience, while descending the narrow steps in the tunnel, Ramachandra Dev stumbled intermittently. 'Be cautious, Maharaj! Ahead, there are broken steps,' came the admonition. Meanwhile, the Dalabehera had already arrived.

In the faint glow of the lamp, the sanctum grew ever more sombre. Dalabehera's silhouette was hard to discern, and Ramachandra Dev could not clearly tell his position.

After offering a respectful salutation to Pataleshwar, Dalabehera produced a modest draught of Charanamrita infused with tulsi leaves, sandalwood and the essence of bel leaf, for Ramachandra Dev. Yet those scant droplets only seemed to inflame Ramachandra Dev's thirst further, prompting an inward exclamation of 'What a fierce thirst!' Taking several sips from a copper vessel, he exhaled a long, relieved sigh and pressed himself wearily against the sanctum wall, content in the knowledge that no pilgrim or servitor was likely to intrude—here, at least, he was secure.

There was no further inquisitiveness in him—only the still, eager anticipation to hear the complete account from the Dalabehera.

The Dalabehera then spoke, 'Maharaj, you have witnessed it all! If such tyranny is being unleashed upon the deities' chosen—the esteemed Pushpalak Puja panda—what fate, then, awaits the other servitors?'

In a tone laden with pain, Ramachandra Dev murmured, 'I see it clearly—most of the servitors now bend in deference to Aminchand. Otherwise, what courage would they have to haul in Patjoshi from the Ratna Vedi? And who exactly is that Mahapatra? I have heard that Aminchand has even bound him with the sacred saree upon his head.'

'Aminchand has ousted Vishnu Paschim Kabat Mahapatra from the post of Parichha and, in his stead, reinstated that impetuous, unruly Madan Mahapatra at the Eastern Gate. The old band of Parichha has vanished entirely, replaced by new men. Wherever the Parichha decree, the servitors follow; yet those who defy them are strictly forbidden from entering the Singhadwar.'

Even the devoted servitors of Lord Jagannath had ultimately thrown their lot in with Taqi Khan. Now, with whom was Ramachandra Dev to wage his solitary battle? He exhaled deeply, a breath laden with the weight of abysmal despair.

The Dalabehera then confided, his tone thick with connotation: 'Some servitor has whispered into Aminchand's ear that the deities have secretly taken refuge somewhere amid Chilika—perhaps on an isolated island, within a reed forest, or atop a remote mountain peak. Consequently, a well-informed detachment of the Maluda's faujdar, led by Bajrakot's Bagha Singh, is now scouring every corner of Chilika. Until the deities are withdrawn from Chilika, they will surely resort to binding him with a leather rope again.'

Yet, the deities had already been spirited away from Chilika, a truth that Ramachandra Dev chose to withhold from the Dalabehera. Trust had become a fragile thing—even his own shadow seemed suspect. What if the Dalabehera, in some unguarded moment, let slip the secret?

Ramachandra Dev, steering the conversation in a new direction, inquired, 'What news of Vishnu Paschim Kabat Mahapatra? Where is he now?'

In truth, Ramachandra Dev had come to Puri seeking an audience with him—hoping, perhaps, for an encounter.

But he was reluctant even to divulge this very purpose to the Dalabehera; his interest in Vishnu Paschim Kabat Mahapatra was not born of any deep attachment—only a flicker of curiosity.

The Dalabehera replied, 'Ah, I nearly forgot the matter of import. Just a couple of days ago, Vishnu Paschim Kabat Mahapatra arrived and took shelter at Santadas Math. It was here—within these temple walls—that he was encountered. He, too, was inquiring about you, Maharaj. He left word—should you meet, send word to him. He has insisted on a rendezvous in Gangapada. He repeated it several times—Paschim Kabat Mahapatra!'

Gangapada? Hadn't he promised to return to Chilika soon?

'Did he proceed straight from Puri to Gangapada?' Ramachandra Dev asked, his voice laced with urgency.

The Dalabehera nodded. 'That is how I remember it.'

There was no time to linger in Shrikshetra. He must depart for Gangapada at once. Yet even this news, Ramachandra Dev was not entirely confident enough to share openly with the Dalabehera—so he remained silent.

Emerging from the sanctum, Ramachandra Dev declared, 'I am off to Cuttack. From there, I must ascertain Taqi Khan's state. Lakshmi Paramaguru departed on the very same day, yet no trace of him remains. Without contacting him, everything is shrouded in darkness. Meanwhile, those servitors who stand with us must be kept united, vigilant. There are some, like Shendha Suara, who care neither for the wrath of the Parichha nor the blazing glare of Aminchand.'

Then, drawing a deep, steadying breath, he intoned,

'Steel your heart, Dalabehera! Shri Jagannath, if he wills, shall soon grace the temple with his presence; The empty throne shall be restored to its fullness. We are but instruments for that divine purpose.'

Outside, the sky wore a variegated mantle of clouds, heavy with the languor of late afternoon. The distance from Puri to Gangapada is, at the least, twenty kos. It was a night of the Krishna Paksha—and who could say what date it was? Perhaps, in three or four hours, the moon would emerge. As Ramachandra Dev gazed skyward, he calculated inwardly that if he departed now, Gangapada might be reached by dawn. Yes—that would be just right. This night! This impenetrable darkness!

Once again, the same dusky, deserted path unfolded before him. The horses' hooves, weary and slow, dragged through the dust. Beneath the pale, mist-veiled moon, Ramachandra Dev appeared like a shadowed spectre, a figure carved from the night itself. Paschim Kabat Mahapatra had never intended to go to Gangapada. Why had he suddenly set forth? The fort lord there had placed a foot in two boats, drinking deep from the waters of treachery—Govind Bairiganjan.

The bitter memory of the battle at Gangapada, fought against Taqi Khan's forces, still lingered fresh in Ramachandra Dev's mind. Had fate played differently, the Mughal power would have crumbled entirely. He could have avenged the treachery and betrayal at the Battle of Tikali in Raghunathpur.

At that time, Taqi Khan himself was marshalling his forces from Rathipur Fort, while Ramachandra Dev, alongside Harichandan of Banapur, had held firm at Khurda's

Barunei Fort. Taqi Khan's strategy had been clear—to shatter Ramachandra Dev's forces at Gangapada, ensuring that the Mughal army could surge forth like a flood towards Cuttack, unhindered. Rathipur posed risks, obstacles. But between Rathipur and Gangapada, the path lay open.

For crossing the Kushabhadra River towards Cuttack, the sole impregnable fortress is Gangapada. Thus, Taqi Khan had invested every ounce of his might to that very point. And yet, as Ramachandra Dev's Dheknia Paikas clashed with the Mughal soldiers, the enemy could not advance a single step. The relentless hail of shattering musket balls and the volley of arrows had rendered the Mughal forces chaotic and disorganized.

In the fervour of battle, Bhagirathi Kumar himself also set out to confront Taqi Khan's commander, Makaram, in direct combat. At that moment, Makaram Khan, riding amidst his encircling cavalry, was launching a fierce and unyielding assault upon Ramachandra Dev. Bhagirathi Kumar sprang onto his horse to aid the Paika warriors from behind.

From behind, Maharani Lalita Devi's voice rang out, sharp and commanding—'Jenamani!'

At those words, Bhagirathi Kumar immediately reined in his steed.

At the fort's gateway stood Maharani Lalita Devi—formidable and fierce as Bhairavi in the guise of Rudrani—and behind her, Bairiganjan followed. In his eyes shimmered a look of bewildered helplessness, as though he had suddenly been plunged into a crisis of faith.

'You called out to me, mother?' Bhagirathi Kumar's voice carried a note of irritation.

Lalita Devi's words struck like a blade. 'You think victory in Gangapada, the defeat of Taqi Khan, will serve your cause? And while I still live, will *yavani* Razia become the Maharani of Khurda? Will her unborn child inherit the throne? Is this truly what your mind conceives?'

Ramachandra Dev's marriage to Razia—a union Lalita Devi could neither forgive nor forget—had festered within her, transforming jealousy into vengeance. A woman consumed by envy burns fiercer than the flames of a scorching summer—more relentless, more devastating.

Like an obedient child, Bhagirathi Kumar turned back, retreating into the fort.

Lalita Devi turned to Bairiganjan and commanded, 'Announce among our paika warriors that a treaty has been struck between Taqi Khan and Ramachandra Dev. Why should they shed blood in vain? The quarrel among these in-laws is nothing but mere posturing.'

Her voice, hissing like a serpent, lent an almost hypnotic cadence to her words. In the very hour of triumph, the paika warriors of Gangapada began to fall back, scattering like a herd of frightened beasts in the face of a prowling tiger. Witnessing their retreat, the fort lords and paikas from neighbouring strongholds followed suit, gripped by purposeless terror. Chaos spread like wildfire. Rumours swirled—Ramachandra Dev had surrendered to Taqi Khan!

At the fort of Bairiganjan in Gangapada, a white flag had already been hoisted in the name of surrender. Bhagirathi Kumar and Bairiganjan advanced—not to launch an assault but to offer felicitations to Taqi Khan. Meanwhile, several of Ramachandra Dev's most trusted generals were captured by the Mughals and executed at Rathipur. Once more, Ramachandra Dev found himself a fugitive, forced to abandon Barunei Fort at Khurda, escaping into the uncertain depths of exile.

And now, Gangapada again—why was Paschim Kabat Mahapatra being summoned there? What purpose would his presence serve?

For the fugitive in disguise, that variegated, dust-choked path offered neither water, shade, nor refuge.

Ahead, perhaps, lay the Daya River; the moon, shrouded in mist, cast a pale glow on its sands. There, like an exhausted infant, he collapsed upon the riverbank. After giving his horse some water, Ramachandra Dev dismounted to grant the creature a few moments' rest—he, too, so desperately needed reprieve.

Amid that enveloping haze, before his tired eyes, Razia appeared, drifting—ethereal and mysterious, like moonlight itself, imbued with boundless sorrow and compassion.

That storm-ridden night, after their meeting at Rathipur Fort, he had encountered Razia once more—this time in the vicinity of Kadam Rasul in Cuttack. Disguised as a dervish—a humble fakir wandering incognito—he roamed Cuttack, ever watchful of Taqi Khan's schemes. He sat apart from the cluster of fakirs huddled together on their blankets. His disguise was flawless—a half-open Quran rested upon a wooden stand, a string of glass beads hung around his neck. Whenever someone approached, he intoned verses in a nasal chant, mimicking the cadence of wandering mystics.

As Razia circled the shrine, she paused, recognizing him instantly. Beneath the folds of her churidar and salwar, her feet—adorned with golden anklets that resembled delicate, petal-like filigree—gleamed in the low light. Though Ramachandra Dev found it too painful to meet her gaze directly, his disguised figure did not escape her notice.

In a steady, purposeful cadence, she finally asked, 'Can one truly be cheated by such artifice?'

Ramachandra Dev offered no reply.

There was no time—soon, the guards and attendants would arrive. Yet so much remained unsaid.

Razia spoke softly, 'How many times have I journeyed to the abode of Ghazisa Pir, offering dua for a meeting with you, only to return empty-handed? And today, after all these days, we meet and not even exchange a word? Did I ever lay claim to the title of Khurda Begum? Why do you remain mute? After all this time… only silence?'

With his head bowed like that of a guilt-ridden sinner, Ramachandra Dev murmured, 'I am granting you liberation, Razia! Allah knows I am not responsible for dismantling your life with the caprice of a mischievous child plucking petals from a flower. Naib Nazim Taqi Khan is toying with both our lives—he has reduced us to mere pawns on the chessboard of politics.'

'Where there are no bonds, how can there be liberation?' Razia's lips curved into a subtle, knowing smile beneath her silken scarf—a smile as enigmatic as a fog-enshrouded, moonlit night.

What answer should be given to this riddle? Ramachandra Dev wondered, unable to fathom it.

Then Razia said, 'Freedom from the knot of bondage is easy enough; but the knot that entwines you with me is, in truth, not bondage at all.'

There was no time now for further words. By then,

the khojas and bodyguards had already arrived at her side. Razia tossed an Ashrafi on the blanket before Ramachandra Dev and moved on, leaving behind a trail of unspoken mysteries in that drenched, starlit night.

In the mist-laden moonlit night, Razia's figure emerged—mysterious, ethereal, sculpted in shadows and light. Ramachandra Dev had never embraced conversion for her sake; rather, he had been ensnared by cunning stratagems, lured by the promise of Razia's presence. None knew the truth—but the all-seeing did. A thought stirred within him—had it been for Razia alone, he would not have hesitated. In this wandering, uncertain, solitary existence, had she been by his side, these moments would not have been so agonizing.

Gangapada still lay far away.

Rathipur loomed in the distance, a dense mass of shadow and foreboding, beyond which lay Gangapada.

Yet Bairiganjan was nowhere to be found in Gangapada. On investigation, he came to know that he had gone to Haridamada Garh, where fort lords from various strongholds had gathered. Their purpose? Unknown. Perhaps a wedding, an engagement, or a sacred Yajnopavita ceremony at the feudal lord's residence.

Surely then, Vishnu Paschim Kabat Mahapatra would also be present in Haridamada Garh. Was it that Paschim Kabat himself had orchestrated this assembly of the fort lords? Perhaps. Fatigued, Ramachandra Dev advanced northward. Ahead lay Mendhashal, and from there Haridamada was only a couple of kos away. Yet uncertainty gnawed at his thoughts.

In the scorching afternoon of Pausha, the bare

branches of the semal and palash trees began to wither under the relentless heat. In the deodar forest, clusters of dry leaves tumbled down—each fallen leaf echoing memories of its own demise. At that desolate midday, accompanied by the lament of mourning doves, a spectral feminine figure emerged—a nurturing paika bride from the village of Malakuda—haunting the wearied gaze of Ramachandra Dev. In those solitary moments, her memory cascaded over him in quivering rivulets, imbued with quiet compassion. Yet there was no time for indulgence in tender sentiment; before him loomed the relentless call of a merciless battle. Mendhashal village lay still far ahead.

Haridamada Garh stood like an unyielding sentinel, its formidable presence crowning the rugged hill that marked the boundary between Khurda and Banki. Beyond the fort spread a tangled expanse—the blended jungle of Kalapathar, Vaidyeshwar, and Chandaka. At the fringe of the village, upon a modest mound, stood the palace of the Dalabehera, Gadadhar Pitambar Rai Mahapatra, its entrance guarded by a chowpadhi. Encircling the palace was a mighty wall of red sandstone, and only two gates— east and west—admitted entry. The eastern portal, known as Singhadwar, featured twin iron-spiked doors flanked on either side by majestic elephant-lion effigies. Although the doors had grown timeworn and the statues marred by splintered fragments, the indomitable pride of Haridamada Garh shone unmistakably from those fierce, regal lions.

On ordinary days, the gate remained unguarded; but today, two paikas armed with bows, arrows, and spears stood sentry so rigorously that not even a fly could dare pass. Such severe restrictions had never before marred the usual flow of people in and out—so the inhabitants of the garh whispered that something exceptional must be unfolding within. Had a Mughal assault been imminent, one could only imagine.

It was said in hushed tones that mighty warrior-lords from many forts had arrived in Haridamada Garh. Amid the murmurs of the people ran the claim, 'I have seen Bangaroba Uttar Kabat!' Some had witnessed it firsthand, others had merely heard the rumour. 'Near the sacred abode of Stambheshwar Mahadev—close to the ever-faithful Nandi—he dismounted, offering respectful salutes along the winding path until he reached the palace.'

'Only you saw it—I did not,' someone protested, 'I was returning from the fields, where the earth lay barren, the remnants of scorched paddy plants stood like charred spectres, though by now the ripened rice would have swayed in the fields.'

'We are all in the same boat,' he added. 'If we are to sink, we will sink together; if we are to survive, we will do so as one. Oh, I have wandered off course! On my way back from the field, I glimpsed Kamaguru Jhapatsingh, the formidable chieftain astride his horse, making his way to the fort. I greeted him with the deepest of bows. He inquired, "Surely you are Govind Uddandaray, are you not? Is your body well? Does all prosper at home?"'

'Yes, indeed!' I replied. 'The land has plunged into disorder; even the gods have sought refuge. The sacred shrine of the Shrivatsa Khandashala temple stands abandoned. Draw your own conclusions from that.'

Another restless soul, eager to share his own tale, spoke of Fatehsingh, the warrior-lord of Baunsagarh. 'Hold a moment, Uddandaray—you prattle on like a toppled clay pot, spilling confusion! Say it plainly—you have seen Jhaptasingh, just as I have laid eyes on Fort Lord Fatehsingh of Baunsagarh. But for Stambheshwar's sake, guard your tongue—do not let these words escape beyond us, for the Dalabehera's man has gone door to door, giving strict warnings.'

The Dalabehera's man Raghu Kuhatsingh had issued a grave admonition: 'What transpires in our halls? Who among the fort lords treads the path to the fortress? Speak not a word—our enemies' spies slither through the streets like vipers. Should these secrets escape, all will unravel into ruin! Remember—walls have ears. Be cautious.'

So the people of the fort adhered strictly to this command, constantly reminding one another that no word of the comings and goings should ever leave their midst. And yet, in hushed voices, the rumours persisted—a fleeting glimpse of Bangaroba Uttar Kabat, the shadow of Kamaguru Jhaptasingh, the unmistakable presence of Fatehsingh of Baunsagarh. All shared a deep-seated anxiety, though the true matter behind these events remained an enigma.

At the far edge of the village lay the Khandadhua Pond—a reservoir where warriors cleanse their blades, its waters bearing silent testimony to countless battles and lost glories. Here, long ago, a chieftain of the Haridamada Fort—fresh from war—had bathed, cleansing the bloodied steel before seeking blessings from the northern shrine of Stambheshwar Mahadev and the southern temple of the goddess Koshalashuni. It was the age of Manasingh and the conquest of Utkal, when the rugged defences of Haridamada Fort proved insurmountable, denying even the mighty Manasingh passage towards Khurda. In those days, the fort lord of this garh was none other than the revered Bhramarbar Pitambar Mahapatra. Ever since, the pond had borne the name Khandadhoya—its banks a haven for dense groves of tamarind, beneath which paika warriors would gather. There, in quiet clusters, they exchanged tales of long-forgotten exploits and unyielding courage—grand accounts of battles won and foes vanquished—though in truth, they had little else to do but weave legends from dust.

Then—hoofbeats! A rider approached from Mendhashaal, the dust rising in thick, sun-kissed plumes, swirling like vibrant bursts of coloured abir in the afternoon light. From afar, his features blurred into mystery, and a lively contest of recognition ensued among those watching.

One voice cried out, 'This is none other than Benu Chhotray of Manikgarh!'

Yet another retorted, 'Ah, your eyes are sharp indeed! Surely, this is Sundar Rai of Bankoi!'

Before consensus could be reached, the rider dismounted upon the Khandadhua Ghats. But he was neither the famed Venu Chhotray of Manikgarh nor the celebrated Sundar Rai of Bankoi.

An unfamiliar man! Judging from his attire, he appeared to be a Western ascetic. On occasion, when travelling to Shrikshetra, such western ascetics would ride in procession—on horse, elephant, or even camel—heading towards Haridamada Math.

A few voices together remarked, 'He does not seem to be merely an ascetic; he must be a noble of some other fort.'

Narendra Agadasingh, his voice trembling, insisted, 'No, he is not a western ascetic.'

Raghu Jena, dismissive of decorum and propriety, casually commented, 'Ha! You speak as if your pot brims with wisdom, Gramps!'

Narendra Agadasingh, despite his esteemed, elderly stature, was known to be quick-tempered. At every opportunity, his hand would instinctively reach for his dagger. The reproach of being called a 'brimming pot' was something he could not tolerate. Although none was at hand—no dagger or sword—he tightened a saffron gamchha around his waist, slapped his right thigh, and lunged at Raghu Jena, provoking an eruption of laughter from the gathering.

Some of the youths cried out in unison, 'Hey, look—chaos has clocked in for its shift!' Tak dhama-dham! Tak dhama-dham! The sound rang out, echoing the rhythmic beats of the paika warrior's arena.

Like salt scattered upon a wound, the raucous hilarity of the young ones—coupled with their interjections—began to temper Agadasingh's fury. But he relented. He loosened the gamchha from around his waist, yet this playful mockery served only to further enrage him. Casting a stern, reproachful glance at Raghu Jeena, he muttered to himself, 'Look now! What a time has come—we are in the depths of Kali Yuga! The elders have lost all honour and respect.'

At Khandadhua Ghat, the horseman dismounted into the water, washing his hands and face, and after sipping a few pinches of water, he came out. The realization dawned—he was no noble or fort lord, but a wandering ascetic. Had he been one, his identity might have been unmistakable. Sadhus and sanyasis, commuting to Haridamda Math, was common enough. The Dalabehera seldom failed to extend his hospitality to them or mingle with them. Yes, he was an ordinary western ascetics. Intrigue hung thick in the air, and everyone wondered how to commence conversation. Thus, together they cried out, 'Salutations, revered elder! Pray, where does your path lead?'

The horseman, however, had no desire to stop and converse. Overwhelmed by fatigue and hunger, his body trembled; in Gangapada, in the Shiva temple, barely two handfuls of dry anna prasad had settled in his stomach. Yet rather than quelling his hunger, the flame of starvation only flared fiercer, leaving his very bowels in disarray.

In a resonant voice, Agadasingh boomed, 'Do you suffer from a profound thirst, sir? But what else might there be in this Khandadhua Pond besides water? Ah, in our childhood, our homes flowed with streams of milk, curd, and sweet, refreshing sherbat known as Navat Pana—alas, those days are long gone!'

But nostalgia could not quench thirst. The western ascetic, now astride his steed once more, finally spoke: 'Is the Dalabehera in the fortress?'

Dalabehera! What business should a western ascetic have with the Dalabehera? This very question stirred doubt in many hearts. Agadasingh pressed on before anybody could utter a word, 'Not even a single fly may now enter the abode of the Dalabehera. Sir, how then shall you approach him?' In a bid to preserve the honour of his fort, Agadasingh added, 'Here, inside our fort—where seventy-one fort lords of Khurda and one hundred and twenty-nine chieftains have gathered—some serious discussions are underway. You are not permitted to enter, sir.'

Seventy-one fort lords? One hundred and twenty-nine chieftains? Such an unbelievable declaration left the horseman dumbfounded.

Yet he did not dare to reveal his identity, for he knew not which faction they belonged to. The only news he required was confirmation that the Dalabehera was indeed present and that other fort lords had assembled there. Nothing more.

'I am but an invited sanyasi—what business have I with fort lords and chieftains?' declared the horseman. 'A mere audience with the Dalabehera shall suffice.'

Agadasingh contorted his face into a scowl and bellowed, 'Did I not say that deliberations are underway within the Dalabehera's abode? Not even a fly could hope to slip inside!'

Agadasingh might have said more, but hands grasped his arm, fingers pinching his back as whispers urged him to silence. 'It is forbidden to let any talk of the fort's goings-on escape! Why must you deliberately reveal such things to a western ascetic?'

The decree of the heralds suddenly echoed in his mind. He spoke with measured restraint, 'It is prohibited to speak of those who pass in and out of the fortress. Yet, many fort lords have reached the Dalabehera's residence. Venerable one, you must proceed directly to the Math. The Mahanta shall see to your needs; all is prepared. The Math stands just beyond that residence. Even a child could guide you there.'

The rider hesitated only a moment before urging his horse forward.

The western ascetic—how would he reach Haridamada Math? And what fate awaited him once he did? The curiosity was irresistible, and the paikas, unable to quell their intrigue, skirted the pond's edge, silently trailing the horseman. But to everyone's amazement, instead of advancing towards the Math, he took the slope leading to the residence.

Surely, some misfortune was imminent due to the intrepid audacity of the western ascetic. No one had foreseen such an outcome. In fact, the ascetic had not even dismounted—a matter of no small consequence indeed. On the route to the palace, travelling by palanquin or carriage was strictly forbidden—let alone riding directly on horseback along this path! How—how had he managed such a feat?

'Ah! That ascetic carries a force within him—I can see it!'

But before he could advance further, at the Singhadwar, two steadfast sentinels thrust forward their spears, barring his path.

'Beware!' they roared in unison.

The western ascetic remained utterly unshaken— neither the gleam of spear tips nor the booming warnings of the sentinels could rattle his resolve. From within the folds of his robe, he revealed a mysterious insignia. At the mere sight of it, the paika sentinels hesitated, their rigid stance softening into submission.

'Open the gates!' the ascetic commanded in a voice that rang through the still air. As if spellbound, the sentinels obeyed without question. The rider advanced, passing through the grand entrance on horseback—an act so natural to him, yet to those gathered beneath the shade of the babul tree, nothing short of astounding. They stood in stunned silence, gazes darting between one another, seeking an explanation for the impossible.

Here, despite the strict orders of the Dalabehera that no one should enter, the ascetic had penetrated the inner sanctum—how, one might ask? For chieftains of other forts and even the mightiest feudal lords themselves would customarily dismount before entering the abode. Among the fortified domains of Khurda, Haridamada fort held a distinct exclusivity. In the era of Telenga Mukunda, the Dalabehera of this fort had once been the Bakshi.

Agadasingh, ever the keen observer, murmured knowingly, 'Ah, this holy man possesses great power! Did you see how he bewitched those paika sentinels with mere dust?'

Within the palace, the ascetic moved unimpeded, passing through two fortified vestibules. The outer chambers belonged to the Dalabehera, Gadadhar Rai Pitambar Mahapatra—his most private sanctum, inaccessible to all but his most trusted confidants. Fierce guards stood watch at every threshold, yet not a single one raised a hand to halt the ascetic. His palm bore the unmistakable mark of the Khurda Maharaja—a sapphire seal, an insignia known to all. Who would dare obstruct him? The moment they laid eyes upon the mark, the command was clear—let him pass.

It was within these outer chambers that visiting feudal lords and chieftains awaited their turn to enter. Beyond the courtyard lay the grand assembly hall—a space of magnificent proportions. Beneath an alcove, shielded by the shade of a Kadamba tree, stood Radha and Krishna. In another recess, the divine tableau of the Vastraharan Leela unfolded. The chamber walls bore brass-studded shields, gleaming swords, and fearsome tiger masks. Under the flickering glow of oil lamps, the snarling visage of the beast, its ivory fangs, and curling tongue seemed alive with menace.

Seated upon tiger pelts and woven carpets, leaning against the thick stone wall, was Gadadhar Rai Pitambar Mahapatra himself. His cadre of warriors, the formidable Dhenkia Paikas, stood guard. Their weapons were mighty bows and lethal khanda blades. In battle, they advanced with tiger-skin helmets upon their heads, their bodies painted in turmeric hues, a blazing vermilion dot adorning their brows. Their colossal presence alone could make an enemy tremble in fear.

These Dhenkia Paikas hailed from Haridamada Fortress—hence, as the Dalabehera, Pitambar Mahapatra donned the tiger-skin helm, transforming into an almost comical figure amidst this unfolding drama. Within his own home, such a warlike display was unnecessary, yet he remained bound to tradition. How could he forsake the symbols of his lineage? Beneath the turmeric paste, the weariness of age lay hidden—the loose skin, the deepening wrinkles. Time had stolen the vigour of his youth, but he concealed it well.

In truth, his head was bald, his silvered hair barely forming a wreath around his temples. His wrinkles, etched deep into his brow, bore the weight of countless battles. And yet, none would dare guess his actual age—four score years and yet the sinews of his arms remained taut, his voice still thunderous. Even now, when he roared from the Singhadwar, his cry carried all the way to Koshalashuni Temple.

His square-cut face, his white-streaked beard, his

fierce, curling moustache—all blended into a portrait of untamed ferocity. In the dust-hued shadows of his features, two burning eyes shone with an undiminished brilliance. Around his wrists coiled silver bracelets, his upper arms were encircled with copper bands, and upon his throat hung rudraksha beads.

It was said that no arrow, bolt of lightning, or sword could pierce his body while he wore his talismans. Truth or myth, none could say—but what remained undeniable was the vitality that coursed through Gadadhar Rai Pitambar Mahapatra, even in his old age.

For had it not been so, how could a man endure so many wars, so many battles, and still walk unscathed? His eyes blazed—not like the relentless heat of noon, but like embers burning in the dusk of an unyielding warrior's soul.

Now, within those once-fiery eyes, the dim twilight of helplessness flickered. Silent as a carved effigy, he sat immersed in thought. Beside him was Vishnu Paschim Kabat Mahapatra, wrapped in a shroud of hopeless silence, his gaze unfocused, lost in regret. For two long months, he had traversed the fortified domains, pleading with their lords, yet all he could muster were seven or eight fort lords— Bangaroba Uttar Kabat, Kamaguru Jhapatsingh, Fatesingh of Baunsagarh, Dianbagha of Gaudiapadar, Kushupala Balwant Rai, the Dalabehera of Kasanda, and the mighty Mattagajasingh of Khuriya. Two esteemed fort lords— Bairiganjan of Gangapada and Ranasingh of Rathipur— upon whom Vishnu Paschim Kabat Mahapatra had placed his deepest trust, had pledged their allegiance yet failed to appear.

The deep, laboured breath of Vishnu Paschim Kabat

Mahapatra only served to render that already oppressive atmosphere even weightier. There was growing doubt as to whether the Maharaj would ever arrive at the fort at all. The few fort lords who had assembled had come only upon hearing the name Ramachandra Dev.

Vishnu Paschim Kabat had dispatched word in Puri, summoning a meeting in Gangapada.

Yet, at Gangapada, Bairiganjan had cautioned, 'The eyes of Mughal spies and warlords rest upon us. If so many fort lords gather here, Taqi Khan will catch wind of it—the entire effort will be undone. Haridamada Fortress offers far greater security.'

His reasoning was sound, undeniably so. But did his warning not also veil a hidden reluctance—an attempt to evade the inevitable? Who knows the workings of fate? The Mughal commander, Taqi Khan, and his forces lay in wait, ever-watchful for the chance to seize Ramachandra Dev. If he were captured at Gangapada, his fate would be sealed— his rule erased from existence. The very roots of power would be cut. Bound in chains, Ramachandra Dev would be taken either to Medinipur or Murshidabad, marking the final chapter of Utkal's freedom struggle.

Bairiganjan had assured him, 'Gather at Haridamada, I shall follow soon.' But he had slithered away—cunning! To promise one path and take another—that was the art of survival in politics. The truly shrewd thrived in deception, their success measured not by loyalty but by calculation. Though he had not marched straight into Taqi Khan's court at Cuttack, he had surely carried whispers to Lalita Devi in Banapur—there was no doubt of it. Perhaps he lingered in the shadows at Gangapada still, biding his time.

As Vishnu Paschim Kabat Mahapatra departed for Haridamada Fort, he had commanded his most trusted paika, 'Should Ramachandra Dev reach Gangapada, send him directly to Haridamada.' Yet whether that meeting ever occurred was a mystery known only to the gods.

In the austere chamber, draped in humble cloth, an empty seat awaited Ramachandra Dev. Upon witnessing that desolate vacancy, Vishnu Paschim Kabat Mahapatra released a long, weary sigh. Outside on the threshold, the lamp flame shuddered in the gusts of wind, and within the house, long, inky shadows swayed, intensifying an already painful, anxious hush. Somewhere on the wall, a lizard scampered with a soft 't-t,' as it passed over the floor.

Pitambar Rai pressed his fingers against the cold stone floor and muttered, 'True! True!'

Several voices echoed his words in confusion. 'What do you mean, True… True?'

Pitambar Rai, eyes cast towards the lamp's wavering glow, murmured, 'The Odias—they are the gravest enemies of Utkal. Not the Mughals. Not Taqi Khan.'

None spoke in reply. No rebuttal, no commentary followed. Pitambar Rai's gaze remained fixed upon the flickering flame. He continued, as if talking to himself, 'Did Kalapahad truly defeat the last free Gajapati, Mukunda Harichandan? When Mukunda Harichandan seized the mighty fortresses of Gauda, it was as if he had planted his banner upon the very chest of the Gauda Sultanate. And yet, in the hour of triumph, treachery struck from within. Ramachandra Dev Bhanja, as if assuming the guise of Vibhishan, turned traitor—sent word to the emperor himself—declared himself king in Mukunda's stead.

Mukunda Harichandan was delivered a vicious dagger thrust from behind by none other than his own kinsman!'

The final flickering flame of Utkal's sovereignty had not been swallowed by Kalapahad that fateful day—it was snuffed out by betrayal. This bitter history had echoed through generations of Dalabeheras, passed down like a lament, lingering in their hearts like embers that refused to die. As another weary sigh escaped his lips, his gaze fell once more upon the trembling flame.

Utkal's fate—its very future—was as fragile and uncertain as that wavering light.

Bangaroba Uttar Kabat Gadadhar Rai, a man of equal years to Pitambar Mahapatra, broke the silence. 'Have you all forgotten the unity forged during the time of Mukunda Dev? When the Mughal subedar Khan-e-Dauran threatened us, three-fourths of Khurda's Dalabeheras, alongside the fort lords of Ranapur, Saranggarh, Dampada, Khalikote, and Banki, all stood together. In name, they fought as one. Yet, when the enemy gasped for breath, the alliance fractured. Just as victory lay within reach, our own fort lords abandoned the battle, turning their swords upon one another over petty territorial disputes.'

A deep wound resurfaced in Gadadhar Rai's memory, a wound etched into his very flesh. His voice carried the weight of old agony. 'The scar on my left arm—pierced by a blade—remains as proof of that war. I stood alongside Mukunda Dev, leading the Dhenkia Paikas beyond Pipili. Khan-e-Dauran dared not advance further. Even as the fort lords withdrew with their men, Mukunda Dev fought on for four more days. But then, from Cuttack, the Mughal army surged forth like a tide. Four days—and then Mukunda

Dev's strength to resist crumbled. The Maharaja was forced to flee, concealing himself for survival. And then, Bharata Patnaik of Kaukalgarh—one of our own—slipped away from our ranks and allied himself with Khan-e-Dauran. The secret was revealed. Mukunda Dev was captured and taken as a prisoner to Medinipur. Utkal's crown was bound in chains. How, then, could the Dalabeheras, the fort lords, and the paika warriors find the courage to fight again? The noble warriors of Kulda, Khalikote, and Chikakol were forced to bow before Mughal rule. Otherwise… otherwise, that fleeting moment of unity could have erased Mughal power from Utkal forever.'

Kamaguru Jhapatsingh added bitterly, 'Utkal's darkest days have always come at the hands of traitors hidden within its own halls. The enemy within is always the most ruinous. If not for betrayal, would this sacred land— stretching from the Ganga to the Godavari—ever have sunk into such wretchedness?'

And now, once again, the bitter echoes of history began to replay upon every effort of Maharaj Ramachandra Dev. Deep in their hearts, all present experienced this with unspeakable dismay—none could doubt it, yet no one dared to voice the thought. The trembling lamp on the threshold and the long, obsidian shadow cast upon the wall seemed to manifest the agonizing duality of their innermost sentiments.

At length, after a painful wait, Ramachandra Dev staggered inside with wearied, heavy feet—a visage as pallid as a withered skull. Recognizing him was not difficult for any soul. All together they rose in unison, 'Jai Jagannath!' In a fatigued tone, Ramachandra Dev answered, 'Jai Shri Jagannath!'

Ramachandra Dev's disintegration was marked by an unyielding, stark frankness, yet within he felt the hollowness of a man utterly spent. There had been a hope that the leaders of the seventy-one forts would gather here—a grand assembly to unveil the strategy for Utkal's struggle for independence. Every corner of Utkal had long suffered under Mughal tyranny; its people were broken by relentless oppression, and the thirst for liberation was infused into every gust of wind and every drop of water. As if summoned by the eerie calm before a storm, Ramachandra Dev had rushed here in search of those familiar faces. Yet, in the oppressive gloom, only seven or eight faces emerged—and with them, his cherished vision of unity was shattered. To him, they appeared like fragmented, broken branches battered by a relentless tempest. The blow of such disillusionment was harsh indeed.

Ramachandra Dev breathed a profound sigh and sank onto his makeshift seat, completely exhausted, as if every ounce of strength had been depleted. In a chorus of hushed voices, the fort lords inquired with anxious curiosity, 'Are the deities safe?'

Even as Taqi Khan's soldiers scoured every hidden corner of the realm in search of the deities, they knew that they were not secure amid the treacherous waters of Chilika. That intelligence, too, had reached them through Vishnu Paschim Kabat Mahapatra.

A faint, brittle trace of a smile flickered across Ramachandra Dev's wearied face—a smile edged with bitter irony. 'The deities are safe,' he replied, 'but what of you? Is Utkal secure? What calamity could befall those whom fire cannot consume, weapons cannot shatter, and winds cannot parch? What could the Mughals possibly do to them?'

At these words, the fort lords fell silent; no one could formulate a reply. They exchanged troubled glances. In that very moment, Vishnu Paschim Kabat Mahapatra regarded himself as partly culpable—the failure, after so many arduous days, to have gathered seven or eight of the fort lords together weighed heavily upon him.

Moreover, the two chief defensive shields of Khurda—and the foremost fort lords, Bairiganjan of Gangapada and Ranasingh of Rathipur—were conspicuously absent. Ramachandra Dev understood the grim implication. In a tone of detached resignation, he asked, 'Surely, Bairiganjan and Ranasingh have not arrived?'

Whispers had it that they were running with the hare and hunting with the hounds. But who would dare answer for this unpleasant question?

Vishnu Paschim Kabat Mahapatra, his voice laden with frustration, immediately replied, 'They did give their firm promise to come.'

'But where?' Ramachandra Dev asked, his voice edged with derision—a question that was less inquiry than a cutting blow. Then, once again, the familiar cloak of darkness settled in silence around them.

That very silence was broken by Gadadhar Pitambar Rai, who, his throat hoarse, solemnly stated, 'Your Majesty, you are the very crown jewel of our clan, our guiding star. There is no profit in concealing our words from you, Maharaj. Most of the fort lords are like a weather vane, turning whichever way the wind of fortune blows—their resolve shattered, their spine of courage snapped.

What had long served as the barrier to their suppressed emotions now cascaded forth like a flood, laid bare by Pitambar Rai's candid confession.

Bangaroba Uttar Kabat then remarked, 'How much longer will the fort lords continue to fight? Their strength lies in their paika warriors, yet every household is barren today. The ravages of Mughal plunder have stripped away all semblance of power. And yet, when the war-horn of valour sounds, when the call comes from the Maharaj, they leap into the fray like moths plunging into a flame. But today, their faith and strength have faltered.

'Why?' came the plaintive query from Ramachandra Dev.

'Ask yourself, Maharaj, and the answer will come,' Uttar Kabat's voice trembled with unease. 'What can we possibly say?'

Kamaguru Neelambar Jhapatsingh, wrapped in his Bhutanese blanket, cut in sharply, 'Why leave the truth half-spoken, Uttar Kabat?'

'Who is stopping you from laying it all bare?' Ramachandra Dev asked, his tone marked by an almost unnatural indifference, as though he were merely an indifferent spectator to this tragic drama.

Jhapatsingh pressed on, 'What will we gain by cloaking our words in secrecy? The fort lords see that while the Maharaj tread one path, the Maharani and Bhagirathi Kumar move in the opposite direction. In an effort to forge unity, the Maharaj dispatches his messengers among the fort lords, yet even the Maharani sends her own envoys to Taqi Khan. Her emissaries roam the forts, stoking the flames of discord among the fort lords and chieftains. After all, Your

Highness is no stranger to the outcome of the battle at Gangapada.'

Jhapatsingh's words, though unpalatable, carried a harsh and bitter truth.

Jhapatsingh continued, 'Nonetheless, we have resolved to lift the Mughal yoke from Utkal. When the call comes, we shall never retreat—but first, let the Maharaj secure his own homesteads. Let Bhagirathi Kumar and Lalita Devi be induced to forsake their self-destructive paths.'

'And if they cannot be induced?' A voice in the assembly asked.

But no answer came.

Restless, Ramachandra Dev rose from his seat, and shortly thereafter, Vishnu Paschim Kabat Mahapatra followed in his wake.

After countless nights steeped in hardship, the sleep he so desperately craved had finally extended its gentle invitation within the residence at Haridamada Fort, cradling him in the soft embrace of a modest cot. The night swayed to the delicate strains of a reed instrument, its melody entwined with the trembling air, as eyelids fluttered in rhythm—yet sleep refused to claim Ramachandra Dev. His gaze remained fixed upon the flickering flame beside his bed, as though in its wavering light lay the answer to an unyielding dilemma.

Before him, seated upon a water platform as solid as a stone statue, was Vishnu Paschim Kabat Mahapatra. In the shifting wind, the flame of the lamp quivered and its shadow danced across the wall. The whole chamber lay in a state of profound silence and suppressed astonishment, while on the leather-bound shields adorning the wall the gleam of brass accents caught the light, as if spectral eyes—mute witnesses to countless victories and defeats—were watching on. In this crisis-laden hour of Utkal's history, they seemed to await, with mounting tension, the decisive word of Ramachandra Dev.

Mesmerized, Ramachandra Dev gazed steadily at the trembling flame and declared, 'I have seen in the Shri Mandir how many of the servitors have bowed in loyalty to Naib Aminchand. Here, too, I witnessed the fort lords, restless and fidgeting.'

Vishnu Paschim Kabat Mahapatra required no explanation. The shifting realities had long unveiled their harsh truths, and he was well acquainted with them. Yet, what counsel could he offer Ramachandra Dev? He had none.

'Only Lord Jagannath knows his own will,' he replied simply.

And then—silence. Deafening silence, heavy and unbroken.

Suddenly, Ramachandra Dev rose and began to pace the chamber, the firelight casting restless shadows that trailed him, as if mirroring the storm within. 'Tell the fort lords—this is not a war for the throne. I do not seek it. I do not desire the crown. I do not covet the kingdom of Khurda!'

Vishnu Paschim Kabat Mahapatra's eyes widened with astonishment. 'Then what?'

Ramachandra Dev proclaimed with a solemn finality, 'Let Bhagirathi Kumar ascend the throne of Khurda—for he is indeed the rightful heir. My sole aspiration is that the soil of Khurda be free, liberated at last from the Mughal yoke. Whether I be deemed a *mleccha* or not, my heart yearns for the day when our beloved deity, Shri Jagannath, may once again be exalted on the throne of Ratna Simhasana, his mighty arm raised in victory in the sacred halls of Shrivatsa Khandashala temple. May peace and independence return to Utkal!'

Ramachandra Dev's declaration struck Paschim Kabat like a bolt from the blue. Never had he expected the Maharaj to relinquish the throne of Khurda with such unwavering resolve and without the slightest hesitation. His heart wrestled with disbelief, yet his mind was clouded by a far graver concern—could Bhagirathi Kumar truly rise to the occasion and lead Utkal's struggle for independence?

Kabat pleaded earnestly, 'I beseech Your Majesty to defer the decision until Lakshmi Paramaguru returns from Murshidabad.'

In a firm and unyielding tone, Ramachandra Dev replied, 'The counsel of Paramaguru is worthy of consideration. But my decision is final. Every fort lord in Khurda, every chieftain, must be informed at once. Who knows when Paramaguru will return from Murshidabad?'

With that, his turmoil dissipated. A deep sigh escaped his lips, and he lay back upon his cot. In an instant, exhaustion claimed him, and sleep—unrelenting at last— draped him in its embrace.

*****

Chapter IV

Amid famine, starvation, exploitation, and rampant plunder that devastated Utkal, the people came to call Bengal's capital Murshidabad by a name borne of that very suffering—a name that echoed through every whisper of anguish and memory. Under the rule of Nawab Murshid Quli Khan, the capital of the Bengal province was shifted from Dhaka to what came to be known as Muksudabad. In this act, his unchallenged supremacy was proclaimed, for it was from the stolen riches of Utkal and the jizya exacted from the pilgrims of Lord Jagannath that this great city was born—thereby enshrining Murshid Quli Khan's name in the annals of history. Near the city's fringes, beside the worn steps of the dilapidated Kachra Mosque, a forgotten tomb—draped in a once-lustrous silken sheet—attested silently to his final mortal remains. On every street of Murshidabad, the triumphant echoes of 'Motamman-ul-Mulk Shuja-ud-Daula Asad-Jung' resounded as if to seal his legacy forever.

For over a month now, Lakshmi Paramaguru had wandered the labyrinthine avenues of this metropolis, nourished by plunder, his eyes drinking in the splendour and untold opulence of a city built upon the spoils of conquest.

Along the royal boulevard, the palatial abodes of the affluent amirs, umraos, subservient feudal lords, and jagirdars, and the shimmering emporiums that lined the banks of the Bhagirathi—all this festooned pageantry forced to mind again the image of Utkal; a land once ravaged by pillage, now reduced to a wretched state of bondage and despair.

At the florist Malini's shop, heaps of vibrant dyes and pigments stood in stark contrast to the barren landscapes of Utkal, where even before the flowers had a chance to bloom, they were swept away in an instant. Malini's kohl-lined eyes gleamed, her lips reddened by betel leaves—but back in Utkal, wives and mothers bore unkempt hair, their faces gaunt with hunger, conjuring a terror as poignant as beautiful.

Rice was abundant here, sold eight maunds for a mere rupee, yet in Utkal, men devoured the flesh of their own kind, driven by starvation. Murshidabad overflowed with grain, drowning in excess, its air thick with the decadence of its privileged. And in the bustling marketplace, crowds hovered like bees around the florists and vendors, enamoured by luxury. Meanwhile, in Utkal, women had no cloth to veil their shame, while Murshidabad's storerooms brimmed with muslin and fine Bishnupuri silk.

Here, rice is available at the modest price of eight man to the rupee, yet in Utkal, the desperate scarcity has driven men so low that, starved of sustenance, they consume the flesh of their fellow beings. In the midst of plenty and extravagant indulgence, Malin's establishment teems with a swirling, impetuous crowd of the decadent, as if all the world's vanity had converged upon that one mercantile haven.

At Kasim Bazaar, within the dwellings of the

storeroom keepers, throngs of Firangi merchants clustered around the cloth shops. They gazed in astonishment as, from a single ring of cloth, a silk saree spanning twelve yards unfolded before their eyes. 'How can such a marvel be wrought?' they murmured softly among themselves, certain that these treasures, bought at a pittance, would soon be exported, producing wonder in the far-off markets of Europe, where such opulence was both rare and marvellous.

Along the royal thoroughfare, elegantly attired men and women rode in palanquins or astride magnificent horses; dignitaries and the common populace alike trundled along in an orchestrated parade. In the midst of this throng, the contingent arriving from Kasim Bazaar—composed of European traders and clusters of footmen—merged with the local procession. In front of every palanquin, guards dashed about, calling out in unison, 'Clear the way!' as any heavyset noble or feudal lord, en route perhaps to Farrabagh Palace, hurried along. Meanwhile, the Arab steeds, with each measured step along the road, sent forth fleeting clouds of red dust from their hooves, as if heralding the passage of time itself.

For more than a month, Lakshmi Paramaguru had borne witness to this vivid pageant. Day after day, he observed these scenes—a ceaseless spectacle of sumptuous excess and piercing despair—and found himself drifting with an indescribable, dust-like melancholy, as if he, too, were suspended in that ever-shifting veil of time and memory.

And yet, one cannot help but ask: why had Paramaguru forsaken the sacred precinct of Shri Jagannath, enshrined across the sacred Chilika, to venture here?

Before Malini's flower shop, beneath the ancient,

sprawling banyan that offered a modest respite by the roadside, Lakshmi Paramaguru sat in quiet reflection, repeatedly questioning his own heart. He had come seeking an audience with the illustrious Jagat Seth Fatehchand—a meeting that held the promise of salvation—but thus far, no such encounter had materialized. The very notion of presenting his humble petition before the court of Shuja Khan, on behalf of Ramachandra Dev, was a matter beyond even his wildest imaginings.

History, however, weaves its own intricate tapestry. Shuja Khan's blood carried within it the subtle strains of Hindu culture. His father-in-law, Murshid Quli, was born into a poor Brahmin family in the South. In that desperate state, driven by hunger and abject poverty, his father sold young Murshid Quli as a slave to a merchant from Isfahan—Haji Shafi. That merchant, in an act that would change destiny, converted the Brahmin child to Islam and named him Muhammad Hadi. Later, he was taken back to his native land, where arrangements were made for his education and advancement.

After Haji Shafi's death, Muhammad Hadi was granted freedom from the bonds of servitude. Returning to his southern homeland, he found favour with Haji Abdul—the Diwan of the Berar region—securing a post in the revenue department. His diligence and innate acumen soon earned him renown, and when word of his expertise in fiscal matters reached Emperor Aurangzeb, Hadi was appointed Diwan of Bengal. Then he soon became, in all respects, the enforcer of Bengal's laws and penalties—a Subedar by title. In those tumultuous times, Murshid Quli installed his son-in-law, Shuja Khan, as the Naib Nazim, the governor of

Utkal. Under Shuja Khan's reign, Cuttack transformed into a stronghold of Mughal subjugation—a legacy that harkens back to the era of Maharaja Divyasingh Dev.

Murshid Quli, it must be said, was not a man of deep religious fervour. Yet, in his time, many temples were torn down to construct the immense Katara Mosque of Murshidabad. The demolition, however, was not undertaken on his instructions; it was the work of the staunch and unyielding contractor Farad Faras. With a zeal bordering on fanaticism, Faras procured the necessary stones by razing the temples that lay in the vicinity—and with those very stones, he erected the Katara Mosque. The Hindu populace was also coerced into labouring for the construction of this grand edifice; it was solely through Faras's relentless imposition that, in the span of a year, this monumental mosque was born.

After Murshid Quli Khan's demise, his son-in-law Shuja Khan ascended as the Nawab of Murshidabad. It was he who exacted the ultimate penalty upon Faras, the builder of the Katara Mosque, for his relentless oppression against the pious subjects. His decree was both swift and unyielding—a sombre reminder that tyranny, however masked in zeal, ultimately calls for retribution.

Shuja Khan was a traditionalist, valuing the preservation of order and stability, yet he did not succumb to the rigid dogma of fanaticism. His approach was measured— guided by pragmatism rather than blind devotion. Though lacking personal reverence for Shri Jagannath, he harboured no enmity towards the deity or its followers. His governance reflected a cautious balance; while he did not actively champion religious freedoms, he did not wield oppression as a means of control. His tenure as the Naib Nazim of Odisha saw the safeguarding of pilgrimage routes, the construction of wells and stepwells for pilgrims travelling along the Jagannath Road, and the eventual cessation of burdensome jizya taxes—a testament to his preference for governance over doctrinal zeal.

Emboldened by this very spirit of intrepid resolve, Lakshmi Paramaguru had journeyed to Murshidabad to entreat Shuja Khan to guarantee the protection of Shri Jagannath. His wish was heartfelt and straightforward: that the deity might once again reign in the temple, that his dignity and safety would not be marred by the fanatical zeal of Taqi Khan, that the grip of Aminchand's authority be separated from the temple's sacred administration, and that Utkal might preserve even a shadow of the independence it once enjoyed in Akbar's time—a freedom unmarred by Mughal tyranny and marauding plunder. Such was the ardour of Paramaguru's aspiration.

He imagined that if the Lord Almighty were to ascend the throne of Ratna Simhasana, every stain of Utkal's disgrace might be cleansed and every regret allayed. Just as sun-scorched earth is transformed by a gentle rain into verdant, tender green, the oppressed soil of Utkal might, in the hope of liberation, once again burst forth in new life. It was this very hope that had propelled Lakshmi Paramaguru to rush to Murshidabad.

Yet even as he set forth, Ramachandra Dev's voice echoed in his memory: 'Your exertions will amount to nought, Paramaguru! Indeed, though Shuja Khan was not fanatical, why should he heed your appeal? And yet, word from Murshidabad had begun to stir: a subtle, indirect struggle for supremacy was unfolding between Shuja Khan and his son Sharfaraj Khan; even the family ties and alliances involving Shuja Khan and his son-in-law Taqi Khan added to the tangled contest over Murshidabad's destiny. In the midst of this internal tempest, within the confines of the Farrabagh Harem, Shuja Khan sat clutching his Quran, rendered inert and bewildered—bereft now of the strength either to subdue Sharfaraj or to marshal the assertive Taqi Khan.'

Yet Lakshmi Paramaguru's self-confidence remained unshaken. He recalled how he had once drawn Ramachandra Dev from Taqi Khan's fierce clutches—that very divine energy, he was certain, would now inspire Shuja Khan to act. There would be assurances about deities' safety, and once again, Lord Jagannath would return to his celestial abode; Utkal's earth would reclaim its long-denied freedom. Jagat Seth Fatehchand, too, would emerge as a principal ally in this noble cause.

Still, despite his perseverance, Paramaguru had yet to secure even a single private audience with Jagat Seth Fatehchand. He had roamed the streets of Murshidabad in disguise, for being recognized would almost certainly have led to a lifetime's imprisonment—a fate already decreed by Shuja Khan's most trusted councillor, Rai Rayyan Alamchand, ever the devoted friend of Utkal.

For how many more days would Lakshmi Paramaguru traverse the roads of Murshidabad as a destitute itinerant kapalika? Is freedom merely a commodity to be begged for, a morsel to be received as alms? Does the honour of Sri Jagannath depend solely on Shuja Khan's caprice?

Even Vishnu Paschim Kabat Mahapatra had, on that day, voiced the same aching query: 'Is freedom nothing more than an object of charity? Had the resolute visages of Utkal's warriors not been so striking, would Mansingh, in his own contentment, have so readily preserved Utkal's independence—even if only within the confines of Mughal dominion? And if they were to concede, would they grant Khurda Raja any right over the Jagannath Temple or accord him the dignified status of royal servitor?

For centuries, the cost of freedom has been repaid in blood; no one has ever attained it through mere supplication. If Taqi Khan could, with sheer brute force, reduce Khurda to Mughal submission, and if Aminchand could be installed as the temple's superintendent, then how could he ever acknowledge Khurda's claim to true liberty?

But how long, he asked himself, would the struggle against the might of the Mughals persist? What of the Odia warriors, the paikas who went without food or proper raiment, their bodies and spirits repeatedly broken by relentless Mughal invasions and looting? Discord festered among the fort lords, castle keepers, and chieftains: some aligned with Taqi Khan while others rallied behind the Maharaj. There were those, seduced by the allure of Lalita Devi, who longed to have Bhagirathi Kumar enthroned as the king of Khurda—their gaze remained unwavering upon the Maharaj, whom they saw as fallen, stripped of both caste and faith.

Ramachandra Dev, seeking redemption, had bestowed the governance of revenue-free Ramachandrapur upon the Brahmins in an effort to mend divisions. Yet among the staunchly conservative, the self-serving, and in the hearts of the general public, lingering beliefs that the Maharaj was a *mleccha* and a *yavana* still carried weight. In such a quagmire, what force could unite and stand against Taqi Khan? Who would take up arms, and who would lead the charge?

These tumultuous circumstances had drawn Lakshmi Paramaguru to Murshidabad. His hope was to draw forth sympathy from Shuja Khan and restrain the incipient menace of Taqi Khan, quelling the rising ire against Shri Jagannath. But fate had not granted him that opportunity.

Now, on the banks of the Bhagirathi, within the Bhairav temple of Kiriteshwari, he concealed himself under the guise of a kapalika—and that was all.

The very thread of Lakshmi Paramaguru's thought snapped unexpectedly. A regal figure—either a king or a zamindar—was riding in a palanquin. In front of it, a contingent of soldiers clamoured, 'Clear the way! Clear the way!' The palanquin halted right before Malini's flower shop.

Lakshmi Paramaguru's eyes widened in astonishment—it was none other than King Padmanabh Dev of Patia Fort!

But what business did Padmanabh Dev have in Murshidabad? What purpose drew him to the Nawab's court?

Padmanabh Dev cloaked himself in a dhoti of exquisite Kshirodri silk, its immaculate weave a whisper of vanished splendour. Over this, he donned an ancient durbari sujani, richly quilted and adorned with brocade embroidery—an heirloom weathered by time, its frayed edges clutching stubbornly to the weight of ancestral dignity. Every worn thread seemed to murmur the unspoken struggles of his lineage, each faded embroidery a silent inscription of the hardships that had trailed his throne.

From the palanquin's ornate frame hung a golden tassel, swaying with intentional grandeur—a meagre flourish of opulence amidst the weary remnants of past majesty. Around his thick, bull-like neck rested a lavish necklace of studded gold, its brazen gleam striving—perhaps too fervently—to overshadow the poverty etched into the very fabric of his garb. His face, chiselled with dignified angles, bore a tuft of hair that spoke of ancient valour; beneath his nose, a refined moustache, as subtle as a whisper of tiger's whiskers, lent him an air of noble restraint. Atop his head rested an intricately embroidered cap, and upon his brow, a long streak of vermilion testified to rites steeped in tradition.

Reaching out to take a bouquet, Padmanabh Dev started to negotiate over its price with Malin. But who would really bargain over flowers when picked by hands tinted with mehndi?

Casting a sidelong, languid glance with her enchanting eyes, Malini remarked, 'What price can a flower ever command?'

The value that Padmanabh Dev placed on the bouquet did not please her. Moreover, his sudden appearance in Murshidabad—and his haggling over such a simple bouquet—seemed no auspicious omen for Utkal. In a flurry of urgency, Lakshmi Paramaguru started trailing the palanquin.

Near the banks of the Bhagirathi, right in front of the Naubat Khana of Farrabag Vilas Kanan, Padmanabh Dev's palanquin came to a halt. From that point, the journey to the palace had to be made on foot. Only those specially designated—Shuja Khan's councillors, such as Jagat Seth Fatehchand, the representative from Ajimabad in Patna, the Naib Nazim of the Utkal Mughal confederacy, or the royal emmissaries arriving from Shahjahanabad, Delhi—were permitted to continue by palanquin from there to Farrabag. Others were expressly forbidden.

Shuja Khan was the very embodiment of a true Nawab, a man of established custom. In his characteristically opulent manner—and having secured his exalted office in Murshidabad—he had dismantled Murshid Quli's splendid palace named Chehel Sotoun to erect his own mansion within Farrabag Vilas Kanan. Nearby, the famed Roshanibagh adored the landscape.

At the entryway beneath the Naubat Khana, two mounted sentries—clad in ceremonial attire—stood firm. On the very tip of each of their horses' bridles fluttered a flag bearing the emblem of the crescent moon. As Padmanabh Dev passed, they inclined their heads in courteous acknowledgement, their vigilance sharpening in recognition of his role as the emissary of Maharani Lalita Pat Mahadevi. In that moment, a sense of dignity swelled within Padmanabh, his posture stiffening slightly under the weight of such recognition. Yet, contrasting this solemn decorum was the comical oscillation of his ample belly—a shapeless mound that swayed, danced, and rolled along the stone-paved path towards the palace. The sight drew amused contortions to the stern faces of the sentries, who exchanged knowing smiles at the unexpected spectacle.

Before setting out for Murshidabad, to secure Shuja Khan's favour, Maharani Lalita Devi had bestowed upon Padmanabh Dev one hundred gold asharfis as a token—a tribute so essential that from Shahjahanabad, Delhi to Murshidabad no one would care even to open their eyes without it.

'These are but mere hundred mohars,' Padmanabh Dev mused silently, 'what share is left for me?'

'Explain it to the Nawab properly, Padmanabh Dev!' came the composed rejoinder. 'Today I have neither a kingdom nor a rule; I have taken refuge in my maternal home at Banapur for the sake of my son. When that auspicious day comes…' her voice trailed into hopeful uncertainty.

'Rest assured—be confident, Maharani! My association with Shuja Khan is not born of momentary passion. Ever since his days as Naib Nazim in Cuttack, we have maintained cordial ties. He shall not dare dismiss my words. I shall return from Murshidabad with a singular royal mandate in the name of Bhagirathi Kumar. Yet you know well the state of his court—corruption pervades from heel to crown. Bribes, indulgences, and flattery dictate every action, and without such underhand dealings, nothing can be accomplished.'

The Maharani leaned forward thoughtfully, her tone tinged with quiet intrigue as she retrieved a wooden casket from the coffer. 'Indeed,' she observed, almost conspiratorially, 'When fate itself becomes a game of chance, why hesitate to wager?' As the lid swung open, Padmanabh Dev's eyes gleamed with anticipation, catching the glint of gold and gemstones within. With deliberate grace, she tilted the casket forward, unveiling a trove of exquisite gold ornaments, each studded with dazzling diamonds, onto the floor before him. 'Take these, Padmanabh! I have no need for them anymore,' she declared, her voice firm with finality. 'Their worth is no trifle—they will suffice for your needs.'

In this high-stakes wager, it was as if Lalita Devi had staked her final chip. Her eyes burned with fervour, coiled like a striking serpent—an intense glare that spoke volumes of her unyielding resolve. In her bare left arm, she clutched a gold talisman studded with jewels, resting against her unadorned body. In a sudden, vehement gesture, she discarded it onto the heap of ornaments and commanded, 'Do not tarry, Padmanabh! The auspicious moment is slipping away!'

In that instant, Padmanabh Dev's eyes flared with awe at the sight of such priceless treasures. Never in his life had he beheld such an array of exquisite gems and pearls—enough, it seemed, to grace the nuptial ceremonies of royal brides beyond compare.

After obtaining a modest sum in Jahangiri rupees towards his travel expenses, Padmanabh Dev remarked gravely, 'Majesty, Shuja Khan may well contrive trouble over Lord Jagannath. The deities, not being housed in the temple, are costing Utkal a revenue loss of ten lakh rupees through the jizya. Shuja Khan will insist that the deities be reinstated to the sacred precincts of Shrikshetra! But I wonder—how can we bring the deities back to the temple? Maharaja Ramachandra Dev has concealed them in a hidden cove.'

Lalita Mahadevi answered in a voice edged with uncompromising severity, 'I have already taken counsel from the eminent elders of the Mukti Mandap Sabha—the Brahmachari and the Mahajana pundits. Their system is in place, and in the deities' absence, Navakalevara—the ritualistic recreation of the wooden icons—may be instituted. Even the Second Indradyumna, Ramachandra Dev, followed this course.'

'But Bishara Mohanty had brought Brahmapinda from Gauda. Where, then, are we to find it now?'

'If the Brahmapinda remains out of reach, we shall avail ourselves of the *brahmashila* or the Shaligram instead.' Lalita Devi added with calm assurance, 'Do not trouble yourself over this matter; simply explain it to Shuja Khan. When Bhagirathi Kumar ascends the Khurda throne, my very first act will be to inaugurate the establishment of the triad within the vacant temple.'

'And Aminchand?' Padmanabh Dev inquired.

'Aminchand shall be appointed as deputy in the Shrikshetra—we have no objection.' She cared little to quibble over any condition that might secure the Khurda throne.

Meanwhile, in the Dewan-e-Aam of Farrabag Palace, upon a marble divan clad in sumptuous velvet—with a lavish, embroidered cushion atop—sat the Nawab of Bengal, Bihar, and Odisha, the illustrious Shuja-ud-Din Motamman-ul-Mulk, known as Shujauddin Asad Jang. Flanking the divan like solemn sentinels hewn from stone, his steadfast attendants maintained a silent vigil, their hands firmly grasping ceremonial morchals—elaborate fly-whisks fashioned from resplendent peacock feathers. With a crown wrought of lustrous pearls perched upon his head and an exquisite jewelled necklace gracing his neck—even as bracelets forged of eight metals adorned his slack arms—the aged Shuja Khan appeared as nothing more than a crumbling edifice of flesh and bone.

Who, upon beholding him now, would believe that in his youth he had been as formidable, unbridled, and equally extravagant? Murshid Quli had left no sons, and for the sake of his daughter Zeenat-un-Nisa his life had been steeped in abject sorrow and ignominy. Since Shuja Khan's days as

Naib Nazim in Cuttack, she had renounced her husband and taken up abode in her maternal home in Murshidabad.

Thus it came to be that Shuja Khan—the very son-in-law—had become an object of his father-in-law's ire. Murshid Quli had long desired to confer Murshidabad's regal title upon Shuja Khan's son, Sharfaraj, a plea he had boldly presented in the Delhi court. Yet, following his demise, the formidable Shujauddin usurped the reins of power over Murshidabad. Even as he anxiously awaited the moment when the flame of Murshid Quli's life would finally be extinguished near his deathbed, his son Sharfaraj was absorbed in the gaiety and boisterous gatherings within the resplendent halls of Farrabag.

'Sharfaraj! You are so preoccupied amidst the dancing mujrewalis, while Nawab Shuja-ud-Daula, over there, has already dismissed you from office,' someone from the council delivered the tidings. Upon hearing that Shuja Khan was to be enthroned upon his grandfather's ancestral throne, Sharfaraj mustered his loyal forces and galloped on horseback to the bustling Chehel Sotoun Palace to confront his father.

Father and son stood with swords raised—two piercing questions in the contest of power: in this political arena, who is the father, and who is the son? Amid the clash of bare blades that day, tears glistened on the widow of Murshid Quli, Nausheri Banu's grief-stricken face. 'I cannot abide a struggle, Shuja—nor can I let Sharfaraj bear witness to a battle over your appointment!' began her plaintive appeal, her tearful eyes delicately veiled by a softly draped dupatta.

Sharfaraj cast a long, searching glance towards his

grandmother. Then, with solemn resolve, he laid his sword at Shuja Khan's feet and turned away, retreating into the extravagant embrace of the Farrabag Palace. From that moment forward, he never set foot in Chehel Sotoun again.

Still, Shuja Khan bore no ill will towards his son; by his paternal benevolence, Sharfaraj was duly made the Nawab of Bengal.

Now long decrepit and worn by time, Shuja Khan recalled days when, during his pilgrimage to Mecca, he had procured a Qur'an—inscribed by the revered hands of Hazrat—for a hundred thousand rupees. That sacred scripture, along with the prayer beads he now passed through his trembling fingers, had been his sole solace. Though the arms that once struck like lightning now quivered feebly, lacking the strength to wield a sword, his attachment to the honour of his office never waned; until his final breath, he could not part with that exalted title.

Before him, upon the lectern, was placed that very Qur'an. Eyes half-shut in silent reverence, he caressed its tassels in quiet devotion. To his right, upon a throne draped in white chadar, sat Haji Muhammad and Jagat Seth Fatehchand; to his left, Muhammad Ali and Rai Rayyan Alamchand presided—his trusted councillors, the sole overseers of his realm's revenues.

Padmanabh Dev stepped forward. Bowing low like a slab of tender meat, he performed three deep kowtows. Beneath the incense-diffused marble altar of the Diwan-e-Khaas, he stood subdued, subordinate as if by destiny. In his hand, he clutched a bouquet of roses; at his side, within a finely woven Benares silk pouch, lay some gold mohars. The councillors measured the sum by the very size of that pouch.

A khadim announced, 'Padmanabh Dev, King of Patia Fort!'

Shuja Khan, his eyes suddenly alert and his trembling lips parting in tremulous command, replied, '*Tashrif laaiye. Mizaaj shareef?*'

'*Huzoor ki meharbani*,' Padmanabh Dev offered with a respectful nod.

Padmanabh Dev, ever at ease in the courtly rituals, assumed his customary station. He placed a bouquet reverently at Shuja Khan's feet—and, with a dismissive flick, scattered the hundred gold mohars offered as tribute by Maharani Lalita Devi.

At the sight of such a meagre offering, the lines upon the councillors' faces furrowed in scorn. Even the khojas and khadims in Shuja-ud-Daula's court would receive a more generous bounty from a king or zamindar.

Haji Muhammad remarked, 'With this, even our stables' horses would fall short of a day's fodder!'

'Isn't that all there is?' Jagat Seth commented dryly. 'For three long years, the annual peshkash of twelve lakh rupees from Odisha has ceased—and from the ten lakhs due as jizya, not even a pittance is paid. Meanwhile, relentless demands pour in from Shahjahanabad, Delhi, pressing for silver from our coffers with one summons after another!'

Year after year, Shuja Khan borrowed on credit from Jagat Seth and sent the ever-increasing peshkash to Delhi. If the regular contributions and jizya from Utkal were to cease altogether, settling the accounts of the Murshidabad treasury and Jagat Seth's ledgers would become impossible. Thus, Jagat Seth's gaze remained fixed on revenue and tribute. He had hoped Padmanabh Dev would present a handsome sum, but upon seeing so little, despair crept into his countenance.

In strict adherence to court protocol, a khoja arrived bearing, on a silver tray, a flowing piece of cloth and an embroidered skullcap, inside which rested earrings studded with precious gems. Treating the tray as if it were a sacred oblation, Padmanabh Dev inclined his head in a ritual gesture. Padmanabh Dev had not expected such a tribute from Shuja Khan's court, yet—with a wily, detached glint in his eye while accounting for the tray's contents—he declared, 'Sir, everything you have said is true. The peshkash from the Odisha suba has ceased. Shri Jagannath is no longer in Shrikshetra—hence, no pilgrims are arriving to pay jizya. Whatever loss the Murshidabad government has suffered is understood fully only by Maharani Lalita Devi. But what power does she wield? She is confined in Banapur, at her father's house, with Bhagirathi Kumar. The Maharani entreats that Khudaband Shuja Khan restore Utkal to its natural, self-reliant state.'

'That is precisely our intention as well.' Shuja Khan responded, his gaze steady yet tinged with melancholy. 'What, then, stands in our way?'

Observing that his remedy was having its desired effect, Padmanabh Dev added in a low tone, 'There was only ever one—and he belongs to your kindred, Majesty. It is none other than Hafiz Qadar Beg, also known as Ramachandra Dev, who lies at the very root of this matter.'

Shuja Khan roared at the mention of Hafiz Qadar's name: 'He is not our kindred—he is an enemy!'

'Exactly so!' Padmanabh Dev remarked softly, 'Had it not been so, why would they have united to extinguish the Mughal dominion in Utkal? Besides, Shri Jagannath, deprived of a proper abode of the gods, dwells in the hidden woodland hermitages.'

Shuja Khan sighed and replied, 'I could never have imagined that Hafiz Qadar would one day display such fierce enmity against us.'

Yet Shuja Khan still harboured hope—he trusted that, in time, Hafiz Qadar and his followers would renew their allegiance to him by severing ties with the disloyal kafirs.

The astute Padmanabh Dev mused quietly, saying, 'Would Your Excellency still consider him kin? In the meantime, having granted a revenue-free village to the Brahmins, he has already restored himself as a Hindu—though most of those very Brahmins still refuse to acknowledge him as such.'

Jagat Seth's voice then chimed in with a touch of incredulity, 'By donating a single village, has he suddenly become a Hindu in the eyes of the Brahmins? Astonishing indeed!'

'This is our predicament.' Shuja Khan exhaled deeply.

'Your Lordship's troubles are the troubles of all Utkal.' In a subordinate tone, Padmanabh Dev continued, 'Maharani Lalita Devi has earnestly entreated you that once Bhagirathi Kumar ascends the Khurda throne, peace shall reign throughout the land. Rather than a customary annual peshkash of twelve lakhs, Her Majesty is prepared to raise it to fourteen lakhs—and she has no objection to accepting Raja Aminchand as deputy of the Shri Mandir.'

But the deities remained in exile, hidden in the

subterranean wilderness. Pilgrims no longer thronged the temple; silence loomed. Was that not known to Jagat Seth?

'Yet what benefit can there be,' Shuja Khan asked, his voice edged with disbelief, 'in installing Raja Aminchand as deputy in an empty shrine?'

Padmanabh Dev replied, 'Maharani Lalita Devi vows to oversee a Navakalevara—a rebirth of the deities through newly consecrated idols.'

Well acquainted with the temple administration, Jagat Seth raised a brow. 'And how shall a Navakalevara be performed while the deities remain secluded in forest sanctuaries?'

'Even Maharaja Ramachandra Dev, the second Indradyumna, pursued the same course,' Padmanabh Dev explained. 'The fact that the Lord has gone into concealment does not preclude a new installation. Such is the consensus of the eminent members and Mahajana Brahmins of the Mukti Mandap.

Shuja Khan, however, cared little for the minutiae of the intricate rituals performed for the kafir deities, or the ceremonial almsgiving officiated by the Mahajana Brahmins. To him, Shri Jagannath was a matter of revenue, not reverence.

'Our intent,' he declared, 'is peace in Odisha. Let Lord Jagannath return to his sanctum. The loss of ten lakhs annually from the jizya weighs heavily. If Begum Lalita can restore harmony and reinstall the Lord in his temple—and if her offer increases the peshkash to fourteen lakhs—then submit your petition. We shall consent.'

For a fleeting moment, Padmanabh Dev felt as though he had captured the very moon in the sky, only to know that dark, overwhelming clouds would soon obscure its light, an outcome he had never truly hoped for.

Haji Muhammad observed gravely, 'The reports from Cuttack, sent by the Shia-Navis, indicate that Ramachandra Dev is indeed spreading this narrative across Odisha—claiming disinterest in the Khurda throne. His sole objective seems to be the expulsion of the Mughals from Utkal. Then, who can confidently assert that Begum Lalita Devi's plea harbours no hidden agenda? Who can assure that father and son wouldn't align against us?'

Could it be that father and son aligned when the question of the throne arose? They had long been sworn adversaries. What was Haji Muhammad suggesting? Shuja Khan still recalled with indignation the day Sharfaraj, in the Chehel Sotoun Palace, unsheathed his sword against him.

He demanded, 'Have the Shia-Navis really sent such intelligence? For the kafirs, nothing is impossible. If a Brahmin priest can convert a Muslim into a Hindu simply by obtaining a village as a gift, then once the throne is secured, why should father and son not jointly raise their swords against us?'

Padmanabh Dev had never expected to be confronted with such a question. With a slight shake of his head, he reflected, *Does Maharaj Ramachandra Dev truly lack any desire for the Khurda throne, or is this merely a rumour?* And if so, what should prevent him from besting Lalita Mahadevi and Bhagirathi Kumar in a single stroke and seizing the throne of Khurda in a swift coup? No—he thought—it was essential that the waters be muddied first, for only then could the fish be caught.

Scratching his ear thoughtfully, he responded in a

calculated voice, 'That Her Majesty and the Prince would rise in arms against His Excellency? That seems far-fetched. If they had such designs, why would they linger in Banapur? Khurda is under Mughal control, with Mir Hashim posted as its commander. Should the faintest hint of disloyalty emerge, Bhagirathi Kumar's dismissal would be swift. And I stand as proof—is there any servant of the Empire more loyal than Padmanabh Dev?'

Shuja Khan mulled over every perspective and came to the conclusion that Padmanabh's proposal was not without merit. In truth, Khurda lay firmly in Mughal grasp, yet with the absence of Shri Jagannath—the divine soul—in his rightful place, the land of Utkal had all but descended into chaos. The annual peshkash of twelve lakhs failed even to yield a single proper coin; the faujdar and his soldiery, accustomed to plundering, pocketed what they could while then burdening the state with their salaries. Moreover, the jizya had been suspended altogether. If we could reinstall Shri Jagannath in the temple by issuing a new mandate, there would be no further difficulty. Padmanabh Dev was a man of unwavering faith—accepting his proposal would bring benefit, not loss.

When Jagat Seth Fatehchand heard that the peshkash would be raised to fourteen lakhs per annum, his tone softened with sympathy. 'There is no mistrust in you,' he pronounced, serene and unwavering, 'but let it be clearly recorded in the petition: an annual tribute of fourteen lakhs will be paid to the Cuttack treasury on behalf of Prince Bhagirathi. Lord Jagannath shall be reinstated in the sanctum at Puri. There shall be no obstruction in the payment of jizya. Should there be any breach of these terms, Prince Bhagirathi Kumar will be summarily dismissed from the Khurda throne.'

Then, after three deep kowtows, Padmanabh Dev intoned, 'The command of the Sovereign rests upon my brow. I shall take full responsibility. How long could it possibly take to sow discord between the two and achieve our aim? The young prince is but a puppet—he sways in whichever direction the strings pull! But that concern may wait.'

The durbar dispersed. Padmanabh Dev would now present the queen's petition in full accordance with protocol. Shuja Khan, his steps unsteady, began to retire into the palace as the assembled councillors bowed in unison and receded into the background. Clasping the ceremonial insignia in his left hand, Padmanabh Dev stood resolute, while his counterparts lagged behind Shuja Khan. With one final bow, he took his leave from the Diwan-e-Khas.

But what was the true purpose behind the cunning, duplicitous Padmanabh Dev's journey to Murshidabad? It was no longer beneficial for Lakshmi Paramaguru to loiter before Farrabagh like a beggar. Drawing words from his mouth was like squeezing water from stone—and if discovered, imprisonment would be inevitable. Without delay, Lakshmi Paramaguru withdrew to his sanctuary: the venerable Kiriteshwari Temple.

Along the banks of the Bhagirathi stood the illustrious Kiriteshwari Temple—a renowned Shakti Peeth, sacred to both the land and the gods. The beloved deity Kiriteshwari, though the fortunes of Bangeshwar had waned, had seen her sanctity remain unsullied. Over the years, numerous Shiva shrines had sprung up around the temple. Among these, one stood devoted to the Bhairav aspect of Kiriteshwari, where

Lakshmi Paramaguru, with a fixed and steady gaze towards Bhairav, softly recites celestial hymns.

Bhuvaneshi Siddhirupa, Kiritastha Kiritatah
Devata Vimala namni, Sanvarti Bhairavas tatha...

In that serene moment, as Lakshmi Paramaguru sat in quiet contemplation before Lord Bhairav, all his agitation and anxious turmoil melted away, replaced by a profound and tranquil peace.

Yet this Bhairav was, at heart, a Buddhist image—one that was once embraced by Hindu traditions in a manner akin to Buddhist orthodoxy. The Bhairav figure adorning the Kiriteshwari Peeth was a silent testimony to that heritage. Here, the Bhairav embodiment was depicted seated in Padmasana, one hand resting gently on its lap while the other lightly touched its foot. It lacked the customary third eye—boasting only two—and its hands hold neither a rod nor a trident. Instead, it resembles a meditative Buddha, enchanting every onlooker. Over time, however, tradition had come to revere this form as the Bhairav manifestation, its meditations and mantras even inscribed in the *Tantra Chudamani*.

But in the precincts of Kiriteshwari, this Buddhist form was often overlooked. Pilgrims would come for the Goddess's darshan, sip the sanctified Charanamrita, and depart. Few would make the rounds to the shrines of Shiva scattered around her, and fewer still to Sanvarta Bhairava's modest abode. The priests of the temple would perform their daily worship with modest offerings—a palmful of water, a few bel leaves placed upon the Lingas—and leave it at that. Sanvarta Bhairava, for all his tranquil magnetism, was treated with similar brevity.

Ever since Lakshmi Paramaguru arrived in Murshidabad, this Bhairav shrine had served as his haven. He unrolled a tattered blanket upon the worn floor of an old choultry, spending day and night there. His only companions were a few gentle pigeons and the soft cooing of their kin nearby. Close at hand lay a *kamandalu* and even a stray trident—a remnant, perhaps, of a wandering ascetic who sought shelter here—but such vestiges now raised little curiosity. Occasionally, a passing pilgrim dropped a coin, a morsel, a folded offering. No one knew when Jagat Seth Fatehchand might grant him a private audience, or if he would at all; for now, Murshidabad was his sole sanctuary.

That morning, while seated cross-legged on his blanket, all of Lakshmi Paramaguru's thoughts were consumed by the wily Padmanabh Dev—what purpose had brought him here, and what hidden designs lay behind his sudden appearance?

'My obeisance, O revered one!' a voice suddenly called out.

Lakshmi Paramaguru turned to see a traveller clad in humble, coarse garments standing before the Bhairav figure. 'Oh—Lakshmiram!' he exclaimed. In this lonesome clime, Lakshmiram was sometimes his only confidant, the bearer of fragmented news of Murshidabad. Already, he had learned from him that Shuja Khan's health was failing.

'Why, Maharaj,' the traveller asked lightly, 'Has Bhairavji been pleased with your penance today?'

Yet, as on previous days, Lakshmi Paramaguru had no desire to idle away time in small talk with the devotee. Today, he was singularly resolved that no attention should be drawn to his presence in Murshidabad, so long as Padmanabh

Dev remained in the city. Vigilance was paramount, for even the walls here seemed to have ears.

With a subtle gesture, Lakshmi Paramaguru signalled the traveller to depart from this place. In his eyes, the man was indeed an oddity—a great ascetic, no doubt, deeply immersed in Bhairav sadhana. Lakshmiram understood—he bowed and retreated, muttering blessings as he slipped away: 'Victory to Mother Kiriteshwari. Glory to Bhairava Maharaj.'

Lakshmi Paramaguru then withdrew into the silent corridors of his inner contemplation. He had journeyed all this way to Murshidabad, hoping to meet Jagat Seth Fatehchand—but not once had he been granted a private audience. Apart from Rai Rayyan Alamchand, no one proved a reliable aide. Although Rai Rayyan harboured a modicum of sympathy for Ramachandra Dev, fulfilling Lakshmi Paramaguru's purpose through him seemed a distant prospect.

In the council of Shuja Khan, he held little sway now—his presence but a shadow among the powerful. The only actual influence rested with Jagat Seth. Shuja Khan's throne itself leaned upon the coffers of that imperial banker. His ties to Delhi's grandees—its umraos, nobles, and ministers—ran deep, and it was only their words, when echoed by Jagat Seth, that Shuja Khan seemed to heed.

Rai Rayyan had promised to arrange a private meeting with Jagat Seth Fatehchand, yet not once had Lakshmi Paramaguru found an opportunity to converse with him. He himself had tried repeatedly to secure an audience with Jagat Seth, for Fatehchand was not unacquainted with him, but the sentries would not allow him to step beyond

Jagat Seth's gate. Where, then, could such a chance ever come?

That day, as Jagat Seth departed Shuja Khan's court in the palanquin, Lakshmi Paramaguru, standing at the gate, raised his right hand in a gesture of blessing, hoping to catch his eye. Yet Fatehchand, unaware, failed to recognize him, offering no acknowledgement. After all, how could he expect to see Lakshmi Paramaguru in Murshidabad?

A deep sigh escaped the guru's lips—one so heavy it seemed to ripple through the temple's old archways.

Had he truly lost the mesmerising force that once wrenched Ramachandra Dev from the jaws of captivity at Barabati Fort, dragging him by sheer will from under Taqi Khan's clutch in Cuttack? Was that spiritual current now dried, dulled by the grime of politics and the abandonment of *swadharma*? Had the divine fire he once bore dimmed within him?

What was the worth now of quiet rituals, of soft bhajans echoing through the secured sanctum, when the lifeblood of the land was drained daily by tyranny? What was the meaning of righteous conduct when life under servitude bore the constant sting of humiliation? Perhaps resistance alone remained the truest dharma in such a world—the only path of sacred engagement. And yet, Lakshmi Paramaguru felt it—a deep and aching emptiness. As though he had been rung hollow by the very age he sought to resist.

Should he, then, walk openly into Shuja Khan's court? Should he, fearless, declare his stance before all? But such a step would surely lead to imprisonment. His name sat high upon the list of rebels marked by the Mughal court. Murshidabad's durbar was not blind to this. Reports from the Shia-Navis had already painted him as the hand behind Shri Jagannath's disappearance from the temple—a whisper that had made its way to Shuja Khan's ears.

And yet… how long would he cower like a fugitive in the temple shadows?

Suddenly, his concentration broke as a vague presence fell over him. For a moment, he feared it might be Lakshmiram—once again come to unsettle him. But it was not so. Startled, Lakshmi Paramaguru found himself face-to-face with none other than Rai Rayyan Alamchand.

'Where have you been—so sudden of appearance?' Lakshmi Paramaguru exclaimed, his voice a mix of relief and reproach. 'I have tried to meet you many times, but my efforts were in vain.'

Rai Rayyan replied in a gentle yet earnest tone, 'I have not had an opportunity for a private audience with you. Given the current circumstances, even meeting with Jagat Seth is no longer feasible. You must leave Murshidabad as swiftly as possible and return to Utkal—this is the only auspicious course for both you and the land.'

Lakshmi Paramaguru asked, 'In other words…?'

'Shuja Khan has accepted the petition of Maharani Lalita Devi,' Rai Rayyan warned, his voice low and guarded. 'In return for the coronation of Prince Bhagirathi upon the Khurda throne, an annual tribute of fourteen lakhs has been promised. On this condition alone shall Lord Jagannath be restored to his temple. Jagat Seth has offered his wholehearted approval. If he learns of your presence here, your arrest is inevitable.'

A heavy sigh seemed to echo in the troubled silence.

Famine stalked the breadth of Odisha like a spectre;

destitution danced in its streets. Even through coercion—through beatings and levies—the previously agreed twelve lakhs remained unattainable. And now Prince Bhagirathi pledged fourteen? Lakshmi Paramaguru could scarcely comprehend it. Would the prince truly reduce Utkal to ashes for the sake of a throne?

'But how,' Lakshmi Paramaguru asked in a tone of wonder and exquisite frustration, 'does the prince intend to bring the deities back to the temple?'

'Maharani Lalita Devi has sent Padmanabh Dev from Patia Fort as her advocate.' Rai Rayyan's voice took on a nuanced, almost conspiratorial lilt as he answered. 'The Maharani herself shall institute a Navakalevara. Padmanabh Dev has given his word to Shuja Khan.'

'Navakalevara?' Lakshmi Paramaguru's voice bristled. 'Where, then, would they find the sacred *brahmashila*—the divine core? Shri Jagannath is no mere idol hewn from timber. And how could a pious, tradition-bound Hindu like Jagat Seth have given his assent to such a travesty?'

'For Jagat Seth, profit is piety. With two extra lakhs added to the offer, sandstone will suffice instead of the *brahmashila*. Shuja Khan seeks revenue. The jizya must be paid. And the Maharani—she desires the throne of Khurda. She is prepared to accept any condition to claim it. . .'

Now it was clear—Padmanabh Dev's arrival was no accident. And yet, in Murshidabad's corridors, the auctioning of Odisha's soul for petty personal gain was something that Paramaguru's spirit could no longer abide by. His soul rebelled against this sordid bargaining. In Murshidabad, no recourse existed to defy it—perhaps in Utkal, retribution might one day be exacted!

'You've done much for Utkal,' he said, the weight of gratitude in his voice. 'For that, my deepest thanks, Rai Rayyan Alamchand. May Shri Jagannath bestow his blessings upon you!'

With that, Rai Rayyan took his leave. Clutching his blanket, *kamandalu*, and worn trident as symbols of his humble but steadfast purpose, Lakshmi Paramaguru, burdened with despair and resolve, stepped away from Murshidabad towards Utkal—a long, arduous journey stretching before him.

Returning in such utter desolation was heart-wrenching. For the first time, Lakshmi Paramaguru truly understood the magnitude of his inner defeat.

*****

Chapter V

Disguise for self-defence! How demeaning it is! Dressed in black rags, a necklace of cheap coloured stones around his neck, long dishevelled locks tumbling to his shoulders, a cloth satchel slung over one arm, and a walking staff in hand, thus wandered Ramachandra Dev through the streets of Cuttack, cloaked as a dervish. Street after street, in search of Lakshmi Paramaguru. It was also imperative to learn of the actual state of affairs at Taqi Khan's court… yet not a single word had reached him about the guru. Had he been taken captive in Murshidabad?

Behind him, the Shia-Navis and spies prowled like bloodhounds, sniffing in pursuit. Ramachandra Dev knew well: in the looming storm that was to break over Utkal, Lakshmi Paramaguru was his sole confidant, his only trusted comrade. Without him, how could a man condemned by the name of Hafiz Qadir, who bore the taint of apostasy, ever rally the timid fort lords, the castle keepers, the chieftains and the war-worn masses beneath his banner?

Though the Mahajana Brahmins had overseen his public penance—though he had donated the revenue-free village of Ramachandrapur as reparation and been ritually restored to the Hindu fold—the common conscience of the people still whispered: *He is a mleccha, a fallen one.* Among the orthodox Brahmin settlements, he remained untouchable. The *Smarta* priests had cemented that belief. In such a world, only Lakshmi Paramaguru stood with him.

But in all of Cuttack, there was no sign of him.

Then one day, as Babaji Gauradas sat beneath the shade of a bakul tree outside the Jagannath Ballabh Math, softly strumming his ektara and humming Sahajia Vaishnava hymns, his eyes fell upon a passing dervish—and he paused, startled. The Math's veranda stretched quiet and sun-dappled behind him, a place steeped in the memory of its founding by Rai Ramanand, minister to Prataparudra Dev, when it had long served as a sanctuary for the Sahajiya tradition. Fakirs, dervishes, bauls—even wandering muramiyas of the Muslim faith—would visit now and then; its doors remained open to all. *yavana* Haridasa himself, en route to Puri, had once lingered here for days. In the woven tapestry of medieval India, such mingling of Hindu bhakti and Islamic sufi devotion created a rare confluence—a luminous meeting point of soul and spirit.

So, beneath the dappled shade of the bakul tree, Babaji Gauradas felt no surprise at the mere presence of a dervish. But his first genuine astonishment arose from the uncanny familiarity etched into the dervish's face. The man, head bowed in quiet contemplation, seemed to wonder whether Babaji might fail to recognize him. Perhaps, he thought, the disguise was too convincing—surely no spy of Taqi Khan would ever suspect him now.

Suddenly, erupting in hearty laughter, Gauradas called out, 'Come now, Fakir! Why do you stand there?

Here, among us, there is no distinction between Hindu and Muslim fakirs or saints. But a fakir, whether in disguise or not, cannot escape my notice!'

In that moment, Babaji Gauradas knew he had correctly recognized Ramachandra Dev. There was an unsettled flicker at Ramachandra Dev's lips, a wordless struggle between relief and dread.

Without any preamble, Ramachandra Dev asked, 'Babaji, is there any news of Lakshmi Paramaguru?' Jagannath Ballabh Math was known as a shelter for Lakshmi, and it was through this sanctuary that Babaji Gauradas and Ramachandra Dev first became acquainted.

Babaji Gauradas replied warmly, 'I met Lakshmi back in Pausha before he set out for Murshidabad; after that, word ceased. But then, one night as some Vaishnavites were returning from Gauda, they paused here. In Remuna, at a modest dwelling, they saw Lakshmi.'

'So it appears our Paramaguru is returning unscathed from Murshidabad!' Ramachandra Dev thought, his heart buoyed by this tiding.

Babaji, with quiet affection, invited him to linger awhile at the Math—to partake in devotional songs and hymns. Yet Ramachandra Dev was not one for devotional singing—his mind was elsewhere, plagued by instability, anxiety, and a persistent sense of foreboding that turned every moment into one fraught with thorns. Were he to sit like Babaji Gauradas under the bakul tree, ektara in hand, perhaps the burning solitude might cool—but there was no time for that now.

Ramachandra Dev then set off towards the Jama Masjid.

Below its steps, there was always a congregation of fakirs and dervishes—a living bazaar of whispers and portents. It was in such gatherings that gossip from the Cuttack province and secrets from the imperial quarters of Lalbagh would drift freely, bearing news of Taqi Khan's intrigues. But that day was a Thursday. The crowd of wandering souls had journeyed en masse to the Eidgah at Kadam Rasul. Only two or three old and limping fakirs remained behind, cloaked in silence, waiting with weary patience for alms from the occasional devout passerby. Now and then, one would mutter softly, *"Ya Allah… Insha'Allah…"*

Ramachandra Dev asked a nearby fakir, 'So quiet today… the place is deserted.'

'Today, the entire congregation of fakirs and dervishes has gathered at Kadam Rasul.' The fakir replied with a low, calibrated tone. 'And what brings you here—to share our share of alms? Go directly to Kadam Rasul, my friend. There, Razia Begum is arriving to offer her prayers—and she gives abundantly. She has a great devotion to fakirs and dervishes. And if you are an accomplished astrologer, all the better. Look at my leg—I can't walk that far. So here I sit, a humble servant of the Lord Almighty, waiting by the mosque stairs, at his mercy. Last time, a fakir helped me there, and Razia Begum dropped two gold mohurs into my little pot! May Allah bless her soul. And you—are you new to Cuttack? I've not seen your face before!'

The fakir's tale seemed to cascade on without end.

In the sweltering, lonely afternoon, the very name 'Razia' echoed like a plaintive dove's cry from some secluded retreat, stirring a deep reverberation in Ramachandra Dev's subconscious. In his most solitary moments, her memory would awaken within him, merging like a vivid rainbow of iridescent bubbles over calm water. He recalled that one time in Rathipur Fort when, quite unexpectedly, he had spent a night in her company. Who could have planned such an unbidden encounter in Rathipur Fort? Was it truly that Razia had come, on that day, to seek blessings at Ghazisa Pir's shrine—or had she come instead to warn him of an impending danger? Perhaps she had come to point out some benevolent threat looming on the horizon.

And yet, in that stormy night, the meeting between Ramachandra Dev and Razia was entirely accidental. Life, after all, is nothing but a tapestry woven from such unforeseen moments, without which existence would become unbearably arduous.

Yet, overcome by that tide of wistful sentiment, Ramachandra Dev found he had no time for such indulgence. Slinging his satchel over his shoulder, he made his way towards Kadam Rasul. There, perhaps, fate would grant him the longed-for meeting with Razia. But would she recognize him—in this disguise? His mind churned with anticipation. And there, he hoped, news of Taqi Khan might also reach his ears.

At the entrance of Kadam Rasul, near the Naubatkhana, a bustling fair of devout souls had gathered: fakirs, dervishes, beggars, and vendors from flower shops mingled. Every Thursday, Razia Begum came here to pray, bestowing generous alms upon the gathered mystics. And on that day, the crowd was huge.

Ramachandra Dev slipped inside and seated himself among a cluster of fakirs, spreading out a black cloth before him. He withdrew a bundle of incense sticks from his satchel, struck his flint, and lit them, planting them firmly in the earth. Smoke curled into rings on the biting breeze. In his worn robes, masked by the quiet, he was indistinguishable from any other mendicant.

Nearby, a fakir recited verses from the Quran, laid on a wooden stand. But no such text lay before Ramachandra Dev. Then a voice barked out: 'Who's this beggar among fakirs and dervishes? Is there no other place for you to beg?'

Though in truth, the difference between a fakir and a mendicant in tattered robes was hardly discernible; only those who intoned the words of the Quran were held in higher regard. How, then, could they tolerate the presence of a beggar among them?

Had his disguise been pierced? Ramachandra Dev rose wordlessly and walked away. Beneath the golden canopy of a kanchan tree to the east of the shrine, he muttered, 'In Allah's world, fakir or beggar—what difference does it make?'

For a moment, he wondered whether it was safe to remain there. Yet, amid the clamour of squabbling fakirs and their mutual insults, no one even noticed the quietly disguised Ramachandra Dev.

Suddenly, a chorus arose from the courtyard as voices cried out, 'Razia Begum! Razia Begum!' By then, Razia Begum had already mounted her vehicle and arrived at the foot of the Naubatkhana at Kadam Rasul; from there, she would walk on to the shrine.

The khojas and khadims began shouting at the top of their voices, 'Clear out! Clear out!' and the crowd dispersed amid the reverberating sacred refrain echoing from their lips: 'La ilaha illallah!'

Razia ascended the marble platform and approached the steps at Kadam Rasul with quiet dignity. For a few hushed moments, she offered her prayer in humble devotion. High above, on the octagonal roof of the shrine, an Arabic supplication had been inscribed—a hymn to Allah:

> *Khak bardam chandni,*
> *Aba aaya Baboon,*
> *Sajuddeen Muhammad Khan,*
> *Har pooja payaamay,*
> *Jisna paaye va tasam.*

(No matter how many prayers one utters, one can never fully repay the blessings of the Almighty. This invocation alone is the measure of His mercy. A lifetime devoted to offering one's prayers—like the fragrant, drifting smoke from incense at His feet—reveals life's very essence and fulfilment.)

Razia lit a small handful of incense and placed it reverently at the foot of the shrine. Then she began the circumambulation of the shrine. During this sacred procession, beneath the sheltering kanchan tree, her steps suddenly halted near the spot where the disguised Ramachandra Dev sat. For an instant, he bowed his head in quiet submission.

In a hush laden with knowing, Razia murmured, 'However deep your disguise, fakir, you are never beyond the reach of my gaze.'

Startled, Ramachandra Dev glanced around and muttered, 'Ah… cursed be it, Razia. Do not sully yourself with disgrace in front of everyone.'

'Indeed!' came a quiet reply, followed by, 'But how

long must this disguise last? One must eventually confront the truth.'

Soon, the hushed exchange between the disguised Ramachandra Dev and Razia began to draw the attention of the other fakirs. Their covert conversation here spelt danger. In response, Razia casually flung a gem-studded ring into his bowl and said under her breath, 'This is my mark—a sign of my seal. Present it when you go to Barabati Palace, and the guards will surely clear your path.'

Razia vanished into the flowing tide of fakirs and mendicants.

Ramachandra Dev turned the ring over in his hand. It held a twilight-hued *sandhyamani* stone—said to preserve a husband's love without end. Razia's wifely devotion—a stroke of fortune more intoxicating than any destiny! A faint, self-mocking smile flickered across his face at the thought.

Barabati Fort had long become the refuge of the abandoned, the captive, and those in need of shelter. There was no place for such souls in Taqi Khan's lavish Lalbagh Palace; Razia herself had forsaken Lalbagh and now resided in one secluded wing of Barabati. While debates on dharma and sacred shastra flowed interminably among the fakirs and dervishes, the intrigues and conspiracies woven within Lalbagh left no room for her. Indeed, she had no desire to remain imprisoned within its opulent cage.

The women's quarters at Barabati lay quiet. Before it lay a blooming rose garden—a true gulistan of roses. In that garden, memories from long ago, when Ramachandra Dev had once been detained within these very walls, stirred in the twilight. He recalled the day in the Gulistan when he first met that mysterious woman—a vision concealed beneath a modest shawl, with a delicate, almost shy countenance reminiscent of a fragment of the moon drifting amid soaring clouds. In his mind's eye, clusters of jewelled recollections silently swam across the canvas of that desolate afternoon.

Outside, the clamour of the armed operatives and attendants had finally subsided. In the heat of the afternoon, all seemed to doze. Disguised as a fakir, Ramachandra Dev advanced towards the zenana of Barabati. At one point, a couple of armed guards attempted to stop him. But when they caught sight of the mark—Razia's seal—they immediately stepped aside. Someone even exclaimed, 'You're headed for Razia Begum's quarters!' Ramachandra Dev then revealed, from his satchel, the ring set with its glimmering sandhyamani gem. The guards fell silent in astonishment. Razia Begum's mark was a signal of her permission. One guard, in a hushed tone, murmured, 'Go… go, my friend— the fates smile upon you! Razia Begum's kind gaze is upon you. Otherwise, who would have procured such an exquisite ring?'

'How long, then, must this disguise persist?' came a sudden, penetrating inquiry. Hearing these words, Ramachandra Dev was momentarily taken aback.

Meanwhile, behind a partition inside a private chamber, Razia sat upon a plush carpet. Outside in the bustling Barabati compound, Ramachandra Dev—still cloaked in his fakir guise—continued on. To a stranger's eye, it might appear they were engaged in some scholarly discussion on sacred texts. But Razia had already shifted the veil—this was politics now.

'Naib Nazim Taqi Khan has returned from Murshidabad with the royal edict.' Razia said quietly. 'Soon,

Bhagirathi Kumar will be consecrated as the Maharaja of Khurda!'

'But as long as the Ratna Simhasana within the Lord's sanctum lies vacant,' Ramachandra burst out, unable to hold back, 'who will recognize his right to the throne?'

Razia nodded. 'In Lalbagh, Patia King Padmanabh Dev and a few other fort lords have been engaged in consultations with the Naib Nazim for days now. There is growing suspicion against me among his closest aides, which is why I have taken refuge in Barabati Fort. However, I have heard from these very trustworthy servants that Maharani Lalita Devi has pledged to restore Shri Jagannath to the temple!'

Caught up in the intensity of the moment, forgetting the perilous circumstances around them, Ramachandra Dev cried out with unwavering passion, 'Impossible!'

******

Chapter VI

After several days of silence, a vibrant stir had swept through Shrikshetra Purushottam—word had spread that the Lord's Navakalevara was imminent. Maharani Lalita Devi had taken the lead in orchestrating the sacred ceremony, while King Aminchand, residing within the holy precincts, was overseeing the proceedings in his role as deputy.

Pilgrim agents, driven by restless purpose, had dispersed in all directions to spread the news.

Meanwhile, by the modest temple of Lord Satyanarayana near Merdarosh, Shendha Suara reclined against the temple wall in quiet contemplation, his gaze drifting skyward, still wrapped in the lingering euphoria of bhang.

While the bhang coursed gently through him, all seemed well with the world. But once its haze began to fade, a heavy stillness crept in—he felt as lifeless as a dead snake. Yet, as if by muscle memory, whenever a pilgrim ambled past, he would stir just enough to mumble in his usual offhand tone: 'How can one proceed without venerating Satyanarayana, my lord? This Merdarosh is our ancient kitchen—the sacred hearth where Lord Satyanarayana and all the gods reside!'

Merdarosh had once boasted a modest kitchen, though the veneration of Satyanarayana scarcely stretched back a century. Still, how could the world sustain itself if a deity resembling Narayana were not enthroned in an empty sanctum to summon the customary trickle of offerings and coin? Pilgrims bowed perfunctorily and drifted onward towards Bat Ganesh. Day by day, the alms dwindled. And yet, by some mysterious grace—perhaps the nod of Chakadola (Sri Jagannath) himself—Shendha Suara was never left famished, however enigmatic the blessing might be.

After one such pilgrim departed, Shendha Suara chuckled to himself, 'As long as my dark Lord abides, this Suara's stomach shall never go empty. Somewhere, somehow, two fistfuls will always find their way into my bowl.'

'And who will drop those fistfuls into your bowl, O great Suara?' came a sharp retort.

It was Kantha Mekap—a pilgrim agent—en route to Garad house, where King Aminchand held his court as deputy, diligently orchestrating the rites of the Navakalevara. Casting his eyes upon the leisurely figure of Shendha Suara at Merdarosh, he inquired casually, 'Has any coin been earned today?'

The sly inquiry ignited Shendha Suara's temper; his brow seemed to blaze with indignation as he responded, his voice rising buoyantly through the haze of bhang, 'I am not here to tussle over an empty deity for mere coin! That's your trade. Your ambitions have strayed—you've bound yourself as Aminchand's flunkey, shamelessly licking up every scrap like one who feasts on the discarded morsels of a Pathan, all in the name of this Navakalevara!'

Kantha Mekap clenched his waistcloth and stepped forward with a sharp crack of his knuckles, eyes blazing. 'Shall I carry your slander straight to His Highness Raja Aminchand? You've grown insolent, Suara!'

Undeterred, Shendha Suara shot back, 'Off you go, to complain to your father Aminchand. I bow to no man's tyranny—indeed, I am a child of the revered Panda!'

Tempers flared, and the verbal skirmish between Shendha Suara and Kantha Mekap quickly escalated, compelling several servitors to intervene before the dispute could devolve into a full-fledged brawl.

Among the servitor community, the Navakalevara had already cleaved hearts into two factions.

One camp argued: this was a double Ashadha, not a leap month—so how could the Navakalevara be enacted? Yet now that the venerable Mahajana Brahmins of Mukti Mandap had granted Maharani Lalita their blessing for the ceremony, what power could now stand in its way? Indeed, most servitors had rallied behind Lalita Devi and Aminchand, their hearts aflame with enthusiasm for the impending ritual. How, they asked, could one dwell indefinitely before an empty sanctum? Without a consecrated deity, how were pilgrims to be drawn, and whence would the offerings come?

However, a small number of dissenters contended that the deity was not merely a mass of wood to be swapped out like an old effigy; they were steadfast followers of Ramachandra Dev and Lakshmi Paramaguru. For some, Shri Jagannath was nothing more than a source of potential earnings—but for the true believers in Ramachandra Dev, he embodied the very soul of Odisha, the lifeblood of a sovereign land, a symbol of unity and indomitable spirit. How could that Lord himself—now concealed in the forested refuge of Tikali—be consecrated anew by Navakalevara amid the secret intrigues that coiled through Shrikshetra?

Though a few Mahajanas of the Mukti Mandap voiced their dissent, armed with scriptural argument and classical precedent against the Navakalevara, the noble clans of the Vatsasa lineage—such as the houses of Nanda and Ratha—having received the favour of Maharani Lalita Devi, chose to disregard their protest altogether. 'Since when did these Gotreya upstarts pass for true Mahajanas?' they scoffed. 'After accepting revenue-free villages from an outcaste like Ramachandra Dev and masquerading as nobles, they've earned little more than the right to warm a seat in the Mandap—not the authority to invoke scripture.'

The astrologer offered precedent: 'There was once a time when the Navakalevara could not be performed in an intercalary month. And yet, when it was at last enacted, the day was an Amavasya—on the 17th day, in the 31st danda of the lunar cycle. Even then, the rites prevailed.'

Thus, those opposing the Navakalevara were reduced to a dwindling minority.

In anticipation of the new consecration, the once sombre and subdued spirit of Shrikshetra suddenly stirred with vibrant expectancy.

It was the sacred day of Shukla Dashami in the month of Chaitra—the moment when the inaugural rites of the Navakalevara were solemnly set into motion. A modest midday dhup was offered to the imagined deities at the vacant shrine. Harihara Pati Mahapatra ascended the ceremonial throne to place the *ajnamala*—the sacred garland of command—into the hands of the Daitas, who would now set forth in search of the *daru*, the sacred timber from which the new deities would be carved.

The temple thrummed with avid servitors.

From within the crowd, Shendha Suara cried out with a mix of mischief and exasperation, 'Oh, Pati Mahapatra, if not upon the deity itself, then from which altar shall you bestow the *ajnamala* upon the Daitas after which they will depart in search of the sacred *daru*!'

Initially, the Daitas had opposed the Navakalevara. But as time passed, they found themselves aligning with the Pandas and priests. Govind Swain Mahapatra, one among them, diligently serving the grand altar, thundered in a resounding tone, 'Do you not see the divine images emblazoned upon the *senapata*?'

With dissent reduced to a scant minority, how could such feeble resistance endure against the unified chorus of servitors intoning 'Hari Bol'? Silently, Shendha Suara withdrew from the sanctum. According to the age-old liturgy, once the decree had been formally granted from the three altars, Bhitarachha Mahapatra was to ceremonially tie a sacred saree around both the Daita and the Pati Mahapatra. Upon the binding of this cloth, the rite of *Daru Sandhan* would thereby commence, following the holy ordinance. Thus, the Daita, the Pati Mahapatra, and the accompanying servitors advanced in solemn procession towards the Anasara Pindi to receive the sarees.

Following the saree-binding and in accordance with ancestral rite, Bhitarachha Mahapatra adorned Deula

Karana, Tadhau Karana, and Khuntia, stationed at the Jaya-Vijaya Dwar, with beautifully bordered gota-kinari sarees. In a similar gesture of ceremonial honour, Padia Karana and Lanka Vishwakarma were graced with cotton sarees, each tied reverently around their brows.

Then, passing through the *jagamohana*, they would proceed towards the Balisahi Palace. There, in keeping with ancestral custom, the maharaja of Khurda was to ceremonially touch the sacred betel nut and hand it to the Rajguru and the Daitas—thus consecrating the commencement of the search for the hallowed *daru*, the divine timber. Yet the Balisahi Palace—once a resplendent royal palace—now lay in ruins, for the Khurda Raja had voluntarily exiled himself. In his stead, Raja Aminchand waited at the Markandeshwar Sahi, at Landa Math, with Senior Parichha Rajguru Gauri by his side. It would now be Aminchand's hand that touched the sacred betel nut, which he passed to Rajguru Gauri, who, in turn, entrusted it to the Daitas.

'Like paupers chasing alms, how many supplicants now sprint towards Aminchand's door!' Shendha Suara grumbled bitterly in impotent rage.

Indeed, today in the sacred temple, Aminchand stood as the harbinger, the enactor of will, the dispenser of destiny! Those very servitors who had once scoffed at him—Panda, Padhiari, and their ilk—now sat in hushed anticipation, eyes lifted in silent supplication, awaiting a flicker of Aminchand's grace. A single glance, they believed, could sanctify their fortunes beyond imagination. Meanwhile, Shendha Suara, along with the handful still loyal to Ramachandra Dev—those who, despite austerity and abandonment, had sworn to reclaim Lord Jagannath, the unconquered soul of Odisha, from his exile among the *yavanas*—stood now at the margins: unwelcome, unheeded, interlopers at a banquet of borrowed light.

As the ritual dictates, that night would be spent at Shri Jagannath Ballabh, and on the morrow, the Daitas and Pati Mahapatras would journey to the shrine of Goddess Mangala at Kakatpur. There, sheltered within the consecrated Deuli Math, they would lie prostrate before Goddess Mangala until late at night, for the conveyance of divine commandments in a dream. This prophetic vision would divulge the whereabouts of the sacred *daru*.

The deity Mangala of Kakatpur and the Deuli Math, nestled along the gentle banks of the Prachi River, shared an enigmatic and enduring bond with Shri Jagannath. This mysterious connection perhaps signified the confluence of divine energies during the Tantric-Buddhist era, when Shri Jagannath absorbed the Shakti principle within himself. Indeed, before every Navakalevara, both the Daitas and the Pati Mahapatra would receive within these hallowed walls a revelatory dream, disclosing the direction and precise location where the sacred *darus* of Lord Balabhadra, Goddess Subhadra, Lord Jagannath, and Sudarshana awaited.

Daita Gopal Swain Mahapatra was a servitor to Shri Jagannath's enclosure. Daitas were the Lord's most intimate attendants. Shri Jagannath was their sovereign lord, though in later rites, Brahmins came to hold ceremonial authority. For this sacred intimacy, it was they who, on Jyeshtha Shukla Trayodashi, following the Badasinghar Bhog, would enact the veiling of the Lord—*bahuta kaṇṭiba*—and the offering of *senapata*. It was they who would draw the *rahurekha* upon the forehead, perform the *chita*, guide the *pahaṇḍi bije*, drape the Lord in *hativesha*, and conduct the Nabajoubana viewing in the Anasara House. Each gesture, each rite, was theirs to perform.

For the sacred *daru* quest, the chief of the Daitas was ceremoniously crowned with a saree tied upon his head—an emblem of office borne by Gopal Swain Mahapatra.

Bishi Mahapatra, acting in his role as Pati Mahapatra, began by bestowing the *ajnamala* upon the Daitas. Then, in ritual mimicry, he offered a garland to Sudarshan's altar. Yet as he did so, his conscience trembled like an agitated serpent; his hands quavered with alarm. *This is no true* Navakalevara—*this will be nothing less than the slaughter of the gods!* Say what one will of Shendha Suara—half-mad, irreverent—but none could deny the iron resolve of his heart. Even as other servitors bowed in silence, it was he who alone roared his truth into the sacred silence.

All at once, Bishi Mahapatra's moral fortitude broke. His hands trembled, unable to steady the *ajnamala*, despite his conflicted feelings as a humble servant of the gods. Yet he had turned his loyalty to Aminchand, receiving a handsome bribe in the bargain. With the promise of the Navakalevara completed, the tantalizing lure of jagir and rich rewards loomed large. Unmoved, Bishi Mahapatra continued, unflinching as he mounted the garland on Sudarshan's altar, never once glancing away.

That night was spent at Jagannath Ballabh, and the very next day, the Daitas, along with Pati Mahapatra, arrived at Kakatpur, their steps heavy with both anticipation and trepidation.

In the sombre recesses of Deuli Math, Bishi Mahapatra lay dishevelled, sprawled in a makeshift surrender on the cool floor. Yet no rhythm graced his quiet contemplation—it was all as though the whole affair were nothing more than a child's play masquerading as a Navakalevara! In such a farce, the deity would be reduced to a mere doll, while Lalita Devi might well assume the role of a regal matriarch. Aminchand was to rule as the deputy of Shrikshetra, and Lord Jagannath would remain lost in some grand wilderness, his Navakalevara incomplete and unformed. There would be no Vishnu-shila inside—so how could Mangala Devi ever bestow upon them the dream-revelation for the *daru*?

Likewise, Daitapati Gopal Swain Mahapatra was himself languishing on the earth, his meagre share of bhog leaving his stomach scarcely filled. And how many more days were they to persist in this charade? He, too, had been richly compensated by Aminchand to bring forth the Navakalevara, lured by the twin temptations of jagir and reward—temptations not easily discarded.

A drowsy heaviness began to cloud the Daitapati's eyes, until at the sound of Bishi Mahapatra's voice his sleep shattered.

'Swain Mahapatra!'

'Hmmm…' came the measured reply as Gopal, the Daitapati, lifted his gaze, his tone edged with anticipation, 'Has the dream-revelation been received?'

In a calm, unwavering voice, Bishi Mahapatra declared, 'Rise, and let us set forth. We shall spin a tale that a dream-revelation has indeed been granted. Loosely woven as these many irregularities already are—why should the smallest hitch perturb us?'

'True! The Mother will never grant her dream-revelation. How long must we lie here, surviving on two morsels of offering once a day?'

In the deep gloom of the math, a solitary lamp flickered, its light casting long, dark, and wavering shadows along the walls, like forlorn spectres in silent lament.

Pati Mahapatra spoke with solemn gravity, 'You know as well as I do—the Navakalevara is unravelling, taking an unorthodox course. For the sake of *daru*, the goddess will never bestow upon us any dream-revelation.'

'Then what shall we do?' the Daitapati murmured with a languid yawn.

'Let us proclaim to everyone that the dream-revelation has been received. At the break of day, after receiving the deity's auspicious darshan, we will depart this place.'

'But...' the Daitapati hesitated, his mind echoing a silent protest.

Pati Mahapatra, however, was resolute. Sensing the inner turmoil of his subordinate, he pressed on, 'Where is Shri Jagannath not present, dear Daita? He is even woven into the very fabric of our self-interest. Come— let us announce that in the *Nairitya*, the southwest, Lord Balabhadra's *daru* awaits, in the north, that of Subhadra, in the *Ishaan*, the northeast, of Shri Jagannath, and in the east, that of Sudarshan. The goddess has granted her dream-revelation!'

'Ah, but merely declaring it does not make it so, my lord,' objected the Daitapati. 'How can the *darus* be found bearing the conch, the discus, the mace, and the lotus? When the goddess has not truly bestowed the dream-revelation, how will these divine symbols appear?'

Though the argument was not without substance, Pati Mahapatra quelled it with cold precision. '*Instead of fortifying our cause, he undermines it from within,*' he mused bitterly. Then, with a tone both persuasive and reproachful, he insisted, 'This is not your station, my friend. Those divine symbols are not etched solely upon wood— they are inscribed in bhakti itself. Perceive with devotion, and they shall reveal themselves.'

Still, the Daitapati pressed, 'You think words alone will make it so?'

'Must you prattle like a scholar, Swain Mahapatra? Have you forgotten the hundred gold mohurs we took from Raja Aminchand?'

The Daitapati countered, 'The bargain is struck— what room is there now for regret? Every Navakalevara is meant to be crowned by a dream-revelation on its very first night. And now, you declare that we've received one, only to depart at once? But heed my words: when the time comes to fell the *daru*, and people gather in the forest, if the sacred symbols are absent, do you think they'll simply let us walk away?'

It wasn't as though Pati Mahapatra had overlooked that particular nuance. Within moments, he allayed the Daita's unrest. 'Indeed... there shall be an anthill by the river's edge, nestled within the grounds of a cremation site. From it, a black cobra would have risen, hood flared in wrath—we shall say we saw it with our very own eyes. Who, after all, would dare doubt a vision so vivid? And should there be a Sahada tree nearby, so much the better; even the presence of a Varuna tree would lend the aura we require. With such omens in place, the signs upon the *darus* shall be plain for all to 'perceive'—exactly as expected.'

Pati Mahapatra had meticulously planned every detail. His logic was incontrovertible—after all, when the very game was but one of play-acting with dolls, what harm was there in a performance executed to perfection?

Then let us proceed at dawn to the Mangala temple for darshan, and embark on the *daru* extraction,' urged the Daitapati. 'There is no profit in tarrying.'

In a surge of fervour, Swain Mahapatra strode resolutely out onto the veranda from the sombre recesses of the math. It was the last quarter of the night, and the morning star shimmered in the eastern sky.

Daitapati gasped in startled surprise. It was as if the twin, watchful eyes of Lord Jagannath were fixed upon him, scrutinizing his petty, self-serving manoeuvres—as though they longed to admonish him, 'Men like Pati Mahapatra have, through countless ages, wielded me as a weapon for their own ambition. Yet you, dear Daita, are truly mine; in the end, you too have…'

In that nascent glow of dawn, it almost seemed as though the Daita could hear a silent reproach echoing in the star's radiance. Like a ghost compelled by fate, he slunk back into the dim interior.

On the eastern bank, amidst the mango groves freshly cleared, the Daitas and other servitors had pitched their Shabara settlement—makeshift, sacred, transient. Among them stood Mahapatra, the leader of the servitor band, who had come for the *daru-chhedana*, the ritual felling of the divine neem trees. And yet, the navel-string of Shri Jagannath's tribal birth still pulsed through this Shabara Palli, no matter how insistently servitors like Pati Mahapatra sought to cloak Him in Vedic vestments as the Purushottam of high Brahmanical lore.

Stepping into the sanctified space of the Shabara Palli, Pati Mahapatra raised his voice in a clear, commanding tone: 'The dream-decree has been received. Waste no time—hasten to behold Mangala, and let us depart promptly.'

At dawn, as the first light caressed the palli, an excited clamour burst forth, echoing triumphantly: 'The dream-decree is here—truly, the dream-decree is here!'

A hush fell as the servitors exchanged glances, their faces frozen in astonishment.

Far away, in Barabati, Cuttack, whispers of the Navakalevara reached Ramachandra Dev through Razia's report. He could scarcely believe it—how could Lalita Devi, by the very word of King Aminchand, journey so far? Perhaps Razia had erred, or maybe it was merely the cunning twist of Taqi Khan's tongue. Yet the preparations for the Navakalevara had advanced beyond anyone's wildest dreams. The common refrain on every lip was, 'The *darus* have been found! All four of them!'

In this grand arrangement, the *daru* of the elder deity Balabhadra was discovered near the cremation ground at Bhogeshwar village, Subhadra's *daru* resided in Beraboi, the dark lord Shri Jagannath's *daru* shimmered along the Prachi at Singipur, and Sudarshan's *daru* lay in the distant precincts of Kalahata. Even Ramachandra Dev had heard these murmurs—the very pulse of the people resonated with this news.

Though Shri Jagannath still dwelled in Tikali Raghunathpur, it was declared that his Navakalevara would be performed. The *mahadaru*—the sacred timber cradling the hallowed Brahmapinda within its wooden heart—was to be cast out from the Ratna Simhasana of the temple and condemned to the wilderness for ages untold. The very soul of Utkal, emblem of its indomitability, would be severed from its cherished earth. And then, after the Navakalevara, who would acknowledge him in the guise of the *mahadaru*?

In a frenzy reminiscent of a mad dervish, Ramachandra Dev clawed at his matted locks in bewilderment—why? Why this betrayal?

A piercing self-accusation surged through his depths. 'You exiled Mahaprabhu for your petty pride,' he seethed. 'To assert your dominion over the temple—to stake your claim—you played the dacoit, spiriting away the Lord from the opulent Ratna Simhasana of the Shrivatsa Khandashala temple... or was it something even darker? Let Bhagirathi Kumar ascend as Maharaja of Khurda, let him be anointed upon the coveted Gajapati throne; let Aminchand seize stewardship of Shrikshetra—if that is truly Mahabahu's will. But tell me, Ramachandra Dev, who are you to stand against destiny? Will you condemn the cherished deity of the Odia people to languish in perpetual exile? Shall mere fragments of timber forever pose as the living Shri Jagannath? And who will believe that He dwells within the sanctum, when His presence endures in Tikali Raghunathpur?'

But where had Lakshmi Paramaguru vanished? Whom should he consult for guidance in this crisis? He had heard that Lakshmi Paramaguru was en route from Remuna on horseback—a ride of two days to reach Cuttack. Some said he had been sighted at a math in Remuna; others believed he had ridden straight to Puri in search of Ramachandra Dev— neither possibility could be dismissed.

Then what purpose was served in loitering among these vagrant fakirs?

Even the fellow fakirs had begun to take him for a lunatic. Heaven alone knew what omens of madness they thought they saw flickering in his eyes.

Surely, Lakshmi Paramaguru must have brought news from Murshidabad! And what promise might Shuja Khan have offered to ensure that Shri Jagannath remains unblemished within the temple?

Lakshmi Paramaguru! Lakshmi Paramaguru!—he was now the sole hope, the one true advisor.

With no time left for delay in Cuttack, Ramachandra Dev himself set forth towards Puri.

Every arrangement for the Navakalevara was now in place. Once the sacred *daru*—gathered from far-flung corners—arrived in Puri, the ancient rites would unfold. The Vishwakarma artisans, adhering to sacred injunctions, would begin crafting the divine idols within the *darugriha*. At long last, the Navakalevara would be ushered in. Upon its completion, Bhagirathi Kumar would ascend the exalted Gajapati throne, consecrated in full regalia, while Lalita Devi would be acclaimed as Rajmata—the royal matriarch. So prolonged had the delay been that Maharani Lalita Devi's patience had frayed to a perilous edge.

Her eyes, fierce and ravenous like those of a lioness, gleamed with unshed tears as she sat upon a solemn wooden seat in the Landa Math, her gaze flicked to the doorway, measuring time by the dwindling light. She waited, restless, for word of how far the preparations for the Navakalevara had advanced.

Bhagirathi Kumar was proving to be a complete

disappointment. Tasked with traversing the sixteen revenue-exempt and paika-settled villages to rally the Mahajana Brahmins and paika sardars to their cause, he had instead vanished—rumour placed him languishing in a gymnasium or ensnared in the velvet shadows of a mahari's chamber. His disregard for Lalita Devi was no longer a secret, and as for the struggle over the Khurda throne, he had made his disinterest crystal clear. To him, the Gajapati seat was little more than a bleached cairn of ancestral bones—and he had no desire to be consecrated upon a grave.

Alas, what misfortune! Bhagirathi Kumar was not ambitious at all—he was content with these trifling indulgences. Had he not sworn revenge for every slight? One could only see the same poisonous blood of decay coursing through his veins.

For how long had the Senior Parichha Rajaguru Gauri been waiting, ready to speak his mind? Yet Lalita Devi, lost in her own ruminations, was unaware of his presence. Sensing the delay, Rajguru Gauri called out without further ado, 'Devi.' At the sound of his voice, the delicate thread of her reverie snapped, and she looked towards him, saying, 'Why are you standing? Please, have a seat.'

Taking his seat with quiet grace, Rajguru Gauri allowed Lalita Devi to proceed. 'We have received word that the *darus* for the ritual have been discovered in the surrounding regions, yet they have not arrived in Puri. Bear in mind—the day after tomorrow is Akshay Tritiya, the very day the chariot ceremonies must commence. Instruct Aminchand to dispatch scouts and determine the cause of the delay.'

The delay in the *daru's* arrival filled Lalita Devi with

unease and a torrent of anxieties. She wondered whether the Daita and Pati Mahapatra had, at the final moment, aligned themselves with the Maharaja. In times such as these, nothing was beyond imagining.

Rajguru Gauri spoke gravely, 'The *darus* for the elder Lord and Subhadra have reached the outskirts of Chandanpur, as we learned yesterday. Yet the *daru* intended for Shri Jagannath lags behind. From every hamlet, villagers are halting the *mahadaru* along its path. Hundreds of devotees crowd around to offer puja, straining at the ropes, each eager to pull the cart bearing the sacred timber with their own hands.'

'So then, Rajaguru,' Lalita Devi asked, her voice kindling with restrained excitement, 'would you say the people's fervour for the Navakalevara is truly ablaze?'

'There is no shortage of fervour… and yet…' Rajaguru's voice faltered—a hesitation. A confusion clouded its timbre.

'Yet what?' she pressed.

In most Brahmin-led provinces, the arrangements for the Navakalevara are being welcomed, even the proposal to consecrate Bhagirathi Kumar upon the Khurda throne meets with little dissent. But among the feudal lords, the chieftains, and the fort lords... disquiet brews. There are whispers of revolt—a coalition in the making.'

Lalita Devi fell silent for a moment. The idea of a united front between these groups was not unthinkable. But even if they did band together, could they truly withstand Taqi Khan's combined power and the might of his loyal garrisons? Yet first—above all else—the Navakalevara must proceed. It is imperative that Shri Jagannath grace the temple with his presence. And yet, the *daru's* arrival is delayed for no good reason. With worship scheduled for tomorrow and Akshay Tritiya the day after—when the chariot construction is to commence—how many days remain before the journey to Sri Gundicha?

In Rajguru Gauri's heart, however, there was not a shred of doubt about the Navakalevara. He had not come here merely to debate; he was convinced it would not be stalled. With a shrewd insight into the capricious nature of public opinion—an enigma as subtle as any riddle—he mused that wherever a cunning man like Aminchand set his gaze, all would follow. After all, how else could one discern the symbols of the conch, discus, mace, and lotus etched even into the trunk of a neem tree? Would villagers intercept the bullock cart to offer worship? And then, would the promise of an unhindered Navakalevara be entrusted solely to Aminchand? Was he destined to become the master of the temple—the appointed governor of the Purushottam Kshetra?

However, Rajaguru's agitation stemmed from an entirely different cause. In conversations with some of the servitors, it became clear that Lakshmi Paramaguru—the elusive one—had suddenly appeared in Puri. Meanwhile, the appointed retainers were scurrying about in all directions, their loyalties divided.

'But where had Lakshmi Paramaguru vanished? How had he managed to elude Taqi Khan's grasp and cloak himself in secrecy for so long?'

'I've heard that he had gone to Murshidabad.'

'But Raja Padmanabh Dev of Patia has just returned from that very city. And he did not forewarn us, for he tarried there for more than a month! We placed a petition before the Nawab of Bengal, Bihar, and Odisha to secure a royal firman—had Lakshmi Paramaguru truly been there, he would have gleaned some clue!'

Even Rajguru Gauri himself would have no inkling of Lakshmi Paramaguru's arrival in Shrikshetra. And yet, for the past few days within the temple, Shendha Suara had taken to roaring in his thunderous voice: 'Friends, I have seen warriors—fierce and formidable! And now, Aminchand, secretive as ever and still shamelessly licking the Pathans' filth, dares to conduct this Navakalevara while the Lord remains hidden from His people? Yes, my brother, my stance is unequivocal! As long as I, Shendha Suara, breathe, there will be no Navakalevara. I'll twist and break their arms!'

'Must you spout such reckless words in your inebriated state, Shendha Suara? Do you have no regard for any higher power? Heed my words and always follow the tide—lest you be swept away!'

One servitor, an ardent supporter of Aminchand, had tried to warn the Suara. But the Suara, brooding in the shadows near Merdarosh, muttered to himself with a burst of glee: 'The Guru has returned from Murshidabad—Lakshmi Paramaguru, in all his splendid abundance! One moment, and the wheel of fate turns in full!'

At these words, the servitors could no longer keep silent. 'Lakshmi Paramaguru went to Murshidabad! And now he has returned to Puri!' came the murmurs, and those servitors who had hitherto kept their lips sealed began to lift their heads in pride. A clandestine council was forming—a plot to foil the Navakalevara. Troubled by this dissonant chatter, Rajguru Gauri hastened to consult with Lalita Devi.

'Who is this Shendha Suara?' Lalita Devi inquired, her tone laced with concern. 'Is Aminchand unable to rein him in?'

'Aminchand has dispatched his men to capture him and bring him to the Garad for trial on several occasions,' Rajguru Gauri replied gently. 'Yet Shendha Suara remains as steadfast as a seasoned wrestler.'

During the Naga Yatra at Haragauri Street, Shendha Suara would appear as a Naga ascetic—an icon of untamed power. With a pot, heavy as iron, bound to his head and the changu's beat echoing behind him, he would stride forth with unyielding pride. In his enraged avatar, even the bravest wrestlers dared not draw near. In a low, threatening rasp, he would growl: 'Go… go, and tell Aminchand that this Suara, devout servitor of the Lords Kalia and Balia, will not go to the man who shamelessly licks the dregs of the Pathan. If anyone dares approach me, I'll break their legs. Mark my words.'

No one dared confront Shendha Suara. When Aminchand pressed them for further details, they merely shrugged—'He must be roaming somewhere far from the sanctum.' Aminchand himself paid little heed, letting the man ramble on as if seized by mad fervour. Would the Navakalevara truly be hindered because of him?

With a note of deep worry in her voice, Lalita Devi asked, 'Will Lakshmi Paramaguru, acting alone, be able to hold back the Navakalevara? After all, the majority of the servitors—the chosen retainers and the venerable Mahajana Brahmins of Mukti Mandap—stand firmly with us, do they not?'

Rajguru Gauri offered a soothing assurance, 'Do not be troubled, Devi. Everything will fall into place naturally.'

As Rajguru Gauri rose to depart, Lalita Devi called out from behind, her tone both commanding and resolute: 'There will be others like Shendha Suara among the servitors, ready to rally behind him now that the esteemed Junior Parichha, Vishnu Paschim Kabat, has taken the reins of command. Inform King Aminchand—dazzle them with the lure of rewards and jagirs until every voice of dissent is stilled. Use every means at our disposal: force, inducement, punishment—and the art of subterfuge, Rajaguru. Once the Navakalevara is flawlessly completed, Bhagirathi Kumar must claim the Khurda throne.'

Lalita Devi's eyes ignited like twin burning embers, their fierce glow reflective of both passion and resolve.

******

Chapter VII

'Has Vishnu Paschim Kabat Mahapatra arrived yet?'
No reply came from Lakshmi Paramaguru; his gaze was transfixed on the flickering flame atop the lamp—a portrait of mesmerized stillness. A moth flitted erratically around the glow, its wings in a tremble, as though ensnared by some mysterious agony. Yet within that agony pulsed a rapturous ecstasy, a delirious exaltation. The flame seemed to beckon, to promise an end through consummation—to be seared, to be charred, to be reduced to ash—that, perhaps, was the destiny of its brief, winged existence, to vanish in a final, transcendental dissolution that epitomized the perfection of its evanescent arc.

Behind him, Ramachandra Dev paced with his arms folded in quiet resignation through the crumbling chambers of the ruined Balisahi Palace, much like that restless moth himself. In the temple of Shyamakali, the toll of the evening arati bells had long fallen silent, and Vishnu Paschim Kabat Mahapatra's arrival had been anticipated for some time. Today, Ramachandra Dev was to render his final verdict—a decision that would not be made lightly.

After a long, anxious wait, amid the disordered

throng of thorny weeds, scrubs, creepers, hedge plants and rank vegetation in the palace courtyard, someone finally began to approach. Ramachandra Dev paused, straining his ears as the sound drew near. Emerging from the dim light, Vishnu Paschim Kabat Mahapatra appeared, his form barely distinguishable in the feeble glow of twilight.

'You should have arrived long ago,' Ramachandra Dev said, his tone tinged with reproach. 'We've been waiting every moment since yesterday.'

With an unsteady, troubled look, Vishnu Paschim Kabat Mahapatra beheld the two men before him. Ramachandra Dev and Lakshmi Paramaguru wore pallid, ghastly faces, their coarse hair and unkempt beards giving them the appearance of a kapalika—mere disguises for what lay beneath.

'I was not here in Shrikshetra,' he explained. 'I have gone to monitor the movement of the *darus*.'

'Ah, the *daru* destined for the Navakalevara!' Ramachandra Dev's voice flared as if ignited by a sudden conflagration. 'Now—where are the *darus*?'

Sinking wearily into a nearby chair, Vishnu Paschim Kabat Mahapatra replied in a tired tone, 'The *darus* for the elder Lord and Goddess Subhadra will reach Atharanala by tomorrow. But the *daru* for Shri Jagannath is delayed yet.'

'But just yesterday we heard that the *darus* for the elder Lord and Goddess Subhadra had reached Chandanpur—and from there, it takes not more than a day to reach Puri!'

'The congregation for the *daru* is immense,' Vishnu Paschim Kabat continued. 'They have been halting them for worship, performing kirtans with cymbals and conch, and entire villages along the route are swarming with people.'

Still pacing, Ramachandra Dev inquired, agitation mounting, 'And is there indeed a vast throng gathering around the *daru*?'

'An assembly of countless people! Do not ask—folks are coming from beyond Utkal, from distant Mughalbandi—the three coastal districts under the direct administration of the Mughal emperors—and far-off lands, all eager to witness the Navakalevara of the gods. The fervour and exaltation among them is boundless; families have even rallied together to haul the bullock-cart laden with the *daru*!

'So long as the *mahadaru* lies cloaked in concealment at Tikali,' Ramachandra Dev maintained with bitter restraint, 'this Navakalevara is no more than an elaborate spectacle—a pious charade. Can they not see it for what it is? And that too, undertaken in a season shunned by the scriptures?'

Vishnu Paschim Kabat Mahapatra answered, 'Aminchand, alongside the imposing Rajguru Gauri, has masterfully launched a campaign by stoking these rumours throughout—to the effect that Shri Jagannath has conferred a dream-decree upon Lalita Devi for the Navakalevara. Who among the people can resist such captivating propaganda? Their ears, sharp as kites, have caught every word—that is the very texture of our folk's temperament. The temple has remained vacant for years, and now even the inner soul of the nation trembles in anticipation of beholding Lord Jagannath upon his lavish Ratna Simhasana!'

Ramachandra Dev countered, 'Yet the deities themselves remain confined within Tikali. Though the *darus* may one day be transmuted into wooden effigies and hoisted upon the hallowed Ratna Simhasana, the *mahadaru* still languishes in the vast wilderness!'

'Your Majesty appears to forget,' murmured Vishnu Paschim Kabat Mahapatra, his tone steeped in quiet conspiracy, 'that even Taqi Khan's network of spies and informants has yet to uncover this hidden mystery. And how would the common people ever come to know it, if at all? And even if they did… what could they possibly do?'

A dense silence descended, broken only by the faint, simmering current of unrest. The moth's restless orbit around the lamp's flame—its wings trembling in a hush of suspended wonder—echoed the inner upheaval churning within their hearts. Against that silence, their fears and uncertainties stood exposed, stark and unspoken.

With his hands clasped behind his back, Ramachandra Dev strode ponderously and murmured with bitter introspection, 'Will such monumental falsehood and deception be forever enshrined in our history—carved out solely by brute force and clandestine conspiracies?'

Lakshmi Paramaguru burst into a wild, almost lunatic laughter—a sound as unpredictable as the mirth of a mad dervish. His laughter, echoing through the deserted quarters of the palace, sent tremors through the very air, while the calm flame of the lamp leapt in the gentle caresses of the night breeze.

'This is not the first time it has happened,' Lakshmi Paramaguru affirmed, 'and it certainly won't be the last. The annals of the ages are steeped in lies, deceit, and the triumph of brutal power. Would you deny such an enduring truth?'

Ramachandra Dev fixed his eyes on the dancing flame, lost in a trance-like stillness, as Lakshmi Paramaguru's probing question echoed within him.'

'It is but the length of time itself that poses the problem,' Lakshmi Paramaguru observed.

Ramachandra Dev paced the stone chamber in slow, deliberate strides and intoned in a dramatic voice 'The artifice of deception and the ephemeral prestige of brute power are, in turn, signed by truth and justice. If darkness were without its subtleties, how might we discern the promise of illumination? Patience, indeed—patience is paramount, O Supreme Guru! History, in one sense, is the test of a man's patience.'

Lakshmi Paramaguru answered with impassioned clarity, 'Were it not for such faith, why would I dare venture towards Murshidabad, mouth agape as if to challenge a tiger? Oh, sinful one—Padmanabh Dev!' That dismal memory of Murshidabad still seared him inwardly.

Ramachandra Dev replied, 'I told you, Paramaguru, that going to Murshidabad would be futile for you!'

But had I not gone, how else was I to catch even the faintest scent of this conspiracy? And how were you to uncover the plot between Lalita Devi and Aminchand for the Navakalevara?'

Yet these arguments drifted into the realm of endless, futile debate—a debate in which Ramachandra Dev's heart found no solace. Ever since returning from Haridamada Fort, his mind had been alight with unresolved turmoil, like simmering embers glowing beneath the ash. Now, seeking clarity, he turned to the counsel of Lakshmi Paramaguru.

'Tell me, where do the minds of the servitors and the commissioned functionaries drift?' Ramachandra Dev demanded of Vishnu Paschim Kabat Mahapatra.

'Except for a few dissenters, the majority have

rallied behind Aminchand; all are agog for the ensuing Navakalevara!' came the reply.

'It is only natural.' Lakshmi Paramaguru interjected wryly. 'To them, the deity is but an enterprise—divinity reduced to daily bread. How long can they endure a barren sanctum, flaunting a thirteen-handed god within a space scarcely spanning twelve fingers, while their stomachs remain hollow from fasting?'

Outside, amid the disordered clusters of thorn-bramble and rank foliage, a figure began to appear—one whose step was unburdened by trivial doubts or petty hesitations. He strode with an air of unruffled assurance.

A spy from Aminchand's camp? Had one arrived, flanked by paikas, to take them by force? Word had already flown across the farthest reaches of Utkal—Taqi Khan's edicts pronounced in chilling clarity: all seditious elements were to be seized without mercy. The rebellion was to be razed, each flickering ember of dissent stamped out beneath the weight of an iron heel. All eyes turned eagerly towards that distant, anxious beat.

Yet Vishnu Paschim Kabat Mahapatra sought to allay the fears. 'Perhaps Shendha Suara is on his way. I had instructed him to come here once the evening arati at Shyamakali Temple concluded.'

'Shendha Suara? Who is he?' Ramachandra Dev inquired, for he was unacquainted with the man.

In the dusky glimmer of lamplight, the threshold gave way to a towering silhouette—Shendha Suara—storming mid-harangue, hurling invective at an unseen foe.

'Oi! Spare us your cheap theatrics!' he barked.

'We've stared down men with thunder in their bones—you're not even a tremor!'

Shendha Suara's visage was a spectacle in itself—weathered, unruly, and utterly singular. But his garb surpassed even that in its eccentricity. Two gamchhas clung to his frame: one cinched around his loins, its tail knotted and jutting like a coiled rope—a defiant spiral of rustic pride. Draped across his shoulder hung another, sodden with sweat, its saffron hue deepened by wear and toil, as though dyed not with pigment but with persistence. His eyes burned crimson, fever-bright, and crowning the tangled knot of his hair was an incongruous garland of jasmine, swaying with every breath like a provocation to order itself.

Ramachandra Dev, inwardly aghast, muttered to himself, 'What purpose does this odd fellow serve? Is this whom Mahapatra brings to confront the cunning Aminchand? Then heaven help us...'

Shendha Suara continued his lone invective in a slurred, disjointed chant, 'Wouldn't I have shattered their limbs!—Ah, but in the haze of bhang and the wild fury boiling inside me, my eyes went blind as I lay in the Merdarosh. The two guards seized me, dragging me off to Aminchand's Garad! Had I been sober, would those damned reprobates have dared lay a hand on me? I'd have snapped their wrists like dry twigs!'

'What transpired?' Mahapatra interjected, his tone firm, yet edged with inquiry. 'For what reason did they escort you to Aminchand?'

Shendha Suara straightened, his voice thick with indignation, each word laced with the residue of insult and defiance. 'Aminchand—seething—demanded of me,

"When did Lakshmi Paramaguru arrive in Puri? Where is he now?" I answered him plainly, "O Naib, speak with sense. Raise your voice, and I shall raise none in return.'"

'Then came the flattery. "Shendha Suara, do not fan the flames. Let the Navakalevara proceed undisturbed. Let Bhagirathi Kumar ascend the Khurda throne—you shall be rewarded, granted a jagir. Your fortunes will turn.'"

'And I said—keep your jagir, and your promises with it! A single grain from Lord Jaga-Balia's offering is wealth enough for me.'

He flung the words like sparks from a whetted blade, then continued, voice rising with each breath, 'That Senior Parichha—he is the rot at the root, smouldering beneath it all! He pressed: "What do you know of Lakshmi Paramaguru and the deposed Maharaj? Bear in mind, Aminchand is now the Naib of Shrikshetra, the custodian of the entire region! Speak, and your reward shall double—otherwise…!'"

'"Otherwise, what then, O Senior Parichcha?" I snapped. "Will you cast me from the temple grounds while Jaga-Balia still abides?" Only then did their tone soften.'

Ramachandra Dev's patience was fraying at the seams. *From where—and for what inscrutable divine purpose—had Mahapatra unearthed this obstinate, bhang-addled buffoon?* He stifled a groan, the question gnawing at him.

But Shendha Suara resumed, his voice now curling into Senior Parichha's guttural snarl: '"You hold every scrap of news concerning Lakshmi Paramaguru and the fallen Maharaj. Relay these details accurately to Naib Sahib!" I retorted, "I've told you once—I keep no tidings of anyone. How many times must I repeat? The Maharaja has renounced caste, isn't that what is proclaimed? And tell me, whose caste did you adopt when you cozied up with Aminchand—feasting on the refuse of the Pathans?" Words slipped in the haze of bhang, and where could I run then? The guards lashed at me with sticks, like beating horse gram to pulp. And still Senior Parichha shouted, "beat him… beat the clown!—exclaiming, "One cannot extract ghee with a bare straight finger!" Yet I held my breath, tensing my arm so resolutely that not even a single muscle betrayed me. Aminchand then called out, "Leave that wretched bhang addict!" Then I left straight for the shrine of Siddha Mahavir. The air was thick with the rhythm of the pakhawaj. Then it struck me—Vishnu Paschim Kabat Mahapatra had summoned me. So I turned this way.'''

With that volley of words, Shendha Suara slumped down, his knees buckling in dejection.

Ramachandra Dev inquired, his voice low yet heavy with gravity, 'What course have the servitors and functionaries chosen in this most sacred of undertakings? Shall they lend their hands to Aminchand's cause, or remain withdrawn in silence? And tell me—now that the deities have been concealed amid the storm of Mughal fury—how shall the rites of Navakalevara unfold beneath such a shroud of secrecy?'

'Your Highness,' came the reply, 'by flaunting the greed for rewards and jagir, Aminchand has brought even the mighty under his sway. Think what these great men will do for their own selfish gains—they wear silver locks on their lips! And what do they do? Wherever Aminchand turns his key, they turn in exact unison!'

'Tragic! Truly tragic!' Ramachandra Dev sighed.

'When the fort lords, castle keepers, and chieftains sway with every shifting wind; when the masses, mad with devotion, beat their cymbals and chant in frenzied welcome of the sacred *daru*; when the sixteen Brahmin provinces and countless feudal lords prepare to receive the Navakalevara; and when the Mahajanas of the Mukti Mandap pore over scriptures to sanctify the rites—what, then, can one expect from these impoverished, famished servitors?'

'Then… what now? Is this not the very crux of our dilemma?'

Shendha Suara thundered, his voice echoing like a war drum, 'But I have made it abundantly clear on Aminchand's very face—so long as Shendha Suara draws breath, this Navakalevara shall not proceed in defiance of the sacred order!'

'What madness is this? Does this deranged wretch truly believe he can stand alone against a vast and organized force?'

Ramachandra Dev turned towards him, his gaze steady, his tone tempered: 'But how? How do you plan to confront this power on your own, Shendha Suara?'

'This is a matter of utmost secrecy,' he replied. 'Must it be laid bare so openly? The Maharaj has asked—and shall I remain silent in response?'

He rose slightly, as if summoning the weight of his words: 'My lord, the arrival of the *daru* alone does not consecrate a Navakalevara. The sacred wood must first rest beside Narasimha and Alamchandi, near the Gundicha temple. Only then—beneath the ceremonial parasol, with the conch, the drums, and the trumpets—shall it pass through the northern gate into the sanctum of the Lord, and be placed within the sacred repository at Koili Baikuntha. That night, I shall act. Not the *daru*, but the wood—we shall spirit it away. Let this remain sealed between us. If you so command, Maharaj, we shall steal it under the cover of darkness. And when the Vishwakarma artisans open the sanctum at dawn, they shall find it empty. We will leave no trace. There shall remain neither bamboo nor the sound of the flute. Why allow needless pandemonium to take root?'

Vishnu Paschim Kabat Mahapatra, visibly startled, faltered, 'It is not without merit. If you can truly carry it through, then let it be done. What do you say, Paramaguru? Should the Navakalevara be halted, the web spun by Aminchand and Lalita Devi shall unravel of its own accord.'

Shendha Suara, emboldened by the moment, revealed the full extent of his design: 'And then our servitors shall proclaim—"How can the Navakalevara be performed in defiance of divine ordinance, while the Lord yet lives? That is why the *daru* must disappear."'

Vishnu Mahapatra then remarked with wry amusement, 'Yes, yes! Once the crow takes flight, the ear is as good as gone. There is no shortage of those eager to believe in such omens. Why else did they throng in droves, beating drums and raising hymns, the moment they glimpsed the conch, the discus, the mace, and the lotus etched upon the wood?'

Lakshmi Paramaguru silently cast his eyes towards the burning flame, lost in an unfathomable reverie—a profound, dense stillness enveloping him.

Breaking that long silence, Ramachandra Dev spoke, 'You are dismissed now, Shendha Suara! Let the *daru* first reach the precincts of the Gundicha temple, only then shall we deliberate upon your proposal.' There was an unmistakable reluctance in his tone, as though the idea had not yet found sanctuary in his heart.

Shendha Suara shook the damp cloth from his shoulders, his rotund buttocks catching the lamplight in a brief, glistening glow, then rose unsteadily and muttered to himself as he disappeared into the corridor's shadows.

Ramachandra Dev watched him go, then spoke, almost to himself, 'So this was the counsel for which we summoned Shendha Suara? Whatever his proposal may be, it is astonishing that he dares to face such overwhelming power on his own. This defiance, this audacity, is what we need most in these times.'

At last, breaking his silence, Lakshmi Paramaguru inquired, 'But, Maharaj, what is your opinion on this?'

Ramachandra Dev ambled with his hands clasped behind his back, lost in thought as if deciphering the answer to a most challenging question. All the while, both Lakshmi Paramaguru and Vishnu Paschim Kabat Mahapatra watched him with anxious anticipation.

Suddenly, Ramachandra Dev turned sharply and exclaimed, 'Impossible! This proposal, as it stands, is unthinkable. I have not abducted the deities like a common thief—I have merely dispelled them to ensure their safety from the Mughal conflagration. To seize the *daru* from its repository—even if it is but clumps of wood—is nothing short of a bandit's act. I am no malefactor!'

'Then?' Vishnu Paschim Kabat Mahapatra queried, his tone edged with challenge.

The moth, drawn in helpless orbit around the wavering flame, at last plunged into its heart, its wings seared, its body consumed in a final, futile tremor. Yet in that descent, in that luminous surrender, it had answered the call of the fire. And in that call, in that act of annihilation, lay the purest consummation of its brief and incandescent existence.

In a tone of precise determination, Ramachandra Dev announced, 'My intent is not to purloin the *daru*. I shall restore the deities from Tikali even before the Shrigundicha procession commences.'

'But Shrigundicha—the chariot festival—lasts only a month.' Paschim Kabat interjected with pragmatic concern. 'Today is Baisakh Ashtami of the dark fortnight; there remains barely a week until Akshay Tritiya, and then nearly a month in Shrigundicha. Would it not be folly to, without proper preparation, extricate the deities from Tikali's sanctuary only to thrust them later into uncertainty and further assault? Since the day the Lord left His temple, Taqi Khan and Raja Aminchand have been prowling like wounded tigers.'

'A discerning man does not commit to action in haste.' Lakshmi Paramaguru observed, The Maharaj's resolve may be sincere, yet have we truly pondered its ramifications?'

Ramachandra Dev replied with deliberate certainty, 'Lord Jagannath is indeed secure in Tikali—but what of the consequences of such security? O exalted Paramaguru, when Aminchand, with his cunning stratagem, anoints Bhagirathi Kumar as a pawn upon the Khurda throne and installs the newly consecrated idol upon the Ratna Simhasana, the people will come to revere it as the true Shri Jagannath. And the sacred *brahmashila*, the *mahadaru*, shall lie forsaken in the wilderness for ages to come. Moreover, once King

Aminchand, through artful deception, accomplishes the Navakalevara, the chieftains and fort lords who now stand with us will swiftly shift their allegiance. For as the Naib of Shrikshetra, he will be perceived as the rightful royal servitor. Taqi Khan's path will then be cleared of all resistance. And when the paikas and fort lords of Odisha begin to accept Aminchand as the Rajasevaka, the royal servitor, whom then shall we summon to forge an unyielding alliance?'

Ramachandra Dev's logic, unassailable in its precision, resonated deeply. Who could guarantee that Shri Jagannath would remain safe in Tikali? The constant dispatches from Jagadev suggested that safeguarding the deities for long would soon become impossible. Inevitably, the faujdar of Chikakol would catch wind of their concealment, and once his suspicions were aroused, would he not strike?

Yet, for now, the deities remained safely ensconced in Tikali. If, through artful cunning, the Navakalevara could be thwarted, then Aminchand would once again stand exposed, treacherous as Shishupala—and the liberation struggle of Odisha would blaze forth in jubilant fervour.

Lakshmi Paramaguru, his voice laced with apprehension, inquired, 'But what if, after the Lord has arrived in Shrikshetra, Taqi Khan should bind him once more with leather cords and drag them away? Do we truly have the strength to resist such an act? The entire land of Odisha slumbers—like a banana grove flattened after a storm.'

'If it is the will of the Divine, so it must be!' answered Ramachandra Dev with silent resolve. 'Who am I to stand in his way? We are but the instruments of an ethereal fancy. Yet, for the sake of my modest pride, I cannot allow the Supreme to be relegated to wander as a denizen of the wilderness.'

A deep stillness then fell over the assembly; each mind sank back into its private reverie. From the dark clusters nearby came the relentless chirping of crickets, mingled with the resonant beat of the pakhawaj emerging from the Mahavir akhara. Over this symphony of nature and distant drumbeats, waves of verses and quatrains rippled, while in the Jega dwellings, music, bhang, and mirth gathered in raucous celebration.

Breaking the hush, Ramachandra Dev declared, 'Hurry, Vishnu Paschim Kabat Mahapatra—depart tonight! Inform, one by one, our allied fort lords and military chieftains of our decision. There is no danger in retrieving the deities from Mahuri to Khallikot; the kings of Mahuri, Khallikot, Ghumsur, and Athagarh will lend us their complete support. From Khallikot to Khurda and Puri, ensuring that the deities reach safely shall be the duty of our lieutenants—even if a handful must volunteer extra effort. Spread the word among the fort lords and the paikas that Bhagirathi Kumar is to be crowned on the Khurda throne without objection. Let the land of Odisha reclaim its freedom, and let Shri Jagannath return from the wilderness to his rightful seat in Shrivatsa Khandashala temple on his Ratna Simhasana. I am willing to be obliterated for this cause!'

This doctrine, he made clear, was no novel conception. Only days earlier, at the fort of Haridamda, Ramachandra Dev had proclaimed his decision. Though the edict left a deep impression on many of the fort lords—whose hearts, in truth, leaned towards Lalita Devi under the pretext that the Maharaja had lost his caste—they did not hesitate to rise against Taqi Khan in support of his unwavering mandate.

Let the Mughal yoke be cast off from the land of

Odisha; may this sacred soil be sovereign once more! In the past, Ramachandra Dev had been viewed as an impediment—his name shadowed by the stain of caste defilement. But under the wise counsel of the Paramaguru, he had atoned: he granted the tax-exempt village of Ramachandrapur to the Brahmins and, through penance, reclaimed his place within the dharma of his forebears. Yet the fort lords and military chiefs were not likely to accept this transformation without hesitation.

For Ramachandra Dev had not severed ties with Razia.

Yet he was not prepared to relinquish contact with Razia. He, ever the incorrigible miscreant, remained entangled in a delicate web—a helpless woman sacrificed upon the altar of treacherous politics. In moments of reflection, Razia's doe-like, surma-kissed eyes would drift before him, deep and unfathomable as dark, sorrowful waters.

Lost in his contemplations, Ramachandra Dev finally stated, his voice subdued. 'Razia was born of a Hindu mother—you know this well, Paramaguru!'

'But her blood carries the lineage of a Muslim father,' came Lakshmi Paramaguru's reply, bitterness tinging his tone.

'Perhaps so,' Ramachandra Dev countered softly, 'but her devotion to Shri Jagannath is unwavering—etched into her very soul.'

'Yet the people will not understand this, Maharaj!' argued Paramaguru, his voice calm yet firm. 'In the realm of politics, so much must be sacrificed,'

'But one cannot forsake the heart and the conscience,'

replied Ramachandra Dev, 'otherwise, it would be nothing more than the policy of a butcher rather than true politics,'

Lakshmi Paramaguru then intoned, 'History itself is the chronicle of such executioners.'

'Indeed,' Ramachandra Dev added with quiet defiance, 'I would not have my name listed among them, Paramaguru Mahashay!'

'Then whom shall you sacrifice?' Lakshmi Paramaguru pressed in what seemed his final inquiry. 'Shri Jagannath or Razia? Odisha's liberation struggle or the frailty of hearts for Razia?'

'In such a dire circumstance,' Ramachandra Dev pronounced, 'I shall sacrifice none other than myself. It is on this very premise that I vowed to restore the deities to the temple and to enthrone Prince Bhagirathi upon the Khurda seat.'

Lakshmi Paramaguru, knowing well Ramachandra Dev's unwavering habit, had no further rejoinder—and silence fell again.

Suddenly, the plaintive cry of a bird outside shattered the heavy quiet. Ramachandra Dev, pacing the crumbling, shadowed recesses of Balisahi Palace, came to an abrupt halt. Fixing his gaze upon Lakshmi Paramaguru, he declared: 'Go forth through the Bishi parganas, across the Karabada provinces, and into the quarters of the Shasani Brahmins—and silence those money-changing Mahajana Brahmins and self-serving feudal lords who, seduced by selfish greed, extol the virtues of Taqi Khan and Aminchand. I know the strength that lies within you. I am bound for Tikali, and by the coming Ashadha Amavasya—at the break of dawn, during *Netrotsava*, the Festival of the Eyes—the deities shall be restored to their rightful place upon the Ratna Simhasana. Accordingly, marshal the servitors loyal to our cause, Vishnu Paschim Kabat Mahapatra! Ensure that every one of them, including Shendha Suara, is alerted. They must see to it that the rites of the Navakalevara are delayed at every step.'

In that moment, Ramachandra Dev's voice resounded with an immutable and resolute decree—a plan he had long since devised.

But Lakshmi Paramaguru persisted, 'Yet will Bhagirathi Kumar truly ascend the Khurda throne? He would be but a puppet dancing to Taqi Khan's tune. How then can the Maharaj's noble vow to liberate Odisha from the Mughal burden ever come to fruition?'

With unyielding finality in his tone, Ramachandra Dev replied, 'Every word of your counsel is duly noted, Paramaguru Mahashay! Now you must accept my decision—it is irrevocable, it is final!'

Looking towards the lamp, Ramachandra Dev beheld the same moth that had once fallen into the lamp's fiery womb—its frail, trembling form writhing in feeble agony, unchanged in its desperate dance. Its delicate wing was gradually detaching, fading into insignificance.

For one whose very being had been drawn to the lamp's inviting light, O Lord, why was it condemned to the consuming, searing flame? What was this struggle, this blaze, this relentless burn—if not a reflection of life itself?

With a long, restrained sigh, Ramachandra Dev stepped away from the sombre darkness. Before him lay an unmistakable sign—a dire summons echoing in the silence.

*****

Chapter VIII

Like a wandering kapalika ascetic, Lakshmi Paramaguru drifted from village to village—traversing the Bishi parganas, crossing into the Karabada provinces, and even venturing into the cloistered quarters of the Shasani Brahmins. The influential Shasani Mahajanas, those learned Brahmins, now wielded considerable sway over society. When they spoke, their every word, like that of Lord Brahma, was heaped with the authority of Vedic dictum, while cultural anxieties and social inertia have twisted every notion of refined thought. In this society, independent reflection and free ideas had no sanctuary at all. Even in the indigenous folds of Utkal's culture, the coordinated, Dharma□inspired generosity has long been lost amidst the relentless onslaught of Pathan and Mughal incursions.

The erudite Shasani Mahajanas, with their labyrinthine smriti texts and scholastic entanglements, had ensnared the natural flow of public life. Because of their incessant prattle, the vibrant blossoming of knowledge— once radiating as brilliant, scriptural scholarship—had now been supplanted by the antiquated charm of priestly rites and paraded as the ornament of the esteemed. Alas, these were truly dismal times! Even within the temple, a new cadre—the Suna Gosain Niyoga—had been quietly installed, not to serve the deity, but to sway the minds of daitas and other servitors, all beyond the public eye. Officially, their role was limited to sweeping beneath the Ratna Simhasana and sprinkling water along the upper rows. But these humble tasks offered just enough occasion to lean close, whisper at the right moment, and gently steer allegiances where needed.

If only these very men among the Gosain Mahajanas could awaken in us a thirst for liberation—a solemn vow for struggle! But alas, when the influential congregations of the Mukti Mandap assembly, swayed by the lure of the Asharfi, endorsed a Navakalevara instituted in defiance of sacred injunctions, how could one fault the humble servitors? Their modest livelihoods depended on the installation of the deities upon the rightful throne—an act that, however compromised, ensured their daily bread.

Aminchand had already showered rewards upon them, promising further treasures yet to come. His allure and influence were not at all inferior to the stirring power of lofty ideas or timeless scriptural verses. And yet, even if the Shasani Mahajanas were to embrace such an imprudent notion without reservation, most of them still could not fully commit their hearts to the Navakalevara envisioned in the chaotic procedures of the Karabaḍa and the Bishi. The deities—ever clandestine and secretive—burdened their consciousness with their very elusiveness. They could not, in good conscience, accept the arrangements being made for this unlawful Navakalevara. Moreover, when even the ruling Gosains remained silent, who among them would dare to protest—let alone mount any meaningful resistance?

In a clear, unflinching tone, Mani Subuddhi of the Vishvanathpur Shasana asserted, 'Paramaguru Mahashay! You are our revered guide—your words are as indelible on our minds as the sacred voice of scripture. We, too, know this is no true Navakalevara, for the deities live on; we shall grant them a living samadhi! Upon that consecrated altar, Bhagirathi Kumar—though little more than a puppet of Taqi Khan—shall be anointed upon the throne. But pray tell, what choice do we have? Rath Babu from Dakshin Sahi roams the Shasani villages, proclaiming that the Almighty has bestowed the realm of Utkal upon the Badshah. Who then dares to oppose this? And whose voice shall be heeded—ours, or that of the Shasani priests and the Danadhyaksha?'

Just the previous night, Lakshmi Paramaguru had taken shelter in the Bhagavata house of Subuddhi; by dawn, a sure and steadfast route spanning five kos lay ready towards Veer Gopinathpur. Meanwhile, discord had erupted between the Danadhyaksha, Damodar Nanda of Shasani village, and certain factions. Though Nanda was a Samanta, he had given his daughter in marriage to the Gotreya Samantas—lured by the wealth of the bride-price—in deference to the traditions of the Nanda-Samanta line. And then, during a conclave of learned pundits, with flagrant disregard for both Nanda and the established Samantas, he was the first to anoint the Gotreya Samantas' foreheads with sandalwood paste. Was such an insult to be borne? For the lure of gold—regardless of caste or antiquity—had long divided the three Samanta factions: Vatsa, Nanda, and Rath, who have held sway for generations. And from whence did this unexpected Gotreya element emerge?

At that very moment, the old and venerable Nari Tihadi had arrived at Subuddhi's Bhagavata house. He had once presided over the Bhagavata recitation of Shri Jagannath Das in the Vishvanathpur Shasana. A Brahmin village—and yet, an Odia Bhagavata! What greater affront to orthodoxy than the public chanting of scripture in the language of the common folk?

At the summons of the Danadhyaksha, the elderly Tihadi was escorted into Damodar Nanda's mandap, where—upon a humble coconut mat spread across the stone colonnade—a cluster of eminent Mahajanas had assembled. In the hazy stupor of bhang, the eyes of the Samanta Gotreyas glowed a deep, ruddy hue, like hibiscus petals.

Oh, what blasphemies Nari Tiwari unleashed! And what of the Bhatta Mishras—those not even counted among the Samanta Brahmins? Could it truly be that the Bhagavata, composed in the vernacular of the Shudras by Jagannath Das, was now being recited along the public road of a Shasani village? If even the great Shrimad Bhagavata was rendered in that common tongue, drawing the most fringe souls to sit upon the royal thoroughfare—what hope remained for the survival of the Aryan, eternal Sanatana Dharma?

Such questions stirred a lively tumult among them.

As Nari Tihadi ascended the mandap, the Danadhyaksha, his tone grave, inquired, 'So—it is true? You brought the oil-pressers' Bhagavata and had it recited along the royal route? And the low-caste folk—the Shudras—listened to its verses?'

A chorus then reverberated in unison, 'Tihadi, have you not sullied the dignity of the Vishvanathpur Shasan, reducing its honour to dust? What remains of its esteem?'

Nari Tihadi, though a Smarta Brahmin by birth and a follower of the Utkal Vaishnava tradition, had ultimately embraced the Gopal Vaishnava sect. He presented himself with little more than a string of tulsi beads around his neck and an Atibadi tilak adorning his brow. In the Danadhyaksha's stern gaze, this austere simplicity seemed to strip away the immaculate aura of the sacred white thread worn across the torso in accordance with Brahminical rites.

Noticing the Atibadi tilak on his forehead, Damodar Nanda burst into laughter and asked, 'What image has been painted upon your brow? Beyond a mere sandalwood speck, what ornament does such a mark bestow upon a Brahmin's forehead? Now even the low-caste folk are beginning to wear such insignia.'

Nari Tihadi remained silent. For this was no simple mark, no mere tilak. It was a dot at the very heart of *nada*—the primordial sound. The phallus, a symbol of virility, poised at the centre of the yonic void: the mystery of creation itself. To reveal its meaning would be unwise—for how could these haughty, self-righteous Brahmins of high social standing, so ensnared in hollow scriptures and caste-bound pride, ever comprehend such profundity? When even among Brahmins, none dared share a drop of water from another's hand—where, indeed, had the generosity of Jagannath culture vanished? Alas!

Nari Tihadi began, his voice steady, 'During the reign of the Suryavanshi emperor Prataprudra Dev, the venerable saint, the esteemed Atibadi Jagannath Das Gosain himself would sit beside Bat Ganesh within the temple precincts, delivering the Prakrit Bhagavata. And it was the Shudras who listened! Yet Sanatana Dharma stood unshaken—no shadow of decline had touched its sacred flame.'

One of Danadhyaksha's council members commented in a rough, derisive tone, 'No wonder then that the Suryavansha vanished from the earth! How could Mother Earth—our own Vasundhara—tolerate such unrighteousness?' Meanwhile, many eyes turned towards a corner of the mandap where, by the Shalagram Shila, an elaborate display of flattened rice and coconuts was underway.

Nari Tihadi continued, 'You claim that it is an offence for the Shudras to listen to the Bhagavata in the Prakrit tongue. But what of Matta Balarama Das—so named for being intoxicated with love for Lord Krishna—who once compelled the temple's lowly to hear Vedantic scripture?'

These are historically acknowledged, fact-based arguments—so entrenched that they could not simply be dismissed by the obstinate narrow-mindedness of the priesthood.

Raising his voice in reversal, Nari Tihadi pressed on, 'Was it not Atibadi Mahatma's impassioned recitations of the Bhagavata that moved Indradyumna the Second to institute the Purana Panda Niyoga within the sanctum itself? Tell me—did the venerable Mahajanas of the Mukti Mandap raise their voices in protest then?'

At this, Danadhyaksha Damodar Nanda exploded, 'It was precisely that lawlessness which incited the Mughal assault! The Lord forsook his Shrivatsa Khandashala temple and vanished into secrecy!'

From near the cluster of flattened rice and coconuts, the members of the council joined in a single chorus, 'it is as clear as the realms of heaven itself! Who could possibly reject this truth?'

No one dared to speak in Nari Tihadi's defence. And so, under the steely, wrathful gaze of the Danadhyaksha and his council, he was exiled from his Shasana and took refuge in this Karabada for many years.

Nari Tihadi addressed the guru, 'Oh, Paramaguru Mahashay! Today, within the Shasan, the authority of the priesthood is at its zenith. The venerable Mahajanas of the Shashan, driven by their insatiable greed for charitable donations, are not shy about turning white into black and black into white. Why, then, should they dare speak out in opposition to the enactment of the Navakalevara? For it is entirely lawful to grant the living deity a consecrated samadhi and institute this Navakalevara—scriptural mandates can even be extracted from our ancient texts in its favour.'

This objection, however, was not unfounded.

Mani Subuddhi murmured, his voice laced with quiet indignation, 'Is this not the truth? Once, Gadadhar Rajguru dared to perform the evening arati without tucking his *kachha*—the pleated edge of the dhoti customarily secured at the waist. Unabashed, he stood with his vestments loosened, and from that day forth, the ritual, once deemed invalid without such adherence, ceased to be questioned. Later, another Rajguru went so far as to pronounce even fermented rice water unfit as a sacred offering, forbidding its use in the Shasana with an iron decree. Yet his aged mother cried out in protest, 'My son, you have laid a ban on Kanjipani— how, then, shall widows and others be sustained?' At once, the Rajguru added a verse, "Safala Kanjika Grahya," as if affirming, 'Yes, partake of Kanji—but be sure to mix in a couple of vegetables!' Today, the people have fallen prey to this corrosive influence of sacerdotalism. These very priests, bought by the royal power, have long since seen the radiance of Brahmatic wisdom diminished by their rapacious greed for charity.'

Subuddhi's words were not lies.

Lakshmi Paramaguru had wandered from village to village, bearing witness to the self-consuming effects of priestly dominance over the masses. The deities still dwelled in the wilderness, and yet, driven by greed for the throne, Lalita Mahadevi sought to perform the Navakalevara outside its prescribed time. Soon enough, Bhagirathi Kumar would ascend the throne as nothing more than a puppet fashioned in the likeness of the unworthy Taqi Khan. Within the temple walls, Aminchand's uninterrupted regime would hold sway. Odisha's honour, pride, and sovereignty would be ground into dust. But who was there to see it? When the illustrious Mahajana body at the Mukti Mandap declared the Navakalevara to be sanctioned by scripture, what authority remained to Lakshmi Paramaguru? The Maharaja had already lost his caste—what value, then, could his protest carry?

The venomous influence of sacerdotal power had rendered an entire once-vibrant community paralyzed. In order to rouse this entranced people from the dust of their downfall and to unite them against the Mughals, Ramachandra Dev had taken an oath—a pledge whose success now filled Lakshmi Paramaguru with tentative doubt. Although these Shasani Mahajanas might indeed awaken public consciousness, in their own selfish greed, they had become nought but servants bought by the might of the royal power.

Lakshmi Paramaguru exhaled a long, wearied breath. A gust of quivering wind sent the steadfast lamp flame dancing, its fickle light casting a long, swaying shadow upon the wall.

'And what now?' Paramaguru asked, his voice composed and deliberate.

Silence reigned for a moment—no one dared answer. Finally, Paramaguru resumed, 'In Murshidabad, I have seen that the Nawabi era of Shuja Khan is now in decline. The rivalry between Taqi Khan and Sharfaraj Khan, contending over the coveted throne of Bengal, Bihar, and Odisha, is gradually smouldering. At this very moment, Mughal power is feeble. If ever there were an hour for Odisha's liberation, that moment is now! You must rouse and organize the popular power, or else this opportunity will forever slip through our fingers.'

'The will of the Supreme shall surely be fulfilled,' Nari Tihadi declared, his voice firm. 'You and I are but facets of this divine orchestration. You must continue your work. It is not true that all these learned Mahajanas are held captive by the Danadhyaksha's grip. Many may harbour doubts: if the deity dwells in a nether realm, then upon what scriptural basis is this Navakalevara justified? And how—after Ramachandra Dev, through penance and charity, reclaimed his Hindu identity from *mleccha* origins by bestowing Ramachandrapur—is he now deemed impure? Even the Shasani Brahmins have granted him absolution.

Mani Subuddhi echoed a similar sentiment: 'We shall act strictly according to the strength we possess. I urge you, as far as you can, to travel throughout the province. All the people of these lands still stand behind Maharaj

Ramachandra Dev. Let them see you and listen to your words to regain their lost courage. But tell me, where is the Maharaj now?'

It was best to remain silent regarding the Maharaja. Lakshmi Paramaguru answered quietly, 'He must be wandering among the paika villages somewhere—who can say? The resolve of the paikas is already all but broken!'

'*Nana srantaya srirasmi iti rohitaḥ shushruma! Charaiveti... charaiveti* (To the weary wanderer, the radiant divine spoke thus: 'We have heard it from the red-hued sage—Move forward... move forward)!' Onward we go, onward we go! Come, keep moving… for life itself is found in movement! He who refuses to move is doomed to remain below!

In that fatigued hour, Paramaguru recalled a great Upanishadic dictum with sombre reverence.

Veer Gopinathpur lay far off. Under the blazing Baishakh sun—Akshay Tritiya long past—the sky was utterly clear, not a cloud to be seen. Not a single drop of rain marred the parched earth. Drought reigned; one could almost hear the steps of desiccation itself. Above, the sky lay bare, while on the slender branches of distant coconut trees the sunlight glinted like a razor-sharp, shining sword. High in the firmament, two stately eagles circled slowly, their wings seemingly weary from the relentless heat. Their pace was languid, as if even they moved in resignation. Along that arduous path—sometimes adorned with golden urns borne upon palanquins and heralded by the blare of horns and drums—Paramaguru journeyed from one Shasana to the next, his presence dignified and serene within the curtained sanctum of ceremony. Accompanied by ceremonial grace, he moved like a living invocation—bearing edicts, honours, and signatures with the solemnity of one ordained to consecrate the sacred rhythm of the realm.

As the palanquin made its way along the road, attendants on either side marched closely together, bearing chaamars with a gold handle. Yet today the oppressive blaze of Baishakh showed no mercy, and the barren fields and withered crops along the way appeared utterly helpless. Even the weary travellers, catching fleeting glimpses of Lakshmi Paramaguru, failed to recognize him; in their eyes he seemed nothing more than a stray, roving kapalika— someone best avoided at all costs. It is better, they thought, not to be seen by such unseemly wanderers.

In every Shasana, the layout remained traditional— there was a Devi temple to the east, a Shiva temple to the west, and in some places even a Dadhivamana temple stood. Before each temple, a stone staircase led down to the sacred kund, the Pushkarini, where pilgrims would wash away worldly cares. Lakshmi Paramaguru himself descended to the ghats, drank deeply of the cool water, and emerged again through the temple's vestibule with a quiet dignity.

Before the closed door of the Goddess's sanctum, Paramaguru took his stand and silently began to intone a mantra, his voice low and resonant: *om uttiṣṭha puruṣi, kiṃ svapiṣi bhayaṃ me samustitam…*

'Is this some kapalika?'

A handful of men sat hunched in a shadowed corner of the vestibule, their dice-board unfurled between them. With every meagre throw, they cried out in vexation—the dice refused to favour them. And then, their eyes turned towards the sudden presence: where had this kapalika come from? If he were to utter some incantation or stir hidden sorcery, might their fortunes scatter like the dice themselves?

Seeking respite, Lakshmi Paramaguru spread his ochre cloth upon the earth and reclined for a brief moment. Among the dice-playing group, one voice rang out with derision: 'The Goddess's arati is done. There will be no prasad now—so why do you continue to lie here?'

They had come to see him as nothing more than a beggar! Had these people forgotten Lakshmi Paramaguru— the man who once drew throngs from every corner just for a glimpse of his divine presence? Today, even when he was close at hand, they fail to recognize him.

In a weary tone, Paramaguru reassured them, 'I am resting for a while. Do not worry about the prasad.'

But meanwhile, the game of dice continued unabated, with voices murmuring in rhythmic cadence: 'Seventeen— just once, clean and fair!'

Alas! Woe unto us! Such was the lamentable state of our Shasani villages today. Lakshmi Paramaguru's chest heaved as a long, shuddering breath escaped him. For generations—since the era of the mighty Bhaumakeshari emperors—Brahmin colonies had been established to 'Brahminize' the land of Utkal, steeped in age-old cultural traditions unaligned with Brahminical orthodoxy. After the completion of Vedic sacrifices, kings would grant parcels of land—fields, orchards, even aqueducts and watercourses— surrounding the sacrificial grounds to the most eminent Ritvik Brahmins. This meticulous deference to sacred duty was untainted by servility or sycophancy; the Shasans stood as bastions of Vedic learning and culture, preserving the independence and aristocratic heritage of Utkal. Many among the Brahmin Mahajanas had served as royal counsellors and generals in times of war. But where have they gone? What became of the venerable Rajguru Godavarivardhan during the illustrious Kanchi campaign under Maharaja Purushottam Dev and the lineages that followed?

'Smash it! A raw blow, and let fortune howl!'

A heated assault upon someone's pawn had just erupted. The clamour of dice players disrupted Lakshmi Paramaguru's meditation, compelling him to close his eyes and feign repose.

'Hey… have you heard?' The conversation twisted mid-game, veering into realms far removed from dice.

'Heard what?'

'It is whispered that Bishi Pati Mahapatra has been graced with twenty acres of revenue-free land by Her Majesty, Maharani Lalita Devi. Can one fathom it? While our Brahmin lords of venerable lineage are awarded fertile expanses in Gobarmunda, it is the humble temple priest, Pati Mahapatra, who receives the annuity for a lush, uninterrupted tract nestled in the marsh-swept lowlands of Jhinkariya Domani.'

'Was it not Pati Mahapatra who discovered the sacred *daru*? Had he not received the annuity, tell me—who among you would have?'

'But there exists no precedent—no decree—for bestowing revenue-free annuity upon those who undertake the quest for the *daru*!'

'Arey, it's a newly minted mandate!' someone remarked with a half-smile, his tone dipped in irony. But the words hung heavy, as though burdened with consequence. He hesitated, his voice retreating into silence.

'Speak up! Why have you swallowed your words?' came a further demand.

Lakshmi Paramaguru, pretending to be asleep with a snore, strained to catch every word of their hushed conversation.

'This is an extremely secret matter. Did Pati Mahapatra and the Daita truly receive the dream-decree from Kakatpur Mangala? They say, for mere spectacle, four logs were felled—carelessly chosen neem wood—in the name of a Banayoga rite! But is this the sacred *daru*, or merely timber dressed in ritual garb? And how can Mangala Devi bestow divine ordination through dreams when the sanctity of Navakalevara lies unravelled? You do not grasp the subtleties.'

'Ah... ah... you do seem exceptionally well informed.'

'And why not? I was in Purushottam. The Daita faction clashed bitterly over the affair. The twenty-acre annuity was bestowed upon them—granted, as they say, for as long as the moon and sun endure. That truth spilt forth amidst their quarrel.'

'Lies... utter lies! How dare you spout such brazen falsehoods?' an old man exclaimed in a drawling, nasal voice. 'I saw it with my own eyes—the sacred *daru*, destined for the elder Lord, transported by bullock cart. Conch, discus, mace, lotus—each emblem etched upon it. Had the Goddess's dream-decree not been in place, would Pati Mahapatra have secured that *daru*?'

At this, laughter rippled through the gathering. Even in broad daylight, a goat seemed to him a cow—his vision pale and faltering. Yet he insisted he'd seen it all: the conch, the discus, the mace, and the lotus, each emblazoned upon that very *daru*.

Someone let out a wry chuckle. 'You can't even distinguish the red pawn from the yellow on a simple dice board—and now this? You claim to have seen sacred symbols? It's pure spectacle, a grand illusion for the gullible!'

'Do you imagine that eyes of mere flesh can discern the symbols of the Divine? Only those blessed with divine sight may perceive them. You lack such vision—hence, you failed to see.'

'Oh, ho!' came a burst of laughter. 'So you claim to possess divine sight, do you?'

'Listen—some servitors within the sanctum echo the same whispers. Entranced by the lure of the throne, Lalita Devi is said to be consigning living deities into samadhi to clear the path for the Navakalevara. Even the high-ranking elders of the Mukti Mandap appear swayed by the prospect of state patronage. Once this Navakalevara is fulfilled, Bhagirathi Kumar will ascend the Khurda throne, and around him shall rise two Shasans—one Lalita Devipur, the other Bhagirathipur. From the mouths of the eminent, drool already spills in anticipation of power.'

'Ah… who can outwit you rascals, bred in the vicious churn of Kali Kala? Ask the Danadhyaksha, Damodar Nanda—if you dare confront him!'

'Enough of your Danadhyaksha! What does one make of those who, drunk on the lure of gold, forge ties with the Gotreya Samanta clan despite belonging to the higher Nanda Samanta? On what moral ground does he even stand?'

Is this then the band of opposers to the Danadhyaksha?

There was discord in the Shasani villages over the Navakalevara! Rumours swirled among the people—that beneath the twilight of ritual, the living deities were being yielded to eternal samadhi. Was there then doubt about this Navakalevara? The conspiracy of Lalita Devi—born solely of lust for the throne—stood as clear as daylight in the minds of the people. It was as if, caught in the surge of the current, Paramaguru had at last clutched a drifting straw.

And from that very moment, Paramaguru strode towards Danadhyaksha Damodar Nanda.

In the mandap, Danadhyaksha Damodar Nanda sat implacably on a deer hide, while near the revered Shalagram Shila on a stone slab, bhang and other herbs were being ground. Before him, on a wooden stool, lay several *Smṛti* treatises—perhaps manuals of ritual procedure—in which the notions of caste and awakened consciousness had been so intricately interwoven that they held sway over every mind. Nanda unrolled a bundle of *panchang* and began to determine what was auspicious and inauspicious, setting the tithis in order. Below the mandap, a few Shudras—the Karabada or Bishar folk—stood awaiting his decree. As members of the Shudra order, they were not permitted to ascend the temple steps.

Damodar Nanda's eyes fell upon Lakshmi Paramaguru. 'Come, please join us! Paramaguru Mahashay, where have you been hiding?'

In Damodar Nanda's piercing gaze, Paramaguru's disguise was uncovered. Hastily, he stammered, 'I wish to speak with you privately!'

Under the spell of his solemn incantations, Damodar Nanda rose and gestured, 'Please, come inside.'

Following him, Lakshmi Paramaguru traversed the outer chamber and, in a deep, pensive mood, seated himself in a wooden asana. Nanda was busy arranging food and refreshments for the guru. With quiet urgency, Paramaguru observed, 'We have little time to settle here; we must depart elsewhere before evening.'

Seated again beside Paramaguru on another wooden seat, Nanda implored, 'Command us, O revered Paramaguru!'

The sudden appearance of Lakshmi Paramaguru—in a state that was at once rugged and grimy—rendered the Danadhyaksha momentarily confounded. Without ceremony, Lakshmi Paramaguru spoke, 'You are a scholar of the Vedas, a master of the scriptures, a Brahmin of noble lineage! But remember, being a Brahmin does not simply mean donning the sacred tuft, nor do the scriptures reduce merely to ritual procedures! Only those who take refuge in the Truth and remain fearless in upholding its honour are truly Brahmins.'

He then intoned the prayer of an ancient Arya Rishi.

Kale varshatu parjanyo,
Prithvi shasyashaalini
Desho'yam kshobharahitam
Brahmanaastu nirbhayaa.

(May the rains fall in season, may the Earth flourish with ripe harvests, may this land remain undisturbed—and may the Brahmins stand fearless, guardians of truth.)

Damodar Nanda replied dismissively, 'Those priestly pundits recite that very blessing every day, intoning it as they lay the sanctified *duba* grass upon the remnants of their auspicious deeds. What, pray tell, is new in that?'

'No, no—that is hardly a benedictory verse. What your Shasani priests chant, with their muddled elocution, is a hollow recital—crafted to flatter and mislead the Shudra patrons. Hear instead the resonant cadence of the Arya Rishis: an utterance timeless and pure. A Brahmin is not merely a bearer of ritual or tufted thread. He is a seer—one who dwells in Truth, unshaken by fear or corrupted by greed. That is the true prayer of the Arya sages.'

Lakshmi Paramaguru's words bore a gravity that Damodar Nanda found difficult to grasp. In a moment of stunned uncertainty, he cast a glance towards Paramaguru—his hair falling in wild, matted waves upon his shoulders, his beard spread across his chest, veiled in the dust of countless roads long traversed. Upon his broad, timeworn brow, a fresh streak of vermilion shimmered—like a flickering flame.

'If a Brahmin, for lust of gold, silences the injustices of royal tyranny,' Paramaguru continued with solemn conviction, 'then how shall society endure? Who then shall safeguard dharma?'

His words hung in the air, and Damodar Nanda, still uncertain of Paramaguru's full intent, inquired, 'Pray, what is your meaning, revered Paramaguru Mahashay?'

Lakshmi Paramaguru answered, his tone both lamenting and bitter, 'What more is there to say? Today, the ritualist, sanctimonious Brahmins are parading about, announcing that the Maharaj has lost his caste—he has become a *mleccha*. And yet, it is by the very means of expiation through charitable offerings, arranged by men such as you, that such a maharaj has been enshrined once more.'

At last, Paramaguru's purpose began to dawn on

Damodar Nanda. With the frankness of a general recounting a battle won, he declared, 'Who does not know that the Gotreya Samantas, driven by their appetite for donations, compelled the Maharaj to atone for his misdeeds? In the third year of Maharaj Harekrishna Dev's reign, the Maharaj bestowed Veer Harekrishnapur as charity and a distinct class of Gotreya Samantas was born. But tell me—do these men possess any nobility of lineage? In which circle of nobles do they count themselves?'

In that unguarded moment, he had entirely forgotten that, seduced by the lure of gold, he himself had offered his daughter in marriage to the households of those very Gotreya Samantas, totally oblivious of his old pledges. In the very act of reminding him, Lakshmi Paramaguru's tongue faltered—he was here to fulfil a purpose, not to descend into petty quarrels.

'From a rational standpoint, I accept your words,' Lakshmi Paramaguru stated firmly. 'But do know this—Maharaj Ramachandra Dev does not covet the throne. Let Bhagirathi Kumar be consecrated as the rightful ruler of Khurda and serve as the royal servitor of Shri Jagannath. Ramachandra Dev harbours no objection. Yet while underhanded stratagems are used to enshrine new deities in Shrikshetra under the guise of a Navakalevara, our sovereign—the Gajapati of independent Odisha—is being reduced to little more than a puppet, a marionette fashioned in the image of the Mughal deputy, the Nazim. It is this desecration of sovereignty against which Ramachandra Dev has declared war. And if, out of greed or fear of forfeiting the revenue-free annuity, you choose silence now—how shall the world move forward?'

'Spare us that snare, Paramaguru Mahashay! You are highly esteemed among the Vatsagotreya Samantas. To stand against your words would be both unthinkable and deeply dishonourable. And when the Lord himself entrusted Maharani Lalita Devi with the dream-decree to enact the Navakalevara—who among mortals could dare obstruct its divine unfolding?'

'And what greater misfortune could befall us than for learned men like you—scholars of the sacred texts—to be swept away by the seductive propaganda of these dubious, lawless rabble, Damodar Nanda?'

In his heart, Paramaguru mused in wonder at the extent to which this debased propagandist discourse on the Navakalevara had spread.

'Paramaguru Mahashay, this is no fabrication—no sordid scheme, nor cunning deceit. By the Lord's own will, Maharani Lalita Devi was graced with the divine ordinance to procure the sacred *darus* for the Navakalevara. Let us not allow scepticism to shroud what heaven has revealed.'

'Yet as the deities remain confined to the nether regions, how can they ever manifest as gods without the hallowed *brahmashila* within? Shall the divine be reduced to woodlanders wandering the forests, while wooden effigies sit enthroned upon the Ratna Simhasana? Would that not foreclose the very possibility of a living samadhi for the sacred?'

'Even the location of the *brahmashila* was revealed to Lalita Devi in her dream.'

A stupendous, cemented darkness of blind superstitions—what truth, what reason, what sense of national identity could ever tear asunder such veils?

'Do you not desire the liberation of Odisha?' Lakshmi Paramaguru's voice broke through with an impassioned plea. 'Do you not long for this land to be freed from the Mughal yoke? Is that not your wish?'

Damodar Nanda, wearied by such unsavoury discourse, was disinclined to debate further. Ever since he had offered his daughter in marriage to the rival faction, certain elements had grown increasingly hostile toward him. If even a whisper of covert council between the rebellious Lakshmi Paramaguru and himself were to reach his concealed allies—be it Aminchand or the Maharani— the entire edifice would collapse.

'But remember,' Damodar Nanda, with a heavy sigh, declared, 'it is by the will of the Divine that this land of Odisha was granted to the Badshah. That its wealth should flow into the coffers of the Mughals—this too is a curse inscribed by Lord Brahma. Tell me, then—who dares stand against it? Who are you to resist? And who am I to defy?

After a long, reflective breath, Lakshmi Paramaguru rose and departed, leaving behind only an overwhelming uncertainty—a path without direction, a destiny uncharted.

*****

Chapter IX

Akshay Tritiya—the sacred juncture for the commencement of chariot construction. From that auspicious day, the pilgrim tide began to swell in Puri, drawn by the promise of divine celebration. The previous year, the grand inauguration had faltered, for the deities were said to dwell in the nether realms. Though the Chandan Yatra had been completed in some form, it bore the weight of absence.

But this year, with the advent of the Navakalevara, preparations for the Rath Yatra surged forth in jubilant splendour, and the Chandan Yatra drew throngs no less immense. During the inner Chandan Yatra, pilgrims arrived in waves spanning five kos, many having already beheld the deities' boat ride upon the sacred waters of the Narendra Pushkarini during the outer festivities. Thus, among them, the insistence on the outer Yatra waned. It was the pilgrims from the Mughalbandi dominions and the Western travellers who arrived in significant numbers. Having fulfilled their yearning to witness the Rath Yatra, they would depart from Srikshetra with hearts content, graced by darshan, and steeped in the sanctity of the moment.

For the entire year, the commissioned servitor

community had remained dormant—hands bound, with no effort made toward earning. Yet now, stirred by the promise of the Navakalevara, most had sprung to life. Those who opposed Lalita Devi and Aminchand might appear outwardly indifferent, but within, a ceaseless murmur questioned whether the Navakalevara would truly materialize. If the living deities remained confined to the nether realms, how could the Navakalevara ever come to pass? Merely because certain Shasani Mahajanas of the Mukti Mandap, having absorbed pearls of wisdom from Aminchand himself, had issued their decrees? Yet, as the influx of pilgrims intensified in Srikshetra, who among them would willingly forgo the earnings owed to them by sacred custom?

Beside the temple steps of Goddess Lakshmi in the open courtyard, a few weary pilgrims from the Mughalbandi sat on low platforms, momentarily alleviating their fatigue amid the sultriness of the month of Jyeshtha.

One such pilgrim remarked to another, as though imparting arcane knowledge: 'This is the glory of Lakshmi Devi! Not even a leaf stirs, yet sitting near the sacred maw of the Mother, one feels the trembling caress of the breeze.'

Meanwhile, amid the multitude, the pilgrim agents—Kantha Mekap and Palia Govind Mahapatra—had already begun their silent hunt for opportunity. Clad in dhotis tightly wrapped to their knees, ochre waistcoats draped over their torsos, sacred tilaks emblazoned on their foreheads, and turbans crowning their heads, they bore on their shoulders emblematic cloths inscribed with the names of gods. Around Kantha Mekap's neck hung a thick Rudraksha mala, its heavy beads bearing silent testimony.

Kantha Mekap then commented, 'Goddess Lakshmi

is the maiden of the *ksheer sagar*, the Ocean of Milk. The sweltering heat will torment the daughter, while the father revels adrift upon the rocking waves! And for that reason...'

'Aha!'—a hushed ripple of sympathy stirred from the devout crowd.

Suddenly, among the pilgrims, Kanchana's mother burst into tears. As if pressed by some unseen force, her sobs grew louder.

'Ah, dear lady! What is wrong? Why are you crying?' Within the group, an elderly woman laid a compassionate hand on her shoulder—a gentle gesture of comfort. Yet none could fathom the sudden grief that had overtaken her.

Though Kanchana's mother and her companion Ambakasi had grown old—their youthful tresses long since silvered—their friendship remained verdant, still vibrant with the freshness of spring.

In that moment, only Ambakasi could decipher the silent language of the tears and halting whispers of Kanchana's mother, a meaning reserved for the intimate bond between a mute and his mother. In hushed, troubled voices, others inquired, 'What has happened? What ails Kanchana's mother?' Her weeping only intensified, unrelenting.

Memories of Kanchana clawed at her heart. Her daughter had sent word that she wished to accompany her mother on the Chandan Yatra. But the overbearing mother-in-law had barred her way. 'And here I am, a mother, beholding the Lord's Chandan procession... while my daughter cries inconsolably, trapped in the entanglements of her marital home—nagging in-laws and endless strife.'

Ambakasi's eyes, too, shimmered with unshed tears.

'A woman is born to leave her mother behind and

take root in another's house. Why, then, dwell on memories and invite grief?'

And one by one, from beneath the veils of many women, muffled voices began to rise in sorrowful resonance. 'There was such sorrow in the heart of the sea—for daughter Lakshmi Devi—but also such boundless affection! In a place where not even a leaf stirs, the wind flows in trembling adoration, whether under the sun's gaze or the shroud of night.'

The conversation meandered wildly—from Lakshmi Devi to Kanchana, from Kanchana to the sorrows of all women. 'These womenfolk are ever a nuisance,' muttered an elderly patriarch. Then, with a sideways glance, he added, 'Yes, Gosain, what were you saying?' Kantha Mekap's talk had been momentarily paused, swept aside by the swelling tide of Kanchana's mother's sorrow.

Kantha Mekap inhaled a pinch of snuff, sneezed twice, and resumed in a low, conspiratorial tone. 'Believe it or not, these are matters of faith. The world itself rests on belief—otherwise, would Dasia Bauri, dazed and half-mad, gaze upon the sacred face of Lord Chakadola, shimmering in his humble bowl of rice? Meanwhile, Lalita Devi reclines upon a cushioned divan in her inner chambers—such a hushed and lonely night. And then, without warning, the entire house is suffused with the intoxicating scent of dayana blossoms.'

Several eager voices murmured in wonder, 'How…?'

'Tell me,' Kantha Mekap continued with quiet fervour, 'where did that fragrance of dayana come from? In her dreams, Lalita Devi saw it all… and there, standing before her, was Mahabahu—adorned in silken robes, yet tarnished! Mahabahu declared, 'How long must I remain in this lowly state? How long will my Ratna Simhasana lie silent in the Shrivatsa Khandashala temple? Am I destined to languish here in this barren wilderness?'

'Oh, Divine One! How much suffering have you endured! How many more days must you remain in this desolation?'—a wavering, sibilant lament rose from many veiled throats, trembling in shared sorrow.

Just then, as though conjured by the sheer emotional weight of the moment, Sendha Suara made his entrance—boisterous and jarring, like an off-key cymbal crashing into a sacred hymn. Turning toward Kantha Mekap, he bellowed, 'Hey, man! You're on fire today!'

Shendha Suara's raucous taunt was aimed at the very sight of Kantha Mekap, whose face bore the delicate touch of sandalwood and whose attire, embossed with sacred names, commanded attention.

But where had this boar come from, suddenly charging in to scatter the pilgrims at such a moment? Many of the servitors like him—opposed to Aminchand and Lalita Devi—were steadily sowing seeds of doubt and distrust among the throngs surrounding the Navakalevara. They, too, spread rumours, claiming that the Lord had appeared in the Chadhaukarana's dream, saying: "Will you consign me to samadhi while I still abide?" And the innocent pilgrims, caught in faith and fevered hope, believed it.

Even Kantha Mekap knew well that this was merely a provisional Navakalevara—and the servitors, too, held that conviction. Yet one wondered how much longer they would remain bound to this desolate realm, suspended between duty and doubt.

'Pilgrims, have you beheld the twelve-armed deity dwelling within a shrine scarcely wider than a single hand? Let us behold the sheep of Kali—come along!' Hayagriva Madhava—once a revered Buddhist figure—had been reduced to a mere beast of this degenerate era.

'Look over there—Bhushand Kak himself!'

Such divine spectacles might fetch a few copper coins, perhaps even a stray pahula. But honestly, all of this was smoke and mirrors—a tangled farce. These people had no urge to witness the supposed sheep of Kali or that mythical twelve-handed deity. No one offered the aṭika bhoga; even the simplest sankhudi bhoga was neglected—every household remained in desperate fasting! And so, regardless of whether the Navakalevara was indeed provisional or not, most of these servants, driven by the pangs of hunger, tirelessly campaigned in its favour.

'Where did that boar appear from, at this very moment, to drive the pilgrims away?' whispered Govind Mahapatra conspiratorially into Kantha Mekap's ear.

Shendha Suara was a boisterous bull—utterly unbridled! Engaging him in discourse bore little promise; the only result would be the shooing away of the Mughalbandi pilgrims.

'Go now, Suara,' Kantha Mekap murmured, his words carefully shielded from the ears of the pilgrims. 'It is time to cleanse the temple floor. The inner pit beneath the sanctum must be purified, and the Ratnavedi requires washing as well. Lord Ramkrishna and Lord Madanmohan are soon to arrive at the sacred Narendra Pushkarini. Why leave your duties behind and come here, only to disrupt our prayers and dampen the blessings we're barely managing to earn?'

From afar, the toll of bells and gongs reached their ears. The Ratna Vedi lay deserted. Yet even so, it was known that Talichha Mahapatra would soon arrive at that forlorn altar, accompanied by bells, ceremonial umbrellas, and a plaintive trumpet echoing through the air. Prasad would be offered. Once the sandalwood had been applied, Lakshmi, Saraswati, and Madanmohan would be adorned with garlands and flowers, and in Ramkrishna's palanquin, the Chandan Yatra would begin its sacred journey. Shendha Suara, the temple's cleaning servitor, was tasked with washing both the inner pit beneath the sanctum and the enclosure surrounding the Ratna Simhasana.

Even in the absence of the deity, throngs of pilgrims crowded around the vacant Ratna Vedi, bowing low and touching it in reverence. After all, the altar remained—and once, long ago, it was the sole embodiment. From that grand pedestal, Lord Narasimha had emerged, granting darshan to King Indradyumna in his leonine form.

And who could say? If Jaga Balia's wish were to stir, might not a Jahangiri coin come fluttering forth amid that reverent crowd? What gain, then, was there in shooing away Kantha Mekap's pilgrims? For he himself peddled Navakalevara in a frenzy of greed. Yet, in truth, within his heart, he opposed Maharani Lalita Devi and Aminchand.

'Well then, Guru—I'll heed your word,' Shendha Suara relented. 'You must come to Siddha Mahavir's abode this evening; the hour of bhang and sacred herbs is nearly upon us.'

After a long search, the Khuntia sevak finally located Shendha Suara. Raising his voice with exasperated vigour, he called out, 'Talichha has already departed with the dhup offering! The cleaning is still incomplete—when will the Mudirasta arrange the Prasad?'

Like an obedient boy, Shendha Suara knotted his towel around his waist. With his plump hips swaying rhythmically, he swaggered off in long strides toward the Bhog Mandap.

'Disaster averted!' In unison, Kantha Mekap and Govind Mahapatra exclaimed these words, and suddenly a sense of calm settled over the crowd.

Kantha Mekap continued, 'Yes, so… I was saying…'

Then someone reminded him, 'Lord Chakadola granted the Maharani a vision in her dream…'

'Indeed, that is so,' came the reply. 'At that moment, she stirred from her slumber as if awakened by a sudden flash. The entire house was suffused with the delicate fragrance of dayana flowers, while a lamp on the wall flickered softly. The Maharani thought, "What strange dream did I see?" In the recesses of her heart, she silently accepted the portent. She whispered, "O Mahabahu, how long will you remain lowly in the nether? I have been saved—but how can I save you? I, after all, am but of the feminine lot. And what strength I possess!" Three days and three nights have already passed.'

'Then?' many asked in hushed wonder.

Govind Mahapatra, hands folded at his forehead in silent supplication, murmured, 'O Mayadhara—the Wielder of Cosmic Illusion—who are we to hope to fathom the mystery of your maya?' In gentle unison, the gathered pilgrims, palms joined in prayer, echoed, 'O beloved one! Your divine mystery remains forever beyond mortal sight.'

Meanwhile, Kantha Mekap, his imagination kindled

afresh, went on: 'Listen to that dawn! In a dream, Mahabahu appeared once more before Lalita Devi and declared, "Establish my Navakalevara. Remember—Kalapahad once scorched me to cinders, and it was Indradyumna the Second who revived the Navakalevara."'

One pilgrim, perplexed, interjected, 'What strange tale is this? Kalapahad—a mere mortal like us—dared to burn the bearer of divine might? Did his crown not burst asunder beneath the weight of such sin?'

'They did indeed burst,' Kantha Mekap affirmed, his tone both grave and unyielding. 'But who among mortals can elude the iron law of karma? Even Narayana is not exempt—he, too, is bound by the consequences of his deeds. In his incarnation as Krishna, Mahavishnu Jagannath once employed a cunning ruse to vanquish Kalayavana. Muchukunda, the ancient king, lay deep in yogic slumber. Krishna, choosing concealment over confrontation, cast his radiant yellow robe over the sleeping monarch and withdrew into the shadows. Kalayavana, deceived by the gleam of the silken mantle, mistook Muchukunda for Krishna and struck in haste. But Muchukunda, blessed with a fiery boon, opened his eyes—and his wrath alone reduced Kalayavana to ashes. Krishna did not escape the echo of that deception. In the age of Kali, the consequence returned. Kalayavana was reborn as Kalapahad—the same who desecrated the divine *daru* form of Vishnu, setting alight the body sanctified by ages of devotion.'

Another pilgrim added, 'The reverent Bhupati Pandit composed the account in his palm-leaf manuscript *Prema Panchamrita*.' He then recited it in the exalted tone of the Bhagavata:

The deceitful act that Krishna wove
Was no true deed of Kshatriya's trove.
Its fruits he bore in future days,
Reborn as Kalapahad ablaze.
As wrath incarnate, fierce and grand
Within the Daru Brahma's holy land.
On Neelachala's hallowed plain,
He seized the god in binding chain.
He set afire each sacred limb,
For karma's course is vast and grim.
When even Vishnu could not flee,
So, what of fragile souls like thee?

Indeed, the Lord's descent into the netherworld is itself the inexorable fruit of karma. None are immune to its grasp—not even the divine.'

'And then?' someone asked. 'Sit, friend. Talichha Mahapatra—the Mudirasta—has yet to enter the sanctum. Had he arrived, the trumpets would surely have announced it. I cannot fathom why the dhup offering is so delayed today.'

Kantha Mekap added, 'The Vaishnava Mahajanas of the Mukti Mandap—those steadfast Gosains and their like—have accepted the Navakalevara. The Navakalevara shall come to pass. But where will the sacred *brahmashila* be found? That time, Bisara Mohanty stole away the *brahmashila*—what of now?'

'Truly, the *darus* shall be obtained! But where can one find *brahmashila*?' came voices in unison— '*brahmashila… brahmashila*!' The very propaganda that the servitors opposed to Aminchand and Lalita Devi had spread regarding the Navakalevara had deeply ensnared the credulous.

Yet Kantha Mekap had long since resolved this very dilemma. 'Chakadola has, in a dream one night, already told the Por Nayak—he, the heir of Bisara Mohanty—that somewhere in secrecy, you shall find my *brahmashila*!"

'Where… where?'

'This is a secret matter. The Por Nayak will not speak to Lalita Devi about it. Then, how are we to know? To speak of it would cause our very skulls to crack open. Hence, the Navakalevara proceeds. Only one who, in a previous life, earned such merit will truly be capable of comprehending this decree! Begin now—offer forth what you can. Don't toss coins like alms—give a proper Jahangiri rupee!'

Inside the temple, the trumpet of arrival suddenly sounded forth.

The midday dhup drifted gently from the temple kitchen. Soon, Talichha would make his ceremonial approach to the Ratna Simhasana. Once the ritual offerings were complete and the three enclosures received their veneration, the Mahajanas would be granted the *ajnamala*. Then, in a palanquin, Ram and Krishna would be enthroned; in the celestial vimana, Lakshmi, Saraswati, and Madanmohan would be installed. The grand procession of the vimana carriers would begin its solemn march toward Narendra Pushkarini.

Pilgrims had gathered from distant lands to behold the grandeur of this outer Chandan Yatra. The *natamandapa* overflowed with fervent devotees, and amid the resonant chants of 'Haribol!' and the piercing waves of ritual ululation, the victorious cry—'Jai Jai Mahabahu!'—rose and rolled like a thunderous ocean tide.

Meanwhile, Kanchana's mother and her companion Ambakasi, having discreetly knotted the ends of their sarees together, lagged behind the crowd. 'One ought not to venture out with such women,' an elderly man snapped. 'Over there, behind locked doors, pilgrims are being herded—what will you see there? Dust and shadows?'

The homa for consecrating the *darus* destined for chariot construction was approaching its solemn culmination. The Padiakarana stood poised with ceremonial sarees, ready to drape them around the heads of the carpenters. For some time now, three pandas, clutching their *ajnamala*, had been waiting at the gate of Balisahi Palace. Once the homa concluded, the chariot consecration would commence. The temple priests continued the sacrificial rite, which was expected to conclude within moments.

The peals of gongs and the resounding call of trumpets drew nearer. Perhaps the throng of pilgrims was delaying their approach. Yet one wondered—was the Balisahi Palace truly so far?

But where was Prince Bhagirathi Kumar? A restless commotion stirred on all sides. As per custom, once the vimanas reached the palace gate, the Maharaja—acting as the royal servitor—was to perform the veneration of the deities. Had he received their *ajnamala* and completed the sacred puja, the people would have recognized and accepted him as the sovereign of Odisha and the Divine's chosen servitor. The entire ceremony had been orchestrated for this very moment. Yet now, at the hour of reckoning, Kumar was nowhere to be seen. Within the palace walls, the wily Aminchand waited. If Bhagirathi Kumar delayed any longer, the ritual consecration of the chariots would fall to him—and with it, his claim to eminence in Purushottam would be sealed. Give him an inch and he would take a mile.

Like a famished lioness, Lalita Devi prowled restlessly through the crumbling remnants of Balisahi Palace—'Where is Kumar? Where has Bhagirathi Kumar gone?'

Chhamukarana surely knew—and it was no secret to Rajguru Gauri. Bhagirathi Kumar was likely lying in Suna Mahari's quarters, where Aminchand had confined him like a tamed parrot in a cage. Yet who among them could persuade Lalita Devi to believe such news? Though she knew, she feigned ignorance and questioned everyone. What was it that she did not know?

There was no longer that resplendent radiance or tenderness on Lalita Mahadevi's face. Her burnished golden form—now marred by the sullied flames of anguish. Tresses that once cascaded like monsoon rivers now hung in disarray to her waist. Those lustrous tresses—which had the power to shame the monsoon clouds—had, in recent years, been blanched to a pallid hue. A few strands of white marked her forehead, while her nose—sharp as the edge of a sword—and the chiselled lines of her face had grown stern and unforgiving. She wore no ornaments on her arms; no bangles, no bracelets adorned her limbs. Even the streak of sindoor that once graced her forehead, as a married woman, had been forsaken these many days, as she had declared her austere vow and preferred to live like a widow. Around her neck hung a rudraksha mala. Had she carried a *kamandalu* and a trishul, clad in ochre robes, none would have doubted she was a Bhairavi, a renunciant. And yet, her eyes no longer possessed the gentle softness of a true ascetic; they were shadowed as if by the dusk. Within them burned the fierce hunger of a midday tigress—the desperate yearning of an ember hidden in ashes, awaiting but the slightest tender caress of a gust.

Inwardly, Lalita Devi murmured repeatedly, as though caught in a trance, 'Poison… the very poison that coursed through his blood.' Her voice, distant and spectral, carried the incantation like an echo from another realm—'Chhamukarana!'

'Devi!'

'Where is Kumar? The homa for chariot consecration is about to be completed. Ram Krishna and Madanmohan have left the sanctum and are heading toward the palace gate, where Aminchand awaits the veneration. Has any word reached you?'

Chhamukarana remained silent, offering no reply. He wondered whether Bhagirathi Kumar would arrive at all. If Raja Aminchand were to complete the rites, then in the quiet recesses of his heart, Rajguru Gauri would surely rejoice.

Lalita Mahadevi raised her voice in a commanding tone, 'Chhamukarana!'

'Devi,' came the respectful reply.

'Why do you stand there like a tethered post? Go—fetch Kumar at once! The vimanas of the gods will arrive any moment.'

A panda stepped forward and announced, 'The homa for the auspicious commencement has now been completed.'

In the chamber of Suna Mahari, deep in the lanes of Chudanga Street, Bhagirathi Kumar sat languidly upon a velvet cushion. His body, draped in rose-tinted muslin, exuded a muted warmth; on his brow, locks curled in a flourish reminiscent of a blooming serpent. Around his neck, a nageshwar garland graced him, and before him lay several empty Muradabadi liquor vessels.

To the rhythmic cadence of the madal's beat, the gentle undulations of Suna Mahari's voluptuous form radiated an enchanted invitation. Her hips and thighs, in their subtle sway, leapt with the eager grace of desire drawn to a flickering flame—poised to surrender at its beckoning shimmer.

Ta jhamjham, ta kattatak. Ta jhamjham, ta dhe!

Yet there was no tawdry allure in Suna's laughter-filled, intoxicated eyes, nor the stirring of her hips. Her dance, it seemed, was no mere display of seduction—it was as if her every movement was an act of ascetic devotion. The meticulously bound composure of her body had unravelled, with delicate petals falling from her gently loosened locks; her steps, once firmly in place, had slipped into disarray. Suna danced as though entranced, and Bhagirathi Kumar watched her with rapt wonder, captivated by the rippling waves of her movement. Was Suna in an ecstatic frenzy today? Sometimes she would surrender herself to the rhythm like this, with such wild abandon that her dance seemed less a performance than a ritual of dissolution.

It recalled that earlier day in the temple—before the sleeping rites of the deities during Badasinghar, before Ratna Vedi—when she had not merely danced but offered herself in a ritual so profound that it transcended mere performance. There were neither the resounding beats of the madal nor the recited chants that evening, yet the rhythm was flawless. In that spellbound moment, Suna's attire fell into a graceful disorder, and in the vortex of her dance, she relinquished all worldly authority. She rendered herself completely—a self-offering so intense it eclipsed the boundaries of artifice. Had someone embraced her? Whose tender caress graced her? Whose fragrance filled this embrace? Where was his subtle touch? Where was her bodice? Her veil? Where… where was it? Nothing remained—only an absolute, profound void! Beneath Ratna Vedi, she lay unaware for what seemed an unmeasured span of time.

From that day forth, Suna embarked upon an exploration of countless bodies—each embrace bearing unspoken promises, every caress a phantom of that tender touch, each lingering scent a pursuit of that elusive essence. And yet, all who came sought only to partake in Suna Mahari's physical offering—admiring the graceful curvature of her form, the alluring tenderness of her body, the flame-like sway of her dance. From Puri to Cuttack, from Murshidabad to the myriad gatherings of impassioned connoisseurs, her praises echoed like sacred refrains. But who truly understood that within her very flesh lay an inward quest—a spiritual penance masked in corporeal expression?

'Suna!' Bhagirathi Kumar called out in a quivering tone. She offered no reply, as if she had not registered the lascivious summons.

Ta dhin, ta katak. Ta tak, ta dhe…

For a few moments, with no attentive eyes upon him, the waiting Chhamukarana, unbidden, stepped inside. Marked with a Hari Mandir tilak upon his brow, a tulsi mala around his neck, and a draped mantle over his shoulder, he appeared strangely incongruous amid that fleeting tableau.

'Manima!' he beckoned.

As the rhythm faltered, Suna stood silently, her gaze cast downward. Suddenly, it was as if she had returned to another realm—a realm of sensual flesh and vibrant desire. Bhagirathi Kumar, too, had been drawn into that parallel domain ruled by duty, discipline, and rivalry. Yet he stood unready for the rupture. In a gruff tone, he demanded, 'Why are you here?'

Flustered, Chhamukarana replied, 'The homa for the chariot's auspicious commencement is nearly over. The deities have reached the palace portal. Following His Majesty's veneration, the chariot construction shall commence!'

'All that bustle will be overseen by Naib Aminchand!' Bhagirathi Kumar interjected, his tone edged with impatience.

At the sight of Chhamukarana, Suna had already drawn inward, cloaked in a profound gravity. In her wake, the madal players silently withdrew from the chamber.

Chhamukarana's voice carried a quiet astonishment as he said, 'Aminchand has long awaited this juncture. And yet, you—as the royal servitor—now preside over the sacred rites of Navakalevara?'

'Not I! Not I!' Kumar retorted, his voice taut with vexation. 'It is the Queen Mother who initiates the Navakalevara...' Bhagirathi Kumar, who once revelled in life's unbridled freedom, was not the one to be ensnared in this labyrinth of courtly machinations.

'Why this grand spectacle, then? Is it not but a prelude to claiming the throne of Khurda?'

Bursting into hearty laughter, Kumar remarked, 'Remember, the throne itself is but a living sepulchre. Let that not be forgotten, Chhamukarana!'

How cunningly Aminchand had reduced the princeling to a mere pet parrot—locked away in Suna Mahari's gilded cage! Chhamukarana stood there, utterly astonished. In history, the decline of a people often begins thus—with the slow erosion of their noble warriors' character. But what answer would he offer to the Maharani when he returned? Would she give credence to Chhamukarana's tale? After all, she trusted not even her own shadow. Aminchand had also already subdued him by flaunting avarice; it was hardly surprising if the Maharani harboured such doubts.

Is this the anointed Gajapati destined for the throne? Is this truly the jewels of Utkal's crown?

'Manima, now come forward!'

'But for the veneration, is it not Aminchand who is meant to be here?'

'It is Your Highness who must serve as the royal servitor and inaugurate the rites.'

'And if not?'

'What a strange question indeed! In the presence of thousands, before the palace—if Manima is to perform the veneration of the gods and herald the commencement of the chariot rites, only then shall the people acknowledge you as king. You shall stand as their royal servitor. For this is the throne of Odisha—if you are not truly the servant of the Lord, of Mahabahu himself, how can you lay rightful claim to it?'

In a harsh, cutting tone, Kumar declared, 'I desire no throne whose reputation is built on intrigue!'

'Do you not seek the throne, Majesty?' Chhamukarana could scarcely believe his ears. What followed was a pointed query: 'Why, then, is the Maharani endorsing this

Navakalevara?'

'The Maharani herself shall answer that question! I will not,' replied Kumar, his voice laced with stern ferocity. 'Will not that Mahabahu—whom she so fervently extolled—be the very instrument of your sordid conspiracy?'

'Manima…'—was this the impassioned prince he strived to calm with judicious counsel? Could such fire be tempered by wisdom alone?

In Murshidabad, Shuja Khan's puppet reigns in Cuttack as Naib Nazim Taqi Khan. His shadow stretches to Puri, where Aminchand pulls the strings. And Aminchand's own marionette dwells in Balisahi—none other than the Maharani herself. And now, I am to be fashioned into yet another puppet upon the throne of Khurda? A theatre of strings and shadows! The Maharani, you, all of you—even Mahabahu has been reduced to a trembling effigy! But I, Chhamukarana, shall not dance upon your stage of deception!'

Raising an empty Muradabadi chalice, Kumar cried out sharply, 'Suna… Suna!'

But where was Suna? It was the Maharani herself who now stood before him—Kali! Bhairavi! In the hush of delay, she had arrived in a closed palanquin, veiled from the gaze of the crowd, to lead Bhagirathi Kumar away from the watching multitude.

'Poison… poison—the very same venom courses through his blood!' exploded Lalita Devi. 'Arise! Come now, Kumar. The vimana carriers can wait no longer. The delay has been far too great.'

Enthralled by the Maharani's incantations, Bhagirathi Kumar gathered at her side, though irritation flickered across his face.

How long, one wondered, would the vimana carriers wait at the gate, the lords borne upon their shoulders? For once the veneration was complete, the deities would proceed to the Narendra Chakada—where, too, the air thickened with myriad rites and ceremonials. At Palia Garabadu's command—the man entrusted with this sacred task—the sanctified water delivered by Jagannath Ballabh was to be transformed into a camphorous elixir. And with that very elixir, each altar inside the enclosure was to be consecrated by the Mahapatra. How long had this chain of symbolic acts endured? To seek its origin was to risk entanglement in a snare of unknowable antiquity. When, indeed, had the mystic confluence of Panchadhyani Buddhism, the wisdom of the Buddha, and the sacred culture of Jagannath merged to engender the Panch Pandavas? Else, what part could those five divine archetypes possibly play in Jagannath's Chandan Yatra? After the camphor ritual, the Panch Pandavas would rise to claim their place upon the ceremonial throne, in the wake of Ram Krishna. Arjuna and Sahadeva might move with the effortless grace of ritual embodiment, but Yudhishthira and Bhima—those weightier souls—would stumble through the festivities. Yet come they must. And then, aboard the trailing vessel, would appear Madanmohan, Lakshmi, and Saraswati—a triumphant synthesis of Buddhist metaphysics, Brahminical imagination, and theatrical pageantry steeped in idol worship. And finally, as dusk pressed in, the Mudirasta would offer prasad to the gods.

Now, Rajguru Gauri, the Senior Parichha, had taken on the mantle of Mudirasta.

And then, the offering—Naib Dashavatar draped the

sacred sash across his shoulder and presented the *bidiya*, a lime-free betel leaf. But this was no mere procession. It was a resplendent exhibition of every creed, every path, every stream of thought.

Thereafter, the servitor entrusted with the betel casket—his shoulder adorned with the sacred sash inscribed with Dasavatara Stotras—would solemnly present the *bidiya*, a lime-free betel quid, as ritual offering. Yet this was no mere procession. It was a resplendent confluence of philosophies, paths, and spiritual currents—a graceful descent of folk culture from its metaphysical heights. Each gesture, each offering, had been meticulously preordained through a labyrinth of remedies and ritual prescriptions, woven into the very fabric of sacred tradition.

Yet, where was the axis of this grand celebration? Where was the royal servitor—Bhagirathi Kumar?

The servitors aligned with Aminchand began to exclaim, 'Ah! A matter of veneration, is it? Is this truly such a grand affair? If the princeling is absent, let Naib Aminchand perform the rite—would the sanctity of the sacred text be defiled?'

Others chimed in, 'Will the vimana carriers bearing the gods aloft in palanquins, be forced to stand in the heated glare of the sun? Their shoulders must soon ache!'

As the number of onlookers swelled, a hushed murmur rose in the crowd: 'This is hardly an auspicious sign!'

Meanwhile, Naib Aminchand, draped in ceremonial silks, waited anxiously, his hope resting solely on the directives of Rajguru Gauri. He knew that the princeling would not easily emerge from the gilded confines of Suna

Mahari's cage.

Rajguru Gauri's sinewed face flared with fire. His eyes blazed with urgency. 'Raja… Aminchand!' he began, then abruptly fell silent.

Before anyone could fully grasp the scene, Shendha Suara—like a wild, unruly beast—sliced through the throng, charging forward with the fury of a marauding bull. A rogue incarnate! This miscreant, as though intent on igniting a fresh calamity worthy of Lanka's ruin, sent a ripple of dread through Aminchand's loyalists.

With eyes narrowing like those of a coucal—piercing, red, and unrelenting—Shendha Suara fixed his gaze on Aminchand and bellowed, 'Well, well! Is that gem ablaze today, or are you trying to summon the sun itself?'

'Damn you—may your mother perish!' Almost instantly, one of Aminchand's adherents snapped back in crude retort. 'What nerve you have to diminish King Aminchand!'

Shendha Suara's cutting remarks, together with the biting jibes aimed at Aminchand, ignited a burst of laughter and mockery among the gathered crowd. Observing Aminchand's bewildered and indecisive state, he taunted, 'Your pulse has turned icy!'

Not to be outdone, Pushpalak Bali Panda's eyes blazed scarlet as he added with satisfaction, 'Well said, my friend!'

Realizing that the hour was growing dire, Aminchand, his tone laced with urgency, turned to Rajguru Gauri and demanded, 'Where is Kumar? The time for veneration is upon us!'

Suddenly, a voice rang out from within the crowd,

'Kumar, Bhagirathi Kumar!' Ahead of his palanquin, the sentries cried, 'Clear the way… clear the way… move aside!'

In a state of bewilderment, Kumar disembarked from his palanquin. With a note of chiding sorrow, Aminchand lamented, 'You have delayed it far too long, Kumar!'

Amid the resonant peals of bells, gongs, and blaring trumpets, Aminchand could not even decipher a reply from Kumar: 'You are all mere puppets! You have reduced even the gods to dolls. What difference would it make if you turned veneration into a mere puppet play?'

At last, the veneration came to its conclusion. In unison, the people raised their voices in exultation, 'Jai Mahabahu! Jai Bhagirathi Kumar!' That triumphant cry resonated through the timeworn, shadowed rooms of the dilapidated Balisahi Palace, reaching Lalita Mahadevi—who had long awaited the sound—with a sense of soothing relief.

Soon, Chhamukarana appeared and announced, 'After the veneration, the deities have now proceeded toward Narendra Chakada. By the grace of Shri Jagannath, the chariot's inaugural ceremony has unfolded without a hitch.'

And now, the hour had arrived—Navakalevara! Navakalevara!

Then, upon the Khurda throne, Bhagirathi Kumar would be consecrated—an event Lalita Devi had awaited with unwavering eagerness.

Her eyes gleamed—serpentine hunger flickering beneath their surface. 'Where is Naib Aminchand?' she inquired, her voice low, deliberate.

Chhamukarana bowed slightly and replied, 'He has, in all likelihood, returned with Rajguru to Santadas Math.

At the Santadas Math, the chamber lay in solemn silence. Below, an exquisite floor covering had been spread out. There, Aminchand—casting his pearl-adorned turban upon the mat—reclined against a bolster, weary and defeated. So much spectacle, so much orchestration—and yet, bribery in the wrong hands and misplacement of intent had turned it all to dust. Was the princeling not detained, if only for a moment? And how, indeed, did Lalita Devi come by the clue to Mahari's concealed chamber?

Rajguru Gauri, wisely discerning Aminchand's unspoken thoughts, leaned close and whispered, 'Fear not, Your Majesty! I, Rajguru Gauri, am a man of steadfast character. Let the Maharani trace the path—I'll pave it in gold.'

He had heard such lofty claims many times before—with thousands of rupees, inducements, and bribes exchanged, each person's true nature long since laid bare. Yet once drawn into the very midst of affairs, there would be no remedy for changing one's course. Aminchand, fanning himself with a peacock-feathered fan, inquired, 'So—now? Bhagirathi Kumar has already performed the veneration and inaugurated the chariot ritual?'

'Let him!' came the sharp retort. 'What difference does it make? The daytime procession is modest and unimpressive, with few pilgrims coming to witness it. At Narendra Pushkarini during the day, they form but a small circle around the vessel. Nor does the ecstatic Mahari dance grace the occasion. But by night, the vessel makes three circuits, and around the sacred pond, throngs gather to behold the dance. The Maharani had arranged the rites so that, during the nighttime ritual, Bhagirathi Kumar would be the sole focus of the grand procession. I have explained it to her, for if Naib Aminchand does not accompany Kumar in the procession, it will seem quite improper, especially when Kumar's coronation on the Khurda throne rests upon his support and goodwill. If he is not seated in the procession, he will take it as a grave insult.'

Drawing deeply on his Muradabadi silver hookah, Aminchand exhaled a curling wisp of smoke. Some assurance settled within him, and he asked, 'Then?'

The shrewd Rajguru cast his gaze about and murmured in a conspiratorial hush, 'There—will you not see it for yourself?'

Yet his eagerness deepened further as he continued in a tone heavy with impatience, 'What is there left for me to witness? I have seen so much already—what more can be revealed?'

Rajguru Gauri spoke softly near his ear, 'I have already instructed the servitors that, while they distribute the Khadi Prasad on the vessel, you must be the first to receive it. For only those royal servitors upon whom Lord Jagannath bestows his grace receive the Khadi Prasad ahead of all.'

Aminchand, teasing, then countered, 'And by receiving the Khadi Prasad first, what kingdom does one gain?'

But he did not concern himself with the ancient traditions of Odisha's history. In those days—the era of Emperor Akbar—utter anarchy reigned, with many claimants vying for the illustrious Gajapati throne. To restore order to this fractious dominion, the imperial court dispatched the Rajput commander, Raja Man Singh, an arbiter vested with sovereign authority. The auspicious Chandan Yatra was in full flourish, its pageantry veiling tensions that ran deep. Amidst this confluence of ritual and royal aspiration, a symbolic offering changed the fate of a nation. Ramai Rautara—serene, discerning, and favoured—received the Khadi-prasad before all others. Man Singh, attuned to the divine pulse, perceived it not as chance but as cosmic ordinance. The grace of Shri Jagannath had revealed itself. With solemn conviction, he proclaimed Ramai Rautara the rightful sovereign of Odisha. The other contender, the son of the independent Gajapati Telanga Mukund, was sidelined, retreating into quiet obscurity in the dominion of Ali. Thus unfurled another scroll in the grand tapestry of Odisha's history, where ritual eclipsed sword and divine will crowned kings.

These historical nuances did not penetrate Aminchand's mind.

Rajguru Gauri explained further, 'Then let us unravel that thread of fate. In the wake of Telanga Mukund's passing, Odisha fell into a twelve-year fugue of disorder. Law gave way to lineage, and from among the shadows rose the son of Danei Vidyadhar—sheltered within the ramparts of Totami Fort. With careful diplomacy, he won over Todarmal and was consecrated as Ramachandra Dev, a sovereign born of compromise and ritual. His reign saw a sacred flourishing. In the temple cities of Khurda and Cuttack, he revived the Banayoga, commissioned icons of the deities, and entrusted Bisara Mohanty, who had retrieved the Brahmapinda, with the mantle of Por Nayak—the guardian of divine rites. Where once the Lord partook in the austere offering of uncooked prasad, Ramachandra invoked a new dispensation—the Sankhudi feast of cooked food in abundance. The ascetics and celibate Brahmins, moved by his devotion and order, hailed him as the Second Indradyumna, swathing him in silk and chanting his praises across the land. Odisha rang with the echo of his name. Yet even as the temple bells tolled in his honour, the other Ramachandra Dev—heir of Telanga Mukund's line—made his way to the imperial court of Delhi, bearing his claim before the throne of Akbar. The Emperor, resolute in judgment, dispatched Raja Man Singh once again to Odisha, bearing a singular mandate: "Crown the one upon whom the divine mark has fallen. Let him be king.'"

What a dramatic turn of events! Aminchand, drawing a deep drag from his hookah, queried in a husky tone, 'And then?'

'It is only he upon whom Lord Shri Jagannath bestows his divine grace that Odisha's true hero is revealed—a chosen soul destined to ascend the Gajapati throne,' Rajguru Gauri intoned, his voice steeped in solemn reverence. 'But how was Raja Man Singh to divine the mark of favour? Quietly, he sought counsel from the pandas and servitors—custodians of ritual insight. Such consultations were not without precedent. In the storied age of the Suryavansha, during the reign of Maharaja Kapilendra Dev, the royal household had fractured under the weight of fraternal rivalry. The throne stood contested, the line of succession clouded. In meditative resolve, Kapilendra devised a subtle trial, one tethered to faith and fate. On the morrow's darshan, upon the sacred Baisi Pahacha, the son who first seized the trailing hem of his dhoti would be deemed the rightful heir. At dawn, as the king ascended toward the Lord's altar, Hamir Dev stood to one side, and on the other, Purushottam Dev—the son of an Odia queen. As they reached the sanctified steps, the loose end of the dhoti slipped free. Without hesitation, Purushottam grasped it. The gesture was simple, but for Kapilendra Dev, it bore the weight of divine sanction. He saw in that moment the unmistakable will of Shri Jagannath—a choice made not by man, but by the deity himself.'

Back in the present, Aminchand's patience had frayed. 'But how did Man Singh determine which Ramachandra bore the grace of Lord Jagannath?' he demanded, wearied by the unfolding lore.

'With the covert instruction of Second Indradyumna, the servitors had choreographed the moment with quiet precision. During the Chandan Yatra, it was ordained that the servitor who bestowed the Khadi-prasad first would reveal the divine will. The one to receive it would be deemed the true sovereign of Odisha. And so the ritual played its part. Seated between the two claimants, Raja Man Singh gestured to the temple servitors: "Bring forth the Khadi Prasad." With practised grace, the servitors stepped forward, anointed the brow of the Second Indradyumna Ramachandra Dev with fragrant sandalwood, and placed the Khadi Prasad before him, while the other watched in silence. In this quiet orchestration, destiny was sealed. Before the sanctified gaze of Goddess Vimala, Man Singh announced what the ritual had already whispered: Ramachandra Dev, Second Indradyumna, was the divinely chosen Maharaja of Odisha.'

'And now?' Aminchand pressed, his throat tight with anticipation.

'Maintain your patience—witness it for yourself!'

By nightfall—four *ghadi* into the nocturnal hours—the moon had risen high above the grove of palms, casting its ethereal sheen upon the world below. Illuminated by the warm glow of torches and the soft shimmer of *baneti* lamps, the night had shed its shadows; it wore the radiance of day. A stately vessel lay moored along the banks of the sacred Narendra Pushkarini. Bhagirathi Kumar, borne aloft in a grand palanquin, had only just arrived to join the unfolding celebration. Around the waters, pilgrims and onlookers from far and wide had gathered, their numbers swelling like a living tide.

From amidst the gathering rose the sonorous strains of bhajan—tambourines pulsing in rhythm with ecstatic chants: 'Jagabandhu, the supreme Lord… Thou, who slayest the crocodile with Thy mighty chakra!' The atmosphere trembled with reverence and exhilaration. Exclamations flared amid the throng—'Isn't this the way kings are made?' 'There stands the princeling!' 'The gods have arrived! What cause remains for delay?' Even the processions from the Suara settlement were now making their way, illuminated by radiant flame.

Other groups had already assembled in gleaming splendour—some lounging heavily in the temple tank, like buffaloes against the water's calm; others swam or splashed about in ecstatic abandon. Whether driven by the bliss of Chandan Yatra or drawn by the lure of material gain, all had gathered under the spell of divine theatre. Ah! The Lord orchestrates this *leela* with cosmic wit—for who, in heart or spirit, would dare forsake such celestial revelry?

Amid the throng, a wide-eyed admirer caught sight

of a young maiden and cried with fervent admiration, 'Exquisite *rabdi*… pure cream!' That was the grandeur of the Suara royal ensemble—who else could stride through such incandescent festivity with such unshakable grace?

From another quarter, a playful voice rang out, 'Pure *chhena*!'—and a roguish wit from a nearby settlement, spying another radiant figure, added with a chuckle, 'That's no ordinary beauty, my friend—that's top-shelf *rabdi!*'

That year, however, the contingent from the Suara settlement began their journey much later than tradition would prefer. Earlier that afternoon, within the rustic confines of the *Jegaghar*, a lavish repast of bhang and indulgent fare had been laid out. Sated and subdued, the revellers slipped into a deep, narcotic slumber. As day softened into dusk, and the air turned the hue of oil lamps, the ever-watchful Nokani Panda commenced his gentle campaign of rousing, pouring cool water over each soul, one by one, with patient grace. Even preparations for the *baneti* and the ritual *gotipua* performances lagged behind schedule. The scrupulous Nata Padhiari, with a discerning eye and delicate touch, was seen weaving brilliant ketaki petals into the braid of a young dancer—a lad radiant with youth and reverie. He was tender toward his troupe. For truly, what had that fleeting world ever offered, if not the companionship of comrades, the intoxicant of bhang, the dance of kites in the wind, and the enduring rhythm of music? The Odia people—once plundered of wealth, their hard-won earnings taken by grasping hands—had not surrendered their nobility. Though the coin had evaded them, their spirit had remained resolute. Within the chambers of their hearts, they had lived as Maharajas still.

Pahili Panda—draped in the guise of a naga—strutted forth with theatrical intent. Yet one could scarcely believe their eyes; he resembled more a writhing eel than a true serpent. A genuine naga, after all, radiates a fierce majesty, the kind embodied by the formidable Shendha Suara, whose arms are stout and sinewed, like the sturdy legs of an elephant. But for reasons unknown, the fervour that once ignited his love for the naga attire seemed to have waned this year.

A voice rang out sharply, 'Is this how you walk in your debut procession? Pick up the pace—are you trying to tarnish the name of the Suara settlement's ensemble?'

'Elephant! Elephant!' roared Shendha Suara.

For truly, without the grand sway of an elephant—a symbol of strength and gravitas—how can a procession ever march forward with conviction?

Near the carved pillars of the *Jegaghar*'s veranda, Shendha Suara—ever restless amidst the multitudes—was seen merrily rocking a young goat, which bleated in mild protest. In a moment of impish exuberance, he offered the little creature two hearty swigs of bhang-infused water and adorned its neck with a fragrant garland of mogra. That little companion, too, was destined to march with the ensemble at Narendra Pushkarini.

'Elephant! Elephant! Who went to fetch the elephant?'

Shendha Suara tightened his wet gamchha around his waist and, rallying his spirits, gathered another and began to shout, 'Elephant! Elephant!'—thus amplifying the clamour as the festive cry soared through the night.

By the time they had adorned themselves and set

forth, three hours had slipped into the night.

The ensembles of the other settlement had arrived long ago, while those of the Suara settlement spent their time casting blame on one another. Now that the procession has reached Narendra Pushkarini, all voices have fallen silent.

It was a matter of the settlement's honour. Pahili Panda might have appeared scrawny—like a mosquito at first glance—but his gait was a marvel to behold. Donning the guise of Parashuram, he vanquished the rival settlement with theatrical grace.

I am Parashuram, the valiant—the thunder-kneed ascetic! Janughanta Parashuram, forged in vow and flame. Who else dares to bear that sacred name?

At length, an elephant was procured from somewhere. Proudly borne upon its back sat Nokani Panda, brandishing the emblem of the settlement's ensemble like a Vaijayanti flag waving in triumph. Ahead of the gathering, three young men—casually twirling their *baneti*—advanced with assured grace.

On either side, the folk of the various settlements advanced in neat rows, garlanded with blooming mogra and keeping perfect time with the rhythmic beat of the changu drums. A pet flame-throated bulbul perched merrily atop one head, while on another's arm, a tiny mongoose shimmered as it looked on—each little creature destined to join the journey to Narendra Pushkarini. Two *gotipua* dancers capered about, theatrically exclaiming, 'O gracious Sumana!'

At the forefront strode Shendha Suara and Bali Panda—Bali, too, proving himself no weakling. In the settlement's festivities, he took on the guise of Veer Hanuman. Both wore twin garlands of marigold about their necks, while atop their heads, ornate pitchers adorned with jasmine sent fragrant garlands swaying in rhythm. Their eyes, flushed crimson from bhang's heady intoxication, carried a swagger that was all their own—Madanmohan's regal stride, Shendha Suara's mischievous flourish. And between them, the little goat walked proudly, bedecked with mogra blooms. And what of it, if it were merely a goat? It too basked in the joy of the occasion.

The onlookers remarked, 'No tiger or lion from the Suara settlement this year?'

'Indeed... their fortunes have thinned of late!'

'But look how the Baseli settlement has outshone them all! Their ensemble boasted the dramatic tones of Telangi drums, several troupes of *gotipua* dancers, and even glittering glass representations of tigers and lions!'

'I tell you, comrade—Aminchand must have oiled more than a few palms to mount such a pageant over ours. The people of the Suara settlement, after all, remain his steadfast opposers.'

Suddenly, with a thunderous outcry, voices roared, 'Move... clear the way!' In that instant, the disciplined order of both the fair and its spectators crumbled into a tide of confusion. Naib Aminchand, ensconced in a stately palanquin, commenced his procession toward the sacred grounds of Narendra Chakada while sentries bearing flaming torches flanked him on either side, rushing ahead in hurried formation.

The buoyant swagger of Shendha Suara faltered momentarily as he stepped aside to yield the path for Aminchand.

'Hey—where is that boar charging now?'

Bali Panda remarked with a sardonic curl to his

voice, 'Perhaps there's purpose to his frenzy.'

Amid the procession, Bhagirathi Kumar—seated in solemn repose atop the stately vessel—voiced his impatience, barely veiled beneath ritual restraint: 'How much longer must I remain here?'

He had been brought straight from Suna Mahari's chamber.

'I cannot say,' Talichha Mahapatra replied. 'The deities' arrival at the vessel is delayed for reasons unknown. I've even dispatched a scout into the chakada to uncover the cause.'

At that moment, a sentinel announced, 'The Mandua Bhog is complete. Now, once the *bidiya* quid is consumed, the deities will finally arrive on the vessel. There is some Rajguru or Mudirasta who is deliberately stalling the proceedings?'

'Hail! Hail to King Aminchand!'

No sooner had Aminchand's procession reached the banks of Narendra Pushkarini than the people of the Baseli settlement raised their voices in acclamation, 'Hail! Hail to King Aminchand!'

Shendha Suara flung open his arms and bellowed, 'I say—who is that rhino daring to sit on the stately vessel? What right has he to do so? Let him face an extraordinary reckoning today!'

With a swift motion, Shendha Suara tightened the gamchha around his waist and lunged to block Naib Aminchand's path.

Bali Panda clutched at Shendha Suara from behind, urging, 'Come now, comrade—don't go, don't go! The Baseli settlement contenders have arrived all bundled up. Besides, this is our rival settlement—they'll turn you into chutney!'

By now, Naib Aminchand had ascended to the apex of the stately vessel. It was for him, and him alone, that Rajguru Gauri—now assuming the mantle of Mudirasta—had orchestrated the calculated delay in the chakada. As bells, gongs, and trumpets rang out, the deities approached in their majestic vessel. Onlookers and pilgrims—forgetting fatigue in their swelling anticipation—cried out in unison, 'Jai Mahabahu!'

While many from the settlements had already entered Narendra Pushkarini, Shendha Suara—his spirit waning—remained reluctant to take the plunge. Stationed on the ghat's steps, Bali Panda called out, 'Come now, friend! Why linger so long at the edge?'

Shendha Suara struggled to hold back a reply; his anger pressed at the seams, barely restrained, as though the mogra garland around his neck had begun to wilt in protest. Nearby, in a shadowed corner beside Bhagirathi Kumar, sat the man known for scavenging the remnants of Taqi Khan—his very presence dismantling the meaning of the moment. Garlanded, crouched as if in offering, his form spoke what Shendha Suara dared not voice. Amid swirling dust and dazzled eyes, Aminchand rose—like a proclamation made flesh—as though to declare: 'Behold! Who is the true master of this hallowed Srikshetra? The princeling is but a token; I alone am supreme. It is for this that the Navakalevara is being ordained. It is for this that the chariot's inauguration has taken shape.'

Behind Aminchand, the chamara bearers waved their fans rhythmically, as though saluting destiny.

Suddenly, Shendha Suara's muscles tensed as he

sprang forward, his intent clear: to seize Aminchand and hurl him into the waters of Narendra Pushkarini. His jaw clenched, his lips ground together. Then he froze, as though searing coals ignited against his skin.

Had Rajguru Gauri, in his avarice, so utterly smothered all sense of propriety?

How was it that when Talichha Mahapatra conferred the Khadi Prasad upon Bhagirathi Kumar and marked his brow with sandal paste, Rajguru then proceeded to offer the same prasad to Aminchand, anointing his forehead as well? Such a breach of sacred protocol amounted, in every sense, to a flagrant violation.

Yet, amidst all this turmoil, the Baseli settlement's people continued to shout their refrain like salt poured over a wound, 'Hail King Aminchand!'

Shendha Suara glowered, his eyes burning crimson as he fixed his gaze upon the stately vessel, uncertain now of what he might do. Sensing the rising tension, Bali Panda grasped him firmly and drew him back into the procession, saying, 'Come on, my friend! Is this spectacle drawing to a close? It has only just begun!'

Khadi Prasad was never meant for Naib Aminchand—such sanctity is bestowed solely upon true royal servitors. How, then, could Rajguru Gauri have committed so brazen a sacrilege?

Slowly, a hushed murmur began to ripple among the onlookers—a silent chorus of unuttered protest, as if the very air carried the weight of a grievance too profound to articulate.

*****

Chapter X

At the storied Lalbagh Fort in Cuttack—where not even a fly was permitted to trespass—the landed aristocrats and jagirdars, having journeyed from far-flung provinces to pay their respects to Naib Nazim Taqi Khan, now wandered the fort's courtyards, their steps marked by a befuddled sense of duty. At times, when a robust musahib or courtier in regal attire caught their discerning gaze, they would bow with long and formal salutations—offering phrases like *adaab arz* and compliments on his refined bearing—murmured softly behind a veil of hennaed trellises or rose clusters, all in hopes of eliciting a whisper of possibility: that, by fate's indulgence, an audience with the valiant Naib Nazim Bahadur might be secured.

With their beards tinged in rich mehndi and handkerchiefs delicately perfumed, the musahibs would respond with an almost unnerving gravity, remarking, 'We ourselves have not yet set foot in the *diwankhana*—let alone attended to others' accounts. Today, Naib Nazim Bahadur's temper is exceptionally fierce; an audience with him would be no mean feat!'

And yet, one could not help but ask—what, truly,

was unfolding within these walls? What strange and fevered excitement had seized the very air?

The entire state of Odisha lay under Mughal dominion and had sunk into an enforced hush—solemn and unyielding, like a charnel ground. Ramachandra Dev was nowhere to be found. In time, Bhagirathi Kumar would be anointed upon the Khurda throne, once the rites of Navakalevara had taken root. Meanwhile, Maharani Lalita Devi and Naib Aminchand, stationed in Puri, were quietly orchestrating the grand arrangement.

The chariot's inaugural ceremony proceeded flawlessly, imbued with untroubled merriment. What cause, then, remained for the naib nazim to fret? Why was his mood so obliquely troubled?

One jagirdar, having furtively pressed a gold ashrafi into the hand of a musahib, leaned close and murmured—almost as if to say—'Even if no formal audience is arranged, at least disclose what this unfolding affair truly is!' He ensured the whispered titbit would soon ripple among the jagirdars, zamindars, and supplicants, granting him the stature of one privy to the secret. Yet the matter was so classified that if even a single ear beyond one's own happened to hear it, the entire edifice of power might tremble. It was a secret to be guarded—and yet, if shared in murmurs, it could elevate one's prestige. Indeed, he could boast of being among Naib Nazim's inner circle; for in a realm where not even a fly was permitted entry, these men alone held the veiled reins of authority.

But what, truly, could that innocent musahib have grasped of all this? What hidden deliberations were unfolding behind the veiled doors of the Diwankhana? The fort's governor, Musharif-e-Khas and his loyal officers, visibly perturbed, fluttered about—unsure whether their orders were being rigorously obeyed beyond the fortress walls. The moment their gaze fell upon a musahib or jagirdar wandering the garden or the perfumed Gulistan, they lunged forward, eager to demonstrate their prowess. The master of the fort was a man of absolute accountability—indeed, who else could wield such sovereign authority? From the central gateway beside the Sadar Phatak to the resounding halls of the Nahabatkhana, vigilance was unbroken at every turn. And yet—how had these men come to be gathered here? What rationale, if any? The musahibs might be pardoned seven indiscretions, but how these persistent aristocrats and jagirdars infiltrated the precinct by bribing the musahibs was hardly a secret to the governor. Upon discovery, they were compelled to part with a few ashrafis to placate him. Better, perhaps, to slip behind a cluster of henna or roses and escape his piercing gaze.

'What is the matter? Speak up, Khan Saheb! Why does the fort today teem with such austere watchfulness?'

Would one dare offer him a bribe on any other day, when even now—a gold ashrafi placed discreetly into his palm—no reply came forth with haste?

'The matter is exceedingly delicate—utterly confidential, indeed. But now that you ask, I may share a trifle. Nobles and ministers have arrived from Murshidabad itself, dispatched by Nawab Motaman-ul-Mulk Shuja-ud-Daula Asad Jang. You grasp, surely, the gravity of their presence? At this very moment, they are seated in secret counsel within the Diwankhana—nothing more, nothing less.'

The musahib knew little beyond these sparse hints—and he carried his own bitter regret, for he had never enjoyed the honour of spending even a single day in the intimate inner court of the naib nazim. With a downcast air and tentative steps, clad in a tailored achkan, he set off in search of another familiar zamindar—one he hoped might secure for him another two ashrafi concessions.

For the assembled jagirdars and zamindars, even this shred of gossip was treasure enough. The one who possessed it would readily trumpet his knowledge before others—each of whom, envious and intrigued, would assume that he alone stood among Naib Nazim Bahadur's trusted confidantes. After all, how else could he be aware of Murshidabad's emissaries, sent directly by the Nawab himself?

But what, after all, was the deeper truth at hand?

It seemed that for most of these zamindars, their very sense of worth was measured solely by their inclusion in the naib nazim's court.

In the shadowed grounds of Lalbagh—beneath the cool, dense canopy of towering deodars—dozens of commoners sat like silent effigies. Rugged, weary, hungry, and parched, their faces bore the imprint of toil and suffering. Perhaps they had gathered to lament their oppression and plead for justice. For in the days when Shuja Khan held the mantle of naib nazim, the gates of the Diwan-e-Aam stood open—a sanctuary even for the humblest soul. Today, those plaintive eyes once more sought entry, slipping a sweet into the hands of the guards, desperate to lay their petition before the throne.

But they could not, unlike their aristocratic counterparts, afford the currency of persuasion—gold ashrafis. At the sight of them, the fort's governor roared, 'Away with them! Who allowed this rabble into the courtyard?'

A few guards, brandishing sticks and spears, surged forward to drive them away—but found, soon enough, that resistance was needless. Sensing danger in the air, the petitioners scattered like startled sparrows. To these guards—merciless by temperament, and known to snarl like beasts at the merest change in weather—the lives of the ragged, famished subjects held no weight. Perhaps those fugitives had come bearing grievances of extortion or violence at the hands of the landed elite, yet such complaints had grown into routine under the Mughal yoke. Why trouble the naib nazim's court with afflictions so familiar, so tediously common?

The fort's governor, Musharif-e-Khas, peered into the inner chamber of the Diwan-e-Aam. On ordinary days, this hall would resonate with the voices of trusted nobles, amirs, umraos, qazis, jagirdars, zamindars, courtesans and musicians—the lively strains of sarangi and tabla mingling with the courteous chatter of attendants. Clad in finely pressed pyjamas and vivid, patterned caps, the khidmatgars, holding peacock feathers as if they were treasured emblems, would stand behind the courtiers on ornate floor coverings like living statues. Other aides circulated glasses filled with wine and sherbet among the councillors and esteemed guests. At a raised dais, upon an intricately woven carpet layered with embroidered cushions, sat Naib Nazim Taqi Khan himself—a figure of flesh and refinement—with his skullcap reclined backwards, adorned by shimmering golden brocade and glittering jewels. Candles and chandeliers suspended from the ceiling lent their light to the hall in a festive, resplendent display, while hookah-bearers presented golden-leaf pipes to rest gently beside Taqi Khan's lips, and the fragrance of Ambari tobacco wove its heady spell through the air.

Yet today the hall was utterly transformed—paralyzed by a heavy, ominous silence. Not even a fly stirred in the Diwankhana. The candles trembled in the breeze, colliding softly as the atmosphere itself seemed to quiver with subdued restlessness. Today, an unmistakable air of melancholy, grave and lifeless, had descended upon the space.

On the plush carpet, the floor covered with a pristine white sheet, lay scattered cushions like fallen soldiers on a ruined battlefield. Behind Taqi Khan's dais, two stalwart guards, spears in hand, stood in silent vigil, their uniforms tightly cinched from waist to shoulder, secured as if protecting the very honour of the fortress. In the hazy half-light, the polished *patka*—sashed from cummerbund to shoulder in a diagonal arc—gleamed with quiet precision, its shimmer a lingering echo of order amid encroaching disarray.

In the common quarters of the Diwan-e-Aam, reclining upon sumptuous cushions, Padmanabh Dev had been lulled into a fitful doze amidst the hush of bolsters and carpet. For him, the gates of Lalbagh remained ever ajar—a silent gesture of enduring allegiance.

'Salam alaykum, Raja Saheb!'

Startled, Padmanabh Dev awoke with a jolt, his doze shattered in an instant. Clutching the hookah hose that he still cradled in his lap between his lips, he seemed as if he might speak at any moment of his mounting concern.

'Assalaam alaykum!'

Musharif-e-Khas leaned in and said in a low, hushed murmur, 'Today, no discourse shall take place with Naib Nazim Huzoor. Why, then, do you persist in waiting idly?'

Padmanabh Dev's response trembled with urgency, 'There was a matter of the utmost importance, Musharif-e-Khas Saheb!'

But was it truly so? Has the Motaman-ul-Mulk descended upon his deathbed? Attaullah Khan and Manikchand had, time and again, whispered the same secret in clandestine tones—but still Taqi Khan found it hard to believe. In these latter days of the Mughal court, where ambition so relentlessly overreaches that a man can scarcely trust even his own shadow, how could one possibly commit to the news of Shuja Khan's final hour?

Indeed, to poison trust is simply another word for politics. Here, human connection, devotion, and compassion are rendered as counterfeit coins—mere folly. To confront one's enemy with a drawn sword is valour; yet such valour, in this age, is no longer politics. When one displays bravery, there is always the risk of losing one's head—but to sever one's head while laughing is the very art of political capability. And if that severed head belongs to one's dearest, most vulnerable, true confidant, so much the better—they must fall first, for they alone know where your true weaknesses lie, where your secret wounds remain hidden.

Otherwise, consider this: after the death of Murshid Quli Khan, when Sharfaraj Khan was to ascend to the throne in Murshidabad, why did Shuja Khan in the Chehel Sotoun Palace raise his sword against his own son, Sharfaraj? Had Murshid Quli's widow, Begum Nausheri Banu, not been present, surely someone must have been struck down by the sword, whether it was father or son. In that tumultuous scramble for power, neither father nor son recognized the other; both, blinded by their ambition, became prey to the ruthless game.

This, indeed, is the politics of capability!

There is no father, no son, no brother, no kin—only blood and sword. To place one's trust or faith in another is sheer folly.

So what occupied Taqi Khan's mind at this moment? He ought to be departing for Murshidabad without delay.

As he ambled along, Taqi Khan suddenly stopped. Turning toward Attaullah, he inquired in a low, measured tone, 'Tell me, is Motamman-ul-Mulk Shuja-ud-Daula truly gravely ill?'

Attaullah's inner irritation mounted with each repetition of this question, as if he silently cursed the endless need to answer, questioning whether Taqi Khan did not believe his words. Suppressing his vexation within, his mehndi-tinted beard and his perfumed handkerchief— whirling about his balding crown in a manner as graceful as it was pensive—led him to reply, 'The state of Motamman-ul-Mulk Shuja-ud-Daula remains as mentioned. Otherwise, why else would Haji Muhammad Sa'ab and Jagat Seth dispatch us with such news?'

Taqi Khan continued, his tone laden with reminiscence, 'I had recently set out for Murshidabad during Zilqad. At that time, Motamman-ul-Mulk had already begun to appear quite ailing. When he spoke, his voice would tremble and his breath catch in his throat—he would even gasp. He could say little beyond this: 'Not one single coin of Odisha's ten lakhs ever finds its way into the treasury! Over here in Shahjahanabad, Delhi repeatedly demands peshkash—the heart finds no repose... Yet, in merely two months, his condition has worsened so drastically. I cannot bring myself to believe it!'

Meanwhile, Padmanabh Dev still waited in the Diwan-e-Aam—a space where, if he were ever granted a private audience with the naib nazim, he would be poised to deliver news of extraordinary import. Today, he had brought yet another 'special' report for him. Although his gaze has always been benevolent, news of this nature was remarkable indeed. In the Mughal court, there was no dearth of hushed intrigues; if such tidings were to secure the Khurda throne, it would be nothing short of miraculous.

'No matter how essential the news might be, when it comes from the direct command of the naib nazim, no one may ever hope for an audience. The Diwan-e-Khas remains sealed off—even to the musahibs, his most intimate confidants. They claim that the indispensable news has come from Murshidabad courtesy of Haji Muhammad's nephew, Attaullah Khan, and Jagat Seth's grandson Manikchand. The influence and prestige of Haji Muhammad and Jagat Seth Fatehchand in the Murshidabad court are no secret to anyone; they are, in effect, the right hand and the left hand of Motamman-ul-Mulk Shuja-ud-Daula Asad Jung. Understand then, the gravity of the situation!'

Padmanabh Dev knew the matter was indeed dire. Surely, even those serving the regime must have heard whispers of this—but what exactly was happening? No one seemed to have learned the whole story. Padmanabh Dev fancied himself no less astute than Taqi Khan, though whispers often dismissed him as a monarch of meagre endowment. Still, Ambition burned hot, and eyes were fixed intently on the Khurda throne. Should the opportunity arise, how soon might Bhagirathi Kumar be reduced to a mere Shishupala—duped, dismissed, undone by destiny? For that, he needed a complete and unvarnished account of all that transpired between Murshidabad and Cuttack!

Padmanabh Dev then, ever dutifully, asked in a subdued tone, 'But what news stirring in the hidden recesses of Lalbagh could elude the eye of the Musharif-e-Khas?'

With a voice heavy with helpless resignation, he answered, 'Only Khudah, the Almighty, knows. Even I am forbidden to enter the Diwan-e-Khas. Forget about the khadims and khidmatgars—no common woman is permitted to enter the Diwan-e-Khas today, for it is strictly decreed by Naib Nazim Bahadur; otherwise, news of this would leak out.'

Yet Padmanabh Dev did not surrender easily. He sank onto one of the regal cushions and drifted off to an uneasy sleep. Alas, today Padmanabh Dev was so utterly neglected—there wasn't even a khidmatgar to fan him.

Inside the Diwan-e-Khas, upon the richly adorned floor with its plush cushions and scattered with embroidered sheets, only Attaullah Khan and Manikchand remained among the esteemed guests—there was no third companion. Outside, two groups of lashkars maintained a strict vigil, and entry was barred to all. On the sumptuous carpet, Naib Nazim Taqi Khan, with his obese frame, now wandered with a weighty gravity, burdened by his anxious thoughts. Today, there was no dance nor music; the courtesan appeared despondent, and in one quiet corner, the tabla, the sarangi, and the tanpura lay abandoned like clay pots discarded after a funeral. A profound and heavy silence had enshrouded the assembly. There was neither a tabla player nor a sarangi maestro, nor even a master of the tanpura—and the ghungroo tinkling at the feet of the mujrewali hung in mute suspension.

There was no bustle in the mehfil; the issue at hand was all too grave. Whether on this side or the other, a decisive verdict was imminent.

After a long, heavy silence, Manikchand broke his calm detachment and remarked, 'What power have we over the will of Khudah?'

Yet again, with a hint of resignation, Taqi Khan asked, 'So then… maut bichhavan—the deathbed—is a certainty? Are the final moments approaching for Motamman-ul-Mulk?'

Taqi Khan repeated his question again and again, as though his repeated inquiries might finally dispel his doubts. He wondered silently—did some strife lie hidden beneath all these machinations?

Attaullah Khan then spoke, 'By Allah Ta'ala's benevolence, may Motamman-ul-Mulk persevere for a few more days. That is what the physicians say. Even the firangi physicians have observed him many times, but he does not trust their remedies. He fears they might have mixed poison into his medicine! In a few more days, as he languishes on his deathbed, his retribution shall be exacted… his illness is nothing more than the ravages of old age!'

Taqi Khan spoke with urgent intensity, 'Are the government's reins now held by Sharfaraj? Has Sharfaraj gained dominion over Bengal, Bihar, and Odisha?' His voice trembled with the weight of his own claim on the Murshidabad throne—a right which, in his eyes, was equally sacrosanct.

Attaullah Khan replied gravely, 'When Motamman-ul-Mulk was in robust health, governance was wielded by Haji Ahmad Sa'ab, Fatehchand, and Rai Rayyan Alamchand. They continue in their roles to this day. Yet the true power—the key, so to speak—is clenched within Sharfaraj Khan's fist. Not solely his own, but that of Lutaf Ali, Mir Murtaza, and Mardan Ali, who have fashioned Sharfaraj into a mere instrument, keeping the real key firmly in their grasp. Indeed, while royal decrees are still sometimes issued bearing the mark of Motamman-ul-Mulk Shuja-ud-Daula, there are occasions when even those come directly from the grip of Sharfaraj's hand.

In truth, the rightful heir to the *masnad* of Murshidabad was none other than Sharfaraj. His mother, the oft-neglected Jeenat Begum—daughter of Murshid Quli Khan—had long cloaked her ambitions in the garb of piety, trailing rosaries and ritual garlands in a theatre of devotion, all the while circling Shuja Khan's deathbed like fate in a vulture's disguise, awaiting the waning breath of Motaman-ul-Mulk.In a trembling tone, Shuja Khan barely managed to whisper, 'Jeenat… you have borne so many transgressions against your soul. Will you forgive me, so that in these final hours I may find even a semblance of peace?'

His voice was faint, barely audible over the low murmur of the hall. The lamp's flame still flickered, and a solitary candle burned quietly—a silent witness as evening had long succumbed to dusk. Nearby, upon an intricately carved ivory Qur'an stand—fetched at a princely sum from

Mecca by Shuja Khan himself—the holy text rested in silent dignity. A Maulvi had recited its verses only moments earlier. Now, in the dimming hush of inevitability, the sacred book stood as Shuja Khan's final refuge—a solitary bastion of faith amid his gathering fate.

Yet Begum Jeenat remained mute, her heart hardened by years of neglect and injustice. Bitterness clung to her heart like venom. How could she now forgive Shuja Khan's failings? With a strained, almost theatrical sorrow, she lifted the draped Maslin over her head and spoke through tears, 'You are my fate—this world and the next. By Allah's grace, may you swiftly recover.' Two solitary tears glistened upon Shuja Khan's pallid brow—tokens of sorrow veiled in ritual. But as if conjured by some hidden fire, from within the deep folds of her shawl, Jeenat's sunken eyes blazed—like those of a famished tigress, cloaked in devotion yet kindled by venomous resolve. Through the lattice of the window, a scattering of semi-dried tresses, like ripened tufts of Kasha blossoms, fluttered across Jeenat Begum's furrowed brow, dancing gently in the night breeze.

A slave girl tiptoed in to deliver a message, 'Haji Sa'ab is awaiting Motamman-ul-Mulk's presence.'

Shuja Khan, his voice barely above a whisper, replied, 'Send him my regards.'

But Jeenat's voice rang out in protest, 'No... no—Motamman-ul-Mulk's condition is exceedingly fragile today. Let Haji Sa'ab come tomorrow.' *Haji Muhammad! Haji Muhammad! You conspirators! Your very presence here—your endless scheming—is meant solely to salvage my feeble-minded Shuja Khan. Otherwise, where would the remnants of marital accord be found?*

Her face furrowed with hardened resolve.

It was Haji Muhammad, Jagat Seth Fatehchand, Rai Rayyan Alamchand—the entire cabal—who had conspired against Jeenat Begum herself, plotting to deprive Sharfaraz, son of her very womb, of his rightful claim to the *masnad* of Murshidabad. Each were complicit in the treachery. Yet Jeenat had stood firm, resolved to resist them to her final breath—for so long as she lived, they would not succeed.

In a voice laden with melancholy, Shuja Khan murmured, 'Sharfaraj! Sharfaraj!'

His every word dripped with regret—how callously had he disregarded his own son? His instincts, however minute, now scolded him. In these final moments, with Allah as his witness, he conceded that the throne of Murshidabad could never remain secure in Sharfaraj's weak hands. He was indolent, capricious—and the very nobles of Murshidabad opposed him.

Once, Murshid Quli Khan had cradled his only daughter Jeenat's son, Sharfaraj, with tender affection, dreaming of the day he would be crowned Nawab of Murshidabad. Yet now, that cherished love had warped into a bitter curse upon the boy's destiny. The cupbearers, the musicians, the dancers—all had swept him into their lavish indulgence. Even now, his harem teemed with a thousand and a half attendants. How, then, could the throne of Murshidabad ever be secure in the grasp of such a feeble man? How might his son, Sharfaraj, ever ascend to become Nawab of Murshidabad? And what of him—how might he ever transform himself into the naib nazim or minister governing Bengal, Bihar or Odisha?

Had Murshid Quli not wronged Shuja Khan?

Shuja Khan, tilting his head askew, fixed his gaze on Jeenat and, in a frail voice, murmured, 'Water… water… I am so parched, Jeenat… where is Sharfaraj?'

Without hesitation, Jeenat offered a flawlessly rehearsed lie, 'He arrived some time ago—but at that moment, Motamman-ul-Mulk was drowsy, and he left. I have told him to return later.'

'Sharfaraj!'

The name died on his lips, heavy with unsaid longing. Now, surely, Sharfaraj must have been indulging himself somewhere—conspiring with self-serving friends, perhaps plotting to whisk away a fair lady from a respectable home in Murshidabad. His irresponsible, unbridled behaviour had turned him into poison in everyone's eyes. Taking a deep, trembling breath, Shuja Khan repeated, 'Sharfaraj!'

The father lay feebly upon his deathbed—was the son not stirred to see him, even for a moment? And yet, had Shuja not spared him even the slightest neglect!

Begum Jeenat, too, waited every moment for Sharfaraj. In these desperate times, even if filial piety failed, the hope of a rightful claim to the throne demanded that Sharfaraj come to Shuja Khan.

'But where was Sharfaraj?'

Inwardly, Jeenat simmered with bitter knowing—when the root is poisoned, the fruit cannot flourish.

Shuja Khan lay still, his eyes dim and vacant, his body inert upon the bed; his mind lucid though his limbs betrayed him. He understood it all too well: he was held captive by the converging will of Jeenat and Sharfaraz. The keys to the governorship of Murshidabad lay firmly in their grasp. Shuja Khan was no fool—for the perceptive, even a single breath of intent suffices.

Taqi Khan wandered through the Diwan-e-Khas, his face etched with worry. In a pensive tone, he spoke: 'So, the key to the Murshidabad throne has slipped into Sharfaraj's grasp. What use is there now in setting out for Murshidabad? Yet that does not mean I hold no claim to the throne. I did not attain the title of Odisha's naib nazim through the sympathy or benevolence of Motamman-ul-Mulk—I earned it through the strength of my own arms: first as a faujdar, then as a diwan, and finally as naib nazim. But for now, venturing there would only ignite a fratricidal conflict. And if such strife were to be kindled during Motamman-ul-Mulk's lifetime, it would not reflect well in the eyes of the influential amirs, umraos, and the people.'

Indeed, meeting with Shuja Khan now would be contrary to Taqi Khan's interests. The last time he sought him out, he was not confined to bed, but his displeasure with him concerning the affairs of Odisha was unmistakable.

Shuja Khan had declared that not a single coin from Odisha had reached the treasury since Shri Jagannath vanished from the temple—and that the annual loss had climbed steadily to ten lakh rupees.

'Return Shri Jagannath to his abode, Taqi,' Shuja Khan exclaimed, his tone rising with fervour. 'When I was Odisha's naib nazim, in the days of Motamman-ul-Mulk Murshid Quli Khan, I had stepwells and caravanserais built along the Jagannath Road. Ram, Rahim, Allah, and Jagannath—they are one! You must recognize this truth. Because of Emperor Aurangzeb's religious fanaticism, the Mughal empire was doomed, and its Hindu subjects became adversaries. Yet it was the Hindus who, from Akbar to Shah Jahan, embodied the formidable strength of the Mughals! You have grievously mistreated the Hindu world by oppressing their adored deity, Shri Jagannath, Taqi!'

For the kafirs, Shuja Khan was exceedingly magnanimous. The Shia and the Sufi, though not lacking in their reverence and devotion toward the idol of the kafirs—Shri Jagannath—found little sympathy in Taqi Khan, for he was a staunch Sunni with an implacable contempt for the Sufis. He deemed it a sacred duty to eradicate the power of the kafirs. Yet even as the state lost a treasure of ten lakh rupees by not restoring Shri Jagannath, unrest and rebellion ignited in every corner of Odisha. It was only then that Taqi Khan consented to reinstall the sanctity of the Shri Jagannath temple in Puri. Were it not for the mounting unrest, he would have razed the temple to dust, just as he did the shrine of Baladevjew at Kendrapada.

Shri Jagannath, it seemed, had faded into oblivion. For the sake of his reinstitution, a new order—Navakalevara—was being arranged. Once that was complete, restoring Shri Jagannath to the temple and then proceeding to Murshidabad might yet prove beneficial. Otherwise, the moment any meeting took place, the old accusations would resurface, the same questions repeated, and bitter objections hurled: 'Odisha is ruined!'

In such circumstances, a journey to Murshidabad would offer no profit.

Upon rising, Attaullah Khan offered a sher—his voice woven with reflection.

Barbaad gulistan karna ho,
Ek hi ullu kaafi hai.

Har shaakh pe ullu baithe hain,
Na jaane gulistan kya hoga.

(To lay waste a garden, one owl would suffice. But now, with owls perched on every branch—who can say what fate awaits this ravaged grove?)

Then he interjected, 'Sharfaraj may serve as diwan in Bengal, but what are the conditions in Murshidabad? What state will prevail when the Nawabi throne of Murshidabad is secured? What use is it to squander time in vain debates? But mark this well—the first right to the Murshidabad throne is yours. Hence, Haji Muhammad and Jagat Seth have sent us to you. If you harbour discontent, then we must consider another course!'

'Another course?' Taqi Khan flashed like lightning, 'Who else could possibly stake a claim for the Murshidabad throne?'

'Why, none other than Alivardi Khan—the Naib Nazim of Bihar, Azimabad,' Manikchand replied calmly.

At these words, Taqi Khan's eyes began to shimmer, turning red like the outer peel of an onion—his excitement mounting with each passing moment. Bihar's Alivardi was yet another thorn—a rival not to be disregarded. Formerly known as Muhammad Ali, a musahib, he had once been supremely trusted as a courtier of Shuja Khan, who now hid behind a mask of courtesy, but beneath that façade was as cunning as he was duplicitous. After Murshid Quli's time had passed, the naib nazim of Bihar was removed, and under Shujauddin's designs, Muhammad Ali was made to ascend that throne. From that insidious musahib emerged Naib Alivardi Khan! Meanwhile, Shuja Khan's right hand,

Haji Muhammad, had been discreetly dispensing vast sums from his treasury to bolster Alivardi's army—and this very intelligence had reached Taqi Khan. Suddenly, the implication of such a military buildup became unsettling. What was Haji Muhammad's true design? It was hard to say—and all of this was but part of the calculated preparation for an intervention in the Murshidabad throne following Shuja Khan's downfall.

Taqi Khan asked, 'Why, in all this, is Alivardi Khan involved? How so?'

Attaullah Khan's reply was unambiguous: 'If you remain inactive and reluctant amid the contest for the Murshidabad throne, then Jeenat Begum's decree alone will not be enough to seat Sharfaraj upon it. Even if the River Bhagirathi turned to blood, Sharfaraj shall never govern Bengal, Bihar, and Odisha! If you do not consent, then it is Alivardi who shall prevail.'

It seemed as if it was not merely an immutable law, but a resolute determination. Attaullah's eyes flashed with fervour.

He had vowed never to forget, nor forgive, the disgrace brought upon him by Sharfaraj. He had sworn by Allah that one day he would avenge that affront—with blood and sword.

Taqi Khan himself was not yet prepared to raise his sword against Sharfaraj, but Alivardi's forces would!

Before Attaullah's very eyes, the self-sacrificing, tragically fallen body of Shabnam—beloved daughter of his own brother—had been laid lifeless upon the ground. It was a silent, defiant protest against the tyrannical Sharfaraj. On that dark day, Attaullah had pledged by Allah's name that he would exact retribution.

Even among Sharfaraj's cronies—those who prided themselves on whispering about which household boasted the most beautiful ladies—a hushed conversation ensued during a gathering. One murmured, 'You must have seen Shabnam—dewdrops—on the grass, oh Nawabzada? But did you ever notice its radiant sparkle in a woman's eyes?'

'Have you seen it, my friend? Where?'

'Why, at Attaullah's brother's, Bismillah's daughter—Shabnam!'

'But Bismillah is none other than Haji Muhammad Sa'ab's son-in-law, the brother of Attaullah Khan,' another musahib commented. 'Would it be easier to bring his daughter into the harem?'

Taking a swig from a muradabadi jar of wine poured into a cup, Sharfaraj declared, 'Send forth a message—I must go personally to Bismillah's mansion to see Shabnam. Dispatch word to Bismillah at once!'

Bismillah, upon receiving such disgracefully scandalous tidings, unsheathed his sword and hissed to one of Sharfaraj's aides, 'Tell Sharfaraj: let him lift the burqa and behold what will fall upon Bismillah Khan's corpse!'

What immense audacity! If such cruelty could be wrought upon the very family of Haji Ahmed, what hope remained for ordinary folk? Haji Muhammad was utterly struck dumb by this insolent exchange.

Meanwhile, Shuja Khan remained silent.

He had lost all power to restrain Sharfaraj from his misdeeds. Shuja Khan knew full well that Jeenat Begum had already bought the faujdars to her side with bribes. In Murshidabad, not even one soul dared oppose Sharfaraj's caprice—who, indeed, would have the courage?

Yet Bismillah's nerve was no less formidable. Sharfaraj's myriad 'friends'—those who used to whisper in his ears like sycophants—assured him, 'Will the diwans of Bengal not present their daughters to the aspiring Nawab of Murshidabad, Sharfaraj? After all, his harem already boasts many daughters of noble lineage.'

That very night, a band of horsemen and lashkars encircled Bismillah's mansion. Along the banks of the Bhagirathi, beneath a garden awash with tented hues, a tent was raised, and Sharfaraj waited in anticipation of Shabnam. 'If the cup may not grace the lips, then let the lips draw near and honour the cup—what transgression lies therein?' he declared.

'Bravo! Bravo!' cried the sycophantic musahibs, their voices dripping with borrowed conviction.

Three days and three nights passed. Yet the grand front door of Bismillah's mansion remained firmly closed. Should the troops now cry 'attack' and tear down the walls?

No! No!—Sharfaraj was a treasure-hunter of beauty, not a common brigand. There was no need for an assault— what beauty could be looted with a sword? Not a single voice rose in opposition to Sharfaraj's lawless indulgence, let alone dared to resist.

Haji Ahmed came to Begum Jeenat with his grievance. But what reply could she offer? Sharfaraj was no ordinary man—he was an unbridled steed, reckless and untethered. Her cool, steady grasp had long failed to rein him in. Within, a bitter flare rose: they were all lackeys in the service of Nawab Shuja Khan. And what worth did that man possess? Nothing, Jeenat thought. Sharfaraj's very blood ran tainted with Shuja's corruption, his lineage loathsome, his impulses unchecked. What other fruit could a poisonous tree bear? Yet it was in this very lawlessness that Jeenat found a strange, perverse vindication—for her own disgraced femininity, silenced and splintered, now mirrored in the disorder Sharfaraj sowed.

After long delays came the dark night. At last, the doors of Bismillah Khan's mansion swung open—and out stepped Shabnam in her burqa, alone. Along the banks of the Bhagirathi, under a tent where a candle burned with unwavering flame, Sharfaraj sat watching, his heart resolved: sooner or later, Shabnam would surely appear! Some moths, drawn to the flickering light, ignited and fell, perishing in their descent. Sharfaraj watched this interplay of allure and self-destruction with habitual rapture. The spell of beauty has ever been such that its irresistible invitation seems designed to set even the tiniest mote ablaze—what fulfilment there is in the blaze, what profound meaning achieved!

Suddenly, the current of his thoughts broke against an unseen rock. His breath hitched as surprise gripped him— who was this woman in the burqa at such an ungodly hour? Aside from her henna-tinted feet and the lush velvet of her turban, nothing else was discernible. A mystery cloaked in silence, she stood—unfathomable, unnamed.

'Who...?' Sharfaraj asked softly.

From behind the flowing burqa, a husky voice replied, 'Let the Nawabzada lift the veil with his sword—he may see, if he dares.'

Ah, whose utterance wove such dulcet enchantment— even the veena blushed at its own imperfection.

Sharfaraj raised the tip of his sword and pulled aside the drapery. In the candlelight, her eyes shimmered like those of a playful doe.

'Y–you… you… Shabnam!' he exclaimed in astonishment.

For a long, suspended moment, Shabnam said nothing. Her eyes remained unmoving, as if carved from stone. *You laid siege to Bismillah's mansion with your lashkars, all to glimpse me. And now? Has your hunger been sated at last?* she thought, the silence between them heavy with unspoken verdicts.

Gently, tracing a delicate finger beneath her eyes, Sharfaraj murmured, 'Yes, Shabnam—I saw it on the petal of a rose, on a tender sprout of grass! But never, ever in a woman's eyes, Shabnam…' His throat constricted with unspeakable emotion.

'Is that enough?' Shabnam asked in a calm, detached tone.

'But where does the thirsting heart find its fill, Shabnam?' he pleaded.

'Yet the capacity of the cup has its limit!'… Bismillah's lineage had been so deeply shamed—they could not endure any longer! Then, as if sealing a lover's kiss onto soft, supple lips, Shabnam pressed the diamond-studded ring on her right hand to her mouth.

Before Attaullah Khan's eyes, the lifeless body of Shabnam—his beloved niece—floated, stranded and still. And above it, as if inscribed in flames, a challenge blazed: *Will you be able to withstand this, Attaullah?*

Taqi Khan—who had been pacing the Diwan-e-Khas in anxious contemplation, uncertain whether setting forth for Murshidabad now was wise—could only watch with troubled heart.

Attaullah, with a note of weary resignation, said, 'Remaining here is fruitless—let us go, Manik!'

Yet opportunity itself seemed to slip away from Taqi Khan's grasp.

Taqi Khan announced, with authoritative resolve, 'In two days we shall set out for Murshidabad. Let both of you ride ahead of me.' After Attaullah and Manikchand took their leave from the Diwane-e-Khas, Taqi Khan called the faujdar and ordered, 'Make all the arrangements for the army. In precisely two days we depart for Murshidabad with no fewer than five thousand horsemen! The journey spans seven days, but we must cover it in three.'

Was this departure really for battle, or what?

'Meanwhile, the fort lords of Odisha and other prominent men are gathering around Hafiz Qadar, united in purpose. In our midst stood the Navakalevara—heralding the commencement of the *safar* in the month of Ashadha!'

'We have no concerns about the Navakalevara. By then, we shall have returned.'

With that, Taqi Khan dispatched the faujdar to prepare the camp.

Barely having drawn back the soft muslin curtains, Taqi Khan, as he advanced toward the palace, suddenly halted in astonishment. Beneath the dim light, a figure cloaked in a burqa—its form resembling an exquisite statue—appeared before him. Lo, how was Razia here, of all places?

'Dear sister, how have you come here?'

'Is it strange for a sister to visit a brother's house

at this hour?' Her doe-like eyes shimmered, brimming with unshed, innocent tears.

'But why, then, at such an untimely moment?' Could it be that Razia had gleaned the hushed confidences exchanged between Manikchand and Attaullah Khan? Had the tightly-held secret already begun to unravel—that five thousand cavalry were poised to thunder toward Murshidabad?

Taqi Khan asked with concern, 'Was no one stopped you?'

'Every door was guarded, but I managed to slip through bearing a dire message, dear brother! I beg you, arrange for my swift departure to Murshidabad!' Her weeping was nothing new—a performance of such tears had already won many favours from Taqi Khan.

Lowering her face into the folds of her burqa, she broke into muffled sobs.

'What happened? How did Murshidabad suddenly enter your mind?'

'It is father's final hour—I cannot bear the thought of not seeing him.' Her plea trembled with raw, aching emotion, silencing every doubt.

Taqi Khan pressed, 'But who gave you this news?'

'Two fakirs came from Murshidabad,' she murmured. 'They said Motamman-ul-Mulk Shuja-ud-Daula is in a precarious state of health.'

Fakirs and dervishes had long visited her, bearing fragments of news like drifting incense. For a soul such as hers—shaped by whispered sermons and a life steeped in religious discourse—this was the rarest, most sacred of tidings. After all, she had once been the beloved daughter of Shuja Khan.

Taqi Khan, his tone gentled by concern, said, 'I have been told that father's condition is serious—yet not as desperate as claimed. Attaullah Khan and Manikchand have come from Murshidabad, bearing news. Were the matter truly urgent, would they not have informed me at once? Still, Father is unwell. I assure you, when his final moments approach, I will make all necessary arrangements for your journey. For now, return to Barabati Fort.'

Razia did as she was told—but beneath the veil, her lips curled into a quiet smile.

To Ramachandra Dev, it was the golden juncture—where fate met ambition, and held its breath.

In Barabati Fort, two devoted fakirs sat in quiet vigil, intently reciting verses from the Qur'an.

*****

Chapter XI

The mind—a lush and yielding cow, breaks her leash at the faintest vow.

At the break of dawn, Shendha Suara and Bali Panda, joined by gymnasium companions and temple servitors, had already gathered on the steps of the sacred bathing platform—the Snanavedi—beating tambourines with fervent zeal. In those early hours, tongues were sharpened by purpose. Once the three altars received their mangalarpan (auspicious offerings), Madanmohan would ascend to the platform above. Meanwhile, nestled among those very steps, the bhang-sodden Shendha Suara lounged in giddy abandon.

Yet in the eyes of the Senior Parichha Rajguru Gauri, the scene struck a bitter note, as discordant as harsh music is to refined ears. Time and again, Pati Mahapatra had been admonished: 'At Snana Purnima, these servitors render no proper service at all. Why, at the break of day, have they gathered on the Snanavedi as if forming a wrestling arena?'

Even the Khuntias had repeatedly pressed the point: Rajguru Gauri was growing incensed. Why have you all been beating the tambourine since morning? Today is Snana Purnima…!'

'Go, go, O Khuntia! Your turn is second. Rajguru Gauri now presides as Mudirasta—strict and unyielding. But what kind of Snana Yatra is this? The deities dwell in the wilderness, in the nether realm. Which deity will ascend the Snanavedi in ceremonial *pahandi*? *The mind—a lush and yielding cow—breaks her leash at the faintest vow…*'

Indeed, the deities lay buried underground. On this Snana Purima, pilgrims would be denied the longed-for glimpse of the famed *hativesha*—the elephant guise they so revere.

Whether it symbolised the ancient Aryan steeds or stood as a marker of Buddhist philosophy, Shri Jagannath had long become the epicentre of a coordinated spiritual culture—a convergence so deeply woven that its origins had long been forgotten. Every year on Snana Purnima, throngs of pilgrims—numbering in the thousands, spanning the expanse of five kos—would flock to the bathing pavilion to behold the deities arrayed in *hativesha*. Many who had come to witness the Chandan Yatra at Shrikshetra even lingered until the Navakalevara. And though the fierce noon of Jyeshtha beat down relentlessly, a large crowd still gathered at Bada Danda— the Grand Road.

Ramachandra Dev, cloaked in disguise, stood apart from the gathering pilgrims, eyes fixed upon the empty Snanavedi. Having made the necessary arrangements here, he would soon set out for Banki, Ranapur, and Nuagarh. Yet the enthusiasm among the feudal lords, chieftains, fort lords and battalion leaders had not yet awakened. Would Mahabahu return to Ratnavedi once more? They regarded

Lalita Mahadevi's Navakalevara as a predestined decree—but if they withheld their complete support, it would not be easy to bring the deities safely from Tikali. Perhaps it might even be impossible!

Within the temple, among the servitors, two factions have emerged: a substantial portion, moved by the enticing influence of Rajguru Gauri, had favoured Aminchand, who had now fully immersed themselves in the sacred undertaking of the Navakalevara. Only a handful—Shendha Suara, Bali Panda among them—remained in quiet opposition. Nevertheless, to sway the public in their favour, both Naib Aminchand and Rajguru Gauri had maintained the natural, unbroken flow of every temple festival. After Chandan Yatra, the Snana Yatra stood as the principal festival. And once the deities entered Anasara—fourteen days secluded from view—the lingering notion of their subterranean retreat would fade from the public's imagination, clearing the way for the Netrotsava.

Meanwhile, the charge to marshal the servitors against this unfolding intrigue fell to Paschim Kabat Mahapatra. Had even a single earnest conversation occurred before the journey to Tikali, Ramachandra Dev would have found full assurance—he would surely have discerned the temper of the servitor ranks. Yet Paschim Kabat remained cloistered within the sanctum, and any meeting with him proved all but impossible.

While the deities remained in concealment, *hativesha* would not take place this year. Rumours of Paschim Kabat's clandestine manoeuvres to obstruct the festival had already reached Aminchand. Had something been enacted against him?

There was no recourse but to wait. With troubled eyes, Ramachandra Dev gazed toward the Snanavedi, lost in thought: 'Mahabahu, when shall your hallowed presence once again sanctify the silent throne?'

The tolling of bells and gongs was soon heard throughout the temple, and mangalarpan commenced. As custom dictated, now the deities were to make their ascent upon the Snana Mandap in *dhadi pahandi*. Yet the deities were absent! Only Madanmohan would be enthroned upon the vedi by the Mahajana Brahmins. In beholding Madanmohan, the devotees' long-cherished dream of viewing the deities in their *hativesha*—the vision of an actual festival—would at last be fulfilled.

With his sacred cane swaying vigorously, Chhamu Khuntia had, time and again, bellowed at Shendha Suara and Bali Panda, 'We shall have Madanmohan enthroned by the Mahajanas! Why do you all sit idly upon these steps, indulging in frivolous pastime?'

As Chhamu Khuntia swung the cane with fierce determination, Shendha Suara, Bali Panda, and their fellow wrestlers pounded their tambourine with equal vigour, echoing his chant in their deep, guttural voices: *The mind—a lush and yielding cow…*

At length, even the eminent Rajguru Gauri was compelled to appear, arriving with a golden cane in hand—a symbol of his unassailable authority in the temple's sacred regulations. Raising the golden cane high above his head, he roared, 'Do you not all hear the clarion call of the Khuntias chanting "Manima…Manima?" The Mahajanas are in the midst of enthroning Madanmohan. The deities have already ascended to their sanctified level—the seventh step! And yet you linger here in irreverent play, mocking sanctity upon these hallowed stairs!'

Yet the chant—*The mind—a lush and yielding cow...*'—rose from his throat with renewed ferocity.

Such insolence—a flagrant disregard for the very power these men were meant to command—this, Rajguru Gauri could not abide. He had already discerned that, in the prelude set by Paschim Kabat Mahapatra, these unruly servitors were eager to spark conflict at every turn.

A Mudirasta by title, a priest by tradition—yet among the people, he had become a mere caricature, mocked and defied! In these troubled times of the Navakalevara, who knows what further mischief they might contrive?

Enraged, Rajguru Gauri cried out, 'Are your ears as hard as stone?'

In response, Shendha Suara stepped forward, muscles taut with indignation. 'Come, Madanmohan—the idols that await are but moving deities! Recently installed, they now stand in the rear row behind the Black God. But the Black God himself is absent—he has gone into concealment. How, then, shall Madanmohan alone be enthroned upon the Snanavedi?'

This argument was irrefutable. Yet, at this moment, it was not merely a matter of logic—it is an order of supremacy, a testament to raw might. In a voice that carried to every ear, Rajguru Gauri solemnly proclaimed, 'The deities have not vanished into hiding! In the temple's *darugriha*, their new forms are being constructed. Today, it is only Madanmohan who will ascend the Snanavedi.'

'But Madanmohan is a recent addition to the pantheon—joined to Shri Jagannath only later through the Vaishnava tradition. Today, it is the *hativesha* of the gods that draws pilgrims in throngs to the Bada Danda—not Madanmohan alone. If the *hativesha* is absent, why mislead the devotees by installing Madanmohan upon the Snanavedi?'

Rajguru Gauri's eyes flared with fury—he knew the meaning of this defiance. 'Who are you to question such matters?' In a fit of blazing anger, he struck Shendha Suara on the forehead with the golden cane.

A sharp stream of blood gushed from Shendha Suara's brow. He made no attempt to stem the flow or dab it away with a towel—he simply fixed his gaze upon Rajguru, his resolve unbroken despite the wound. For one who cared little for life, what was a few drops of blood? Let him please Naib Aminchand with a couple more lashings if needed be! But who among them could silence Shendha Suara now? What was Madanmohan to do in the midst of the sacred Snana Yatra? Were the pilgrims scorching under the sun to witness them, or to behold the gods in their *hativesha*?

Bali Panda, seizing his tambourine with both hands, raised it aloft and bellowed, 'Bloodshed! Bloodshed!' Today, the Snanavedi should have been cleansed with eight pitchers of camphor-water! Yet it is stained with the blood of Shendha Suara. From the very cane of Rajguru—Aminchand's nefarious lackey—blood was spilt!'

On Bada Danda, before the Snanavedi, a resounding murmur swept among the gathered pilgrims: 'Bloodshed! Bloodshed! A terrible ill omen!'

Some of the akhada wrestlers, muscles taut and arms bared, readied themselves to attack Rajguru Gauri. With a fierce bellow, Nokani Panda thundered, 'Blood pours from Shendha Suara's brow? I'll set your senses straight!'

Nokani Panda was truly a man of the arena—once his fury ascended, it was nearly impossible to rein it in.

In response, Shendha Suara swept him into his embrace and murmured, 'You'll soon sully your hands if you continue. Leave him be—his time is yet to come. Greatness lies not in the act of slaying, but in the endurance to bear. You dishonour your rank by unleashing force upon these lowly keepers. Only the revered Lord will understand!'

With the demeanour of a condemned man, Rajguru Gauri lowered his head and, like a guilty criminal, turned away toward the sanctum. Striking Shendha Suara to make him bleed was deemed unseemly—he now felt the act had crossed a line. The temple drums, once thunderous, fell into sudden silence.

The temple servitors took their positions—it was now impossible for Madanmohan to ascend the Snanavedi. The sanctum required purification—his presence was impossible while blood defiled the ritual.

Among the pilgrims, voices rose in an agitated murmur: 'Bloodshed at the Snanavedi! Is this not a dire, ominous sign? The deities dwell in realms afar—how could Madanmohan ever come to the vedi? Did Shendha Suara utter anything vile?'

The fervour swelled, gathering dangerous momentum. Should the pilgrims breach the sanctum, an assault on Aminchand would no longer be unthinkable. In every mind, one thought rang clear—he was the architect of this desecration.

Ramachandra Dev, standing amidst the swirling

crowd, beheld the impassioned scene with a mix of bewilderment and solemn duty. Deep in his heart, he felt a quiet reassurance: this people were not yet defeated; their spirit of resistance remained unbroken, and their intrinsic discernment of right and wrong had not ceased.

From that avid gathering, Paschim Kabat Vishnu Mahapatra emerged, seized Ramachandra Dev by the arm, and said, 'You must depart at once, Maharaj! Matters here are growing increasingly grave—I shall see to the unfolding events here!'

The pitiless noon of Jyeshtha!

Under a sky barren of clouds, fire rained down from above. Beneath, fatigued earth shimmered like a blue mirage. With his left palm, Ramachandra Dev wiped away the rivulets of sweat cascading from his brow. His horse was spent, and Athagarh still lay far ahead… His body began to shudder with thirst on this road, devoid of water and shade—a path that stoked an insatiable yearning. 'O Shri Jagannath, why must life's initiation be so unrelentingly harsh?'

After the calamity on Snana Purnima, Ramachandra Dev had left Puri behind. Today was Anasara Dwadashi. He recalled how Talichha Mahapatra and Padhani, accompanied by resounding bells, gongs, trumpets and parasols, would commute to the king's palace with as many silver platters as there were members in the royal household. There, the saree once graced by the king's touch would be bestowed upon the Daita, Pati Mahapatra, Swain Mahapatra, Tadhau Patnaik, Deula Karan, and Talichha Mahapatra. This was the rite of Anasara Dwadashi. Perhaps Anasara is itself a symbol—a confluence of the Shabara or feral aspect of Shri Jagannath with Brahmanical culture. In some primordial age, did not Indradyumna, in his quest for Jagannath, drape a saree about every seeker's head? Could this be the memorial of that very moment?

But today… the path was long, barren of shade and water, and choked with dust.

There were only a few days remaining until Shrigundicha or Rath Yatra. Had he not wasted time in Banki and Ranapur, he would have reached Athagarh by now. Surely, Lakshmi Paramaguru must be awaiting his presence for a meeting. Yet no one seemed to know why a message was dispatched from Athagarh; even the paika bearing Paramaguru's note could offer nothing further.

That very day in the battle of Chhatradwar Valley, when the kings of Banki, Ranapur and Nayagarh had risked their very lives to aid him, deeper treachery unfurled. In Chhatradwar, in a moment of base betrayal, Baxi Benu Bhramarabara turned traitor, while Lalita Devi conspired with Taqi Khan. Ramachandra Dev found himself trapped and imprisoned in an iron cage, amidst which the trust among the fort lords had all but vanished. A clandestine intrigue was afoot. All waited, wondering where fortune would flow like water; above all, Taqi Khan's terror was shattering their resolve.

And yet, in the midst of that fearsome gloom, stalwarts like Shendha Suara and Bali Panda emerged, steadying Ramachandra Dev's wavering heart. Before his very eyes, the vision of the sacred Snanavedi floated into being—Shendha Suara's defiant, unyielding spirit vividly on display as blood streamed inexorably from his brow before the humbled Rajguru Gauri. Bali Panda roared out, 'Bloodshed! Bloodshed!' while the subdued, anxious murmur of the pilgrims echoed this call.

Ramachandra Dev spurred his exhausted horse with a determined kick to its flank. The beast surged forward, sending up a billowing cloud of scorching dust beneath the blazing sun.

In Banki, King Shrichandan declared openly, 'A traitor within is worse than a thousand Ravaṇas. Whom shall you rally, Maharaj, against the might of the Mughals? Were we not your comrades during the battle at Chhatradwar?'

'This was the old tale from the era of the Ramayana. Had there been no internal foes, how could the Pathan and Mughal invaders have subjugated this land? But I do not claim the throne of Khurda, Shrichandan! If I am destined to fall, I shall not bemoan or regret it. Bhagirathi Kunwar is the rightful heir to the Khurda throne. Let him, with valour, recline upon the royal seat, let Mahabahu return to the silent temple—and once more, may the land of Utkal be free!' Thus Ramachandra Dev repeated his earnest words, echoing among the fort lords and chieftains. Some had pledged their full support; others had chosen to evade; still others had explicitly refused to confront the Mughals—arguing that endless resistance had worn them down. For spirit alone cannot sustain a people. 'Look at the paikas—their bellies empty, wages withheld, fields barren… Chhamun! They no longer possess the strength to combat. Please stop aimlessly drifting through a fog of despair.'

Yet, at length, Shrichandan offered his reassurance: 'When war breaks out during the return of Mahabahu from Tikali—if Taqi Khan's troops dare to raise their hands to bind him in leather straps once more—then the paikas of

Banki will fight them, spilling their last drop of blood. Just observe what others say.'

Somewhat buoyed by those words, Ramachandra Dev made his way to Ranapur. There, the local chieftain, Dhananjay Deo, too, seemed reluctant to appear openly. How can one feud with a crocodile whose lair is in water? A nation cannot hope to survive on morale alone—life demands both strength of arm and the wealth to sustain it. Throughout every village, the prophetic *Malika* now spread the dire prediction, "The Mughals shall devour Utkal's wealth," and with each recitation, the collective resolve crumbled a little more.

'Will Utkal ever be free? Chhamun, you flail ineffectually amidst this fog!' came the bitter refrain.

In a weary, studied tone, Ramachandra Dev repeated those well-worn words again and again, 'Whether Utkal remains independent or not, let Mahabahu return to Shrimandir. While the Mahabrahma still abides, the three *daru* blocks shall be drawn forth and installed upon the Ratna Simhasana by Naib Aminchand—and yet, the *mahadaru* shall forever lie abandoned in the dark stronghold! Such a thing will never be possible!'

The pronouncement was inviolable. Dhananjay vowed, 'From Kalupada to Tangi, amid the clusters of bamboo, our paikas from Cuttack will contain Taqi Khan's forces. Let us have tidings from Ganjagarh. Mansingh of Ganja, alas, sits too comfortably in the lap of Maluda's Faujdar.'

'But we shall not be able to bring Lord Jagannath on the Cuttack-Chikakol Road, Dhananjay,' Ramachandra Dev warned. 'Bringing the deities that way would invite a rear attack by the faujdar of Chikakol. With Taqi Khan pressing ahead and the Chikakol faujdar dogging their steps from behind, our forces are sure to be crushed in a pincer movement.'

Before Ramachandra Dev's eyes, the familiar scene of Chhatradwar swam unbidden.

'Then?' Dhananjay murmured.

Should he reveal to Dhananjay the very route of the gods' return? But in these uncertain times, whom could one trust?

Ramachandra Dev answered gravely, 'Keep your paikas armed in the stretch between Kalupada and Sunakhala. The fort lords of Kuhudi and Tangi will assume responsibility over that sector. On the day of Netrotsava, it is certain that Mahabahu will arrive at Shrikshetra. From today onward, keep your paikas at the ready—the month of Jyeshtha is already halfway spent.'

At Nayagarh, the local chieftain Mandhata echoed the same sentiment.

Among the feudal chiefs and fort lords, there was a constant tug-of-war between conflicting 'yes' and 'no'—an indecision that haunted their hearts. Yet, among the paika villages and common folk, Ramachandra Dev had kindled a new hope: a vision that, emerging from the vast wilderness, Mahabahu would return to claim the Ratna Simhasana; their barren hearts would, at long last, be filled. After a protracted night, they would witness the sunrise of a new dawn.

In numerous villages, however, the pilgrim agents dispatched by Lalita Devi to herald the Navakalevara had scarcely managed to spread their message—many were barred from entry altogether.

'Remember,' some cried, 'the deities have retreated time and again in the face of Mughal onslaughts, only to return once more to the Ratna Simhasana! What sort of Navakalevara is this? The gods are coming back. The throne of emptiness will be complete. And while the deities still walk among us, you plan to lay them to eternal rest—you wretched miscreants!'

Though no formal summons had come from their commanders, across the villages, paikas gathered before the shrine of their village deity—engaging in playful skirmishes and swordplay. In hushed tones, the stirring strains of the Kavach Bandhan hymn began to ripple through the air.

> Southward, I kneel where Vimala reigns in glory,
> At Badabada, her service is famed and unshaken.
> Hold high the banner of her mighty chieftain.
> In battle, let him conquer and guard the realm!

Utkal was the realm of Shri Jagannath. He would return to that exalted, vacant throne—and how could the paikas ever remain silent then?

The passionate fervour of the masses had both enchanted and bewildered Ramachandra Dev. For Shri Jagannath was no aloof deity; instead, he was an intimate companion, a member of their very inner circle—a national guardian. Once exiled, he was now returning among his people. In every direction, joyful anticipation festoons the air with celebratory welcomes.

Mahabahu was coming back.

Who had spread such news in every quarter? Who had stirred such tremors in every heart? Each time Ramachandra

Dev pondered this riddle, he became ever more entangled in its trickery. Deep inside, he wondered—how did one man's whisper ripple into mass belief? Who could ever unravel this mystery? Perhaps only he—enthroned within the heart's sanctum—could trace its elusive thread. Everywhere in Odisha, the anxious refrain rang out: 'Mahabahu shall return! Mahabahu!' The clamour to inaugurate the Navakalevara appeared to be nothing more than a ruckus—a puppet show contrived by Naib Aminchand and Lalita Devi.

The horse's pace was noticeably slowing.

Along the sunbaked path of life, beside the roadside stood a sal tree whose broad, tender leaves draped like a soft shawl—an echo of verdant memories from ages past. Beneath its cool, soothing shade, Ramachandra Dev paused to give the weary horse a moment's rest. He patted its neck time and again. The animal, as if understanding the intimate silence of the gesture, seemed to say that this journey—bereft of shelter, water, or true respite—was merciless. Yet, now was not the time to falter. The horse scratched at the dry earth with its hooves. Foam now lapped from its mouth, a silent testament to its thirst.

Then, urging the horse onward in search of water, Ramachandra Dev pressed forward. His throat, too, grew parched, drying with each heartbeat. The narrow trail wound through a thick, tangled forest of brush, past groves of bamboo—before emerging onto a rough, stony road that stretched away into the distance. The oppressive heat recalled the lingering sultriness of the Anasara days! It felt as if an invisible hand clutched his very neck, the relentless glare of the sun compressing him from all sides. Oh… where had the doves gone on this sweltering afternoon—he mused, for not even their gentle cooing could break the spell of this languid, numbed midday—a day as solitary as it was scorching.

His eyes were not deceived, though—could this be the fabled Brahmarakshasa? A spirit? A phantom? Tales of such monstrous beings emerging on desolate afternoons had once haunted his childhood. Now they seemed to leap and bound in the heat. Rubbing his eyes, Ramachandra Dev peered into the shimmering haze. No clear form stood before him; he had never witnessed a man towering eight or ten hands high, and then the figure reappeared, advancing in long, measured strides. Perhaps it was only a trick of the light, an illusion conjured by the dense, tangled forest. But then, where did that elusive shape flee from the path, vanishing into the deep woods? And why, indeed?

Somewhere nearby, the horse suddenly caught a scent—a hint of water—and let out a sharp whinny. Its cry sent a shiver through the woodland floor. In the distance, like a dark, sinuous outline resembling the lashes of a watchful eye folded into dream's hush—a shadow, serpentine and subtle—emerged along the boundary of the forest. There, a waterfall flowed, its cascade carving a cool passage along the grove-lined banks. It reminded him of that tender, pleading gaze of the young paika bride in Malakuda village as he beckoned for water on a blazing day. In the maelstrom of life's ceaseless struggle, that visage of hope may have once taken wing, but still, the gentle cascade flowed on as though poured from her clay vessel. As if those mournful eyes, it seemed, now took shape along this secluded forest path.

Ramachandra Dev dismounted. He washed his hands and face, drank deeply to quench his thirst, and then offered water to his horse. The exhausted animal, its eyes lowered in contented repose beneath the cool shade, stood still for a moment—it, too, needed rest. Ramachandra Dev had set forth from Nayagarh at dawn without so much as a pause, and it was now clear that reaching Athagarh before nightfall was a distant hope. Weary himself, he leaned against a sturdy sal tree. In the gentle murmur of the waterfall, he heard the sweet cadence of sleep's lullaby. And yet, even with his eyes lowered in exhaustion, true respite remained elusive.

No sooner had his eyes closed than an oppressive question stirred in his heart: Why had Lakshmi Paramaguru so urgently sent word that he must reach Athagarh without delay? Why now? Had the feudal lords of Mahuri or Khalikot withheld their cooperation? Or had some other difficulty emerged—perhaps the faujdar of Chikakol had at last uncovered a vital clue? Paramaguru had further conveyed that someone, having journeyed from Barabati in Cuttack, had now reached Athagarh, bearing tidings from Razia itself. Yet what those tidings entailed remained veiled in uncertainty. And was Taqi Khan summoning arms beneath the old banner once more?

Trouble crept into Ramachandra Dev's thoughts as the steady clatter of his horse's hooves shattered his drowsiness. Opening his eyes, he scanned his surroundings with fresh alertness. There it was again—the towering silhouette he had glimpsed before in the tangled depths of the jungle, looming eight to ten hands high, now seemed to cling to a sal tree by the waterfall, wearing *ranpa*—two wooden legs—elevated in such a way that one might alight upon them and appear impossibly tall. Its rippling muscles tensed under loose trousers, its body bore scattered markings like splashes on canvas, and atop its head rested a turban, from beneath which dishevelled locks fell, clinging damply with sweat. *Oh... in this guise, I nearly mistook him for a Brahmarakshasa!* A quiet smile flickered through him. The man paused as if to sip from the modest pool of water, then reclined into the cool refuge beneath the tree's shade by the cascade, silently murmuring, 'Ugh, this heat!'

He had embarked from Kamagarh at daybreak, only to be met with a barren landscape—no water in sight. Evening would find him at Ratagarh. His mission was simple—deliver the *shiali* knot to the chieftain of Ratagarh. From Kamagadh to Ratagarh, from village to village among the paikas, the *shiali* knot was passed along like a secret token. In the effort to forge a unified nation, the chieftains would extol bold words of oneness while the paikas, binding *ranpa* around their limbs, circulate the *shiali* knot—be it from one chieftain to another or even to feudal lords. Its emblematic message was clear: *We too are ready.* Thus, from one village to the next, a silent proclamation of impending rebellion—or even full-scale war—would be unfurled in the ancient, time-honoured manner of the paika army.

The paika, unfastening the *shiali* creeper from around his waist, carefully counted the knots already tied. It seemed that since morning, he had traversed an expanse equivalent to fourteen kos. From Ratagarh, another paika would be dispatched by the chieftain—that was the pact.

Suddenly, amid the hush of wilderness, a human voice startled him.

Ramachandra Dev called out, 'Who are you? In this searing heat, where are you headed? How far have you come?'

The man had traversed fourteen kos on wooden

legs—what was this stranger's intent? Could he be aligned with Maharani Lalita Devi?

Ramachandra Dev suspected the man was indeed a paika. In times of tumult, one would seldom travel so far unless necessity demanded. When the country teetered on the cusp of unity, the *shiali* knot would circulate as a herald. He surmised something momentous lay on the horizon; after these long days of silence, a storm was bound to arise—but from which quarter? Could it be from the camp of Lalita Devi?

The paika gave no reply, studying Ramachandra Dev with silent caution.

Glancing toward Ramachandra Dev, the man too harboured private thoughts—he mused that divulging secret matters in the company of an unknown stranger was unseemly. Who could tell if the man before him was aligned with the Mughals? Spies, he knew, were scattered in every corner of their ranks. Yet, in these days when the nation stood united, what was there to fear? The *shiali* knot sailed quietly from village to village; now, what could trouble them? Let the lurking spies, and the Mughals learn their tidings—that Mahabahu was returning to the vacant throne. This so-called Navakalevara, he thought wryly, was nothing more than a puppet play contrived by Lalita Devi and Naib Aminchand. Otherwise, how could Mahabahu appear in dreams to the exiled Maharaja and ask how he might grant him samadhi, when he yet abides?

At length, the paika answered, 'Are you a spy, perhaps? Well then, why fear? Listen—this Navakalevara that Maharani Lalita Devi is orchestrating is merely a puppet show. Mahabahu is indeed returning to the vacant throne!'

Ramachandra Dev's tired eyes suddenly flared with unexpected zeal as he demanded, 'How did you come by this knowledge?'

What a naive soul was this! he thought. How could a man—privy to the very gossip known even to the rustic women of Odisha, and, as a horseman, not privy to such critical news—keep such valuable intelligence? He seemed every bit a chieftain or a feudal lord, with scruffy beard and alert eyes that gave him away. But did he not keep this news guarded, or was this a game? A decoy meant to draw truth from him? Let it be. What's the use of fear now? You birth sons by the roadside, then cower at witches?

The paika continued, 'You know nothing. The Maharaj is now somewhere in exile. One night, in a dream, Mahabahu spoke to him: "I am veiled in secrecy. While I dwell among you, are you not giving me samadhi and ushering in a Navakalevara? I am returning to my Ratna Simhasana." At that very moment, the Maharaj was alone at the chowpadhi of the chieftain of Bhaunriagarh, amid a night so desolate it scarcely had a sound.'

The Paika gathered his breath.

How astonishing! The genesis of these sub-stories, these legends—they do not merely rule over facts. Rather, they weave a tapestry of poetry and imagination, an intricate web of dreams. Yet beneath their delicate allure lies a fragile essence of truth that touches the common heart with inexplicable depth. A truth so profound, it outlives the scaffolding of history itself.

Ramachandra Dev found himself utterly spellbound.

In a rambling, impassioned tone, the paika went on, 'At that very moment, the Maharaj's slumber shattered like fragile glass—while a lamp burned upon the altar, not a soul stirred in the depths. And how had that garland of fresh dayana blossoms come to rest at Maharaj's head as he slept?'

'By the gods,' Ramachandra Dev exclaimed, 'it is told that the Maharaj, having uttered the Kalma, was wed to the *yavani* queen. He is a *mleccha*, and you claim the Lord himself granted him vision?'

'Tell me, master,' the paika inquired, 'whom do you call a *mleccha*? A man is never *mleccha* in his conduct, but only in his thoughts. Otherwise, would the *yavana* Salabega or the untouchable Dasia Bauri—the crazed one—be counted among the foremost devotees of Lord Jagannath? Would the Lord himself receive offerings from Dasia's modest bowl? Whether he stands as the Maharaj or recites the Kalma, he remains but the sole servitor of Mahabahu.'

'And what of Lalita Devi? Of Naib Aminchand?'

'*Mleccha*—they are *mlecchas*, in the true sense!' At his loud cry, the lonely woodland trembled, as if in response. 'For would they ever orchestrate the practice of consigning the deities to eternal samadhi while yet alive, dancing to the paltry refrain of the Mughals?'

Ramachandra Dev gazed at the paika in rapt wonder. These very souls were the indomitable, indestructible spirit of a suffering Utkal. In them resided pure thought, an unclouded, detached vision, boundless patience, and infinite endurance! Amid all the downfalls of eras and the ever-changing winds of fate, it was they alone who had safeguarded Utkal.

As the paika's words tumbled on in their incoherence, Ramachandra Dev's curiosity deepened.

'And then?' he pressed.

'Then—what more could there be?' the paika replied. The Maharaj left his bed and stepped out. The night thundered overhead, and in the sky, two shining lights appeared. But these were no ordinary stars—they were the very celestial, rounded eyes of Mahabahu. The Maharaj was astounded.'

Reflecting on how legends, spun from one soul's imagination, can among the people morph into a truth even mightier than truth itself, Ramachandra Dev was filled with silent wonder. Whose fancy had birthed such marvels? Never before had he seen such twin lights in Bhaunriagarh, nor found a fresh garland of dayana flowers at his head. And yet, on every tongue, this tale had grown to be truth beyond truth.

'Then ...' Ramachandra Dev's voice resonated with deep inquisitiveness.

'Closing his eyes, the Maharaj resolved in meditation, "O mighty-armed one! Mahabahu—where shall I seek you? How shall I begin the search? Where have you concealed yourself? How can I possibly search for you?" From the vast silence, a voice answered, "In each era I have veiled myself thus! King Indradyumna once built a temple here with a thousand Ashvamedha sacrifices in his attempt to draw me forth—yet could he ever capture me? Could I be found in the temple of Indradyumna, when my dwelling lies far beyond in the humble hovels of the Shabaras? I am not to be discovered in mantras or sacrifice. I reside only in love—in tenderness and devotion. Indradyumna allied with the Sabara king, and so I revealed myself. And then Indradyumna sought a boon that none among his descendants should ever live to claim me as their own!'

'But why? This very Suryavanshi king—Indradyumna—who raised the Shrivatsa Khandashala temple in honour of Mahabahu, he sought a boon to be without heirs?'

'Had Indradyumna left behind heirs, they would have claimed Shri Jagannath Mahabahu as their own deity—one not born of the Bhils or the Shabars. In him, the Aryan Indradyumna and the Shabar are united as one indivisible incarnation! He is not merely Aryan, nor utterly non-Aryan.'

'And then?' Ramachandra Dev's curiosity only deepened.

'The Maharaj, with a humble plea in his tone, said, "What trial has Mahabahu set me?" Again, a heavenly voice answered, "Only Indradyumna? Once, Kanchiraj Ratnagreev journeyed from the south to seek my darshan. He, too, performed his thousand-Ashvamedha rites, yet my darshan eluded him. Once more, I veiled myself in secrecy. This ritual, this homa, is the custom of the Aryan Brahmins—but I am not found in the yajna or homa. I exist instead in the heart, in the very breath of life. Ratnagreev fasted for five days and five nights—hungry and parched—and then I granted him my darshan. From the attack of the *yavana* Raktabahu to that of the *mleccha* invaders, I have hidden myself time and again. And each time I revealed myself anew, in fresh form and with renewed sentiment. I was once *mahadaru*, then transformed into the Trimurti, and later into the Chaturdha Murti! I shall also bestow my darshan upon you in my Chaturdha Murti. I find no greater solace than remaining ensconced in the wilderness instead of dwelling in the Shrivatsa Khandashala temple. But now, the onus lies upon you—so that I may never again be bound by the *mlecchas*' leather ropes."'

Silence fell from the void.

'Then?' asked Ramachandra Dev.

What fertile imagination could give birth to such a tale? Yet on every tongue, this blossomed into a legend—a truth that now outshone the ancient canon of history.

'Then... don't you see? The *shiali* knot is being passed along!'

'But why?' came the inquiry.

'From one chowpadhi to the next, the chieftains pass along the *shiali* knot to hold back the *yavanas*.'

'Will this not herald a mighty unity across our land?'

'Yes—unity, or something that resembles it. The feudal lords and chieftains will gather the paikas and position them between Khurda and Purushottam. And should the Mughals dare once more to strike against Mahabahu, the answer will be written—not in words, but in action. A decisive clash awaits—and the resulting bond may be called unity, or whatever you choose to name it.'

Ramachandra Dev then asked, 'But in Purushottam, Lalita Devi and Naib Aminchand are orchestrating the Navakalevara. Once it is consummated, the crown shall pass to Kumar, the rightful king. And here you are, passing on the *shiali* knot.'

The paika glanced around furtively. The ceaseless chirping of crickets and the soft cooing of pigeons deepened the stillness of the wilderness. Meanwhile, the horse stamped restlessly on the parched earth—as if hammering against the oppressive silence.

Should he reveal all these matters to an unknown rider? Who could say which side he belonged to? Perhaps he was a spy—yet if he was, what harm lay in speaking plainly? The very news that now echoed from one household to another throughout Utkal—the word resounding along every road—must not be withheld, even from a stranger, regardless of his affiliation.

'Tell it to someone, will you?' the paika dared. 'If the story spreads, you'll be branded a traitor to Shri Jagannath. There will be no Navakalevara—no, it simply cannot happen. If our living deity remains among us, then by what decree can a Navakalevara ever be proclaimed?'

'Beyond the grove, following the ritual severance of the *darus*, preparations for the renewal of the divine forms are already underway within the temple's hallowed *darugriha*.'

'Whence do you come? Are you not one of the Odia people?' The paika marvelled at the man's utter ignorance.

'I am from Mugalbandi and I am bound for Athagarh—to serve among the king's cavalry. But what is it that has transpired?' Ramachandra Dev inquired, his curiosity tinged with a hint of mischief.

'Mahabahu appeared once more in the Maharaj's dream, proclaiming that on the sacred day of Netrotsava, he would come forth to grace the Ratna Simhasana. Then, how could the Navakalevara be ordained? Speak of this to none—let it remain concealed.'

How many unknown souls had heard this and vowed never to utter it again? Their number knew no bounds. Mahabahu shall return—the message was spread without restraint. The openness, yet the steadfastness of their hearts, was remarkable! Their loyalty was absolute, their resolve unshaken. And with regret, Ramachandra Dev acknowledged that he was the jewelled crown of countless such starved paikas. Though his body—half-starved, its strength all but broken—was wearied by hardship, his mind was replenished by this thought. Even amid penury, their spirit remained indomitable. Fields lay barren, homes crumbled, wages had been withheld for years by the chieftains—who, after all, had little coin to dispense. And yet, their life force was unconquerable. They had vowed their all for the liberation of Utkal, for the honour of Shri Jagannath. This was the unconquerable soul of Utkal.

The paika, turning restlessly on his side, eventually dozed off with his arm for support. Bhaunria from here spanned perhaps a couple of kos; When the sun's blaze softened, he would once more fasten the *ranpa* around his feet and begin his journey.

Yet Athagarh lay far beyond. Whether Ramachandra Dev would reach Athagarh before dusk remained uncertain. After quenching his thirst with pure water from the waterfall, he remounted his horse. Together, they crossed the stream below the cascade, and the horse trotted away, leaving a billowing cloud of reddish dust behind.

There was still some time before sunset. In the forested valley of the hills, dusk descended like liquid darkness, interspersed with sporadic glimmers of light. The heavy, warm breath of the woods rendered the twilight almost oppressive. In the west, the looming shadow of the Ghumsur mountain range signalled the imminent arrival of night, while in the east, over the wooded hills between Banapur and Athagarh, the last golden rays of the afternoon clung desperately. Athagarh lay but two or three kos away—there was hope of reaching it before sunset.

On that desolate forest road, suddenly a figure

on horseback emerged from the front. It was as if this horseman, too, was in a hurry to find refuge before nightfall. In the fading sunlight, his crisp pyjamas, intricately woven fine jacket, and the turban atop his head marked him unmistakably as a Mughal royal. How then did Taqi Khan receive word of preparations for Mahabahu's return from Tikali? Sooner or later, news must reach him. For Mahabahu would not venture into Shrimandir in the dead of night like a wily rogue. Conflict was inevitable. War was certain. Ramachandra Dev, along with the fort lords, the chieftains, and the feudatory chiefs, had been preparing for this inescapable struggle for countless days. This, indeed, would be Utkal's final liberation battle! Mahabahu himself—the symbol of that quest for freedom, the commander of the campaign—would lead the charge... So why, upon seeing this Mughal horseman, did Ramachandra Dev suddenly find himself stricken with terror?

Suddenly, Ramachandra Dev cried out in a resounding voice, 'Jai Shri Jagannath!'

Some pigeons took flight into the deep darkness of the forest, their wings streaked with the riotous colours of sunbeams that were sinking upon them—a vivid splash of light on feathers. Life itself seemed a grand jest. How strange that in this quiet, velvety moment, he must once more unsheathe a sword thirsty for blood!

Ramachandra Dev had drawn his sword, ready to strike at the mysterious horseman. In response, the rider too quickly drew his blade from his belt—a flourish of swaying ornamentation—meeting Ramachandra Dev's weapon with his own, and then burst into a wild, almost maniacal laugh.

At the instant of recognition, Ramachandra Dev

cried out, 'Oh! Mir Habib Saheb! You are here! I never expected our paths to cross in this manner.'

Never in his wildest imaginings had Ramachandra Dev expected to encounter Mir Habib in this forested expanse between Athagarh and Banapur.

Mir Habib calmly sheathed his sword and remarked, 'You drew your sword with such immediacy!'

'Recognizing you from afar was never easy,' Ramachandra Dev replied. 'Who knows—perhaps you are one of Naib Nazim's spies?'

'Then?' came the prompt.

'Then in this desolation, nothing more remarkable could present itself than a head rolling about,' Ramachandra Dev answered, though he added, 'But Mir Saheb, what brings you here so suddenly? This is hardly the Chikakol-Cuttack thoroughfare; you surely could not be returning from Chikakol. So tell me—has Naib Nazim Taqi Khan dispatched you to monitor our movements?'

Ramachandra Dev could not be entirely convinced by such speculation. At Barabati in Cuttack, Mir Habib was known as Taqi Khan's indirect rival—no less a formidable foe. His gaze was also fixed upon the throne of Naib Nazim in Cuttack.

'You're right to suspect,' Mir Habib replied. 'But I was not sent by the Naib Nazim; I was dispatched by Razia Begum.'

'Razia?' Ramachandra Dev's weary eyes suddenly sparkled with astonishment.

'Indeed,' Mir Habib continued. 'I have little time for idle chatter. In Utkal, with the kind of unity that is gathering, it is unsafe for any Mughal faujdar or subedar to travel alone by day. I must reach Khurda by nightfall. Absorb everything from Razia Begum's letter… For if Lakshmi Paramaguru had not been present at Athagarh, I would have been languishing in confinement under Jagadev's orders!'

'But how did you learn I was to be found in Athagarh?'

'Do remember—Naib Nazim's spies are every bit as deft and discerning as yourself. That is why Razia's stern command demanded that this letter be placed in your hands by mine alone. In Ranapur, Banki, Nayagarh—I combed every corner until I reached Athagarh. The moment word spread of my arrival, two of Jagadev's paikas seized me. It was only my old ties with Lakshmi Paramaguru that saved me... Never before have I felt such a breath of unity stir through Utkal.'

There were many rumours, and numerous counsels had been exchanged. In this treacherous strife, Mir Habib too stood to profit—a quiet, encouraging force. But there was no time to lose. By then, the sun had already sunk behind the dense Ghumsur mountain range, leaving the western sky a vast ocean of blood!

Pulling a letter from his belt, Mir Habib advanced toward Ramachandra Dev. With eager anticipation, Ramachandra Dev unfolded the letter—a few lines written in Persian: 'This is a golden opportunity for you—perhaps one that shall not come again. The Naib Nazim has marched to Murshidabad with five thousand horsemen. There, for the sake of the *masnad,* a civil war will break out. In Cuttack, they number scarcely three thousand cavalry and two thousand infantry; your forces can easily seize them.'

This letter could not be false—it bore Razia Begum's

signature and the unmistakable stamp of her seal. There was no cause for doubt. Mir Habib, after all, was Ramachandra Dev's sole well-wisher in Barabati, Cuttack—a friend loyal to Taqi Khan and had been working covertly to unseat the Naib Nazim. His behind-the-scenes ties with Ramachandra Dev were strong indeed.

A surge of fervour filled every fibre of Ramachandra Dev's being. What a golden opportunity indeed!

'Khuda Hafiz…' Mir Habib called as he spurred his horse toward his destination. Ramachandra Dev shouted after him, 'I shall never forget your kindness, Mir Saheb!'

By the time Ramachandra Dev reached the gates of Athagarh Palace, dusk had descended in full. As his horse climbed the slope toward the gateway, two guards stepped forward to block his passage. On either side of the Singhadwar, torches burned steadily, casting flickering light into the deepening gloom. In the blur of shadows, it was nearly impossible to discern familiar faces—yet his voice, refined and unmistakable, was enough to confirm who he was.

'Open the door!'

That command, so ingrained in his voice, brooked no refusal. The guards, well accustomed to obeying his orders, swung the door open immediately. Ramachandra Dev spurred his horse onward and rode briskly inside.

Night had fallen long past.

In the nageshwar garden of the palace, on a low verandah, Jagadev and Ramachandra Dev sat together. On other evenings, this very spot would resound with musical gatherings—a delight for Jagadev, a connoisseur of melody. But tonight, there was neither festivity nor company. By the glow of oil lamps, Ramachandra Dev appeared restless and troubled, while Jagadev's full lips curved into an enigmatic smile. Yet, was this a time for mere merriment?

Ramachandra Dev spoke with urgency, 'You know the state of affairs well, Jagadev! Today is Anasara Panchami—The Phulari ritual is upon us! Even in the absence of the divine, the authorities would have planned to accomplish the customary rites, including anointing all three altars with sesame oil and choa camphor, and crowning each with a garland of fresh dayana flowers. We have merely eight to ten days left to Nabajoubana Darshan. It will take no more than four days to bring the deities from Tikali to the Srikshetra, once they are seated in the chariots. The Khurda route is safe; yet from there to Pipili, we must brace for fierce resistance. Word is that Taqi Khan presently commands five thousand horsemen and three thousand foot soldiers at Murshidabad. Even so, breaking through the Mughal forces in Cuttack to reach Puri will not be an easy task. Every moment now is priceless. So tell me—why have you summoned me from Athagarh in vain?'

No answer came from Jagadev. His lips bore only a mysterious, secretive smile. But surely, this was no time for levity? Exasperated, Ramachandra Dev pressed, 'Why do you remain so silent, Jagadev?'

In his eyes shimmered a playful, quiet resolve, and Ramachandra's restlessness grew. After casually brushing some stray locks from his square brow, Jagadev replied, 'Will you be delayed if you wait until dawn? Surely, you find shelter at night somewhere!'

'But this was not my path. From Nayagarh, I would have journeyed directly to Mahuri, then Kashimpeta, onward to Ramagiri—and only then to Tikali! Last time at Tikali, during battle, Vijay Raju of Rajamahendri and Harihara Vishwasray of Jayantgarh betrayed us at the final hour! Yet Raju and Bahubalendra of Kashimpeta had honoured their vows completely. This time, from Tikali to Mahuri, they are our principal allies. I rely heavily on the support of the valiant Khond battalion of Kashimpeta. I would have set forth regardless of the night and darkness. I have no wish to squander time idly here.'

With a gentle, knowing smile, Jagadev said, 'Lakshmi Paramaguru will provide the answer. At his command, I have dispatched a messenger. Otherwise, I had never even contemplated you. Paramaguru will disclose all you seek.'

Ramachandra Dev countered, 'But let not the evening worship of the Paramaguru leave my patience exhausted. If this is merely an empty jest, then I have no need for respite—for even in this darkness, I shall find the path to Tikali with ease.'

Jagadev answered firmly, 'Maharaj, bringing you here for idle laughter is neither within my courage nor my power! Remember how, before the Mughal tumult— in the aftermath of the Raghnathpur battle—our council was held at Barunei Fort to devise measures to safeguard Mahabahu. That very day, with Pitambara Mangaraj of Kuradamalla and Shatrughna Dalganjan of Champagarh present, I declared: should the Mughals again reach Srikshetra, then until Mughal rule subsists in Utkal, Mahabahu must be left entirely within the sanctuary's care. Others had protested, but you remained silent—I took it as your consent.'

'And what of that?' Ramachandra Dev asked in a tone of quiet puzzlement.

Jagadev responded, 'Wait until morning; you shall then find a solution to this quandary.'

Unable to bear any longer the weight of the unsolved puzzle—and eager to extinguish his mounting anxiety—Ramachandra Dev, restless and irritable, began pacing under the pavilion. In the evening breeze, the rich fragrance of the nageshwar grove filled the air—a scent that, after countless ages, now hinted at a long-awaited union. The soft, marble-like murmur of leaves stirred the promise of an impending rapprochement.

Moved beyond measure, Ramachandra Dev's heart swelled with emotion.

'Ah! Razia!' he murmured inwardly, as if in a sacred echo reverberating within his very being.

In such fragile moments, as the last rays of twilight faded, before his eyes would float the inexpressible sorrow of Razia—a pair of eyes so deep and unfathomable that no visible anguish could ever seem to find the right path to express itself. Tears gathered like pearls upon silken eyelashes.

It was notoriously circulated throughout Odisha, across village courtyards and royal halls, that in the tender embrace of Razia's love, Maharaja Ramachandra Dev forsook his dharma. But what was it about such ardent attraction—a passion born out of countless subtle appeals—that transformed mere fondness into an all-consuming devotion? Razia had bewitched him; to deny that enchantment would only be to deceive oneself. Yet it was not merely the allure of the flesh, but the pull of the heart toward Razia that captivated him. In the lonely struggle for life, she was not just a fellow soldier in time but his faithful spiritual companion. No wonder his soul was restless for her; in moments like these, the painful separation from Razia would promise an immortal reunion. Perhaps it was for that very reason that she would approach so earnestly into the desolate chamber of his heart at these solitary hours.

By his feet, a single nageshwar flower fell.

Absent-mindedly, Ramachandra Dev stooped to pick up the flower—and with that small act, the overwhelming emotion of moments before seemed to be momentarily severed. He was quickly drawn back into the bitter reality surrounding him. *Oh! The dawn is still so far off—indeed, it feels endlessly distant.*

He now found himself amid the dense bamboo forest between Banapur and Athagarh—a cool, verdant wood far removed from any settlement, stretching from Khalikot in the east to Ghumsur in the west.

Arriving at the edge of the forest, Jagadev dismounted and said, 'Let's descend here, Maharaj! There is no safe route for horses through these thickets of thorny bushes.'

Ramachandra Dev remarked wryly, 'Not even an ant could traverse these brambles. Yet tell me, what purpose compels you to bring me into such a tangled forest?'

Jagadev's lips played that mysterious smile again. On another day, Ramachandra Dev might have delighted in the vibrant, wild chorus of this rugged woodland bathed in the golden glow of dawn. But now, everything about the forest filled him with pain. Jagadev remained silent.

Was there even time to waste another moment? Only yesterday had been the day of the Phulari rituals, and today was Anasara Shashthi. How many days remained in their grasp?

Surveying a modest settlement, Ramachandra Dev inquired, 'This village seems newly established—its people appear to be architects and sculptors. From where, amidst this forest, have these settlers—the artisans—emerged?'

Jagadev answered, 'Come, we are far overdue. This village has been named Mathura! I have settled it by granting the craftsmen from Puri and Bhubaneswar ample work and land.'

'Is a temple to rise here?' asked Ramachandra Dev.

'Come along…' Jagadev trailed off. Since yesterday, he had been dancing around such questions; every inquiry only met with an enigmatic smile upon his lips.

Was it a dream—or truth?

Ramachandra Dev could scarcely believe his eyes.

Deep within that dense forest stood a temple, its edifice constructed of khandolite and spotted limestone, soaring to nearly thirty hands in height. It was almost unbelievable that such a sight could be real!

In that age, the hereditary guilds of architects from the Bhubaneswar–Konark era had vanished. Their time-honoured traditions and masterful craft had dimmed into memory. Konark stood as the last flickering flame of Utkalian architecture and sculpture. Thus, although this temple bore no trace of the Bhubaneswar–Konark stylistic idiom, it had been built in accordance with the classical canons of sacred construction. Above the Padmapidha—the lotus-petaled base—rose the jangha or thigh of the temple, from which the walls ascended to nearly twelve hands. Above these, three-tiered cornices crowned the elevation, yet they remained uncarved. No radiance had been etched into its stone—its bones held silence.

Ramachandra Dev beheld the temple with wide, astonished eyes. Jagadev then explained, 'On the day Mahabahu journeyed to Tikali, the cornerstone of this temple was laid. The builders were brought in, and a new settlement was established. Khandolite stones were hauled from the Nayagarh hills. It was vowed that the temple would be completed within a year. Consequently, all the tiers remain plain—they could not be further carved with intricate brilliance.'

'Which is why, even the *kalash* atop the spire, and the crowing dome remain unrealized,' Ramachandra Dev commented softly.

Jagadev gazed raptly at his own creation and said, 'There is no particular style, no refined craftsmanship, no deliberate artistry here—only the spontaneous outpouring of a devoted inner essence. The artisans have toiled day and night to create this; one could scarcely believe it without witnessing it firsthand.'

Yet the temple's architecture did bear the subtle touch of artistry. Its facade was framed by seventeen pillars—each one a testament to delicate, intricate workmanship.

'But why build such a temple amidst this tangled mass of thorny bamboos? In whose eyes is this edifice meant to be seen?'

Jagadev replied, 'Do you remember well the day I spoke, when, as the deities were being transported to Chilika from the Barunei-Cuttack Palace, I had declared that should the Mughals once again launch an attack against Mahabahu, I would transfer them en masse from Puri to the remote wilderness. You thought that was merely a passing thought—yet it was my resolute vow.'

Within the temple, near the Ratnavedi, Lakshmi Paramaguru had already instituted the consecration rites and commenced the homa, following the prescribed method. Jagadev beckoned, 'Please come forth; the oblation has begun.'

In that instant, Ramachandra Dev grasped the solemn weight of his summons to Athagarh. As Lakshmi Paramaguru, with deliberate intonation and with ghee offerings, recited the sacred hymns, the surrounding woodland seemed to resound with divine echoes:

Prathamam shuklavarnabham sharadendu samabhramam
Araktaksham mahakayam phata vikatamastakam
Dvitiyam pundarikaksham kalajimuta sannibham
Atasi pushpa sankasham padma patrayatekshanam
Tritiyam svarnavarnabham padmatrayatakshena
Vichitra vastra samchhanna harekayurabhushitam.

Around the sacrificial altar, artisans stood in silent attendance, their heads adorned with freshly draped sarees. Ramachandra Dev, overcome by a sense of disquiet, found himself unable to muster the courage to approach the Ratnavedi. Even amid the familiar assembly at the *jagamohana*, he felt the hesitancy of a man unworthy of partaking in such a sacred offering. In his heart, he wondered, would his presence be deemed appropriate during such an auspicious rite? In the eyes of the people, he feared he had strayed from dharma, the sacred path.

Stepping quietly outside, Ramachandra Dev looked upon the temple spire bathed in the faint gold of early sun and asked, 'What do you mean, Jagadev? Having come from Tikali, do you propose that the deities shall remain here?'

Jagadev answered gently, 'That is precisely why this

ceremony is being held. And yet, I know full well that you would never grant your blessing for it.'

Ramachandra Dev countered, 'If the holy *brahmashila* continues to remain hidden in these wild reaches, then only wooden effigies will be installed in Shrikshetra. To the simple, devout folk yearning for liberation, such a farce would be an offence—yet, Jagadev, it is unnecessary. For now, our chosen deity, Shri Jagannath, shall indeed be enthroned on the Ratna Simhasana of a free, independent Utkal. I fear, however, that your Ratnavedi might remain a barren void forever!'

The oblation rites had reached their solemn conclusion.

Not long after, Lakshmi Paramaguru approached Ramachandra Dev and Jagadev with the yajna charu (sacrificial gifts) in hand, trailed by the tireless artisans.

Jagadev observed with quiet conviction, 'The Ratnavedi of the Great Void does not lament its emptiness, Maharaj!'

Lakshmi Paramaguru, addressing Jagadev first, pronounced, 'Yet the Ratnavedi of the heart, Jagadev, never remains vacant! In time, Mahabahu shall, unfailingly, ascend to fulfil this vacant throne.'

Later, as dawn yielded to a cloudless blaze gathering overhead, Ramachandra Dev raised his gaze to the heavens and silently pondered, 'I have but one week left! At every step between Khurda and Pipili, conflicts will erupt. The spectre of interdiction looms large. Yet, even so, the deities must be conveyed to Shrikshetra during Nabajoubana Darshan!'

Ramachandra Dev's train of thought suddenly

snapped. In response, Jagadev shouted at the top of his voice, 'Victory to the Third Indradyumna, Maharaja Ramachandra Dev!'

How wonderfully capricious are Jagadev's ways! The artisans, joining in with raised voices, echoed, 'Victory to the Third Indradyumna! Victory! Victory!'

Ramachandra Dev retorted with playful defiance, 'Where stands the illustrious founder of the Yadu lineage— the exalted Second Indradyumna, Maharaja Ramachandra Dev himself? And where, tell me, is Hafiz Qadir—faith-abandoned, peerless only in estrangement?'

A wry, self-mocking smile played on Ramachandra Dev's lips as he continued: 'Today, I am bereft of all resources—stripped of all but my devotion and gratitude, Jagadev. But hear me now—let Paramaguru bear witness, and let all my people heed this solemn word: Shri Jagannath Harichandan Jagadev of Athagarh shall henceforth be hailed as our cherished exemplar—upholder of honour, shelterer of spirit. From this day, and each year hence, the temple's pinnacle shall ring with the chinaras' cry in his name.'

And in a chorus of high, elevated voices, the artisans intoned, 'All praise to our exemplar—our sheltering brother! Victory to Jagannath Jagadev Harichandan!'

The sound of their acclamations, like the resonant blast of conch shells, filled the quiet forest realm.

With resolve rekindled in his heart, Ramachandra Dev mounted his horse and set off along the road to Tikali.

*****

Chapter XII

'Jaguni… Pati Mahapatra…!'
Ramachandra Dev, with his left palm held close like a funnel to his lips, projected his voice in a sonorous tone, 'Jaguni… Jaguni!'

His call rippled through the timeworn Shiva temple, echoing off vine-draped stone and shadowed grove before dissolving into silence. From the temple's loftiest spire, a clutch of pigeons took flight, each feather touched by the dawn's first golden breath. Hidden deep within the sanctuary's crumbled hush—shielded from the vigilant gaze of Chikakol's faujdar—the deities held their silent vigil.

Not far off, some of the Daitas, along with other servitors—Patis and Mahapatras—had established a humble quarter known as Shabara Palli. Its roof bore a delicate veil of mist, as if spun from the very breath of early fog. Long ago, Jaguni had set out towards the Shabara Palli to summon the Mahapatras into the sacred precincts of the temple; for without their arrival, how could the deities possibly leave their altars? In readiness for the divine host, three royal palanquins stood before the temple's threshold. Jagadev had seen to every detail—paikas from Tikali had long been stationed in preparedness, their resolve steadily wearing thin. Clad in martial splendour, they bore the blowpipes upon their shoulders, the ancestral armguards across their chests, a formidable mace in one hand, a khanda and curved knives at the waist, and crowned their heads with ethnic plumes—as if embarking upon a consecrated campaign of war. Indeed, if not a war journey, what else could justify such an array? Poised to counter any assault against the gods, their armour glimmered in the morning rays as the day ascended. And yet, still the gods abode upon their altars— unbidden, unswayed. So, if the Daitas failed to appear, who would escort the gods into their hallowed vimanas?

Today was Anasara Dashami, and within the sacred realm of Shrikshetra, the *chaka bije* ritual would unfold. Near the Dhukudi Gate, the Daita would roll three chakas (wheels) and place them upon the Anasara Pedestal, whereupon the three deities would be solemnly enthroned. After the long, lingering melancholy of Ansara, it was as though the latent might of Mahabahu would finally awaken from its torpor. Tomorrow, Ekadashi would dawn!

Later, the Daita, together with the Mahapatra servitors, would jointly offer sandalwood upon the three altars of the Anasara House. This sacred chandan, prepared by the Daitas, would be presented alongside Pati Mahapatras' own camphor and kesar—a ritual act that vividly signals the harmonious confluence between Shabara and Brahminic traditions in the veneration of Shri Jagannath. It is as if this ceremonial method itself stands as a symbol of that cultural synthesis.

When the sandalwood was offered, the temple courtyard erupted with the resonant peal of bells and gongs, the stirring strains of the kahali, and the rhythmic beat of Telangi drums, all interwoven with the lilting refrain of 'Maṇima… Maṇima' emanating from the Palia Khuntia. Even from the secluded depths of Tikali in that solitary woodland, Ramachandra Dev seemed to hear the jubilant, celebratory clamour of the ritual.

Then would ensue Dwadashi, Trayodashi, and Chaturdashi—those final ritual thresholds. After the sacred seclusion of the fourteenth night, dawn would break upon Chaturdashi, ushering in the divine spectacle of Nabajoubana Darshan. And then, the resplendent Rath Yatra—its five intervening days charged with anticipation and ceremonial stirrings.

Ramachandra Dev grew restless and troubled. Should the gods not be led to the Ratna Simhasana in Shrikshetra before the Nabajoubana Darshan, then Aminchand would consecrate the Navakalevara effigies! And who, then, would accept these idols bearing *brahmashila* as the embodiment of the sacred *mahadaru*? All the strife, every measure of preparation, every ritual exertion and martial undertaking would be rendered in vain, leaving the deities forever marooned in this barren wilderness, exiled as forlorn wanderers of the forest.

Yet still there was no sign of the Daitas, and the sun climbed ever higher overhead! By day's end, at the very least, they must reach the grove of Goddess Kalua Devi in Karaṇḍimal. Who could tell how long it would take to negotiate the intricate Mughal formations stretching between Khurda and Pipili?

At this moment, Taqi Khan was stationed in Murshidabad, accompanied by a host of more than half a battalion of horsemen and a regiment of soldiers. Moreover, those who had once betrayed during the Chhatradwar valley battle were now advancing of their own accord to render military aid. Vijay Raju of Mahendragarh, who had been conspicuously absent last time, had now sent forth his Telangi contingent—ready, if needed, to escort the forces all the way to Puri. From Tikali to Karaṇḍimal, these soldiers vigilantly guarded each valley. And not to be overlooked, the formidable Bahubalendra of Kashimpeta had exclaimed, 'Remain unafraid, Maharaj! Chikakol's faujdar shall not even lay a hand upon you.' His forces, too, were entwined in the watch over the valleys.

Harihara Vishwasray, the lord of Jayantgarh's impregnable fort, had personally deployed his garrison with impressive might in the Tikali forest. Shingaraju of Ramagiri, ever the steadfast ally of Ramachandra Dev— who, in the Chhatradwar valley battle, sent forth his tiger-hide-clad Khond battalion—stood ready. Their bodies, anointed with oil and turmeric, bedecked in tiger skins, with faces fierce as a tigress and voices that roared like wild beasts, made even the Mughal lashkars' hearts tremble at the sight of their valour. They, too, would encircle the gods as they marched toward Puri. In addition, the martial contingents of Jarada, Surangi, Aṭhagarh, and Mahuri had converged. The route to Karaṇḍimal lay unimpeded, and beyond that, the valiant chieftains and paika warriors of Utkal would await. Should battle erupt in Khurda or Pipili this time, Ramachandra Dev had vowed to exact retribution for the past defeat at Chhatradwar—but this was not preparation for total vengeance against previous wars. It was solely to ensure that, before the emergence of

Nabajoubana Darshan, the gods might ascend the Ratna Simhasana.

Between the thick, entwined limbs of two stately sal trees, scorching rays—like the fervour of midsummer fire—descended upon the dilapidated Shiva temple, dousing its ruins in an almost celestial blaze. From Tikali's stronghold, the resolute Govindray had already visited twice, inquiring, 'Why this delay in movement? We must reach Goddess Kalua Devi's grove by tonight—and it would be even better if we could also cross Karandimal. Yet even at the very beginning, such tardiness has set in!'

At every corner, paika warriors stood ready, shifting their stances with measured precision. Their impatience grew as the delay stretched on.

Again, Ramachandra Dev's voice rang out forcefully: 'Jaguni… Jaguni!' But no answer came.

Through the quiet canopy of the forest, a distant murmur stirred the air—an echo gaining presence as it drew ever closer.

A quarrel simmered between Jaguni and the Daita Pati Mahapatras—a delicate dance of reproach and urgency.

'Go... go! Nothing of consequence awaits you with these people in this frantic rush!'

'Why raise your voice like that?'

'Come now, you obstinate soul! Flaunt these bloodshot eyes elsewhere!?'

Jaguni countered, voice laced with pleading duty: 'Prabhu, this is no time for rage. It is about ensuring that the gods take their rightful place in the palanquins and return to their realm today. The Maharaj has insisted since yesterday—tonight, they must reach Karaṇḍimal. Yet even now, leaving this very spot has been delayed.'

A Daita snapped back, 'Oh, you blustering oaf! Shouting in anger gains us no attentive ears. Who's to say that Mahabahu won't set out in the palanquin today? Shall we then forsake our daily ablutions—our very bathing rituals?'

'Ugh! Since dawn, it's been nothing but bathing!'

Since the dim light of early morning, the Daitas and Patis had set out—with a towel wrapped around each shoulder and a water pot in hand—walking nearly a kos to the waterfall where abundant, fine sand lay in quiet abundance. This was their daily ritual: ambling near the falls, attuned to the shifting directions of nature, and spending a brief, indulgent moment in the calm cascade—not out of mere necessity, but as a cherished luxury.

Just as Jaguni moved to speak again, one among them interjected in a raised, decisive tone, 'That accursed Jaguni! Unbridled as ever, he veers beyond counsel. Persisting in defiance brings no advantage. Let's move with haste—time truly has slipped away!'

In the profound silence of the dense forest, their determined exchanges could be heard clearly amid the rustle of leaves. Still, albeit belatedly, the Daitas were on their way back. Extracting the deities from the temple and seating them in the palanquin was no trivial matter—indeed, it would demand considerable time. With restless urgency and mounting anticipation, Ramachandra Dev advanced ahead to hasten the return of the Daitas and their retinues.

Trailing behind Jaguni, the Daitas navigated the winding, uneven forest paths. Around their waists, traditional sashes and neatly folded towels were tightly secured—so snug that their rounded belly seemed to swell further. Damp cloths rested heavily upon each shoulder, while the Patis bore Ramanuji tilak upon their foreheads. Around their necks, the sacred *ajnamala*, whose ropes had once commanded divine movement, now hung limp—a sign of both honour and exhaustion.

But there was no ostentation in Jaguni's attire— he still bore that solid, square, and diminutive face, unchanged though faint traces of illness had begun to show. Ramachandra Dev had heard that in Malagiri, Jaguni had suffered for many days, only to recover just a short while ago.

Nor did he adorn himself with modest embellishments—no delicate earpieces nestled in his large ears, fashioned with Saradei's tender sisterly care, nor that exquisite golden necklace, its beads shaped like coriander seeds and wrought in intricate design, which she had lovingly commissioned for him. After all, what use were the earnings of a humble household, if not to secure such tokens of affection?

Jaguni had once retorted with a playful chiding, 'Sister! Your neck is utterly bare…' He punctuated his words, inadvertently touching a particularly sensitive spot in her delicate heart, while Saradei, on the other side, turned away quietly, letting tears stream down her face in hush—in memory of her husband. In that golden necklace—lost now to distant exile—lived the lingering presence of Saradei. For Jaguni, her memory was an invaluable treasure.

On days, as memories stirred within him, Jaguni would sit on the crumbling steps of that Shiva temple, remove the golden necklace from around his neck and examine it as if beholding it for the very first time. He would turn it over in his palm, and in that moment, Saradei's tender, flowing eyes—brimming with nurturing affection—would seem to shimmer into view.

Yet, amid this swirling storm of events, Saradei herself had mysteriously vanished, lost somewhere in a fever until she fell into an inky unconsciousness, and thereafter, no word was heard of her. The recollection of her absence would fill his heart with a deep, poignant ache.

Lifting his gaze from the necklace, he would behold the two immense, commanding eyes of Mahabahu. In them, it would seem as though Saradei's caring, empathic gaze was reflected with boundless compassion. That very necklace had been the enduring link to her—a symbol of their bond. But after his arrival in Tikali, for the sake of the customary rites mandated for the deities, Jaguni had long since divested himself of that necklace and his earpieces. Gone were the elegantly curled locks and the dark, swirling tresses that once graced his brow. One day, in a sudden whim akin to the practical style of the Daita and Pati Mahapatra, he had his hair tonsured in a rounded manner atop his head, with a few stray strands dangling to his shoulders. Usually, Jaguni would tie them up neatly, but today, in his haste, his damp braid lay haphazardly, a tangle of disarray.

Balanced atop his head now was a huge, perfectly ripe jackfruit, and pressed against his arm, he carried another. Trailing behind him came the Daitas and the Patis, steadily making their way. Jaguni remarked, 'Look at the enormous jackfruits! I am but one man—how much can I possibly lift alone? What if you could carry one or two of these? After all, tomorrow is the Chandan Ekadashi. Tomorrow is Chandan

Ekadashi. We were meant to offer jackfruit and banana—but the bananas are nowhere to be found. So the jackfruit shall be placed before the deities as bhog.'

'Surely, you are a wrestler! With such a distance to cover, how can we bear the weight of these heavy jackfruits?'

They had nearly reached the temple now.

Not to be outdone, Jaguni called back over his shoulder, 'Why do you trudge along with the swagger of Madanmohan? The hour wanes—how late it's become! Lost amidst these winding vines, we scarcely notice the passing of time!'

Ramachandra Dev interjected sharply, 'You have all delayed long enough. We must reach Karandimal by nightfall!'

Jaguni, now spent and breathless with indignation, let loose his long-held lament: 'Mahaprabhu! Since rooster-crow, I've been hollering— "Hurry up, move your feet! Time's slipping like sand from a clenched fist. The Maharaj, poor soul, must be sitting wrapped in worry like a monsoon cloud. And these idols? They ain't no wooden toys to sling over shoulders and toss on palanquins like festival baggage. The elder Lords rest in sacred enclosures—those altars need care, rite, and time, not slapdash tamasha." But who's got ears for truth? These fellows sit squat and stubborn, like swamp buffalo soaking in a forest spring—thick-skinned and deaf as a gourd to any whisper of urgency!'

The Daita, Bhavani Swain Mahapatra, snapped with biting sarcasm, 'We've witnessed grander spectacles than this! And now you strut about, parading your authority—on what strength? A belly filled with parboiled rice and soured horsegram curry? Spare us the theatrics!'

The quarrel flared up once again. The esteemed Bishi Pati Mahapatra threw in a barbed remark, 'Far too clever by half—yet wisdom remains conspicuously absent.'

Refusing to relent, Jaguni added, 'Listen, Mahaprabhu! We would have traversed many kos of road already!'

'Don't waste time on bickering!' Ramachandra Dev commanded in an imperious tone. 'Come, come—hasten with all due readiness! Time is slipping away. Who knows how many hours of the night will pass before we reach Karaṇḍimal? Travelling through the forest by the light of a torch is hardly safe.'

Bhawani Swain Mahapatra wiped away the beads of sweat pearled at his brow with the damp towel and murmured reassuringly, 'Do not fret, Maharaj! Time follows its own course, as does man. Eventually, at some crossroads, the two paths are destined to meet.'

The Daitas and the Pati Mahapatras then proceeded into the temple to attend to sacred rituals, while Jaguni, swaying his waist and chest in mirthful revelry, began joyfully striking the gong. After the proper rites at the three altars were meticulously observed, the Daitas and the Patis, amid the wild, ecstatic peal of Jaguni's gong, brought forth the deities and enshrined them in the palanquins.

In unison, the paikas of Tikali let forth a cry of triumph, chanting: 'Jai Shri Jagannath! Glory to Mahabahu!'

Every particle of the forest seemed to resound with that jubilant acclamation.

These were not mere gods hidden away in a crumbling Shiva temple; they are embodiments of that immortal, invincible spirit. Though amid hundreds of assaults, there had been moments when brute force and the ruinous power of misguided devotion appeared to triumph, the ultimate, magnificent power of the divine endured in the end, ever enthroned in eternal majesty upon the Ratna Simhasana—the source of fearlessness and the fountainhead of liberation.

The paikas lifted the palanquins onto their shoulders with solemn grace.

Ahead of the palanquins—his feet bound in *ranpa*—Jaguni swayed forth like a wild, unbridled storm. From his throat rang the resolute cry, 'Jai Jagannath! Jai Mahabahu!'

His exultation reverberated across the forested expanse; his voice, echoing off the mountains, swelled into a doubled, triumphant tone. The Daitas and the Patis lagged behind, swaying their ample forms onward with ritual fervour as they trailed after the paikas. Meanwhile, Ramachandra Dev rode slowly on horseback behind the palanquins. Though there was neither fear of attack from ahead nor from behind, his eyes remained ever watchful. On either side of the palanquins, clusters of armed paika soldiers advanced in formation—more than ample to confront any foe in this wood—and the passage to Karandimala lay secure.

The shadowed forest trail began to steam beneath the burning mid-afternoon sun, and those entrusted with the palanquins grew weary. Yet valley upon valley, fresh contingents of paikas stood ready—each squad relieved by the next, hoisted aloft in solemn continuity.

Still, Karandimala lay distant.

But where, one might ask, were the common folk—the tender-footed children, the frail women, the worn men, the stooped elders—the devotees? How had they come by word of Mahabahu's resplendent return? Perhaps it was the pealing of Jaguni's gong and the myriad voices chanting 'Jai Jagannath' that had lured them. In this barren wilderness, they had never before heard such a jubilant acclamation— 'Jai Jagannath… Jai Jagannath!'

From the tangled forest emerged throngs of devotees, streaming forth like a vast column of ants, crying out: 'Hold, O bearers of the palanquin—just a breath, for eyes that seek his hallowed presence. We heard he dwelled among us, cloaked in wilderness and shadow. Now, he proceeds to the temple—where else shall his mercy be glimpsed? Grant our mortal eyes a moment's fulfilment.'

It was clear the day would soon wane amidst such delays. Jaguni had issued strict orders—the palanquins must never be laid down, save for the necessary transfer of burden from one set of devoted shoulders to the next. But even the most resolute paikas, loyal in sinew and heart, were drenched in the stifling heat and humidity of Jyeshtha. At every shoulder-change, the fresh bearers would entreat, 'Let us pause for a moment in the shade! It's only a night's march to Karandimala.'

Yet Jaguni, rising upon the *ranpa* like a seasoned commander, barked with resolve, 'No, we cannot delay!' Then, with his gong ablaze in sound, he roared—'Jai Shri Jagannath...!' His cry echoed, again and again, across the assembled devotees: 'Mahabahu is returning! To his Ratna Simhasana, within the sacred Shrivatsa-Khandasala! Do not obstruct his path any longer.'

'We have come from afar to witness his divine vision and sanctify our souls!'

But who would heed their plaintive appeals? The

palanquins surged ahead. Those swept along the path Shri Jagannath had trodden were sanctified with the dust of his passage upon their foreheads. A wilted flower from the ground sparked scrambling; a single thread from the *ajnamala* was seized with reverence.

Observing the teeming devotees as if they were a marching line of ants, Ramachandra Dev's thoughts stirred in deliberate cadence, 'Is this the very self-abnegation of a simple, devoted people? A snare of superstition? Yet for generations, Sri Jagannath has embodied the indomitable power of the soul—the deity for the seeker of liberation. How could he repudiate such a sublime force?'

Yet would he be able to fulfil his solemn vow— to bring the deities to the Ratnavedi before Nabajoubana Darshan?

But Karandimala still lay far off—no sign of it appeared. Here, where the forest offered no cooling shade and sunlight scattered over lost, wild expanses, the destination remained elusive.

At the foot of the mountains, within the penumbra of dawn, Karandimala revealed itself—the grove of Goddess Kalua Devi, where, through a tangle of leaves, a tender flush of light drifted gently into view.

The paikas who bore the palanquins had scattered here and there, taking brief rests. The previous night, torches and lanterns had been mounted to tree trunks; now their glow had gradually faded. Along the mountain valley's passage to Karandimala, the paikas from Mahuri stood ready to hoist the palanquins once more.

Ramachandra Dev inquired, 'Jaguni, why do we still delay? Tonight, we must reach Pipili! Crossing Pipili will embolden our hearts. We have already endured two watches of the day from here!'

Yet Jaguni was at an impasse—if only the Daitas and their retinues would proceed! Today was Anasara Ekadashi, after all! Wherever the gods may be, their divine ordinance remains unswerving. One Daita was busy grinding sandalwood and snapped, 'Had the deities dwelt within the temple, I'd wager that the Ghatuari group would have been grinding sandalwood at home four days ago. There, in the Anasara House, we would smear it upon the three altars. Is this sandalwood, or merely wood from the sal trees?'

From Tikali, Jaguni had gathered wood of the purest sandalwood. But one of the Daitas scoffed that it was nothing but sal wood? Ah, but a clumsy dancer always finds fault with her crooked courtyard! With a fierce retort, Jaguni bellowed, 'You've got the frame of a charging rhinoceros! Are you grinding sandalwood in a wild, haphazard flurry or pestling bhang? Don't you know what time it is?'

Irritated by his own unpracticed hands as he ground the sandalwood, the Daita's inner vexation spilt over, and in a loud voice he cried, 'Off with you, you lazy simpleton! Do you think we're mere sandalwood grinders?'

It was true that the Ghatuaris—those skilled in the art of rubbing sandalwood on a *sila pua*—flat grinding stone—would never be satisfied with such crude methods. But where would they even find a proper grinding stone, a polished one? This wasn't some herbal powdering, and what of the accompanying mortar? Instead, from somewhere in the grove, Jaguni produced a smooth stone and handed it over. How, then, can proper grinding be expected?

Another Daita interjected, 'Enough of this sandalwood! In keeping with the prescribed rites, we'll simply apply a thin smear on all three altars. This isn't the Shrimandir where Raghav Das Math sends seven and a half *ser* of sandal! Will the king now dispatch that weight himself? It takes the Ghatuaris four days to prepare enough paste for the three altars. So let's make do with what we have!'

After so much rubbing, sweat beaded on the Daita's brow. Jaguni then said, 'Hold on…I've saved some camphor and kesar too; mix those in as well.' Ever mindful of the deities' strict ordinance—after all, how could one offer only sandalwood on an Ekadashi—he had collected camphor and kesar, blending them into the ground sandalwood. Together, the Daitas and the Patis applied this sacred mixture over the three altars, while the jackfruits Jaguni had brought were ritually offered as bhog and then consumed in the holy flame.

A Daita remarked, 'And how are we to offer a *bidiya*—the lime-free betel quid, as ordained?'

Jaguni, unfailingly resourceful, had bundled three pieces of *bidiya*—wrapped in sal leaves around his waist. Producing from his cache a few dry *bidiyas*, he cautioned, 'Hold on… don't make a fuss. I've brought along some *bidiyas*.' Though, ironically, the betel pieces resembled the sal leaves in appearance!

After crossing Karandimala, the procession's pace slackened. With each step, urgent voices rang out: 'Stop—stop! Hold the palanquins! You're about to bear them away upon your shoulders… wait! We've come from afar—to anoint our eyes with his celestial countenance.'

Like streams of ants, multitudes of devotees swarmed to catch a glimpse of the divine, their voices mingling in reverent clamour. The resounding cry of 'Jai Mahabahu!' echoed through the firmament and along the gentle breeze.

But who had brought word of Mahabahu's triumphant return—the tidings of his mighty, resplendent presence? Indeed, it was Ramachandra Dev himself who heralded the divine resurgence—from Tikali's hallowed precincts to the sacred soil of Shrikṣhetra. The forts, chowpadhis, and paika hamlets quivered in readiness—as if the very soil had heard the gods stir.

Ramachandra Dev was suddenly reminded of the paika he had met by the cascading stream between Nuagarh and Athagarh, striding on *ranpa*-bound legs, passing from chowpadhi to chowpadhi like a wandering sentinel. He had proudly declared, "Mahabahu once graced the Maharaj with a divine vision in his dreams—I can scarce abide remaining hidden in this vast wilderness. I shall return to the sanctified precincts at Shrivatsa Khandashala, to the Ratna Simhasana!"

Yet no such divine command had ever graced his dreams—whose imagining, then, had spun itself into the fabric of legend?

Now, Mahabahu was returning from exile in the *Mahakantara*… If fortune permits, may a mortal witness this spectacle with his very own eyes.

Immersed in ecstatic revelry, Jaguni roared joyously—his gong resounding as he cried, 'Clear the way… clear the way… clear the path!'

Even the paika sentinels strained to hold back the ever-swelling tide of devotees. If each step were delayed any further, it might take three or four days to reach Puri; by then, the grand Ratha Yatra—preceded by Netrotsava—

would already be underway. And so, Ramachandra Dev, momentarily confounded by duty, gazed upon the unruly throng with mounting concern.

In that very moment, a clarion call rang out, 'Clear the way! Give us passage! Chariots! Chariots!' As the crowd gradually parted, three-wheeled bullock carts emerged, their wheels creaking as they halted. Now the deities would travel not in the palanquin, but upon rope-drawn ceremonial platforms all the way to Shrikshetra! A flurry of shoving and tugging over the chariot ropes ensued.

But where did that ketaki garland appear from? For the Daita contingents were festooning the deities' heads with fragrant ketaki wreaths. Jaguni, standing tall atop the chariot of the elder Lord, bellowed proudly, 'Jai Mahabahu!'
In thousands of voices there arose an echo, swirling like the surging tide upon the vast ocean, chanting, 'Jai... Jai...'

This unstoppable journey—a triumph rising from a land once marred by defeat and disgrace to the newborn, awakened soil of Utkal—seemed destined and irresistible.

All three chariots surged forth like arrows loosed from a bow! Group after group of devotees pulled them along; as one team relinquished its grip on the rope, another eagerly took hold.

Quietly, Ramachandra Dev mused to himself that organizing the journey by transporting the divine in a chariot had proved far more expeditious. At this breakneck pace, it would scarcely be long before nightfall found the deities reaching Khurda.

From countless throats, the unified cry soared high, 'Jai Jagannath!'

Where once lay doubt now shone an indomitable

vigour, that very life force—a vitality revived as though by Mahabahu's miraculous touch, rekindling life as if defying death itself.

Is Shri Jagannath merely the cherished deity of Utkal? Is he venerated only by the Hindu faithful? Observing the throng, Ramachandra Dev felt that he stood as the very embodiment of his people's life force. Throughout the ages, by taking refuge in him, the history of an entire nation has played out—an epic renewed with every mere glimpse of their divine presence. It is not a mere clamour for a deity; it is the unerring, fervent articulation of a people's soul. In infinite moments of crisis, their hearts rise with courage as they utter, 'Jai Jagannath!' This is no ordinary acclamation—it is the resounding affirmation of their vital power.

Together with the crowd, Ramachandra Dev joined in the jubilant chorus, 'Jai Jagannath!'

Amid the tumult, countless carts broke down; yet new ones—new chariots—seemingly appeared from nowhere. Ropes snapped and were immediately replaced, and by dusk, hundreds of torches had been lit. The triumphant chariot of Mahabahu continued its march, fueled by the very energy of his people.

In the distance, through the haze of dark, clouded skies, Khurda-Barunei-Cuttack emerged like a distant beacon in twinkling light. The paikas, brought along from Tikali, were soon to be marshalled from this very ground into a formidable formation.

Summoning a fort commander, Ramachandra Dev issued his order in a firm, reasoned tenor: 'Construct a *soochivyuha*. The deities will remain in the centre, while three elite contingents advance ahead, led by three Champatis.'

But, amid this sprawling multitude, where were the Champatis? Where was the Jogania? Who among them would measure the land by the span of seventeen hands and marshal the formation? Through the surging noise, the fort commander was busy seeking out those daunting Champatis.

News had reached Ramachandra Dev from every quarter: Khurda would be the first bastion where the Mughals must mount their resistance. Beyond Khurda lay Pipili. In Khurda, forces led by Faujdar Hashim Khan—with the stalwart company of Lalita Devi and Bhagirathi Kumar, their paika warriors at the ready—awaited to confront him. The moment they had crossed Karandimala, Mahabahu's triumphant return to Shrikshetra was no longer secret. The Mughal faujdars soon realized that this was not merely a celestial reentrance, nor was it a spontaneous religious uprising; it was nothing less than treason against the Mughal realm—a resounding summons from the land of Utkal to overthrow Mughal rule. Consequently, the moment word reached from Taqi Khan's spies, they plunged headlong into preparations for resistance.

Naib Aminchand had declared emphatically, 'Kumar! Your future, your very claim to the throne, depends on this Navakalevara. Should Hafiz Qadar's conspiracy succeed in thwarting it, then you must accept that all hope of the throne is lost. Do you understand, Kumar?'

Bhagirathi Kumar had come to Khurda, destined for sacrifice—as expendable as a goat offered for bali—accompanied by the paika contingent of Lalita Devi.

After crossing Baghamari, Ramachandra Dev had instructed his commanders to array the deities' chariots within the *soochivyuha*. For there was insufficient space for the expansive *ardhachandra* arrangement that they desired, and beyond the paika regiment lay a vast, unarmed, and disordered multitude. It was proving impossible to marshal that heedless throng into any coherent chain. Now, if in Khurda the well-drilled Mughal forces—united with Bhagirathi Kumar's paika contingent—should combine to resist, what fate would befall them? The very thought left Ramachandra Dev nearly speechless with apprehension.

Before him, Khurda's flickering torches shimmered across the dusk-lit horizon—perhaps the fiery line of Mughal battalions. They stood, weapons raised and ready to strike!

Meanwhile, Ramachandra Dev found himself estranged from the surging mass. The Mughal host loomed ahead, their cannons loaded to repulse the advancing throng. But did this inattentive, unarmed multitude even fathom the threat? One cannonball—its roar echoing like a colossal tree crashing down—would smash the entire unprotected crowd, silencing once and for all the jubilant chorus of 'Jai Jagannath.' And then, who would restrain them? How could an unarmed, defenceless throng fend off such a blaze of violence, a bloodthirsty army? Surely, they were destined to plunge into an abyss of certain death. The very prospect sent a shiver of disquiet through Ramachandra Dev's soul.

Grasping the reins of his horse, Ramachandra Dev paused—time suspended in a breathless hush. Yet he knew well: can a chariot, once stirred, ever be stilled? The journey, once begun, must find its stillness only at the destined end, not along the way.

And yet! Before the chariots, the disordered multitude reached the outskirts of Khurda almost unbidden. Even the paika contingent under Bhagirathi Kumar's command joined in the resounding chorus of 'Jai Jagannath' and mingled with them. Then, as if swallowed by the mists, Bhagirathi Kumar himself suddenly vanished without a trace in Khurda. Under the leadership of Faujdar Hashim Khan, a formation of two hundred warriors had been arrayed to stem the tide of the divine procession—but when they witnessed Kumar's paikas abruptly switching sides, that formation fell into utter disarray.

The slumbering dark suddenly kindled into fervour with voices rising in a thunderous crescendo, as they cried out, 'Jai Jagannath... Jai Mahabahu! All hail the mighty Gajapati, Maharaja Ramachandra Dev!'

Tomorrow was Dwadashi!

That very night, it was imperative that they reach Pipili—lest the gathered Mughal legion, arrayed in an impenetrable defensive cordon, thwart their hopes. In truth, this was to be the final stronghold of the enemy's resistance. The envoys had long since brought word of this development.

For if they tarried any longer in Pipili, it would be impossible to arrive in Shrikshetra before the Netrotsava, and the entire endeavour—the grand campaign—would crumble into defeat. In the guise of Navakalevara, a few wooden effigies would be enthroned on the Ratna Simhasana, and the deities, bearing within them the hallowed *brahmashila*, would be abandoned along the roadside! It was, therefore, essential that they reach Pipili tonight. There, an ultimate trial awaited them in battle.

Ramachandra Dev, turning on his steed, fixed his gaze upon Lord Jagannath. In the tremulous glow of the flame, he discerned the resolute aura in Mahabahu's ketaki garlands—imperishable emblems of triumph adorning both arms. In his eyes blazed the call to battle: O faint-hearted one, how long will you flee? The hour has come for open combat! Where will you hide, clutching your breath as refuge? There is no need for it—this is not merely a return journey; it is the liberation march of long-oppressed Utkal! Though our people are unarmed, they possess a strength of spirit second to none!

Without delay, Ramachandra Dev commanded his commanders and battalion leaders, 'Khurda is expended! Now, onward to Pipili. Tonight, we shall reach Pipili!'

Amid ecstatic tumult and voices that split the heavens with cries of 'Jai Jagannath! Jai Mahabahu!', the chariots surged toward Pipili.

A short distance away lay Pipili, where the first light had begun to spill. The eastern sky would soon be robed in vermilion—so vivid were the signs of a bright dawn inscribed upon the unclouded heavens. Ramachandra Dev had received word from Pipili's envoys: under Maluda's faujdar and Hashim Khan, nearly a thousand armed Mughal soldiers were arrayed along the Pipili–Puri road, stationed to the south, prepared to intercept.

Ramachandra Dev then took stock of his own paika warriors—their numbers would have been no less than three thousand. And alongside them marched countless supporters, forming an impregnable human wall, surrounding the deities and hauling the chariots forward. In unison, they sang and played their instruments—pakhwajs, cymbals, jhanjs intermingled with the strains of devotional hymns, bhajans, and kirtans.

Who could say that the singing of such kirtans and

hymns had rendered the Odia people feeble? Through these stirring strains of devotion, they had forged an invincible force of life. True, the paikas were armed, but in the face of the Mughal artillery—cannons and muskets—their mere arrows, spears, and swords might scarcely hold their ground. In front of Goddess Shubhadra's chariot, some of them leaped and swayed almost in a wild dance; while the formidable Khond battalion under Ramagiri's Shingaraju, their shoulders laden as if carrying the weight of a hundred battles, their bodies anointed with oil and turmeric with faces as fierce as those of tigers, let out piercing cries and vaulted upward with a fervour that seemed touched by the very essence of the divine.

Halting the three chariots for a brief moment, Ramachandra Dev gathered his generals, fort commandants, and battalion chiefs. They needed to consult on how best to face the Mughal formation in Pipili—a force that, while perhaps not yet fully recognized by all, was no secret to them. The tidings of the Mughal advance had already reached their ears.

Balendra, the battalion leader, known for his mastery in forming battle arrays, spoke with serene intensity, 'Without a proper strategic formation—the *soochivyuha*— we cannot stand against them. A Champati or battalion chief shall stand at the fore with a tapered lance in hand, flanked by twenty paika warriors behind him. Armed with daggers, katars, axes and other fearsome instruments, they will wreak dread upon the enemy ranks. The veil of deception—a *chhidrapata*—would unfurl before the enemy. At the signal of Champatiray's roar, hidden reserves shall emerge from secret recesses and launch our assault.'

Ramachandra Dev replied, 'Call it a *soochivyuha* or any other formation—it is unyielding. Yes, the Mughals have their cannons and muskets. But our people—pakhwajs slung over shoulders, jhanjs ringing in hand. Among these paikas, most bear only swords, or bows and arrows. A few carry a lone-barrel musket. Can such modest arms ever stand against a full Mughal regiment?'

Atri's Narendra, an aged veteran of many campaigns with a square, weathered face, a lion-like moustache, and a long streak of vermilion adorning his furrowed brow, bellowed, 'No war is won by weapons alone!'

'Then, what is our strength?'

With ardour wrapped in calm, he replied, 'I have fought many battles, and learned that victory is not wrought by steel alone, but by courage and by morale. That spirit— we possess in abundance. In the battle at Gangapada...' The tale hung suspended. Then, striking his chest with sudden zeal, he continued, 'Even if cannon fire rends our bodies, it cannot extinguish the spirit of this nation. Let us invoke the name of Durgamadhaba—and press onward, Maharaj!'

One of the battalion leaders then spoke in a quiet but resolute tone, 'They may wield cannons, but we command an ocean—the ocean of our people. Like waves crashing against artillery fire, this ocean will disperse the enemy, leaving them as nothing more than frail straws carried away by the tide. Now, do not delay, Maharaj! For after today, the day after tomorrow shall be Anasara Chaturdashi— when the sacred *chaka apasara* is offered, and at dawn, the Nabajoubana Darshan begins. There is no time left for hesitation.'

Today was Dwadashi.

On this sacred day, the chief servitors of the deity would traditionally have their foreheads adorned with a royal sari by the king. But here, no saree was to be found, nor were the illustrious Tadau Patnaik, Talichha Mahapatra, Deulakarana, or any other venerable servant present. Instead, Ramachandra Dev himself took it upon his hands to drape a flower garland around the necks of the battalion leaders and fortress commanders. For today, these were the true servants of the gods.

With a resounding chorus of 'Jai Jagannath!' they set forth at a brisk pace for Pipili. As the scorching afternoon slowly gave way to the encroaching shade of the deepening sky, the three chariots reached Pipili amidst an ever-growing throng of devotees. Once hidden away in some secret retreat, the deities now returned boldly to ascend the Ratna Simhasana at the Shrivatsa Khandashala temple. Whispers stirred among the people—was this Navakalevara nothing but a hoax? How could an emblem of the divine be hastily replaced while the gods still walked among the living? Through the vast skies and gentle winds rang out the triumphant cry, 'Jai Mahabahu! Jai Jagannath!'—the pilgrims journeying for Navakalevara had now joined the surging tide.

Meanwhile, the battalion leaders from distant Nimapada and Kakatpur, who had been seated away from the fray, arrived with their paika contingents in tow. Although these troopers might seem little more than ceremonial scaffolds—with their vividly painted thighs and vestments splashed in bold hues, their timeworn turbans, daggers at the waist, and swords in hand—they were unmistakably armed as paika warriors. When the need arose, they would burst forth from the gaps in the ranks to engage the Mughal forces from both flanks.

So formidable was the skill of the generals, fort commanders, and battalion chiefs that they could bring hostile artillery to silence in mere moments. Once the enemy's cannonry was neutralized, the paikas would swiftly rout the Mughal host, ensuring that the deities were delivered safely to the temple well before the unfolding of Nabajoubana Darshan.

From atop his horse, amidst the vast ocean of his people, Ramachandra Dev surveyed the movements of the Mughal forces with a keen eye. A sudden assault was not his chosen course—his aim was resistance. Yet a quiet dread stirred within him: if Mahabahu were halted along the Pipili route, and this forced theatre of new effigies in the name of Navakalevara were imposed upon the people, how could the nation ever embrace it?

Since dawn, the Mughal host—and their cavalry—had been awaiting orders to begin their assault. Remarkably, even the paikas in Bhagirathi Kumar's contingent had, against all expectation, joined forces with Ramachandra Dev's own soldiers. At the very forefront of the Mughal army stood two formidable cannons, flanked behind by a pair of artillerymen who stood like figures in a painting, with the cavalry corps arrayed further back, followed by the foot soldiers. The plan was clear: the cannons were to open the way, and then the cavalry and infantry would surmount the enemy's position. The horses, having stood since early morning, grew restless and began pawing the ground – a silent testament to their impatience—while even the Mughal formation's resolve seemed to wane.

There was a tense pause as everyone awaited the command from Faujdar Hashim Khan. Yet even he, standing immobile like a statue on his horse behind the artillery, seemed perplexed by the moment. A veteran of many battles—and a man who had led his men on numerous occasions—Hashim Khan knew that the very instant the cannons were fired, the unarmed throng would scatter in chaos, as swiftly and surely as clusters of banana trees are uprooted in a storm. His experience foretold that both the enemy's paikas and the assembled men would collapse in no time. And yet, despite the odds, the adversary remained steadfast—so steadfast, in fact, that he could not bring himself to issue the order.

Before them stood the certainty of death—yet not a flicker of fear. The unarmed multitude, radiant in their death-defying splendour, left the commanders dumbstruck, paralyzed by the sheer majesty of resistance. Only a swelling ocean of barehanded souls surged ahead, unwavering. The paikas held back, encircling the chariots, forging a bastion of defence. And still, before the cannons, the unarmed tide rose—undaunted, unyielding. How could he have commanded cannon fire upon such an ocean of unarmed souls?

Amidst this charged atmosphere, Jaguni, his chamar fluttering as he danced and leapt, cried out in fierce jubilation, 'Jai Jagannath!'

Thousands of devotees, entranced almost hypnotically, repeatedly intoned, 'Jai Jagannath... Jai Mahabahu!'

What need of cannon—he would collapse even at the crack of a lone-barrel musket. And yet, not a single furrow of fear marked his brow. He stood resolute, his face serene—untouched by dread.

Aminchand, however, pursed his lips in disapproval,

wondering why Faujdar Hashim Khan stood like a statue upon his horse. What was he waiting for? What did it all mean?

Then, mounted upon his own steed, Aminchand rode forth and seized the Faujdar's rein. 'Sir,' he said with quiet urgency, 'signal the cannons to fire. The moment they thunder, our enemies shall be driven— scattered like chaff upon the wind, the road to victory laid bare. They are ill-armed and shaken; at the first volley, they shall break ranks and vanish. What cause remains for delay?'

Hashim Khan, his voice weighted with concern, replied, 'Naib Saheb, I have fought many battles, yet never have I witnessed such a fierce, impassioned spirit of *jamhuriat*. Look how far our gaze carries—see how they're converging upon these two cannons. Some will fall, yes, but how quickly will they render both guns useless? We ought to have brought more cannonballs and gunpowder, Naib Saheb!'

'Then?' Aminchand's voice was thick with agitation.

'I'm waiting for them to make the first move!'

It seemed that a fierce contest of wills was unfolding on both sides.

A few battalion officers urged Ramachandra Dev, 'What are we waiting for, Maharaj? Dusk is falling! Who knows when the battle will commence, yet we must reach Puri before night is over. At dawn, the Nabajoubana Darshan awaits—after which, the Netrotsava begins!'

Ramachandra Dev, his breath catching in solemn urgency, said: 'Don't you see, officer, what lies ahead— cannons, muskets, volleys of gunpowder! Even two cannon blasts will bring hundreds of our people to their knees!'

'Yet behind them, thousands endure—undaunted by death,' the battalion officers remarked, their voices edged with steel and reverence, 'they remain steadfast before the cannons. Maharaj, behold the depth of our resolve!'

Numerous ketaki wreaths and countless white lotus garlands lay strewn upon the dust-stained idols, adorning them in sacred bloom. Jaguni's fervent cry of 'Jai Jagannath!' echoed without cease. On the chariot of the elder Lord, he danced in unabashed ecstasy, swaying the chamar before the deity.

After a lengthy wait, the people's composure showed signs of strain. Suddenly, without any regard for Ramachandra Dev's lingering doubts, the three chariots began to advance. Like surging waves crashing upon a shore, the collective roar of the crowd erupted in a resounding chant: 'Jai Jagannath… Jai Mahabahu!'

For generations, the very souls of the Odia people had absorbed this sacred refrain—an incantation that, like the *beej* mantra chanted in the Mrityunjaya yajna, continued to reverberate deep within their subconscious and now kindled a fresh reservoir of strength and valour.

From behind, a timid voice bellowed, 'Cannon! Cannon!'

Yet the chariot-pullers, inflamed by fervour, heeded no warning. If the cannons were discharged, hundreds would fall instantly—but behind them, thousands more stood ready for resistance.

Aminchand cried out, 'They're advancing, Faujdar Sa…H…B!'

Faujdar Hashim Khan looked on in dismay as the

people surged forward, rendering any hope of halting them futile. All the enemy's cannonballs would be in vain against such an unyielding mass.

Then, in unison, both cannons thundered forth!

Like clusters of uprooted banana trees, some innocent men at the front toppled as the tide of devotees—a mighty torrent, like water spilling over a breached embankment—advanced unimpeded. The blast of the cannons was soon drowned by thousands of voices echoing, 'Jai Jagannath!'

'Clear the way! Clear the way!'

From behind, a Mughal lashkar on horseback was bellowing, 'Clear the way… Clear the way…' Two hundred horsemen thundered in the rear, surging in support. They carved through the crowd, advancing with remorseless force. This was, unmistakably, the Mughal army, which had arrived from Cuttack. And yet, curiously, they did not attack. But with cannons ahead, poised to fire, had they unleashed their assault from behind, Ramachandra Dev's paika warriors—and the unarmed throng—would surely have been crushed.

Ramachandra Dev was struck dumb with astonishment. It was none other than Razia! Close at hand, just behind her, rode Mir Habib Khan.

On Razia's burqa-draped face burned an expression of steely resolve—a scowl beneath a regal Chandrahar, with no earrings and a delicate nath adorning her nose; not a single fresh flower marred her austere mien. On first encounter, one might mistake her for a young cavalryman. Razia was arrayed in a sharply tailored pyjama, paired with an embroidered sadri. A gleaming sword swung at her hip, and a proud pagri crowned her head. This martial countenance was beyond anything even Ramachandra Dev had dared to imagine.

Right before the cannons now stood Razia and Mir Habib Khan. Their unexpected appearance left Faujdar Hashim Khan bewildered. How could they be here? Had Naib Nazim Taqi Khan issued fresh orders?

Enmeshed in the solemn trance of duty, the steadfast Razia suddenly hurled a javelin with deadly precision at Hashim Khan's chest. The aim was infallible. Hashim Khan staggered—then began to fall from his horse—his foot, clad in intricately embroidered shoes, still caught in the stirrup. Mir Habib Khan raised his sword and struck a decisive blow upon the cannoneers.

'Jai Jagannath!' rang out as, with resounding vigour, Ramachandra Dev's paika warriors surged forward in relentless charge. The assembled throng held firm, and the sacred circle encircling the deities' chariots remained unbroken. The juggernauts trudged along, crushing and stamping the Mughal lashkars beneath their mighty wheels. Ahead, the path to Puri lay clear and unobstructed.

*****

Chapter XIII

At Singhadwar, on the holy Baisi Pahacha and beyond the outer wooden platform, throngs of pilgrims had gathered for darshan, and indeed Mahabahu had returned—enthroned upon the hallowed Ratna Simhasana!

Today, being Chaturdashi, the ritual of *chaka apasara* lay in wait. Upon dispensing the final *dakshina*, each pilgrim awaited the sight of the Nabajoubana Darshan. Yet the servitors tarried. Though the eastern vault now shimmered with golden light, the darshan remained unbegun.

Time and again, Talichha Mahapatra's voice resounded, 'Paniapaṭ… Paniapaṭ! Where is the Ghatuari? Ghatuari? The sandalwood has not arrived!'

Who could have divined that Mahabahu—resplendent and eternal—would so abruptly descend to reclaim the Ratna Simhasana, unbidden? There stood Shendha Suara, the appointed servitor for today's saree ritual, murmuring with quiet pride: 'I have earned the honour of adorning the head with the sacred sari.' This, indeed, was his badge of pride.

Gauri Patjoshi Mahapatra, chief of the *chhatis niyoga*, had been drawn into service by Naib Aminchand, with a handsome bribe pressed into his palm. Repeatedly, and without restraint, Shendha Suara had declared to Patjoshi's very face: 'Go on… leave! I've served under Patjoshis far weightier than you. Like you, I am a servitor entrusted with the saree rite—but I am no lackey of Naib Aminchand!'

His assigned duty was to wash the stretch from the temple tank to the threshold of the sanctum. But the wet dhoti clinging to his limbs refused to descend below the knees. His *langot* was cinched tight, though the back remained exposed, and around his waist was tied an ochre gamchha. He muttered with irritation, 'No matter how hard I scrub, this pigeon filth just refuses to come off!'

After so many days, at last there was an opportunity for a proper, heartfelt cleansing of the pit within the temple tank and for sweeping the temple floor. From the early hours of Trayodashi, the Sudha Suara contingent customarily cleared the debris from the Anasara Pindi before the Nabajoubana Darshan; the Anasara bamboo matting would be removed. Yet, with an entire *paher* still remaining, the ensconced deities appeared upon the Ratna Simhasana— almost unbidden—a sight no one had dared even to dream! Even as the number of servitors aligned with Naib Aminchand dwindled, a few still proclaimed, 'Once those cannons along the Pipili road fire with a thunderous boom, everything will be cleared away—they shall be trampled and scattered to pieces.'

'Without a proper Navakalevara, how can these uninitiated deities be restored to the hallowed Ratna Simhasana?' they exclaimed.

Amidst all this murky politics, there was no haste in cleaning away the debris from the Anasara Pindi. Disputes among the servitors had sapped all insistence or enthusiasm regarding the Navakalevara. Layers upon layers of dust had accumulated in the pit inside the temple tank, and heaps of shattered remnants lay scattered upon the Anasara Pindi.

Shendha Suara, drenched in sweat, laboured on—pouring pail after pail of water from the kalash as he scrubbed the tank. Yet he refused to move; he was as resolute as vigilant Hanuman—indeed, a most tenacious soul.

'Hey, Paniapat, what are you gaping at, standing idle? Pour the lime water over the broom, Palia Mekap, and begin the sandalwood offering! How much longer until the Netrotsava?'

'Why are you so full of counsel? I am serving here with diligence, I tell you—there's not even a trace of that pigeon stain giving way!' Shendha Suara remained immovable; until his heart saw fit to change, he would not leave the tank.

At the inner wooden platform, Changada Mekap's voice rang out in alarm: 'Where have you gone, oh Nidhidatta Mahapatra? Where is Hari Khuntia? The mouth-washing—*prakshalan*—has not yet been done, the lip-cleansing remains incomplete, and the tilak is yet to be applied! And look here—the crowd for the common darshan grows ever larger!'

One of the Daita servitors exclaimed: 'Yesterday, on Trayodashi, the khadi offering was not performed. And now—how can *kanaka* arpan take place today? Wasn't it the Ghatuari who was entrusted with grinding kohl, hingul, and musk since the previous night? This is like thirst demanding to be quenched—then dig a well already! No sooner had the deities arrived than the Sahana Mela—the common darshan—unfolded. Tell me, when does *kanaka* arpaṇ ever occur amid this?'

Shendha Suara swept the tank with his creaking broom, its bristles rasping against stone. No matter how diligently he scrubbed, the tank never appeared clean enough by his exacting standards. After so many days, he had reclaimed his rightful token of service. And today, with both the principal and its accrued interest, he finally savoured the fruits of that long-denied right—like a famished cow greedily swallowing fresh grass.

Hearing the Daita servitors' grievances, he remarked: 'By all means, Mahapatra, I have toiled in this very tank for countless days. You, too, as a Daita servitor, have long rendered your duty at the Anasara Pindi. But tell me—have Mahabahu's great, rounded eyes ever sparkled like a jewel, or has his divine countenance ever bloomed with that tender, tremulous smile, without *kanaka* embellishment—without the sacred ornamentation adorning his blessed form?'

Shendha Suara paused and, clutching the broom in his armpit, cast another searching glance toward the deities. The ketaki wreaths adorning Mahabahu's crown now lay shattered to pieces; the garlands around his neck had been torn away. His very form bore the dust and scars of battle, and even the Boirani silk he had donned at the outset of his journey from Tikali was in tatters—scattered and dishevelled, his uttariya adrift. For he was not merely a silent witness to this liberation struggle of the Odia people— he was not only the chariot-warrior, but the charioteer of this epic. Ramachandra Dev, his paika warriors, and this indefatigable, fearless populace are but instruments in the Divine Symphony.

After the arrangement for the Sahana Mela, once the throng of pilgrims thinned to a more mature gathering, the Netrotsava would be observed. Already, the servitors had assembled. The Paniapat and the Ghatuari stood poised with a silver urn of sandalwood paste at hand; the contingents of Palia Mekap had arrived as well. After the sandalwood was received, the officiating Mahapatra would perform the rites in the presence of the Daitapati. Once the ceremonial anointing (Mailam Arpan) of the Triad with sandal paste and other scents was complete, the garments of ten Boirani silk would be offered—three for each deity, and one for Sudarshan. Thereafter, Pati Mahapatra would perform the evening arati and invoke with akshata, camphor, and kahali. Finally, Datta Mahapatra's measured preparation of kohl— crafted with a tripartite measure of silver—would be applied meticulously, the three puja pandas using three sacred beams of *til* to adorn the deities' eyes. This was the holy ordinance of the Netrotsava.

Now had arrived the moment for the servitors to reap their well-deserved reward. Yet no special darshan with *dakshina* was held. They had received no earnings from the pilgrims—not yet. The throngs of pilgrims, defying the prohibitions imposed by the Gochhikars and the Khuntias, now stood like an army of ants along the Baisi Pahacha, their numbers so vast that a platter could be slid from the inner platform all the way to the Garuda pillar. In the ceaseless, echoing cries of 'Manima… Mahabahu!'—after days of silence and stunned reverie—the very corners of the *jagamohana* had erupted into song.

But when would the Netrotsava occur? Even now, the Nabajoubana Darshan had not been accomplished. 'Oh,

Shendha Suara, have you left your eyes at home? Look—Paniapat, Palia Mekap, Pati Mahapatra—all have already gathered. And yet you persist here in the tank, clattering away with your broom. Do you suppose the Netrotsava will be completed in such a state? Is this truly what the throng of pilgrims has come to witness?'

At that moment, the impassioned calls of 'Manima! Mahabahu!' suddenly fell silent. Then, near the Jaya-Vijaya Dwar, the sonorous voice of Patjoshi Mahapatra boomed: 'Where has Rajguru Lakshmi Paramaguru gone? Summon him forth! Let him bear witness—for he has become our Rajguru. But is he to arise solely to drag down Sanatana Dharma? Summon him! What am I to do if I see it? Have I not seen it with my own eyes? Have I not known it in my own heart?'

A murmur of disquiet rippled through the assembly. Had something gone amiss? The entire gathering was in uproar.

A ring of servitors encircled Patjoshi Mahapatra, their voices rising: 'Temple purification! Temple purification!'

Even the Khuntias, waving their twin canes and jostling the pilgrims near the inner enclosure, cried, 'Shuddhi! Shuddhi!'

Yet why must the temple undergo ritual purification at all?

Near the Jaya-Vijaya Dwar, the refrain remained unchanged: 'Where is Lakṣhmi Paramaguru?'

Patjoshi Mahapatra hollered, 'How can he appear now, when Sanatana Dharma itself is about to drown? Has he become Rajguru merely to smear soot on the very lips of Sanatana Dharma?'

Then, as if propelled by an unseen force, Bali Panda surged through the throng assembled in the *jagamohana*—shoving, prodding, and pressing his way into the tank. Seizing Shendha Suara by the arm, he dragged him forward and cried, 'Come, O valiant one! The celestial clock has begun its measure. Behold what unfolds before you—and still you linger here, scrubbing at stone with your broom!'

'What's happening? What is the matter?'

'Come now—see with your own eyes! What can I say? Patjoshi Mahapatra has declared there shall be a ritual purification of the temple—the tank will be washed anew, and lime will be applied once again.'

Bali Panda, snatching him with a swift grip, hauled him out from behind the inner platform.

Gosain Suna, who was cleansing the Ratna Simhasana with a folded silk cloth, murmured inwardly, 'Had that rhino not arrived, no one would have stirred this stagnant mass by even an inch from here.'

Inside the *gumat* at Singhdwar, in the shadowed recesses near the sacred statue of Patitapabana, Ramachandra Dev stood on one side, and nearby, Razia. She was garbed in the same crisp pyjama and embroidered sadri—but now, no sword swung from her waist, nor did she wear a pagri upon her head. Instead, her hair cascaded in delicate, curled tresses reminiscent of a priestess's, and on her cupped palm she bore a ring studded with an indranila gem.

Before Razia's eyes, the vision of Mother Kanchana of Murshidabad shimmered in the hush between worlds—a final, bittersweet plea drifted through the air: 'Should you ever be granted darshan of Shri Jagannath, please, on my behalf, present this ring set with indranila upon his

Ratnavedi. Though I am a Brahmin, I never had the fortune to behold his merciful countenance. You, however, must seek him—be sure to glimpse that Neelagiri—the god of sapphire hue. He is the very dawn of every night; a moon that soothes every sorrow.'

That indranila-studded ring is to be offered today as a genuine gift.

'Today, I shall behold Shri Jagannath to my heart's content.'

Yet a shadow of doubt flickered across Ramachandra Dev's eyes as he glanced about and murmured, 'This Patitapabana—truly Mahabahu himself, a living embodiment of Lord Jagannath! In his very sight, the blessing of darshan is bestowed.'

With eyes wide and glistening in innocent wonder, Razia turned toward him and asked, 'But tell me—today, as I come before the Ratnavedi, shall I not behold him? Is not the time granted for darshan, upon the offering of ceremonial gifts, meant equally for every soul—from Shudra to Brahmana alike?

What answer could Ramachandra Dev possibly offer to Razia's innocent question? In the intervening time, his own *yavana* identity had somewhat faded from the public consciousness. But Razia—she remained unmistakably a *yavana*... and who would come for a darshan clad in a sharply tailored Muslim pyjama and a sadri shimmering with zardozi embroidery?

Throngs of pilgrims, pressed together like a stream of ants, ascended the Baisi Pahacha. They smeared its sacred dust upon their foreheads, hands folded in supplication, calling out—'O Manima, Mahabahu!'

'Hey there—drop it! Drop that Jahangiri rupee or an eight-anna! Where are you strutting off to, jingling like that? Won't you pay the ceremonial offering?'

A tug-of-war had broken out among the servitors, each vying for their share of the offerings.

'Oh, you obstinate Mohanty! By what right do you demand the offerings? This is clearly Akhanda Mekap's service—and it isn't even your turn today.'

Bauri Mohanty, clutching a four-anna coin given by a pilgrim, pressed it against his waist and tried to steady himself. But another servitor snatched the coin away and mocked him: 'What kind of servitor are you? You've not been granted any farmland, nor do you wear proper clothes. And you must earn a meagre ten rupees a year by delivering wicks for temple lamps. Who are you to claim the ceremonial dues?'

Bauri Mohanty faltered, his tongue tripping over his words. He stammered, 'Oh—oh, L-Loki Mahapatra! P-please… spare me the prattle—do not boast at dawn. I have seen countless servants, braver than you. Today, at the Netrotsava, I must receive a small piece of *kakara* and half an *arisa* as my *khei*—my share of the offering. I—I'm not part of the ceremonial darshan, so what makes you think you are? You still have a multitude of pilgrims to collect *dakshina* from. What loss will you incur by sparing one? Return—return my f-four-anna!'

For days on end, these servitors had languished in the agony of famine-like neglect. Today, at the moment of the Nabajoubana Darshan, their service was reduced to petty tugging and quarrels. Amid such clamorous chaos, who would even keep Ramachandra Dev's noble countenance in view?

Yet all eyes were fixed upon Razia—her sharp, well-tailored pyjama and her striking Muslim attire commanded the gaze of hundreds, as if they would engulf her with their very sight. She could feel the sting of reproach in their eyes, each gaze a silent accusation.

Ramachandra Dev proclaimed with conviction, 'This Patitapabana—the purifier of the fallen—is none other than Shri Jagannath!'

'But then…' Razia's voice, laden with soft protest, faltered…

'Come, return, Razia,' Ramachandra Dev insisted. 'Our Nabajoubana Darshan has, after all, taken shape along the Pipili route.'

Yet Razia stood as immovable as stone!

'Today, I must behold Shri Jagannath with my very eyes,' she swore, as though taking an irrevocable oath.

In that indecisive, duty-stricken moment upon the Baisi Pahacha, the throng of pilgrims roared, 'Temple purification! Temple purification!'

Bali Panda, tugging on the arm of Shendha Suara, cried out in a gruff voice, 'Open your eyes—behold the glory of your Maharaj! Mani! Do you recognize who's beside him? Look at the audacity of this *yavana* woman—she's entered the sanctum! The Maharaj has brought her inside the temple!'

'Her bosom swelled like twin shields of brass! Oh, my goodness! Will this boy, meant to wield the staff, feast on fish instead?'—such was the irreverence in Shendha Suara's eyes toward the Maharaja. If not reverence, then nothing but a dismissive gesture toward Razia! Never in his wildest dreams had anyone imagined such a scene within the temple. Even as Maharani Lalita Devi abided in the royal Balisahi Palace, the Maharaja dared to bring this *yavana* woman into the sanctum for darshan? This was entirely unexpected—beyond even Shendha Suara's wildest imaginings. The Maharaja was the royal servitor to Lord Jagannath; a man, after all, would his feet not slip? And slip they did. Atonement was made; a village was donated—sin was absolved. But what of this *yavana* woman?

'Damn it! Is this *yavani* here?' cried Shendha Suara.

At the Baisi Pahacha, amidst the bustling crowd of pilgrims, even Jaguni stood speechless, unable to offer a fitting reply. Razia, beside Ramachandra Dev, seemed oddly out of place in his eyes. As he lifted his gaze toward a sky burdened with heavy clouds, memories of Saradei's words and presence flooded back. The deep, onyx waters of Chilika, the whispering breeze along the bank, and that solitary, humble dwelling—how ungrateful he was! Never had he once considered the plight of the one who had offered him refuge. What, he wondered, could have become of that modest roadside inn by now? In Jaguni's mind, the image of the wan, almost sickly Saradei drifted as if on an errant raft, while all around, the foreshore lay covered in sand, bordered by a grove of casuarina and cashew trees. In the dense tangle of casuarina leaves, the wind raged wildly, as though pummeling its head in a fit of madness.

Never—not even for a single day—had he served his benefactor, Saradei; instead, he flitted about like a shadow inextricably attached to Ramachandra Dev. Was it for this very reason that Saradei had been barred from entering the temple? Never once had she beheld Lord Jagannath seated upon his hallowed Ratna Simhasana—the fulfilment of her deepest, most cherished desire—and yet today, as if by some capricious twist, here in the sanctum stood *yavani* Razia, aligned with the Maharaja himself! He had heard whispers that the Maharaja had renounced his caste, but to see his intellect thus forsaken was something he could never imagine. No—indeed, his work here was done. The mighty Mahabahu, armoured in strength, had arrived at Neeladri, his resplendent abode, and ascended once more to his solitary Ratna Simhasana, triumphant and unchallenged. Soon, the land of Utkala would taste freedom. He must now set out in search of Saradei. Amid the uproar, Jaguni almost heard her faint, drawn-out cadence—'Ja...gu...ni...i...'

Brandishing their twin canes, the Khuntias drove the pilgrims back—the sanctum must be sanctified. Only then could the hallowed rite of Netrotsava unfold in its full glory. In its wake would follow acts of adoration and veneration, culminating in the Mahasnana—the Great Ablution. Thereafter, the deity would be ceremonially anointed in the sacred rite of Mailam Arpan, adorned in divine vestments. Then the morning arati, long delayed, would rise in a radiant offering of flame and fragrance. Once the cleansing and consecration were complete, the *ajnamala* would be borne to the waiting chariots. The colossal chariots would then be drawn toward the Singhadwar. Upon Grand Road, the faithful surged in waves—an ocean of devotion, swelling and breaking in ecstatic rhythm.

Yet the Netrotsava remained unfulfilled. The sanctum lay untouched. Only the temple servitors cried out in anguish, their voices echoing through the corridors of ritual: 'Sanctify the temple! Purify the temple!'

Descending the steps, golden cane in hand, as though

fresh from the conquest of a formidable fortress, Lakshmi Paramaguru made his stately entrance. Mahabahu's Neeladri Vijaya—the glorious homecoming of Shri Jagannath—was hailed as his singular achievement. Yet now, an unwarranted delay threatened to dim the splendour of the celebration.

Approaching Ramachandra Dev with a gravely earnest tone, he inquired, 'How has Razia Begum come to be here? With that, the sanctification of the temple shall commence—do you not understand?'

Ramachandra Dev fixed his steady gaze upon Lakshmi Paramaguru, and to answer such a question was beyond his immediate contemplation. Paramaguru's eyes fell downward, as if in that silent gesture lay an unspoken acknowledgement— the reserved decorum of a royal mentor compelled him to show due respect for the sentiments of the people of the realm. Was it not clear to His Majesty what discontent and dissension the very presence of *yavani* Razia had ignited?

'Today, during this ceremonial darshan, the gates remain open to all,' declared Ramachandra Dev with quiet assurance.

'But what of Razia—the *yavana* woman—does she belong here?' retorted Lakshmi Paramaguru sharply, his voice ringing with a crisp, resonant tone.

'Had this *yavani* Razia not stood resolute before the Mughal cannons on the warfront at Pipili,' Ramachandra Dev countered, 'we would be toying with wooden effigies in the temple sanctum, masquerading it as Netrotsava! And the divine forms, carved from the sacred *darus*, enshrining the *brahmashila*—the hallowed core—would lie strewn in dust along the Pipli road, desecrated and forgotten.'

Lakshmi Paramaguru responded, 'In this war for

dharma, the Maharaj and Razia are only instruments through which destiny plays its tune.'

Soon, the debate between Paramaguru and the Maharaja stirred a rising wave of intolerance among the people. Murmurs of dissent grew louder: 'Let the temple be purified and the rites proceed—how long will this delay drag on?' Their handsome earnings were being needlessly obstructed. Who, amid this unrest, would willingly relinquish today's hallowed offerings drawn from the Nabajoubana Darshan and Netrotsava?

Ramachandra Dev then replied, his voice steady as stone, 'I indeed fought for the cause of dharma—but not for blind fanaticism. In invoking the noble banner of dharma's protection, you have—perhaps unwittingly—become zealots who betray the very essence of humanity!'

Caught off guard, Lakshmi Paramaguru stammered, his eyes fixed upon Ramachandra Dev. 'Let us end this argument here! If Razia leaves the sanctum, the temple's sanctification shall proceed.' Yet even these words faltered, catching in his throat.

Against a cloud-laden sky, the sacred flag atop the Neelachakra fluttered wildly—its restless ripples heavy with foreboding—now, what remained to delay?

Ramachandra Dev exhaled deeply, and with quiet resolve, he urged, 'Come, Razia—let us return. The temple sanctification must now begin!'

With Razia shunned and cast aside, Ramachandra Dev felt no desire left for the Nabajoubana Darshan. Silently, he murmured, 'May your honour be safeguarded, Lord Jagannath!'

Yet, where was Razia? Amidst the clamour of

disputes with Lakshmi Paramaguru, she had long since withdrawn from the statue of Patitapabana. At the moment of her departure—beneath the Baisi Pahacha—she left behind a palmful of pearls, gems, and manikyas. Among them gleamed the gold ring, studded with the Indranila gem—the one she had meant as her true offering. In the ensuing frenzy, servitors scrambled to seize the trove, hastily tucking the glinting fragments into the folds of their waistcloths.

'Razia… Razia…!' Ramachandra Dev cried out. But by then, she had already slipped from the temple and been lost amidst the throng along Grand Road.

Ramachandra Dev's struggle had reached its close; his vow was fulfilled. Now, the time had come for Bhagirathi Kumar to be anointed upon the throne. Yet a deep regret remained in his heart. A deep wound had been struck upon his soul.

Dharma had curdled into fanaticism, and freedom had been twisted into the mindless indulgence of a few sanctimonious zealots. Even friendship had turned traitorous—a hard-won triumph slipping away like sand through clenched fists. For those who had faced death in defence of his honour, the majestic Singhadwar of Shri Jagannath—the Lord of boundless compassion and universal embrace—now stood barred. This was not Sanatana Dharma—it was blind fanaticism incarnate! What sort of haven of fellowship had it become? The landscape of wisdom had withered into a barren terrain of aimless wanderers. Lord Jagannath, silent and unyielding, bore witness to this travesty—a culture of camaraderie, affection, and deep-rooted tradition reduced to a superficially intriguing puzzle, its true spirit scarcely found among the common masses.

Like a raging storm, Ramachandra Dev surged forth from the *gumat*. The moss-covered, crumbling palace of Balisahi loomed ahead—its shadows cool with the touch of death.

'Bhagirathi Kumar! Bhagirathi Kumar!'

His cry reverberated through every forsaken nook of the desolate abode, only to fade again into a profound, icy stillness. Through the deserted corridors, Ramachandra Dev wandered, restless, calling out—'Bhagirathi Kumar! Bhagirathi Kumar!'

It was within these very walls of Balisahi Palace that Bhagirathi Kumar once resided, alongside Maharani Lalita Devi, during the sacred rites of Navakalevara. Yet after Ramachandra Dev pierced through the Mughal encampment at Pipili and arrived in Puri, the prince had vanished—leaving behind no trace, no whisper of his whereabouts.

And where, too, was Lalita Devi now?

'Arrange the coronation, Devi... Maharani!' Ramachandra Dev roared. But no answer came—Lalita Devi was nowhere to be found.

In a crumbling chamber of the harem, her lifeless form lay sprawled; upon her blue lips, a diamond ring remained pressed, as if sealing her final breath. She had watched, in her final moments, helplessly, as every endeavour, every fragile aspiration, slowly unravelled. It was said that Ramachandra Dev had ascended to Shrikshetra among the gods—and upon hearing this, Lalita Devi surrendered to death.

The revelation struck Ramachandra Dev like a thunderclap.

Her face, hardened like the scorched afternoon sun, bore the marks of vengeance. The lines etched across her features had deepened with fury. Amid the murk of clinging seaweed and damp, shadowed gloom, the diamond ring glowed fiercely—its light reminiscent of the blazing, resolute gaze of a defiant spirit.

Ramachandra Dev stumbled out of the residence, as though escaping a spectre.

But Jaguni—where was he?

He remembered—after entering the temple with Razia for the Nabajoubana Darshan, Jaguni had vanished from sight. Had he, even in the guileless gaze of Jaguni—his only ally in this unending struggle—become an outcaste, estranged from his own kind?

'Jaguni! Jaguni!'

Even amid the deafening chaos, there lingered the chilling silence of death.

Amid the overwhelming tumult that belied a deathly, cold silence, Ramachandra Dev tugged at its tangled, wild strands clinging to his brow. With a voice rising in anguished repetition—as if a drowning man clutching at a fragile reed—he cried: 'Razia… Jaguni!'

Today marked Pratipada—the first day of the lunar fortnight.

Following the sacred ordinance, the temple priests—*ajnamala* garlands draped over their arms—walked in measured steps toward the chariots assembled near the royal quarters. Each garland, drawn from its altar, was bound to its corresponding chariot. At the seventh step, conches and gongs burst forth, saturating the air with sacred sound.

And in that divine uproar, Ramachandra Dev's anguished cry dissolved into the celestial tide— 'Razia… Jaguni…!'

*****

Black Eagle Books

www.blackeaglebooks.org
info@blackeaglebooks.org

Black Eagle Books, an independent publisher, was founded
as a nonprofit organization in April, 2019. It is our mission
to connect and engage the Indian diaspora and the world at
large with the best of works of world literature published
on a collaborative platform, with special emphasis on
foregrounding Contemporary Classics and New Writing.